TRAIL

OF

DECEPTION

C. L. BREES

ISBN-13: 978-0-578-81760-6 (Paperback)
Library of Congress Control Number: 2020924353

This book is a work of fiction. Names, characters, places, and events are products of the author's imagination or, if real, individuals are used fictitiously. Any resemblance to actual persons, living or dead, occurrences, or locales is entirely coincidental.
C. L. Brees

Printed and bound in the United States of America
First Printing: April 2021

Copy-edited by Dominic Wakeford
Front cover image by Bookcoverzone

www.clbreesauthor.com

To Jesse:

Thanks for all your love and support, and for pushing me to keep being the best version of myself.

"Things are not always what they seem; the first appearance deceives many; the intelligence of a few perceives what has been carefully hidden."

—Phaedrus

TWELVE YEARS EARLIER

THE COLD WEATHER HAD SNAPPED AFTER an endless, brutal winter. The days of below-zero mornings were gone, and with their departure, the misery of home confinement disappeared right along with it.

The sun hovered in the western sky as Gemma tugged at the rickety door of her favorite hangout—the abandoned sawmill—just on the outskirts of Cedar Lake. She pulled the handle, and the hinges of the door squeaked. First Gemma, then Christian, and the two faded into the void of obscurity.

Christian lit his flashlight and aimed the beam towards the ground. "Tell me again why we're here?"

"Tradition. What? Tell me you aren't scared of the dark . . . are you?"

"What? No. I just can't imagine why, of all places, you'd want to celebrate here."

A low chuckle escaped her throat. "We always come to escape reality. And don't deny it. Besides, I brought booze."

"I can't believe I let you talk me into this."

A grin graced her face, and they continued further into the belly of the factory. Dust particles wafted in the still air, and with each step, the decrepit building let out creaks and moans. The uneasiness sent the hairs on Christian's arms on end. Something about the mood on this night was different. He stopped and waved the flashlight around. Near the stairs to the loft lay an overturned chair.

He grabbed Gemma's forearm and pulled her back. "That wasn't here the other day."

She turned her head towards his voice. "We aren't the only ones who come here. Now come on, I need a buzz before my curfew time hits."

Hesitant, he relaxed his hold, and Gemma raced ahead towards the staircase. Gemma's foot met the first tread, but a rustling overhead stopped Christian once more. He tilted his head back slightly, and a gruesome sight he never expected greeted him.

He gasped.

Gemma stopped and turned. "Anderson, what now?"

Speechless, his shaky hand pointed the light upward, and Gemma did the same. When the lights met midair, there hung the lifeless body of a young woman from the rafters. Gemma froze and let out a scream. One so loud anyone within a few hundred feet of the place would have rushed to her aid.

Christian raced up the stairs, yanked her arm, and dragged her away from the horrific sight. Time floored the brakes, and the two stood underneath the swaying body. Neither of the two best friends uttered a word until they came and came direct.

"We . . . We need to find help," Christian said.

Gemma released the breath she had held but never diverted her eyes away.

"Did you hear me? We need to call the police."

That word—*police*—snapped her from the shock.

"No. Are you crazy?"

"What do you mean, no? We can't leave her here like this."

Gemma shook her head and walked back along the path they used when they arrived. With each step, her momentum grew, and soon she was in a full-speed run for the exit.

Christian tailed, doing his best to keep up with her. She tripped on the loose gravel and face-planted into the muddy trail only a few feet from the bushes where they stashed their bikes.

His heels dug into the soft soil, and he slowed into a jog until he came to a stop. Gemma moaned and shifted herself around while Christian hovered above. She grunted between heavy breaths, and he crouched to help her get into a sitting position.

"This is insane, Gemma. Why are you running?"

"I . . . We . . . Was that Lindsay Ross?"

Christian paused and cocked his head away. "I think so. Look, we aren't leaving here until someone finds her. I'm calling the police."

He pulled out the prepaid phone his grandmother had gifted him for his birthday the month before, and he pressed his fingers against the keypad. Nine-One—suddenly Gemma swatted the phone out of his hands.

"Are you insane? What about your dreams of becoming a constable? Hm? What about getting the hell out of Cedar Lake? You're willing to throw it all away over a dead girl?"

"But . . ."

"No buts. We get on our bikes and never speak of this again. We were never here. You understand?" Gemma asked.

Grudgingly, he nodded and mounted the seat of his bike.

Darkness was closing in on Cedar Lake, and so were their curfew times. Gemma pedaled ahead of Christian, and he turned his head for one last look at the building. They continued along the dirt trail that ran parallel to the abandoned railroad tracks in silence.

PART 1

FRIDAY
REGINA, SK

"We can't see the true characters of those who lurk in the shade until they are exposed to the light..."
—Nanette L. Avery

ONE

THE CORRIDORS OF REGINA MEMORIAL HOSPITAL had quieted after an unusually hectic Thursday evening in the ER. Gemma flipped
open the last patient chart, made a few annotations, and passed off her patient
load to the oncoming nurse.

It had been an agonizing twelve hours. Gemma tore away the protective paper gown and latex gloves and tossed them into the biohazard bin as she dashed
for the locker room. Her eyes were heavy, and the only things Gemma wanted for the next twenty-four hours were her bed and a hot shower. Ten steps away
from freedom and a familiar voice pierced through the calmness.

"Williams. Wait up."

Her white tennis shoes skidded against the buffed floor, and her head spun
around. In the distance, running down the hallway, was none other than Daniel,
a medic she'd grown close to over the last four months. Something about him
was off, though. His jovial smile, which greeted her daily, was gone, and in its
place was a sense of urgency.

To keep things lighthearted, she joked. "I told you, I can't go day drinking with you."

The seriousness in his eyes remained. "It's not that. A guy is asking for you in room three."

"What guy?"

His shoulders raised. "Couldn't say. We just brought him in."

"And he asked for me? Why?"

"Don't know that, either. Look, time's running out for this guy."

"Huh?"

"We found him two blocks away in an alley. Four stab wounds to the abdomen. Doesn't look good."

With her attention refocused, the two hurried along the corridor back to the ER. "And he's asking for me?"

"The only thing he's said in the last ten minutes was your name. Your full name. An ex-boyfriend?"

Gemma picked through the various faces from the last two years of dating in Regina, but no one stood out. "Who knows? I haven't had the best track record at picking quality men."

Daniel pushed the door open, and Gemma raced in. When her eyes locked onto the man's face, she gasped and covered her mouth. "Taylor? What . . . what are you doing here?"

The man reached out, gasping for air. Death was imminent. Gemma stepped closer while her colleagues raced to insert IVs and barked orders amongst each other.

He pulled the oxygen mask away from his face, and Gemma leaned closer to his face. He gripped her hand and pulled her forward. The stench of alcohol on his breath assailed her nose. Amidst the chaos, he whispered in a weakened voice, "It wasn't suicide."

Gemma struggled to free herself, but for a dying man, his grip was superhuman. Daniel rushed to Gemma's side and wrapped his arms around her waist. Eventually, she freed herself from his clutches.

"Who? Who didn't commit suicide?"

He labored for the name to cross his lips. "Lindsay."

"Lindsay, who?"

With a labored breath, he said, "Ross."

The name shook her, and her legs wobbled as she backed further away. "What? Hhh–how would you know that?"

The machine beeped faster, and the all-too-familiar pattern of beeps signaled he was fading fast. "Taylor, what makes you believe she didn't kill herself?"

His eyes widened as the injection of morphine hit his system. "I . . . I was there. Stop him."

His body seized, and as the violent shaking increased, a glob of blood expelled from the corner of his mouth.

"He's crashing," a nurse alerted the room.

But mere seconds later, the machine belted out a long, high-pitched screech, and a doctor forced Gemma and Daniel into the hallway.

"You can't be in here," the nurse barked.

"But—"

"No, Gemma. No."

Her back slammed against the wall, and her knees gave out. Her limp body slid along the wall. "This has to be a dream. I'm not here. You're not here. None of this is real."

Daniel crouched in front of her. "This *is* real, though. Who the hell is he, anyway?"

Her breaths shortened, and she said nothing for several minutes. Anxious voices shouting over the constant ear-piercing tones from the machines were the only noises she focused on. Daniel sat on the cold linoleum floor next to her, and moments later, the door swung open.

He jumped to his feet. "So?"

Without a word, a tall nurse shook her head and walked away, onto another situation. The deafening noise from the machine stopped, and Gemma snapped out of the trance she had somehow gotten sucked into.

Still haunted by Taylor's words, she planted her palm against the wall and hoisted herself from the ground. And once back at eye-level with Daniel, she turned, and their eyes locked.

"You want a lift?" he asked.

"I—I just need some air." Without a goodbye, she rushed away down the hallway and out of sight.

TWO

THE DOORS OF THE ER SLID open, and a spooked Gemma hesitated just outside the door. Her head turned from one side to the other, certain a swarm of people would be passing through the area. But to her amazement, the parking lot was quiet. Too quiet. Especially after the roller-coaster night she suffered. No nurses rushing from a break, no ambulance wheeling in another patient. Nothing except birds chirping in the trees around the hospital.

From the corner of her right eye, she spotted her perch—the smoker's corner—a place where she spent too many nights contemplating her life choices. And for only the third time since her internship began, there wasn't a soul around to distract her.

She made a beeline for the set of benches, whizzing past a parked police car and an ambulance while the golden rays of the morning sun beat down against her face. She dug into the deep pocket of her scrubs, and the familiar sensation from the rubber case skidded across her fingertips.

Her hands trembled as she typed in her passcode. This wasn't the way she expected to spend the next day off, but there was only one person she could turn to at a time like this—Christian.

The phone rang twice, and it connected.

"Gemma? What's good?" Christian asked.

She stuttered but squeaked out the words. "We have a problem."

"Not again," he sighed. "What now?"

Paranoid, she scanned the area once more. "No, not over the phone. We have to speak in person."

"Never good when you go all cryptic on me."

"It's serious. Where are you?"

"I just walked into headquarters. Another night in the books. Aren't you off work yet?"

She flipped open the top of her cigarette pack and propped the phone against her ear. Three remained in the box. She wedged one between her lips and inhaled the white smoke into her lungs. "Yeah, but I'm sitting outside the ER on a bench. Look, can you swing by here before heading home?"

He moaned. "It's that serious it can't—"

"No," she cut him off. "This can't wait. I'm aware you think I'm a drama queen. And, on any other day, I'd admit you're spot on. But this time . . . look, we need to chat in person."

He grunted. "Be there in less than ten. Don't move."

She lowered the phone away from her ear and took another drag. Her eyes closed, and the vivid recollection of *that* May evening in 2009 took over. She remembered the tingles slithering along her arms, the freshly cut timber and marijuana mingling in the air, and then Lindsay's lifeless body swaying from the rafter.

Her eyes sprang open and walking her way was Daniel.

Shit.

He plopped next to her and reached down for the cigarette she had squeezed between her index and middle fingers.

"I've told you a hundred and fifty times, you got to quit this shit. It'll kill you." He tossed the butt to the ground and squished it into the dusty dirt beneath his feet.

"Hey! I wasn't finished."

"You are now."

In typical, standoff fashion, she crossed her arms across her chest, and a groan escaped her lips. "Whatever."

Daniel hadn't known Gemma long enough to gauge normal and abnormal behaviors. Still, one thing was obvious: what occurred in the ER was troubling. "Gemma, you can talk to me. What's going on?"

She exhaled and nodded.

"So, what's going on? That guy back there. What did he mean when he said it wasn't a suicide?"

Her foot bounced, and her body tensed. What was there to say? Better yet, how much could she say? Officially, neither she nor Christian was at the sawmill the night Lindsay took her life.

A groan preceded a quick answer. "Something back home."

"You want to talk about it?"

"Not really."

He reached for her hand and gave it a tight squeeze. The medic was never one for putting pressure on anyone. This was a prime example of him not overstepping the boundaries of friendship.

"I'm here if you need to talk. Okay?"

"Thanks. It means a lot."

"And you'll be okay? You're not suicidal or anything, are you?"

She squinted her eyes. "What? No. I'd never."

The shoulder mic screeched out, and he leaned his ear closer. In an instant, he jumped to his feet. "I gotta go. You promise me you're good?"

Her patience grew thin, and she snapped. "Daniel, everything is fine. I'm fine. All I want is to get home, sip on a glass of wine, and forget this morning ever happened. I'll call you later. Cool?"

His eyes widened, and his lips separated. "Yeah, whatever works for you. I hate it when you get cranky. Some rest might do you good," he said as he replied to the dispatcher and walked away towards the ambulance parked near the door.

She watched as the ambulance flipped on the lights and siren and sped away. With Daniel out of sight, she reached for a fresh cigarette to finish what he spoiled. Just as the flame ignited the end of the stick, a familiar silver sedan with tinted windows pulled along the curb.

THREE

CIGARETTE SMOKE WAFTED AROUND HER HEAD as she watched the driver's side door open. Like a dramatic scene from a movie, she watched Christian step out and tear away his sunglass from his face. It didn't matter how many times she blinked; everything happened at a glacial pace until the door slammed closed, and at once, everything returned to normal.

Christian sauntered her way, shaking his head with every step he took. He hovered over her, watching as she took another puff and exhaled.

"You know, one day those are going to kill you," he joked, but deep down meant every word he said.

"If you touch my cigarette . . ." she said. "Besides, something's going to kill us all, so spare me the lecture."

Christian grinned and slid the arm of his sunglasses between two buttons on his uniform.

She took another drag, and her foot bounced. "We got bigger problems."

He folded his arms across his chest and kicked his right foot out to the side. "Yeah, you said. So, spill it . . . what's so important it couldn't wait until I had a shower and a little sleep?"

"The second of May, that's what couldn't wait."

The color drained from his golden-brown face, and his body collapsed down next to her on the bench. "What d'you say?"

"Don't make me repeat myself. Someone knows we were there."

"Who?"

"Remember Taylor Jackson?"

Christian searched through the countless faces and names in his head. "Taylor. Taylor. Skinny kid? A year behind me in school?"

She nodded. "Yeah, that's him."

"How could he know we were there? What aren't you telling me?"

She tossed her cigarette to the ground. "Taylor Jackson just died in the ER less than an hour ago."

He cocked his head and stared at her. "He's here? In Regina? Why?"

"Beats me. It can't be a coincidence, though. How does one end up stabbed two blocks away from the same ER I work in? He must have been looking for me."

"Let's say he was. How does any of that make you believe he's telling the truth?"

"Why would a dying man say, 'stop him,' if he didn't have some information? I'm telling you, there's more to this."

"What else did he say?"

"Stop him."

"Who?"

"Christian, if I had the answers, I wouldn't have called you."

Christian bent forward and covered his face. He massaged his temples and turned to Gemma. "I'm starting to see why you're freaking out. But what can we do?"

"Do you want me to answer that?"

Christian stood up. "You can't be serious. You want to go back to that hellhole, don't you?"

"It's the only way. Of course, this time, we could give Pearson a warning we're coming."

Christian sat back next to Gemma, and neither of them moved for what seemed an eternity. The conversation dwindled, with the two speaking less than a handful of words over the next few minutes.

How was Christian going to tell his best friend he'd kept a secret from her the last twelve years—that it was him who phoned in the anonymous tip which led the constables to find Lindsay?

With a last glance, he turned to Gemma. "As much as I hate this, there's no other choice. The question is: do we have the strength to do what needs to be done?"

FOUR

CHRISTIAN'S KEYS CLANKED AS THEY LANDED in the bowl next to the front door. With bloodshot eyes and a pounding head, the only remedy was a hot shower and a comfortable bed. Yet, somehow, he couldn't shake the aftermath of that distant evening in 2009. It consumed his every thought.

He unfastened the top button of his uniform, slipped off his black boots one by one as he ambled between the foyer and the living room, and he fell hard against the soft armchair. He glanced at his watch. 8 a.m. This was rush hour around the house. Between the hustle of dressing upstairs and brewing coffee downstairs, the house was always chaos. But on this morning, that flurry of activity was non-existent. He peeked over the chair towards the kitchen. His eyes homed in on the coffeemaker which sat untouched.

Something's not right.

Christian made his way to the base of the stairs. *Where the hell is Ginger?*

Their two-year-old German Shepherd greeted him every morning at the front door. However, something was off.

He called out. "Ginger? Ginger, girl, where are you?"

The silence persisted.

He ascended two steps and called out again. "Ginger? Adam? Anybody home?"

A door upstairs creaked, and the pitter-patter of paws against the hardwood floor resounded off the walls. Ginger appeared from the darkness with a wagging tail and her tongue hanging out. She plopped down at the top of the stairs.

Relief washed over Christian, and he crouched down, clapping his hands together. "Good morning, princess. You gonna come say hello?"

Ginger barked twice and raced down the stairs into Christian's open arms. After a hellacious night and shocking morning revelation, her relentless licking against his sweaty cheek provided him with just what he needed: a smile.

He often played rough, something to drain her excess energy so he could get a few hours of shut-eye. But this time he cradled her face in both hands, closed his eyes, and asked, "Where's your other papa? Huh? Still asleep?"

Christian hadn't noticed, but Adam stood propped against the railing, watching the loving exchange. "He's right here," Adam said as he descended.

Christian grinned. Busted. He planted a kiss on Ginger's head and stood. "Didn't notice you there; otherwise, I would have kept my fat mouth shut."

Christian wrapped his arms around Adam's neck and kissed him gently on the cheek.

"Is everything okay?" Adam asked.

"Huh? Oh . . . yeah. Crazy night, but I'm home, so that makes everything all right."

Adam cocked his head. "It's just we expected you a while ago. I got concerned."

"Gemma called."

"Everything good?"

"I think so. She's shaken up, needed someone to talk to."

He chuckled. "Rough night at the ER?"

Christian smiled and lurched his shoulders upward. "Something like that."

Adam moved towards the coffee maker with a spring in his step, inserted a coffee pod, and pressed start. "I have to admit she's holding it down there. Didn't think she had it in her."

With the mug in one hand, Adam swung his free arm around Christian's neck again, and the two stood gazing at one another. Then the haunting memory of Lindsay Ross's lifeless body hanging from a noose reappeared, and Christian shook his head hoping the image would disappear . . . but it didn't.

He retreated. His breaths were shallow, his face grew flushed, and his hands trembled. Adam recognized all these red flags; something wasn't right.

"Whoa," Adam wrapped his arm around Christian's back. "You okay?"

"Yeah, I had a rough night. That's all."

Christian stumbled back to the armchair. As he dropped, Adam crouched until their eyes met. "Babe, I've known you long enough to decipher when something's eating away at you. After those guys attacked you outside the shit bar, we promised each other we'd always be honest and speak our minds."

Christian took in a deep breath and exhaled. "We did. I've been honest and open with you about everything since. It's just . . . there's no delicate way to say this."

"Whatever it is, it can't be that bad."

Christian closed his eyes and turned his head away. "Suppose the only way is to blurt it out loud."

Adam led Christian by the hand to the couch. "You can tell me anything. No judgment. No pressure."

"Something happened this morning. And it dredged up a horrific event from my past."

Adam leaned in. "Oh, God."

Christian shot him a dirty look. "Hey! We agreed . . . no judgment."

"You're right. You're right. Go on."

"I stopped by the hospital because there was a stabbing over off of Thirteenth Street this morning."

"Okay. It's a rough neighborhood. Shit like that happens. But that can't be what has you stressed."

"Gemma called me because the victim, a guy by the name Taylor Jackson, we . . ." he paused and caught his breath. "He's from Cedar Lake."

Adam's stoic expression troubled Christian. "You heard me, right?"

"Yeah. I'm processing. Does either of you have a clue what this guy was doing here? And, more importantly, who stabbed him, and why?"

Christian shrugged. "No clue. I went back and offered to assist, but I'm maxed on overtime, so they gave it to the day shift crew."

"Probably for the best. Were you close with this guy?"

Christian remained in a trance. "No. He's just another ghost from our past."

"So why'd he show up here looking for Gemma?"

As much as Christian wanted to keep Adam out of this, it was impossible. Not only did Adam understand Christian better than anyone, but he'd pester him until he came clean.

"He had a message for her."

Adam sat next to Christian on the arm of the chair. "Okay."

"He said two things: it wasn't a suicide and stop him."

His curiosity piqued. "Who didn't commit suicide? Stop who?"

"Do you remember when we drove up to the sawmill in Cedar Lake?"

"Wow, that's a blast from the past, but sure, I remember it like it was yesterday. What does that have to do with a guy being stabbed?"

Christian ignored his question and pressed on. "I was distant, and you asked me what I was thinking about. Then I said there was an incident . . ."

"Right. And if I remember, you said one day you'd tell me."

"Well, as much as I don't want it to be, the day has come."

Christian carried on for fifteen minutes, unleashing the secret he'd carried for too many years, about what happened that evening at the sawmill.

"And this guy, Taylor. How does he factor into this?"

"Only one way to find out," Christian said.

"You don't mean . . ."

"Might be good to pay my dad a visit."

"Every time you return to that broken place, something bad always happens. Aren't we supposed to be saving up our vacation time for our trip to Mexico?"

"Mexico might need to wait. I owe it to Lindsay to discover the truth about what happened. If you're not interested, I could just do this on my own . . ."

Adam waved his hands in front of himself. "Like hell. I remember what happened last time I let you go back alone. Not this time; count me in."

"Tell you what. Let me get some rest, and then I'll reach a decision when I'm in a better frame of mind. I might even be able to call Pearson up and have him do a little digging."

Adam placed his hands against Christian's shoulders and rocked back and forth until they reestablished eye contact. "You could. He was your biggest ally in Gemma's sister's case. And what else could he possibly be doing in that town? Just promise me one thing."

Christian's eyes wandered away. "What's that?"

"Promise me you will be here when I get home."

A gentle shake took him by surprise, and he glanced back into Adam's eyes. "Okay. Okay. Relax. I won't leave without you. You and I, we're a phenomenal team, and this isn't something I could do without Regina's best cyber forensics guy by my side."

Adam blushed. "Flattery will get you nowhere and everywhere at the same time."

FIVE

THE BUZZING OF HIS CELL PHONE against the nightstand stirred Christian from a less than restful siesta. He strained to open his heavy eyes and grunted as he rolled onto his side. His hand thumped against the reclaimed wood of the nightstand, and he let his hands wander towards the vibrations.

"Anderson," he said with unevenness in his voice.

"Shit. Did I wake you?"

He squinted at the clock on the nightstand. 4:22 p.m. "It's all right. I need to get up anyhow. What's up?"

"I'm outside."

"What?" In an instant, the grogginess wore off.

"Yeah. We should discuss what happened this morning a little more. I'm torn on what our next steps should be."

Christian stumbled to his feet and towards the window. With one quick motion, he drew the curtain. Just like she said, there she sat on the hood of her Toyota, the phone pressed against her ear.

"Jesus, Gemma. Next time a little advanced notice. You act like we're still in high school."

"You're upset."

He sighed. "I'm not."

"No, I've done it now. I pissed you off. I should have called. But Christian, we can't keep putting this off."

"Give me a minute, and I'll be down."

He tapped against the red button, tossed the phone onto the ruffled duvet, and slid into a pair of gray sweatpants and an old, wrinkled police academy t-shirt crumbled on the floor next to the bed.

Christian grumbled a slew of swear words under his breath all the way from the second floor, down the stairs, until he reached the front door. He took a long breath, closed his eyes, and exhaled. As Christian wiped the crust that clung to his eyelashes, he tugged at the front door, and it swung inward.

There was Gemma, toting an oversized bag and complete exhaustion written on her face.

"Hey," he said.

"You look like hell, Anderson."

"Could say the same about you. Have you even slept since this morning?" Christian asked.

She shook her head. "I tried. I couldn't get her face out of my head. Not even a Xanax would put me down right now."

He hung his head and stepped aside. "I sincerely hope you aren't taking that crap."

"Chill. It was a joke. I swear you're too literal."

Christian closed the door behind her and led the way into the kitchen. "I'm a constable. It's my job to be literal." He rummaged through the fridge and yelled around the door. "You thirsty?"

No reply.

He peeked his head from around the door and watched as she dug through her purse and pulled out a screw-top bottle of wine. She set it on the counter, and their eyes locked. He grinned while she twisted the top off.

"What? I came prepared."

With two full glasses of cheap white wine, they retreated to the living room and clanked their glasses.

"To Taylor," she said.

Christian pulled the glass away from his mouth without taking a sip. "I've made up my mind. Tomorrow morning, I'm leaving for Cedar Lake."

She took a long swallow. "Wow. You decided that quick. How long are you going for?"

"Long enough to snoop around a little, ask a few questions, check on my dad, and then get the hell out of there."

"Can I ask you something?"

He nodded. "When have I ever said no?"

"What makes you believe this is more than what it is? Let's face it; Lindsay wasn't the most popular person in all of Cedar Lake. I can name a dozen people who were glad when she died."

"Same. And that's the problem. So many people had motives to harm her, and you're still sitting there thinking it was suicide."

She shrugged and took another sip of wine. "I mean if someone released my diary to the entire school . . ."

"Point taken. Still, why would Taylor travel all the way down here? How did he know where to look for you?"

"It's no secret where I am now."

"Further to my point. Taylor works up the courage to trek all the way here, only to meet a grim end two blocks from the hospital. Why? Why come to you?"

"I'm just as baffled as you. I ruffled a few feathers in Cedar Lake before I left. After what happened with my sister, it's likely Taylor thought I was someone he could trust to expose the truth."

Christian took a sip of wine and his face puckered. "Ugh, where did you get this?" Beer over wine was more Christian's speed.

She snorted. "Yeah, it's not for everyone. You want a beer instead?"

He nodded. "Thanks."

As Gemma returned with a cold beer, she slid into the chair just as the jingle of keys at the front door alerted him Adam was home. He set his beer down next to the full glass of wine and jumped to his feet.

Ginger barked and raced down the stairs to wait for Adam at the door. Christian hung his head and shook it. *Why does he get all the love?*

The door swung open, and Ginger jumped up and spread her paws against Adam's chest.

Adam's eyes lit up at the sight of his four-legged friend. He focused his attention on her and not the more significant event Christian and Gemma plotted in the next room.

Christian appeared around the corner. "Hey, wasn't expecting you home so early."

Adam patted Ginger on the head and stood. "It's a quiet day. Took an hour of leave just to check on you."

He wrapped his arms around Christian and peered over his husband's shoulder. To his surprise, sitting in the living room was Gemma. "Do I even want to know?"

"It's nothing. I mean, it's five o'clock somewhere, right?"

"I love how you use humor to mask your devious plotting. Seriously, what's going on?"

The whispers drew Gemma to the edge of the wall, and she peeked around the corner. "You two do a horrible job of keeping a low profile."

"He thinks we're up to something. But we're not . . . are we?" Christian asked.

She shook her head. "Can't a girl just come by with a bottle of wine and chill?"

"Sure she can, unless a long-lost acquaintance shows up in town, gets stabbed, and the only thing he can say is your name right before he flatlined," Adam said while the color drained from Gemma's face. "Yeah, I heard all about this Taylor guy. What I'm curious about, though, is what you two are scheming?"

Christian and Gemma exchanged glances, and the silence endured. At last, Christian couldn't withstand Adam's stare of death any longer and conceded. "As we talked about this morning, I wasn't sure if I needed to return to Cedar Lake. I mean, that's a long drive, and I could try to convince Pearson to just do it for me."

"Yeah, you said you'd sleep on it. Hold up, you've made up your mind already . . . haven't you? You two *are* planning a trip back home? Aren't you?"

Doing his best to keep a poker-face, Christian skirted around the truth. "I haven't decided. Right now, we're drowning our worries in the bottom of a bottle. You could always join us, and we can figure this mess out . . . together."

Adam was the master of the resting bitch face, no matter the situation. Yet there was always one thing that could melt that miserable look from his face: Christian and his sense of humor.

"Actually, a beer sounds good right about now. It's never fun being the only sober person in the room."

The bottlecap from the cold Heineken crashed against the granite countertop, and Adam dropped the question Christian hadn't prepared to answer. "So, this girl Lindsay, what was she like?"

He swallowed hard. Like most people walking the earth, Lindsay Ross had two sides to her. On most days, she was an amiable, spirited, life of the party girl who got things done. But there was another side to her. A side that seldom reared its ugly head. Lucky for Christian, it was something he never experienced. Unlike many students at Cedar Lake High, he considered her a friend.

"She was, well, Lindsay. I don't know the best way to describe her. Gemma? You have anything you want to add?"

Gemma, never one to suppress her opinions about people, put it all out there. "She was a no-good, lying, backstabbing slut."

Christian's jaw dropped as he slid the bottle into Adam's hand. The two exchanged a quick glance, and Adam took a chug.

"Not a fan, I take it?" Adam asked when he came up for air.

"Not after what she did to me."

"What d'you mean?" Adam asked.

"Bitch was the editor of the school newspaper. In grade eleven, she ran a story about underage drinking on school property."

Christian returned to the couch and plopped down. "Not this again. Gemma, like most people we went to school with, you broke the rules, and she exposed you. You can't blame Lindsay for that."

"The hell I can't. After her little exposé, they suspended my friends and me for a week. An entire week."

Adam took another chug. "To be fair, I have to side with my husband on this one. That's what reporters do. They find a juicy story, run with it, and things come out. It doesn't always end pretty."

With a pouty face, Gemma crossed her arms over her chest. "I disagree. Some things are best left private. Now I'm not saying she deserved what happened to her, but perhaps her meddling ways had something to do with it?"

That was all it took to send Christian's mind into full-fledged investigator mode. Was Lindsay working on something that led to her death somehow? After all, she was well known around town for leaking people's darkest secrets in the school newspaper or her online blog.

"You think her blog is still active?" Christian asked.

"From twelve years ago? Doubtful."

"But you could get to the entries somehow, yeah?"

Adam cocked his head and gazed at Christian's puzzled face. "Care to share what you're thinking?"

"It's nothing. Listen, we should probably eat and get some rest. That six-hour drive is a killer."

***

AFTER DINNER, THE TWO HAD THE house to themselves, and with it came the freedom to speak without eavesdroppers. As Christian stood in front of the mirror, Adam walked up from behind, the electric toothbrush protruding from his mouth.

"You're keeping something from me," he whispered.

"She had a point. It never dawned on me that her reporting could have been the reason she died."

"That's pure speculation. And I can't have you getting ahead of the evidence . . . not again."

"I'm not—"

"You are. You said it yourself—people hated her, hell, they even released photocopies of her diary for everyone to read. That right there could have been enough to send anyone over the edge."

Christian continued brushing his teeth, ignoring everything Adam had said.

"If we're going to do this. If I'm going to help, then we need an agreement."

"What kind of agreement?"

"That there won't be any shenanigans this time. Cool?"

His eyes darted away. "You're right. Fighting over this won't find the truth. You have my word—no going rogue this time."

PART 2

SATURDAY
CEDAR LAKE, SK

"But those with an evil heart seem to have a talent for destroying anything beautiful which is about to bloom."
—Cynthia Rylant

SIX

THE ENTIRE DRIVE TO CEDAR LAKE, Christian couldn't take his mind off what Gemma had said the night before.

Could it be possible Lindsay stuck her nose into something that got her killed?

The brick Cedar Lake RCMP detachment came into focus, and he set aside the dark thoughts that had consumed him the past six hours.

After everything that happened two years ago, this was the one building he never expected to step foot in again. At least not in this lifetime. Yet here he was. However, this time was different. Was it because the people involved weren't family? Or perhaps the entombed resentment, the one he clung to for years, had waned the moment he made amends with his father and came to accept the truth about what happened to his mother?

Whatever the reason, he went into this investigation mindful he was doing the right thing: uncovering the truth about another tragedy from his past. At this moment, returning to Cedar Lake was where he needed to be.

He spotted an empty parking spot next to the front door and aimed the car between the faded white lines. Before he threw the gearshift into park, he did a double-take at the facade of the building.

Something's different.

Then it hit him. The bushes were green, and bright pink and yellow flowers jetted out from the red brick planters abutting the building. He examined the bricks closer and noticed the grunge that once clung to the mortar had vanished. Could it be Pearson allowed himself some free time to bring the place back to its former glory?

The engine switched off, and Christian reached down to release his seatbelt. Before he could depress the button, Adam grabbed his forearm.

"You sure you're ready?"

With a simple nod and a smile, he unbuckled himself. "I owe it to Lindsay to expose the truth, not to mention we still need to figure out a few other things."

"Such as?"

"Why was Taylor in Regina? How much did he know? And did what he knew get him killed?"

"Well, seems like we have a lot of ground to cover and only a few days to do it in. So, shall we get in there and get started?"

Without saying another word, Christian clutched the door handle and popped the door open. He slid the arm of his sunglasses into the front of his polo shirt and slammed the door closed.

Christian skirted the edge of the front fender, still fidgeting with his wallet, sunglasses, and smoothing out his semi-wrinkled shirt. His worries consumed him to the point he missed the slimmer, more cheerful, Constable Pearson propped against the brick wall with his left leg crossed over his right.

Pearson's memorable booming voice took Christian by surprise. "How was the drive?"

Christian took one more step and jumped back, almost losing his balance as he did. He clutched at his chest with one hand and planted his other on the hood of the car. "Shit. I didn't see you there."

Pearson pushed himself away from the wall. Christian moved faster, and the two men met halfway. Christian extended his hand, but Pearson had something else in mind. He widened his arms and embraced the petite Christian.

"It's been way too long," Pearson said as he squeezed tighter.

"Yeah. It's been since the reception two summers ago, right?"

Christian pulled away and tried to keep the conversation going.

"Right. But geez, look at you. You've been taking my advice and looking after yourself."

"That's the goal. The doctor put me on a diet last year. Said if I wanted to live past forty-five, I'd had better make some serious life changes."

Adam yanked a laptop bag from the backseat, and the door made a thud as it closed.

Pearson leaned in. "Ah, you brought your trusty sidekick."

Adam approached and extended his hand. "Luke, always a pleasure. And no, he won't be laid up in a hospital bed this time around."

Pearson let out a chuckle under his breath. "Hey, what d'you say we get inside and find out what we're working with?"

They tailed Pearson as he walked through the front doors. Inside the lobby, Christian glanced around. Things had changed. They had replaced the old, hard plastic chairs with more modern, comfortable ones. The once-paneled walls had been freshened up with several coats of alpine white paint. And after twenty years, the mustiness was a thing of the past.

"When did you find the time to do a little remodeling?"

"Ah, well, as the smallest detachment in Saskatchewan, we're last on the list to get anything done. Looks sharp though, huh?"

"I'm impressed."

They congregated near the glass partition where the same constable Christian met years ago slouched in the chair. Christian cracked a half-smile and raised his hand to wave, but the man turned his scowling face away.

Some things don't change.

The door leading to the heart of the station popped open, and Christian and Adam entered. While the rest of the detachment had received a refresh, the desks were untouched. The same hard, plastic chair with the matted cushion awaited him.

His eyes wandered around the open floor plan, and two boxes sitting on the edge of Pearson's desk caught Christian's attention.

"Are those . . ."

"Yeah. More than I expected, to be honest."

Christian cocked his head to the side. "Why you say that?"

"Well, come on, it was a suicide. It's not like we investigated a murder or anything."

As much as Christian hated to admit it, Pearson had a point. What was there to collect? Her clothes, the noose, a few interviews, and an autopsy report?

"Suppose it's better than having nothing at all," Adam chimed in.

Pearson sat in his chair, which was barely hanging on. "One thing I'm curious about that you didn't clarify last night—why the sudden interest in something from so long ago?"

Christian pulled the chair out and lowered his ass against the scratchy fabric. "I didn't want to discuss too much over the phone. Gemma had an unexpected visitor."

Pearson leaned forward across the desk. "Oh?"

"Taylor Jackson."

Pearson's back crashed against the back of the chair. "Taylor? The same guy who was released from prison six weeks ago?"

"I had no idea, but yeah."

"And he's the reason you want to reopen this case?"

Christian nodded. "Yeah."

"Christian, you can't trust a word that comes from that idiot's mouth. Let me guess—he gave Gemma some tear-jerking story, and she called you in hysterics?"

"Well, you're half-right."

"I don't understand."

"Taylor Jackson . . . he's dead. He's lying on a cold slab at the Coroner's office in downtown Regina."

"Damn. What happened?"

"Four stab wounds to the abdomen. A passerby found him in an alley two blocks from the hospital where Gemma works."

Pearson's tone was bitter, almost callous. "That's a shame. Can't say I'm shocked his shady past caught up with him. I still don't get how his death would persuade an experienced investigator into rushing all the way back *here*."

"I haven't finished. Chill out. He made a deathbed confession to Gemma. Said Lindsay's death was not a suicide."

"How would he know?"

Christian shrugged. "He told her he was there. But there's something else."

"Okay?"

"Taylor said, 'stop him.'"

"Him? Him who?"

Christian shrugged. "Wish I had an answer, but hopefully, something in one of those boxes offers me a hint."

In a complete change of topic, Pearson blurted out. "Dinner plans?"

Christian exchanged a glance at Adam. "None yet."

"Let's do dinner. Say around seven?"

With every passing second, Pearson waited for an answer. The clock on the wall ticked away. It was now 2:17 p.m. "Yeah, we can make that work. We just need to settle in at my pop's."

"Great! You guys have fun sifting through these old papers, and I'll catch up with you this evening. And if you plan to reopen the case, I think it may be a good idea to stop by and visit with Mr. and Mrs. Ross first."

"Yeah. Just don't know how they'll take the news."

"I always say to plan for the worst and hope for the best. There's no other way," Pearson said.

Christian scooted out the chair away from the oversized desk and stood. He extended his arms outward, and Pearson handed over the first banker box. It was heavier than Christian expected.

"Whoa," he exclaimed.

"You need to hit the gym. Changed my life," Pearson replied.

"Hilarious. But since you brought it up, I just have to tell you this new looks suits you."

"Six days a week in the gym, no more junk food, and getting in at least seven hours of sleep every night. But, hey, that's shit we can discuss over dinner. I bet your dad is eager to reconnect."

"I hope so. We haven't talked much recently on account of my new work schedule. But it'll be good to check in on him and witness firsthand his new alcohol-free life."

Adam interrupted. "Christian. You think it's smart to take all this evidence to your pop's? It's all we have left."

Christian and Pearson exchanged glances. "It's just him there. And, besides, he isn't at all interested in any of this stuff. Trust me, it'll be fine."

SEVEN

CHRISTIAN DROVE ALONG HIS CHILDHOOD STREET. The barren trees from his last visit now were abundant with foliage, and the scene brought a sincere smile to his face.

He pulled the sedan into an open parking spot across from 522 Second Street. On his last visit, the house had seen better days, and Christian expected to find nothing had changed. As he glanced around, his eyes widened, and his mouth fell open.

The junkyard had disappeared. The screen door, which on his last visit barely clung to life, was brand new. Even the house color had gone from a dingy gray to a deep navy blue with glacier-white trimming.

Adam bent his head over and caught a glimpse out the driver's side window. "Your dad's been busy."

"Yeah. I'm impressed. It's getting closer to its glory days."

Just as Christian reached for the door handle, the house's front door opened, and two figures appeared onto the front steps. He pulled his hand away and slouched in the seat.

It was his father, standing with a mystery woman he'd never seen before. Christian studied her. She was shorter, with a darker complexion. He watched as his father stroked the woman's upper arm while her hands flailed about. This behavior was an all-too-common sight whenever Christian responded to domestics. And whatever they were discussing appeared heated.

Adam leaned in and whispered, "Who's the woman?"

Christian didn't answer. He only stared as his father, Matthias, placed both hands against the woman's face and pulled her in towards him. His head cocked to the side, then bent forward. And then it happened—his lips landed on hers.

Christian squinted his eyes and jerked the door handle. Without bothering to check for oncoming traffic, he dashed for the front yard. As his father pulled away from his public display of affection, Christian locked eyes with the man.

"Uh, hey, Pop," he hollered across the yard.

The woman pivoted, and Christian watched the rosy color of his father's face drain away. His father squeezed his eyes closed and inhaled deeply. "Hey, Christian. I wasn't expecting you."

Christian stopped at the base of the stairs and leaned against the iron railing. "I wanted to surprise you. Surprise!"

His head turned towards the woman who now sought refuge behind Matthias. Christian extended his hand. "Hi. We haven't met, I'm Christian . . . Matthias's son . . . from Regina."

Her muscles relaxed, but the dumbfounded glare in her eyes said more than words ever could have. She had no idea who he was. Did she even know Matthias was a father?

"His . . . son. I, I had . . .Oh, where are my manners? I'm Joanna."

Christian restrained the built-up words he wanted to unleash and instead offered a half-smile and a glance in his father's direction. "It's nice to meet you. I hope my visit isn't interrupting anything."

"No, no. I'm late for an appointment," Joanna said as she descended the stairs. She glanced up at Matthias. "I'll call you later."

Matthias nodded his head, and she scampered away to her car parked in front of Christian's. As she sauntered across the lawn, Christian never took his eyes off her. Then something moving in the distance caught his eye—Adam leaning against the open passenger door, waiting.

"Shit."

Christian rushed across the patchy lawn and back to the car.

"I'm so sorry, Adam. It's just . . ."

Adam waved his hands in front of his body. "Hey. No need to explain. I get it. You probably haven't seen your dad with another woman since, well, since your mother."

He kept his head down, resting his ass against the warm metal hood. "Why am I getting so bent out of shape over this? It's been twenty-six years. He has every right to move on with his life. I've moved on with mine, so I should let him do the same."

Adam slammed the car door and walked around to the front of the vehicle. "You're in shock. That's all. Now, let's not make him any more uncomfortable than he already is. Okay?"

Christian raised his head. "Yeah."

Christian smiled as Adam ran his hand across his back. He turned towards the house and smiled. "We should get started."

The couple unloaded the boxes from the backseat and walked towards the house. As they inched closer, Christian spotted his father pacing, nibbling away at his fingernails. Something he was all too familiar with.

Matthias stopped the moment his son and Adam wandered up the walkway. In a slow descent, the older man struggled to find the words. "Christian, I didn't mean for you to—"

Christian interrupted, "Pop, it's fine. I promise. You're allowed to fall in love, or lust, or anything you want. I just wasn't prepared to meet her. That's all."

"That's all? You sure?" he asked.

"Yes, Pop, I'm sure. You must tell us more about Joanna."

A smile graced Matthias's face. He swung one arm around Christian's neck and pulled him in tight. Ever since the day he came out, and the perpetrator of his mother's disappearance and death confessed, Christian and his father had grown closer. Not to say things were perfect, but they were heading in the right direction.

"Well, come in, come in. I bet you're both exhausted after that car ride."

"Wasn't too bad this time, since I brought along company," Christian said.

Matthias turned to Adam. "You keeping him out of other people's business?"

Adam chuckled. "That'll be a snowy day in hell."

"Sure would." Matthias closed the door and glanced at the two boxes they carried. "So, what's with the boxes? Another case Pearson couldn't solve?"

Christian flashed a half-smile. "Eh, these. Yeah, this is from a cold case from 2009."

"Why do you have them?" Matthias asked.

"There's been a recent development, and something about it tells me this case isn't what it appears to be on the surface."

Matthias cocked his head. "2009. What happened in 2009?"

Then he glanced at the name written on the side of the white box.

ROSS, L.

The old man wiped his forehead. "You're not."

"I am."

"Why? It was suicide, wasn't it?"

Christian sat his box on the floor of the foyer. "It's Cedar Lake, Pop. Not everything around these parts is so simple. We should sit."

Matthias bowed his head and heaved a loud sigh. Christian gazed around; the house had changed so much since his last visit. The soiled carpeting had been ripped up, the random holes punched in the wall had been patched, but best of all, that stench of urine was a faded memory.

Something inside his father had changed in the last two years. Christian wondered whether burying the past was the motive behind the change, or was it his new lady friend, Joanna?

Christian sat next to Adam on the couch while Matthias sat in his favorite recliner. The same one where Christian remembered him passing out, night after night, in a drunken stupor.

"So what event are you referring to?" Matthias asked.

"Do you remember Lindsay Ross?"

Matthias tilted his head, and the name registered. "Ah, pretty girl. Daughter of David Ross. Didn't she used to come around?"

"Years ago, but yeah, we hung out a few times."

"It's a damn shame, you know, taking her life like she did."

"That's the reason I'm here, Pop. I can't be sure she did."

Matthias shook his head a few times. Once the disappointment wore off, he turned to Adam. "Thought you said you were keeping him out of other people's business?"

His lips quivered. "I said it'd be a snowy day in hell. Christian gets something in his head and . . ."

Matthias turned to his son. "You'll never change, will you?"

The spotlight was on him, something he hated. He quickly changed the subject. "I hate to impose, but would it be okay if we stayed with you for a few days? Two, three days, tops."

"Here? You want to stay here?" Matthias asked.

"I mean, if it's too much trouble, we can get a room somewhere."

The man waved his hands. "No, no. I want you to stay. I'm sorry, son, but I packed all your things away and converted your old bedroom into a guest room."

Christian grinned. "You kept all of my stuff?"

He nodded. "In the attic."

"And you're *sure* you don't mind the extra house guests?"

"You're my son, and you can come here and stay as long as you want."

Christian smiled. It was the first time, since he deserted his father years ago, that a sense of welcoming filled his heart. The couple grabbed the boxes from the floor and made their way for the staircase.

"Pop?"

The old man struggled to get to his feet from the chair. "Yeah?"

"Would it be okay if I use the dining room as a base of operations if I promise to clean up afterward?"

"Base of operations? What are you expecting to find, boy?"

Christian shrugged. "Well, anything can happen. Is it okay or not?"

"I can't think of a reason you couldn't."

EIGHT

THEY CLEARED THE TABLE AND SIFTED through the boxes. They held your standard contents for a suicide investigation: the coroner's report, a few sealed brown paper evidence bags, and seven manila folders. Christian fanned through them, and every name jogged some distant memory.

"Something interesting?"

"Just these names. I recognize them all."

"Should make this easier, yeah?"

There was a pause. "Don't count on it. These are people I had hoped I'd never run into again in this lifetime."

"Who?"

"Just a couple of girls, who were the fakest people you'd ever meet."

"Ah, I take it they were in the popular clique?"

Christian dropped the folders on the table. "What gave it away?"

"You. You always say things like that when it involves those kinds of people."

"What kind?"

"The ones who project a sense of perfection, when in fact they're miserable inside."

"It's more than that with these two. They made my life a living hell in high school. I don't know how I can face them."

Adam rested his hand against his husband's shoulder. "That's why you have me this time. I don't know any of these people, and they don't know me. Besides, your life is amazing. You save lives every day. You're the perfect husband, and I'm lucky to have you. That's realness and not some fake shit you find on Instagram."

Whenever Adam paid him a compliment, Christian blushed. He had spent the better part of ten years with the belief love would never find him. And then Adam happened, and it turned his life upside down.

With a subdued grin affixed to his face, Christian replied. "You gotta stop with all these compliments. But you're right. With you here, I'll survive this mini high school reunion. Especially if it means finding the truth."

"That's the spirit. So where should we start first?"

"With the easy ones—The Ross family."

***

CHRISTIAN REACHED OUT AND PRESSED THE doorbell of the two-story house on the outskirts of town. David and Maureen Ross had money and never held back their need to flaunt it in the faces of the less fortunate residents of Cedar Lake. Christian glanced over at Adam, and the black North Face backpack caught his eye.

"What's that for?"

"We came for electronics. Just have some evidence bags in here, gloves. I know it's been twelve years, but there could still be trace evidence, you know."

"You look like a Jehovah's Witness."

Adam's lower lip curved down. "Thanks, I guess."

A rustling at the door quelled their playful banter. The deadbolt unlatched, and a familiar face stood before Christian.

"Can I help you?" the man asked.

"Chad?"

"Yeah? You are?"

"It's me. Christian Anderson."

The scruffy man scanned him from top to bottom. It had been more than a decade since the two spoke last, but with each passing second, something clicked, and his face lit up.

"Christian. You and Lindsay were in the same class at Cedar Lake High, right?"

He nodded. "We were."

"Gosh, I haven't heard your name in ages. You still living around these parts?"

Christian wasn't a fan of small talk. But he politely answered, "I'm actually in Regina working with the police service these days. This is my husband, who is also a constable."

Chad extended his hand, and the two men shook. "Good to meet you."

"Likewise."

"So, what brings you by?"

"Some additional information about your sister has come to light, and I hoped your folks were around."

Chad glanced over his shoulder. "Yeah, they're in the den watching TV. You guys are welcome to wait inside while I grab them."

With nothing more than a head nod, Christian and Adam stepped into the lavish house. Chad hung a left into an adjoining room, leaving the two alone in the foyer.

"Nice place," Adam said.

"Not my style. Too cluttered. But something in here has changed. This foyer isn't how I remember it from the last time I was here."

"You think they'll remember you?"

Christian shrugged. "Hard to tell. Twelve years is a long time. They must both be in their sixties by now. Hell, Chad was only two years ahead of me in school, and it took him a minute."

"Surely they'll remember you. You and Lindsay were tight?"

"*Tight* is a stretch. We were acquaintances. She stayed out of my way, and I hers."

"Hey, I never asked, but what kind of guy were you like in high school? And don't say a jock."

He chuckled. "Nah, I didn't belong to the muscle-heads. I was more reserved. I kept a low profile, and that's how I liked it."

Adam moved his lips. But just then, Mr. and Mrs. Ross rounded the corner.

"As I live and breathe, Christian Anderson. It's been far too long," Mrs. Ross said. While there was a hint of excitement in her voice, her resting bitch face masked the jovialness well. Some things had not changed one bit.

"Mrs. Ross, Mr. Ross, thank you for taking the time to speak with us," he said. "This is my husband, Detective Sergeant Adam Prescott. He's here to help me with the reason for my visit."

The atmosphere in the room changed in an instant. Mrs. Ross clung to the diamond-studded cross around her neck, and Mr. Ross shifted his eyes away. After an awkward moment of silence, Mrs. Ross eventually spoke. "Your husband. Can't say that's how I envisioned your future. But, anyway, what brings you back to Cedar Lake?"

"There's been a recent development into Lindsay's death. Do you both have a few minutes?"

Her name generated a reaction. "Sure. Yeah, of course. Something happen?"

"Might be best if we all take a seat," Christian said.

Christian and Adam trailed the couple into the adjacent room. Adam nudged Christian in the arm, and there weren't enough words in the English language to describe the sheer terror written across his face. The only thing Christian could do was mouth the words, *I'm sorry.*

They entered the room on the older couple's heels, and Mr. Ross extended his arm towards two oversized chairs near the fireplace.

"Have a seat," Mr. Ross said.

"Thanks," he said as he sat. "Are you acquainted with Taylor Jackson?"

Christian watched closely, hoping the name would produce some response. But to his disappointment, there was none. "I can't say that we are. Does *he* know something about what happened?"

"We're still gathering information. He's just a person of interest in the case."

"Sorry, I wish we could be of more help. But why are you asking about this guy, Taylor? Lindsay killed herself."

Christian's lips curled down. "I've read the report, but I believe otherwise. I believe Lindsay was murdered."

Mrs. Ross gasped and clung to her husband's arm.

"I'm sorry to be so blunt, I just wanted to throw that out there, so you were aware we are looking at this from a different angle. I have to ask, though, what was Lindsay's state of mind in the two weeks leading up to her death?"

"A little withdrawn. But focusing on her studies. I'm guessing you were the same way, right?"

He nodded. "Yeah. Exams were coming up. Our entire futures hinged on getting the perfect scores."

Adam butted in. "I understand your daughter was the editor of the school newspaper. Correct?"

Mr. Ross folded his hands in his lap and leaned forward. "She was. Oh, she loved it. That was her plan, you know, to leave for Regina and study journalism at the university."

"Did she have a laptop? Cell phone?"

"Well, sure, only the best for our little girl."

Christian wasn't sure where Adam was going with his questions but scooted around in his chair as he continued to rattle questions off.

"Do you still have those?"

Mrs. Ross slid her arm free and affectionately caressed her husband's wrinkled hands. "We kept her room the way it was. You're more than welcome to have a look around if you think it'll help."

"Thank you, it would help a lot. Would you mind if I borrowed those items?"

There was hesitation in her eyes, but Mr. Ross nodded. "Sure. Take whatever you need to nail the bastard who did this to my little girl."

"Chad?" Mrs. Ross called out.

A moment later, the stocky man with a full beard reentered the room. "Yeah?"

"Can you escort this constable to Lindsay's room?"

"Sure." Chad and Adam ascended the staircase just outside the den, leaving Christian alone. Their icy stares sent a shiver down his spine, but having known them for over twenty years, he accepted the fact: this was just who they were.

Mrs. Ross kept her eyes on Christian and called out. "And Chad. Give the nice constable her laptop and cell phone. Okay?"

"Sure thing, Mom."

NINE

ADAM FOLLOWED CHAD UP THE STEEP staircase to the second floor. The two exchanged no words until they reached the last door on the left.

"This is it," Chad said as he pushed the door inward.

Adam delivered the forced smile he practiced and perfected throughout his career as a constable. He crossed the threshold, and stepping inside was like a throwback to 2009 all over again. The room was impeccable. Posters of Lindsay's favorite celebrities and Polaroid photos of the few friends she had dotted the walls. But more notable were the framed awards, which she had arranged in a grid pattern. Without ever knowing her, a clearer image of Lindsay Ross formed in Adam's mind. She was a perfectionist.

Chad waited outside in the hallway but kept his eyes on Adam's every move. "Laptop's on the desk, chargers and cell phone are in the top drawer."

"Thanks."

Adam sat his backpack on the hardwood floor and plucked a fresh pair of latex gloves from the half-empty box. Chad spoke up, which baffled Adam.

"What's that for?"

Like most cyber guys, Adam never developed the ability to comfort people using his underlying charm. If he had to explain things to people, shutting off the tech speak proved his greatest weakness. Computers were more his interest. "Evidence preservation."

"Evidence! Whoa, you said you wanted to have a look at her stuff, now you're calling it evidence."

"It's just protocol."

Chad wasn't convinced. "What aren't you telling us?"

"Did anyone threaten your sister in the weeks leading up to her death?"

Chad shrugged and leaned against the door frame. "She . . . she was always sticking her nose into people's business."

"Is that a yes?"

His lower jaw quivered. He blinked more often. Chad Ross was holding something back.

"Chad, I'll level with you. I can't help you and your family uncover what happened to your sister if you don't tell me what you know."

He sighed. "You can't repeat what I say to my parents, okay?"

"I can't promise it won't come out. But what I can promise is that I won't tell your parents what we discuss. Deal?"

Chad hesitated. Was it possible that Christian's mastery of convincing people to spill their guts had somehow rubbed off on Adam? Either way, whatever Adam said convinced Chad to lower his guard.

"She was working on a story. Something big."

"Any idea what it was?"

"No idea. I caught her a few times sneaking out. Sometimes she wouldn't come back until after three in the morning."

"Did you ever follow her?"

He shook his head.

"Did she keep journals? A camera? Anything that you know of?"

"We turned all of those over to the constable in charge of the investigation.

Haven't seen them since."

"Okay. Christian and I must have missed them. Did your sister have any enemies you're aware of?"

He scoffed. "My sister pissed off damn near everyone in this town at one point or another. Although there was an incident a week before her death in the school parking lot. I wasn't there, but it was the talk of the town for a few days."

"Was it serious?"

"Nah, just a spat between Lindsay and her ex-best friend, Angela."

"What about?"

"A guy. Linus Roussin. He's the bartender over at McGinty's. You know the place?"

That name stirred up unpleasant memories from Adam's last visit to Cedar Lake. The helplessness of watching Christian lie in the hospital bed, broken and bruised, returned.

His voice trembled, and he replied with one word. "Yup."

"That's all I know. If you need more details, I'd start with those two."

"Angela, does she have a last name?"

"Martin."

"Anything special about her I should know?"

"Christian should remember her. But she's the mayor's daughter. My advice—tread carefully."

Adam jotted the two names in his pocket notebook. "Got it, thanks. I'll only be a few more minutes, and I'll get out of your hair."

"Sure. Take your time. I'm right down the hall if you need anything."

Chad tapped his hand against the door frame and vanished from view. Adam carried on, removing his evidence collection kit from his backpack. Four anti-static bags, two Faraday bags, tape, and labels to record which cords went with which device.

He chugged along, taking his time to collect things the right way. Even though this wasn't an official investigation, if the day ever came where it was, he could say with certainty that he followed evidence collection protocols to the letter.

When he was finished, he gave the room one last look over. On his first step towards the door, the floorboard under his foot squeaked and slid.

What the . . .

He pressed his hand against the wood, and it jiggled ever so slightly. He had a pretty good idea of what he had stumbled upon.

Sneaky. A hidden cache.

He rifled through the bag, on the hunt for his trusty pocketknife to pry the board loose. Somehow, Adam must have spent too much time away, and soon three familiar voices grew louder in the distance.

Shit.

Adam hastily slid the blade between the seams, pried up the floorboard, and without looking, scooped whatever hidden items were there into his last antistatic bag. He tossed the evidence into the backpack, replaced the board, and by the time the Rosses arrived at the door, he zipped the backpack closed.

Adam stood, hiding the knife behind his back. Maureen Ross stared him down before she crossed her arms over her chest. "We were worried you got lost. Did Chad help you find everything you needed?"

"Yes, ma'am, he did. Sorry if I worried you. I lost track of time reading each of the awards she won. You two must have been proud."

"She was a fireball," David Ross said. A genuine smile graced his face.

Christian wrapped up the conversation, which gave Adam time to retract the knife's blade and discreetly slide it into his back pocket.

Christian glanced at Adam, who picked up on Adam's cue; it was time to go. "Well, Mr. and Mrs. Ross, thank you so much for your time. Once I have an idea about whether Taylor was telling the truth, I'll be sure to get in touch."

Christian gripped the door handle while Adam pulled a business card from his wallet. "And if you can think of anything else that might help us, please, don't hesitate to call."

"We will. And thank you for taking a second look into this."

"I owe it to Lindsay and your family to do right by her. If there's more to this, then you deserve the truth."

The door closed behind them, and as much as Adam wanted to share what he found with Christian, he held back his excitement.

As the car backed down the driveway, Christian exhaled. "I wasn't expecting them to be so . . ."

"So, homophobic?"

He nodded. "Of course, look at where we are. This is blue-collar territory. Our kind aren't much liked in these parts."

"Eh, it is what it is."

"Did you find anything useful on your search?" Christian asked.

That broad grin, the one that no matter how hard he tried to suppress, appeared across Adam's face.

"Well?"

"I got what we came for."

"Then why the shit-eating grin?"

"I may have also walked out of there with something not even the Rosses knew existed."

"Well, don't leave me hanging. What d'you find?"

Adam unzipped the backpack and pulled out the bag he'd hastily filled. "Let's have a peek," he began. "Got a couple flash drives, an audio recorder, and a few SD cards. It's not much, but sure as hell must be important to hide under the floor."

"Under the floor? Tell me you didn't destroy their property."

He shook his head. "I destroyed nothing—the board just popped out."

Christian shook his head.

"I'm serious. They'll never know. Now can we get back to your dad's house so I can uncover what was so secret that Lindsay needed to hide it?"

If Christian replied, Adam wasn't paying attention. The whole time Christian backed down the driveway, he couldn't divert his eyes from the fluttering curtain from the second story. The harder he stared, the more confident he was someone was watching. And the eeriness sent a shiver down his spine so intense he glanced away.

TEN

CHRISTIAN'S WATCH BEEPED. FOUR O'CLOCK SHARP. With the first box in hand, he rounded the corner and sat it on the table's edge. He glanced over his shoulder and found a distracted Adam, who methodically laid out the endless supply of necessary equipment.

"Don't forget we have dinner plans in less than two hours," Christian reminded him.

He glanced up. "I haven't, but we should at least do a light dive to get a better sense of what we're working with."

"Agree."

But Adam wasn't letting his concern about the evidence go. "With your dad having a girlfriend, I have concerns that leaving this out in the open isn't safe anymore."

Christian brushed his hyperactive discomfort aside. "We haven't officially reopened Lindsay's case. Plus, I doubt anything we find in these boxes isn't already public knowledge anyhow."

Adam pointed to the array of flash drives, her cell phone, and laptop laid out on the table. "And these?"

"Yeah, those will never leave our side," he said, his tone changing. "Don't get me wrong, I love and trust my dad. But since no one knows about the peripherals, we can't risk them falling into the wrong hands."

Adam nodded and slid the laptop from the plastic evidence bag. Before losing himself in copying the hard drive, Adam broke out a brush, fingerprint powder, and tape roll. A laptop sitting around, more than likely full of incriminating evidence—he was sure someone had tried to access it within the last twelve years.

The dusting took a few minutes, and as he raised the brush for the last time, six pristine prints dotted the lid. After lifting the prints, he began copying the hard drive.

Adam sat at the table, watching the progress bar fill in. Then a name popped into his head, and he turned to Christian. "Hey."

"Yeah?"

"Ever heard the name Angela Martin before?"

Christian's piercing eyes locked with Adam. "Remember those fake people I mentioned?"

"Yup."

He turned around the picture he held in his hand and pointed. "She's one of them. Along with her queen bee, Heather Grant."

"It might be smart to chat with her at some point."

Christian picked up a photo of Angela, which sat on the table. It was a more recent photo, one he had snagged from her public Facebook account. He never understood why people were so careless with their private information. Christian managed not to sidetrack himself and glared at the photo. The very idea of facing her tightened his stomach muscles to the point he crouched forward discreetly.

If Adam brought her up, he must have a credible reason.

"Can it wait until tomorrow? That visit with the Rosses wore me out."

Adam glanced at his watch. "Yeah, I mean, you're right. Pearson's on his way over, and the case has already sat dormant for twelve years. Another day won't hurt."

Christian nodded and continued reading through the case files.

They left the conversation at that, and Adam sat idly by as the process finished up earlier than he expected. When he transferred the copied hard drive over to his laptop, he immediately ran into his first snag.

"Damnit!"

While pinning photos of persons of interest to the wall, the outburst sent Christian's head spinning. "Whoa, whoa. Relax. What's up?"

Adam banged his hand against the table. "Someone wiped the hard drive."

"What does that even mean, *wiped*?"

The frustration spilled from Adam's mouth. "It means we're screwed."

Christian slid the photo of Angela Martin back onto the table. A few footsteps later, he towered over his husband, who raked his fingers through his thick hair. This wasn't the first, nor would it be the last, time Adam worked himself up over a case.

Christian placed both hands firmly against his shoulders. In a reassuring voice, he said. "What if Lindsay did it?"

Adam buried his face in his hands, and Christian rubbed his husband's back. This was one of his biggest complaints about working with his husband—any time there was a hiccup, Adam would unleash his frustration out on him. Not on purpose, but Christian hated it with a passion.

Christian closed his eyes and sucked in a calm breath. Then a subdued, baritone voice spoke. "Maybe she did. But why?"

"Could be she foresaw what was coming?"

Christian shrugged. "I mean, you've met the locals; it doesn't take much to ruffle their feathers, but once you do, you're bound to get a few threats. Might have better luck with the flash drives?"

After another deep breath, Adam reached for the first flash drive. He retracted the USB and slid it into the reader. Even though this illegally obtained evidence would never hold up in court, he still followed the protocols and made a copy.

The process was quick, and soon a window popped up on the monitor. His eyes scanned the names assigned to each folder. They weren't what he expected on a typical teenage girl's storage device.

"Hey, you want to look at this?" he asked.

Christian smiled. "You got something?"

"Yeah, but maybe you can help make sense of this."

Christian returned to hovering over Adam, and he glanced at the screen. "What am I looking at?"

"The names. Blondie? The Boss? Squirrely? Any of those names pop out at you?"

"No clue. But let's start with The Boss."

Adam moved the cursor over the yellow folder and double-clicked. A slew of more folders appeared, but one, labeled *Scandal*, caught his eye. "Hmm."

Inside the folder was a single Word document titled *She's a cheater*. Adam double-clicked the familiar blue icon.

It was a rough draft of a newspaper article. Adam read the headline out loud. "Cheating Scandal Rocks Cedar Lake."

Adam peered over the monitor. "Do you remember this article?"

Christian pulled out the seat next to Adam. "Nope. And I don't remember any cheating scandals either."

Christian noted the date just below the heading. April 6, 2009. She wrote the article less than a month before he and Gemma found her hanging in the sawmill.

He perused the rest of the article, and when he reached the end, he slouched in the chair and folded his arms across his chest.

"I had no idea any of that was happening."

Adam glanced away from the monitor, and their eyes met. "Seems like this gives the 'Queen Bee' a motive to me."

Christian scoffed. "Yeah, it's always the popular ones who are into all sorts of shit."

"How about this guy, Principal Lowry? You think he's still around?"

He managed a shrug, but before he could respond, a thumping at the front door cut him off.

"What the—" Adam jerked in his seat.

Christian jumped up, and as he moved towards the door, his watch beeped. Six o'clock. From the top of the stairs, his father's booming voice echoed down. "Are you expecting someone, Christian?"

"Pop—scare the shit out of me, why don't ya. Yeah, it's probably Pearson."

Christian choked on his words as Matthias's heavy footsteps stomped away from the landing. Shaking his head all the way to the door, he pulled it open. Pearson's broad shoulders blocked Christian's view beyond the door frame, and he took two steps back just to get a full glimpse of the giant.

He smiled, and his eyes traveled from the man's head to his feet. The constable appeared to be in a rare, relaxed mood. From the indigo V-neck to the fresh boot cut Levi's, it was a side of Pearson that Christian hadn't experienced before.

"Hey," Christian said. He balled his hand together, and their first bumped mid-air.

An infectious smile graced his face. "Yeah, I know. I'm early. Hope I'm not interrupting anything."

"Nah, you're good. We stumbled on something and, well, you know the rest."

Pearson nodded.

"Well, come in. Mi casa es . . ." Christian trailed off. Spanish wasn't his strong point.

Pearson wiped his feet on the doormat and stepped in. "Let's stick with English, yeah? French, Spanish, never quite caught on with me."

Christian smiled and closed the door. They made their way towards the dining room. "How'd things go with the Rosses?"

"Other than their subtle dashes of homophobia, I think it went well."

"Damn, I should have warned you. They may be the richest family in this area, but they aren't the most open-minded. You still got the laptop, right?"

Adam replied as he clicked through more folders. "Ah, we got it. Except there's one slight problem: someone wiped the hard drive clean."

"As in deleted?" Pearson asked.

Adam grinned. "You catch on quick, Luke."

"So finding any information is a no-go, I take it?"

"Not exactly. We have this saying back in Quebec, *L'habit ne fait pas le moine.*"

Christian lowered his head and shook it from side to side. "Adam, why must you be a showoff?"

"Impressive, but as I explained to your husband, French and me, not friends. But there must be a point to your proverb, right?" Pearson asked.

"It means there's more to Lindsay than meets the eye. She must have either wiped it herself, or she sensed her fate was unavoidable and copied all of her files before hiding them."

"Basically what he's trying to say is he found where she hid all the good stuff and . . ."

Pearson interrupted. "Stole it?"

Christian glanced at Adam and raised his hands in front of him. "Hey, he said it, not me."

"I didn't steal it. They gave me permission to remove anything electronic-related from the room. They never said I couldn't pop up a floorboard and look around."

Pearson grinned. "They never said you *could* either. You understand all of this will be inadmissible in court if we find anything."

"I do. But if we play this right, all this stuff may be irrelevant to building a case. We've already found a few people with motives," Adam said.

"Like who?"

"Like Heather Grant, Angela Martin, and even perhaps this Principal Lowry. You know any of them?"

"Yeah, I know 'em all. Lowry's still principal over at Cedar Lake High. Angela Martin is the mayor's daughter. And Heather, well, she and her husband, Peter, run the pharmacy in town. What do those three have to do with this?"

"I'm glad you asked. Turns out, Heather and Principal Lowry had cooked up a scheme in 2009 to alter provincial exams for any grade twelve student—at a price."

Pearson cocked his head, and the wheels turned. "One word comes to my mind: illegal. Yet, I gotta ask, does Lindsay offer any proof to back up her claim?"

"I haven't gotten that far," Adam said as he waved his hand over the pile of flash drives and SD cards. "There are hundreds of gigabytes for me to sift through. I know you wanted to take us out but staying in might be a better plan."

Constable Pearson pulled out a free chair and sat. "Well, you don't think Christian and I are going to make you do all this by yourself, do you?"

Adam glanced around at their faces. "Hell no. We're here to help, aren't we, Christian?"

Christian nodded coyly.

"And Adam, I got plenty of places on speed dial for takeout. Now I understand how you'd suspect a motive with Heather and Lowry, but how does Angela fit into your suspect list?"

"Right. Chad Ross told me she and the victim had a fight in the parking lot a week before she died."

Christian tapped his finger against the table. "I remember that fight. Angela accused Lindsay of stealing some guy, but I don't remember his name offhand."

"Sure, you do. He's the same guy who had you jumped outside McGinty's two years ago," Adam said.

"Linus."

"That's the one. Most murders happen because of three things: money, drugs, and love."

"Yeah, well, which of those was the reason Lindsay's life was cut short?" Christian asked.

He glanced around at their faces, yet neither of them offered a response.

Christian leaned forward and rested his elbows on the table. "Buckle up, because the more we learn, the more I foresee shady characters trying to stop us."

ELEVEN

KEYS CLACKING FILLED AN OTHERWISE SUBDUED room. The sun dipped below the horizon over an hour ago, exposing the breathtaking nighttime sky which Christian remembered gazing at as a child.

His eyes burned from staring at a computer screen for the last three hours, and he pressed hard against them with the palm of his hand, hoping to relieve even a little pain. It didn't help. He blinked twice and turned towards the archway between the kitchen and dining room, where he found his father, watching over everyone as they pecked away.

Christian couldn't take his eyes off his old man, even though Matthias hadn't noticed his son watching him. As he studied his father's face, he realized he'd missed some minor details yesterday.

His locks were a bit grayer, and sure, those stubborn bags underneath his father's eyes sagged more. These were things one expected from anyone in their mid-sixties. But then that devilish grin grew on his face, and Christian remembered the last time he saw it: three decades ago. When his mother, Sarah, was still alive. A time before the bottles of cheap whisky sucked his father's soul away.

But it was back, and to Christian, that meant only one thing; that genuine happiness had returned.

Christian soaked up the innocent moment a few seconds longer, as his glasses slipped from his fingers and crashed against the keyboard. Matthias jumped in surprise. "Sorry, Pop. We didn't wake you, did we?"

He pressed his palm against the wall and pushed his body off the wall. "Nah, couldn't sleep. Must be old age setting in."

Christian chuckled.

"But from the looks of it, you three have seen better days. Might do you all some good to get a good night's rest and pick things up when your heads are clear."

Christian shook his head disapprovingly. "No time for sleep. Taylor didn't drive all the way to Regina for shits and giggles. He came with a purpose: to warn us to stop someone."

Matthias approached, pulled out a chair, and scooted next to his son. "My boy, you can't do this to yourself. You're smart," he said as he glanced around the room. "You're all smart. But we all know if you cram, you'll fail."

"Another hour, Pop, then I promise I'll call it a night. Okay?"

"Okay, another hour." The old man stood and walked across the room. He stopped, rested his hand against the plasterboard, and hesitated.

Christian, hell-bent on figuring out what happened to Lindsay, had returned to clicking away through the droves of files when a movement caught his eye.

"Pop?"

His father glanced over his shoulder. "Hmm?"

"Did you need anything else?"

There was a moment of silence, and then out it came. "Can we talk for a minute? In private?"

The clattering of fingers hitting the keys ground to a halt, and all eyes focused on Christian. He swallowed hard and pushed himself away from the table.

"Sure."

Christian followed his father along the dimly lit hallway into the kitchen. His father never asked to speak privately before. He wiped his damp hands against his shirt and took a deep breath to quieten the heartbeats banging against his eardrums.

Is he dying? Does he know something about Lindsay?

The thoughts swirled, and all he could do was keep asking himself a shit-ton of 'what-if' questions in his head. His father stopped and leaned against the kitchen counter.

With a quiver in his voice, Christian asked, "Pop . . . what's going on?"

Matthias bowed his head and exhaled sharply. "I think we need to talk about earlier."

Part of him was relieved, but the other part of him cringed at the direction the conversation was heading—uncharted territory for the Anderson household.

With hesitation in his voice, Christian replied. "Before you say anything, I want you to know I'm cool with you and Joanna."

Matthias raised his head. "You—are?"

"And I'm sorry about earlier. But I promise you, Pop, it was just shock . . . nothing else. It's just, I've never seen you with anyone besides Mom, and that was so long ago."

Matthias smiled, and tears grew in his eyes. "You mean that?"

"I do. I want what's best for you. And if Joanna makes you happy and keeps you out of trouble, then yeah, I'm good." Christian took a few steps towards him. "You're happy, aren't you, Pop?"

"She's a special woman, you know."

"I'd love to get to know her a little more while I'm back if that's okay," Christian said.

"How about tomorrow evening? She has a daughter close to your age; I could invite her, too."

Christian scanned through everything he needed to do the next day, but some stuff could wait. He wanted to appease his father and thank the woman who kept him on the right path. "Tomorrow evening's perfect."

"And if you get a lead?"

"Then it'll have to wait until Monday. You and me, we're spending at least a little quality family time together."

Christian reached out and wrapped his arms around his father's neck. Never the most affectionate when it came to his family, Christian turned a corner in his life. Gone were the days of invisibility, negativity like he didn't matter. For the first time, his father noticed him—the real him—and nothing would ever take that away again.

Christian loosened his embrace and stepped back. "Well, I should get back to work. Unless you wanted to talk about something else?"

"I think we about covered it."

Christian smiled and turned back for the archway. Halfway there, he stopped and cocked his head over his shoulder. "And Pop?"

Matthias didn't reply.

"I'm so proud of the progress you've made."

***

CHRISTIAN SLID BACK INTO HIS SEAT. He'd been gone long enough that the screen went black. He tapped the spacebar, and the screen awoke from its brief slumber. Before he plunged back into the endless drafts of articles Lindsay had written for the school paper, he glanced across the table at Adam and Pearson. The two remained engrossed in whatever they were doing, so much, they neglected to notice Christian had returned.

He drummed his fingers against the table. The table vibrated, and it snapped Adam out of his deep concentration. His eyes peered over his monitor towards Christian, and he smiled.

"Everything all right?" he asked.

"Yup. Did I miss anything in here?"

Pearson removed his headphones, unplugged them from the computer, and set them on the table. "I found something interesting."

"Thank God. I don't know how much more of this toxic-positive writing I can take."

"I gotta warn you, though, you won't like it, and having no audio doesn't help."

"It can't be *that* bad," Christian said. He stood and walked around the table and stood behind Pearson.

With all eyes on the screen, Pearson restarted the grainy video footage he uncovered on one of the SD cards. For the first ninety seconds, the video wobbled, like whoever filmed it walked with the camera at their side.

Then the shaking stopped. In the backdrop was a familiar setting; the alley behind McGinty's Pub on First Avenue. As the camera zoomed and focused, three silhouettes appeared outside the backdoor near the dumpster.

"What is this?" Christian asked.

"Just wait for it."

Christian waited, and just as Pearson promised, he got a better idea of why the video was valuable.

Immediately, the camera picked up two familiar faces. "Is that . . ." he paused. "That's Lee White."

"In the flesh. I told you, you wouldn't like it."

The camera panned, then zoomed out, and standing next to Lee was another face Christian would never forget. He gulped before running his fingers through his matted hair.

"That's Taylor."

"Explains how he's involved."

"But who are they talking to?" Adam asked. He pointed at the hooded figure standing with their back to the camera.

"You'll see," Pearson said. Those two words were becoming his personal mantra this time around. "Shouldn't be long now."

The calmness on-screen changed, and the hooded man lunged at Lee and Taylor. But his intimidating stance didn't last long when Taylor reached behind his back and pulled a handgun from his waistband. Still, the entire time the mystery man never turned his face towards the camera. He backed away with his hands in the air.

"He was always the quiet kid in school. The one you never expected any trouble out of. But now. Now that harmless image I've had of him all these years is tainted."

They watched a few more seconds, and just as Christian let out a yawn, the hooded figure turned, and the camera caught a crystal-clear frame of his face. Pearson paused the video and cocked his head over his shoulder.

"Now, do you understand why I played this?"

Christian choked on his expletives. "Chad Ross. That dirty lying bastard."

PART 3

SUNDAY
CEDAR LAKE, SK

"Things come apart so easily when they have been held together with lies."
—Dorothy Allison

TWELVE

A POUNDING AT THE FRONT DOOR awoke Christian from a less-than-stellar night's sleep. As he rolled onto his side, he grabbed his cell phone from the nightstand. 8:15 a.m.

"Ugh. It's too early for this," he groaned.

He slid on his jeans and tee before staggering along the short hallway to the stairs. Another series of raps at the door echoed through the house.

He muttered under his breath. "I'm coming. Jesus."

Without checking, he flung open the door and standing there was Gemma, with an overnight bag in hand. His crusted-over eyes widened, and he gave her a hard stare up and down.

"What the hell?"

"Surprise!" she exclaimed.

"Why are you here?"

"Is that any way to greet your best friend?"

A sigh escaped from his mouth. "When she shows up, unannounced—it is. So, let me ask again: why are you here?"

"I told my boss what was going on, and she compromised. I find someone to cover my shifts, and I can take a few days off."

"And since you're standing before me, I take it you found an unfortunate soul to cover for you?"

"Bingo. So, are you going to invite me in, or do I have to stay on the front steps?"

He lingered, reluctant to step aside, but Gemma had a way about her that always forced him to give in. He extended his arm, and she breezed through the front door and dropped her bag on the foyer floor.

Like Christian, this was her first visit to Cedar Lake since her sister's death at her own father's hands. She gazed around the foyer.

"Your father's been busy."

"He's got a girlfriend now, so I'm sure this transformation had a lot to do with her."

"Aw shit. Go ahead, Mr. A. Where's Adam?"

"Hopefully still asleep, unless your drum solo with the front door woke him too."

"Stop being so whiny," she said. "Ooh, before we do anything else, there's something I need to talk to you about while we're alone."

"Coffee first, then we talk."

Gemma followed him toward the kitchen, and with every step she took, the changes continued to impress. "I just can't get over how clean the place is. Do I detect a hint of citrus in the air?"

"Like you said, the old man's been busy."

"Speaking of . . . where is he?"

"Probably the same place I should be. Asleep."

She shook her head. "Funny. His car isn't in the drive."

Christian pressed 'brew' on the machine and leaned against the counter. "He might have needed some alone time with Joanna?"

"That must be the girlfriend?"

"Nothing gets past you."

"And? Do you like her?"

He shrugged. He didn't want to appear overly enthusiastic, but he also didn't want to seem like a cold-hearted ass. "Our encounter was brief, but any woman who can keep my father sober and keep this house immaculate . . . well, she's a keeper."

Their small-talk continued back and forth while the coffee brewed, and Christian handed over a mug for Gemma.

"So, what do you need to talk to me about?"

"It's about Cassidy."

Christian took his first sip. "Okay. And this involves Lindsay in some way, I take it?"

"Not sure yet. Do you remember that party we went to after prom?"

"Come on now, how could I forget that night? The fight in the Ridgeway Inn parking lot. The in-between is a blur—too much booze."

She snorted. "Well, that fight was because of Cassidy. It seems drugs weren't the only thing my sister couldn't break herself away from . . ."

He took a longer sip. "Charles?"

She shook her head. "Worse. Much worse." Her calm demeanor swung as quick as a winter storm in mid-January, and soon pools of tears flooded her eyes. Christian set his mug on the kitchen counter and rushed to comfort her. Whatever she had to share must be significant to bring his otherwise-carefree friend to tears.

"You should sit," he said. He wrapped his arms around her shoulder and pulled out a bar stool for her.

Gemma wiped away the tears that now streamed down her cheeks. "Jesus, why am I even crying?"

"You lost your sister. Anyone would do the same if they were in your shoes."

"I miss her, you know."

He nodded. "Just take your time. There's no rush."

"I never told you this. Hell, I never told anyone this."

"You can tell me now."

"I just wanted to honor her memory and not let it be marred by what happened."

Listening more than he spoke, Christian held her hand while Gemma struggled to find the words to express what she needed to get off her chest.

Then the words came. Four words that changed everything.

"She was a prostitute."

Christian couldn't speak. He sat there with a blank stare across his face as Gemma continued to detail the years of torture her sister endured at the hands of their mutual foe. But he hadn't heard a single word after the big one; prostitute. How had this major news flash evaded him in the time since they found Cassidy's body?

Finally, there was a break in the story, and Christian pulled out the other barstool and sat. "And you believe Lee White was behind it?"

She nodded.

"And the brawl in the parking lot? What was that about?"

"Do you remember they wouldn't let us in the room?"

"Yeah. She just handed over a bottle of booze, and we got trashed in the courtyard."

"Yeah, that's because Lee didn't rent the room for an after-prom party. He rented it because he expected my sister to . . ." She paused.

"To what, Gemma?"

"God, I don't even think I can say it out loud. Lee rented the room so five guys could have an orgy with my sister."

Fourteen years was a long time to remember every detail about just another boring night in Cedar Lake for Christian. Slowly, fragments about that night filled in. But Christian kept his mouth shut and focused on getting his best friend to unload the burden she'd carried with her for so many years. "This is tough, I get it. But you know I'm here for you. I promise once you let all of those pent-up emotions go, you'll be on the road to better days."

After a few slow breaths, Gemma continued. "Things got out of hand with one of her johns that evening. And when Charles showed up, things escalated."

"That was Charles?"

She bobbed her head. "He took the first swing. Then the second. But the john wasn't playing games. He pulled a knife on Charles, and if Cassidy hadn't stepped in when she did . . ."

Christian squeezed his eyes shut. "Things would have been bloodier."

They sat in silence. Christian kept his eyes shut. But then a faded memory snuck up on him. "I remember. Someone slapped her, didn't they?"

"Yeah, Charles did. That was all there was to the fight, and the sex-crazed guy fled on foot. The next day, Charles begged with his father to let her go."

"Did he?"

"Yeah, but by then, the damage was done. Her drug use grew more intense and frequent. She stopped caring. Not just about people, but about life. And I sat by and watched my sister waste away into a zombie."

The anger bubble burst, and the all-too-tough Gemma bawled even louder. With her face buried in her hands, there wasn't much Christian could say to take away her pain. He did the best he could to console her. She let out a scream just as Adam appeared at the base of the stairs, watching the dramatic scene unfold.

Adam made a move towards them but stopped before he even took his first step. Christian motioned with his head and pointed towards the living room. Adam needed nothing further and vanished from sight.

A few minutes went by, and Gemma came up for breath. "I don't know what's gotten into me. Why now?"

"You've kept all this hurt and anger bottled up so long, you were bound to explode at some point."

"I lied. I didn't come to tell you just that. I could have done that over the phone."

"Then why did you come back to this shithole?"

"Because I'm concerned."

"About?"

"You."

"Me? Why?"

"How soon you forget the last time you went head-to-head with Lee. You ended up in a hospital bed, and I damn near lost my life at the sawmill."

"But you didn't. I didn't. We survived."

"Barely."

"Gemma, listen, bruises heal, and I swear my days of going 'rogue' are far behind me now. This time, I'm going by the book."

"I'd love to believe that, Christian. But I know you better than you know yourself. Besides, this is Lee White we're talking about. The guy who calls the shots around these parts. The same guy who ordered an attack on you just because you were snooping around. You can't take him on alone."

"Are you telling me you believe Lee White is involved in what happened to Lindsay?"

Her shoulders lurched upward. "I sure as hell know he had his hand in turning my sister into a whore."

Her nostrils flared, and Christian needed to divert the topic away from her arch-nemesis before she lost her cool. "Hey, I know you want to talk about Lee White, but do you remember a guy named Chad Ross?"

"Yeah. Everyone knows Chad. Hell, everyone knows his family too."

"What's your take on him? Is he the type of guy who could be mixed up with Lee White?"

Gemma paused and studied Christian's face. He was never one who could keep secrets well.

"What aren't you telling me?"

"Huh? Nothing. I just want your opinion."

"No, you know something. It's written all over your face."

"I'm just . . . curious."

"You want my censored or uncensored answer?"

Christian stood from the stool and planted a hand on his hip, and cocked his head. "What d'you think?"

"Uncensored it is. I don't trust anyone in that family. For starters, I hated Lindsay after her little news piece almost got me expelled. Then, Mr. Ross, he's just a piece of work."

"How so?"

"It's hard to explain. This town, the people, they all bust their asses to make a few dollars. Were you aware that over sixty percent of the town is living below the poverty line? Or that we lost close to a thousand residents after all the jobs vanished?"

"I had no idea it was *that* bad. What does that have to do with the Ross family?" Christian asked.

"You don't know . . . do you?"

Christian shook his head.

"David Ross sold the sawmill and a few other businesses around town right before the global recession in 2006. But then the lawsuits came that summer, and by fall, it closed."

"You're telling me he sold the sawmill? Before Lindsay's death?"

"Yes. As far as I'm aware, no one bought it. The place had a bad rap for the accidents, so Ross abandoned the place."

"So in a nutshell, David Ross is the reason behind Cedar Lake's downfall?"

"You bet your sweet ass he is. But it's not just that. It's the way they flaunt their wealth around town while everyone else suffers. Jesus, I've gone off on a tangent. Sorry."

"It's okay, Gemma."

"Now, tell me about Chad Ross. And don't tell me *nothing* because I've grown very good at telling when you're about to lie or are lying."

Christian closed his eyes. The very thought of dragging Gemma into another mystery involving Cedar Lake's finest citizens troubled him. Not because she hadn't matured the past two years, not even because she wasn't a trained investigator. It was her instability that lay at the heart of his hesitancy.

"Well. . .?" she chimed in again.

He opened his eyes. It took just a millisecond for the words to fall from his mouth. "I can't tell you."

"Why not?"

"Because."

"Not an answer. Is Chad Ross involved or not?"

"You're going to badger me until I tell you, aren't you?"

"Hmm, yeah. That's how it works."

"Why do you care so much? You said it yourself how much you hated Lindsay. Why are you suddenly interested in determining if her death was a murder or suicide?"

"Two words: Lee White. If he's responsible, I want to be here when you take him down."

"Gemma . . ."

"I deserve the satisfaction of seeing that asshole's face when you slap the handcuffs on him and toss him away in jail. He stole my sister, and I've suffered in silence every day because of it."

She had a rational argument. After everything the bastard put her through, she *deserved* to be there to bask in the glory and watch as the arrogance on his face vanished when Pearson hauled him away. But first, Christian had to find something to support that Lee White was involved in Lindsay's death. And in this early stage of the investigation, they lacked evidence to suggest her death was anything but what it appeared to be—a suicide. Moving beyond the circumstantial evidence so far had proved more difficult than he could have ever expected.

He stood. She watched. He paced the floor, circling around the kitchen in a tight formation. To involve her or not involve her was weighing on his every thought. Then he stopped and stared into her eyes. "Gemma?"

"Yeah?"

"There's something I need to show you."

"Okay. What?"

Two words dropped from his mouth, what he referred to as Pearson's mantra. "You'll see."

THIRTEEN

GEMMA FOLLOWED CHRISTIAN INTO THE DINING room. He pulled out the same chair Constable Pearson had occupied only a few hours earlier. As she lowered herself against the wooden seat, Adam snuck past on his way to the kitchen.

Moments later, Adam appeared in the archway with a mug in his hand, and even though he was well aware she was there, he had to put on that goofy shocked expression. "Gemma?"

She turned around and smiled. "Morning sunshine."

He scanned both of their faces as Christian pried the laptop open. "What are you doing here?"

"I had a couple of free days, and what better place to be than here in Cedar Lake."

"But you hate it here and swore you'd never step foot in this town again."

"Things change."

"Well, while this place wouldn't be my first choice for a getaway, nonetheless, welcome home."

She smiled, and he moved closer to the table. "Dare I ask what you two are scheming now?"

Christian interrupted. "I think we should show her."

Adam understood what Christian was eluding to, and his eyes widened. "You sure that's wise?"

"Who else knows this man better than she does?"

Adam shrugged. "Your dad? Pearson? We could just go question the man ourselves."

They carried on, back and forth, but fed up, Gemma interjected. "Guys. Who in the hell are you talking about? And what exactly do I need to see?"

Christian cued up the video and hovered over her as she clicked play. Her eyes studied the video, just as the trio had the night before. When his ugly mug focused, Gemma noticed Taylor standing at the man's side. Her jaw dropped as Christian reached over and pressed pause.

"Taylor? You're telling me he was involved with Lee?" she asked.

"Appears so. But from your expression, I guess you had no clue either."

"No. Never. Sure, the guy was a loner and stoner, but to stoop this low?"

"Oh, he goes lower. Just keep watching."

She pressed play, and from the foyer, there was a pounding on the door. She flinched, and Christian rested his hand on her shoulder. "It's only Pearson, I'm sure. Relax."

Adam hurried away while Christian watched as Gemma's eyes fixated on the video in front of her. And even as Pearson entered the room, hugged Christian, and called out her name, never once did her eyes deviate from the screen. Instead, she lifted her index finger, signaling she needed another minute.

And a minute was all it took before her back slammed against the chair. She had reached the climactic ending of the video, which left her with more questions than answers.

"What. The. Hell?" she asked.

"And good morning to you, too," Pearson mumbled under his breath.

She lifted her head, and her eyes lit up at the sight of Pearson's face. "Luke. I didn't even hear you come in."

Pearson gave her a coy grin and quickly changed the subject. "Are you guys sure you want to drag Gemma into this?"

"There's something I should confess. The reason this is so important to us," Christian began.

"I assumed there was a reason. Should I sit for this one?"

Christian nodded.

"I'll get you some coffee," Adam said. He darted away, leaving Christian unsure if his husband wanted to avoid being there when he broke the silence about what he saw that mild May evening. Or was he just being polite?

Constable Pearson sat down next to Gemma and folded his hands atop the table. "Well?"

Christian stumbled on the first few words, but then it came out. "We were the ones who found her hanging, and I'm the one who phoned in the anonymous tip to the police."

Christian watched as Pearson grappled with understanding what Christian confessed to. The constable's eyes darted back and forth between both of their faces. "You're serious . . . aren't you?"

"Dead ass."

"Why didn't you come forward before today?"

"I was eighteen. I was afraid they'd try to pin a murder on us. But now I understand it was wrong of us to leave the scene."

Christian nibbled at his fingernails, and his foot bounced while he waited for Pearson to unleash his full fury on them. But to his surprise, he got the opposite.

"It's not a crime to discover a dead body, Christian. Should you have stayed, hard to say. But you did the right thing by calling it in."

The weight of a twelve-year secret unloaded, Christian clutched his chest. "I can't believe I kept that secret all these years. I just assumed you'd lock us up for fleeing a scene."

"Nah. But I need to ask; you remember anything from that night that seemed odd?"

Christian closed his eyes, and a thousand images flashed before his eyes. And then there it was. The image he tried for years to bury in the back of his mind, front and center now. He allowed his mind to rewind to ten minutes earlier to the bike ride to the sawmill.

With his eyes still closed, he began to speak. "I remember it was an unusually mild evening, and I was still reeling from knowing graduation was less than a month out. Gemma's riding beside me along the dirt path. We're both smiling."

Pearson lowered his voice and spoke in a calm, whisper-like fashion, almost as if he were some trained hypnotherapist. "Where are you heading?"

"To the sawmill. It was tradition when something good happened; Gemma always dragged me there. I hated that place. I tried to weasel my way out of it, but . . ."

Pearson and Gemma sat and listened as Christian continued.

"But Gemma insisted."

"Then what happened when you arrived?" Pearson asked.

"We stood at the main door. The area was quiet. A little too quiet given how beautiful a day it was, I suppose I expected more of our classmates to be there. Anyway, we walked in, and the dust particles floated in the air, and the building moaned. My heart is racing. I'm scared."

"Of what?"

His shoulders lurched upward. "It's my damn intuition kicking in. Then I remember the overturned chair next to the stairs; it was out of place."

Gemma confirmed. "I remember that."

"Then something told me to look up. And I did." His voice cracked, but he continued with the story. "There she was. The noose dug into her neck. Her face was a pale-blue, and all I could think about was getting her down from there."

"Then what?"

"Then I remember Gemma screamed, we ran, and we both swore never to speak about it again."

"But you called the police at some point?" Pearson asked.

"Yeah. When we hit the corner market, Gemma continued on home. But I waited until she was out of sight and used the payphone to phone it in."

Christian opened his eyes, and he wiped away a lone tear. He glanced over at Gemma. She never glanced up after he stopped speaking. She just kept her head down, staring at her hands folded in her lap.

"Did you ever get the sense someone else was there?" Pearson asked.

Gemma shook her head. "No—it's like Christian said, the place was calm. The chair was always in the loft, but the moment I spotted it overturned at the base of the stairs, I just assumed things might have gotten a little rowdy the night before. Nothing to me seemed out of the ordinary, but then again, I had smoked a little weed and had a glass or two of wine before we got there."

Christian disregarded her admission. "All these years, I've wondered about that chair. But after countless sleepless nights, I concluded she must have used it to hoist herself into the noose, and she kicked it over. It must have been my way of making it seem like what it was . . . a suicide."

Pearson reached out and grabbed Gemma's hand. "You've been awfully quiet. Is there anything *you* want to get off your chest while we're all being open and honest?"

Her expressionless face met his. Yet, she shook her head like she had nothing else to contribute. That was until Christian nudged her. "He should know about Cassidy and what Lee White did to her."

"What's he talking about, Gemma?"

She turned her head, and that infamous icy stare burned into Christian's eyes. "I told you that in confidence."

"I trust Luke, and I think you should too. What if he's still doing that to other girls as we speak? It won't bring Cassidy back, but you have the chance to exact your revenge on him. Here. Right now."

She inhaled sharply and exhaled. "Lee White is running a prostitution ring, or at least he was back in 2009. I know because Cassidy was one of his girls."

Pearson had no words. He just gripped her hand tighter.

"I'm only speculating here, but after seeing that video of those three together, it raises questions about what exactly they were up to."

"Was Lindsay going to use it to expose them?" Pearson asked.

"Why else make it? I think the only way to get answers is if we start asking questions. And by we, I mean me," Gemma said.

Christian scoffed. "Now, who's going rogue?"

"I'm not. I'm just trying to protect you. I might get some straight answers out of him if he doesn't think the police are involved."

"You could always wear a wire?"

She shook her head and waved her hands in front of her body. "Absolutely not. If I'm going out there, I'll get you the information you need. If he searches me and finds a wire, you can kiss your answers goodbye."

Things went quiet, and from the other side of the room, Adam's soothing voice pierced through the silence. "Is it safe to return?"

Christian waved him in, and he handed over the coffee he pretended to fetch. "So, what we need now is a game plan. Do we go as a group, or divide and conquer? All those in favor of staying together, raise your hand."

No one did.

"Well, the divide has it. Pearson and I will pay a visit to Angela Martin. As of now, she has the weakest motive to kill Lindsay."

"Wouldn't it make more sense to start with those who have the strongest motive, like, say, Lee White?" Gemma asked.

Adam waved his hand. "Let them squirm a little. If we want answers, we start low and hope those people talk to other people. If we play our hand right, they'll lead us straight to the top of the food chain."

Christian nodded along to his words and offered a few of his own. "He's right, Gemma. We could head over to the café and grab a coffee. You know, strategize our plan there."

And with their plans in place, everyone geared up for a day none of them would soon forget.

FOURTEEN

CHRISTIAN PUSHED THE DOOR INWARD, AND the bell attached chimed twice. The café was a hive of activity for so early on a Sunday morning. Then it dawned on Christian that Cedar Lake was nothing like Regina. People arose early here, and with nothing better to do, they all amassed in one of the few places open.

Christian released his grip on the door, and it slammed closed behind him and Gemma. His eyes widened at the line of eight customers, which snaked back to the corner of the room.

"Was this place always so popular?" he asked. "I've been gone so long I've lost those memories."

Gemma smiled. "Are you ever going to let the guilt of leaving this place and starting a better life go?"

"Someday. But today isn't it," he said.

The aroma of sweet coffee in the air brought back vivid memories of spending hours here after school studying filled his head. Then a booming, familiar voice interrupted his happy recollection. His eyes glanced upward, and standing in front of them was Principal Lowry.

"Christian Anderson?" the man asked.

Christian nodded, all the while studying the man's face. He'd grown older. Christian remembered his chestnut brown hair, which had now faded, leaving a few streaks of gray lining the sides of his temples.

The pleasantries moved on to Gemma, but no matter how much Christian wanted to be polite, he couldn't take his eyes off his face. A nudge in the arm jostled him from his daze.

"I was just telling Principal Lowry how wonderful things have been in Regina. Wouldn't you agree?" Gemma asked. Her face said more than her words ever could. *Snap out of it.*

"Right. Yeah, I mean, it'll never compare to Cedar Lake by any means, but Gemma and I have both found what makes us happy."

The line lurched forward, and the routine small talk continued. Then Lowry said it, something so absurd it took them both by surprise.

"I never pictured the two of you as a couple. Hmm. But glad to hear you two are settling down."

They swapped glances and laughed in sync.

"You are so off the mark there," Gemma said.

"I don't mean to laugh," Christian tried to compose himself. "I'm married, but not to Gemma. Someone else. A colleague I met through work many years ago."

Lowry's face turned redder than a beet, but he smiled and let out a chuckle. "I just assumed you two were an item back in high school. You were always inseparable."

The awkward laughter wrapped up, and then it hit him; Lowry was right. It was easy to mistake them for a couple. The chatter trailed off, and after a few minutes, they found themselves next in line.

Christian watched as the man paid for his order and tossed a few coins into the tip jar on the counter.

Lowry turned. "Hey, I'd love to hear more about what you two have been up to since high school. If you have time, join me."

Gemma began to object. "Well, we . . ."

But Christian had other plans, and his dominant voice overpowered hers. "What Gemma was saying is we'd love to. There's so much we want to fill you in on."

His lips curled outward and upward into a grin, and something in the man's cobalt eyes had Christian squirming in his seat. Somehow, he buried his discomfort and flashed a smile in return as he and Gemma approached the counter.

With Lowry out of earshot, Gemma leaned in close to his ear. "What the hell are you up to?"

"Nothing."

She crossed her arms across her chest while he ordered. "We're supposed to be planning our next move, not catching up with our high school principal."

Christian waited to respond while Gemma placed her order. As he handed the barista a twenty-dollar bill, he reacted. "Gemma. This man stood up for us countless times in high school. I think we can give him ten minutes of our day."

She huffed. "Ugh, fine. Just so you know, I can count on both hands stuff I'd rather be doing instead."

"This will make his day. Hell, it might even make his entire week."

Across the room, Christian found Lowry amongst a room full of people. He set up shop at a four-top table, with his laptop open in front of him, typing away.

Their eyes connected, and Lowry closed the lid. Christian pulled out a chair for Gemma, and they both sat across the table. For a few seconds, no one spoke. But being the social butterfly he believed he was, Christian interrupted the awkward silence.

"So, what's new around Cedar Lake High?"

Lowry's cell phone chimed. "Ah, same old. We finished the new science lab we tried for so many years to get up and running."

Another chime from his cell phone, but he never took his eyes off Christian.

"Wow! I remember you fought hard to get the funding for it. I sure hope it helps get the kids motivated. There's been a shortage of good constable candidates around Saskatchewan the past ten years. A state-of-the-art lab will be a great asset in getting kids involved in criminal justice and forensics."

Lowry smiled. "Gemma," he began. "Rumor around town says you started nursing school recently. How's that going for you?"

"Dreams do come true." The cell phone dinged for the third time, and Christian interrupted.

"Do you need to check that? Might be important."

His once peaceful eyes changed. Now his pupils flared, and Christian questioned why he even bothered asking. "Probably just the ex-wife wondering where I am. Part of the reason she's an ex. But enough about her, what brings you both back to town after so long?"

The conversation shifted into territory Christian wasn't comfortable sharing. Not because he was hiding anything from anyone, but frankly, it was no one's business what *really* brought him back to Cedar Lake.

He concocted a story in his head. "Just came up to spend some time with my pop. Since the wedding, I haven't seen him, and I, well, *we* wanted to check in on him. Make sure he's been doing alright."

"Ah, right. I've seen your father about town a lot; he's doing much better. I take it you've met Joanna?"

There was that name again. How did the entire town know about Joanna except for him? Just like he had with his father, Christian buried the simmering resentment. "She seems like a nice lady. We didn't get to speak much, though."

"Oh, you'll love her. Bit of a past that one has, but her good heart makes up for it."

His message only made Christian more hell-bent on learning everything about her. But not from his father, and what better person than the one sitting in front of him. "We all got one, but is there something I should know?"

"Eh, nothing. I didn't mean it to come across like that. Haven't we all done something in life we regret later?"

Christian nodded. "I hear ya. So what else can you tell me about her?"

"She's an elder on the reservation. Her daughter, Anwaatin, she attended Cedar Lake High, but she graduated a few years ahead of you. Maybe your paths crossed at some point?"

Gemma turned her head away. Her head bobbed back and forth until she turned around. "Wait. Did she go by Ani?"

Lowry nodded. "That's her. So, you knew her?"

"Her and Cassidy were close a long time ago. But something must have happened because one day, she just never came around anymore."

The cell phone sitting on the table dinged in rapid succession, and Christian glanced down at the screen. Several messages filled it, but there were no names attached to them, which meant Lowry had adjusted the settings to not display them.

Why would he do that? Perhaps he values his privacy? Or worse, he's involved in something illegal and doesn't want those close to him to have access?

He ignored his wandering mind and caught the tail-end of the discussion at the table.

"Gemma? Your latte is ready."

She jumped to her feet and back across the crowded café, leaving Lowry and Christian alone at the table.

That's when things took a different turn. One that blindsided Christian.

Lowry leaned across the table and, in a lowered, gruff voice, asked, "A little birdie told me you paid a visit to the Rosses yesterday. How'd that go?"

Christian checked over his shoulder. Gemma stood at the counter, making small talk with another patron, something Christian should have expected as she was acquainted with so many people here.

Meanwhile, the situation at the table grew more uncomfortable, given he had no idea how to explain why he'd gone there. Also, why was Lowry so interested in it to begin with?

At first, Christian stuttered. "I, um, I hadn't seen them in so long."

Pull it together, Christian. That's not a convincing cover.

Lowry pressed the rim of the mug to his lips, patiently expecting an answer.

"I needed to pay my respects. Lindsay and I were friends. But after her death, I didn't attend the funeral or pay my condolences to the family after it happened. The only thing I cared about in 2009 was getting the hell out of town as quick as I could."

The mug hit the table, and it shook. Lowry crossed his arms over his chest, and out came that devilish grin from earlier that raised the hairs on his arm. Gemma's unmistakable laugh echoed through the café, and Christian turned his head over his shoulder. *Let's go, Gemma.*

Lowry reached across the table and gripped Christian's forearm. "Listen to me good. You will stay away from the Rosses. If I hear you've been snooping around again, I'll—"

Even though the exchange shocked him, Christian remained defiant to get to the truth. "You'll what?"

"It'll be the last time."

The two men locked eyes. How was it possible this passive man, one he trusted for all those years, was threatening him? Gemma's cheerful voice in the background diverted his gaze, and sensing her return, Christian eased the tension in his shoulders.

Lowry released his grip on Christian's arm, and his husky voice returned to the pleasant one from before Gemma walked away. He smiled, took a sip of his coffee, and said, "Well, I'm sure they appreciated you stopping by."

He finished up his phoniness in time. Gemma tugged the chair, but before her ass hit the seat, Christian jumped up and put the chair between him and Lowry. He rested his hands atop the varnished wood and stared across the table.

"Well, we've taken up enough of your time. Thanks for letting us hang with you for a little bit and catch up."

Her head swung upward, and she said nothing but the shock in her eyes spoke loud and clear. Christian continued.

"I forgot we need to get over to the grocery to pick up some stuff for this dinner we're having with my dad and Joanna tonight."

Lowry swapped glances between Gemma and Christian. "Ah, well, great catching up, even if it was only for a few. But this is a small town; we're bound to run into each other again."

With only a head nod, Christian turned away with Gemma walking at his side. A heaviness followed him to the door, and before they reached the exit, Gemma piped up. "What's going on?"

"Nothing. Keep walking."

"Come on, I've never seen you end a conversation so abruptly."

Gemma began to turn her head back towards the table, but Christian stopped her.

"Whatever you do, don't turn around. Keep your head forward while we talk. Okay?"

There was a tremble in her voice now. "Yeah . . . okay."

"He knows I was at the Rosses yesterday."

Christian opened the door for Gemma, and she walked out first. He hesitated with his hand on the door. Something told him to turn around one last time.

As he turned his head, his instinct was right—his former principal had eyed him all the way to the door. Christian gave the man one final look-over as Lowry lifted his cell phone from the table and pecked away at the screen. He stepped over the threshold, but what he just experienced left an uneasiness in the pit of his stomach.

There's something not right about any of this. And I'll figure out what he's hiding.

FIFTEEN

CROSS TOWN, THE POLICE SUV PULLED up outside a quaint lakeside residence situated a few kilometers south of downtown. With one swift move, Pearson slipped the gearshift into park and killed the engine.

"Now remember what I said . . . let me do all the talking," Pearson asked.

"Of course. I wouldn't even know where to begin with these people."

"I'm sure you could think of a few things to say. But please . . . don't."

They slammed the doors shut, and Adam took a deep breath. A delicate scent of lavender filled the air, which brought a smile to his face. He walked along the gray cobblestone path flanked by multicolored flowers, doing his best to catch up with Pearson. As he stepped onto the porch, Adam pinned two labels on Angela Martin: control freak and perfectionist.

"Pretty place," Adam said.

"Someone sure put a lot of time and effort into making this place nice. The contrast between being a have-lot and a have-not."

Before they started up the stairs that led to the wraparound porch, the country-style screen door flung open, and a tall, bearded man in glasses appeared.

"Morning, constable. Something I can help you with?"

"Morning, Linus. I'm here to speak with your wife. She around?"

Although Adam had never set eyes on the man before, the name provoked him.

Linus . . . *the* Linus. The same guy who coordinated the vicious attack on Christian two years earlier and got off without a charge or citation.

Adam dismissed his personal grievance and instead focused on listening. An old saying, one his grandmother taught him long ago, stuck with him in every case. *When you shut up and listen, you learn a lot.* If he didn't listen, he'd never find the opportunity to poke holes in anything Linus said.

The tall man leaned against the wooden railing; his body language reeking of smugness. "Girlfriend, we haven't made things official yet. Why you looking for her? She in some sort of trouble?"

"No, nothing like that. We had some questions for her regarding Lindsay Ross and—"

Linus balled his hand into a fist and gritted his teeth. "That bitch? Even in death, she still haunts me."

Stunned by his sudden personality shift, Pearson tried to quell the hostility. "Now, Mr. Roussin, there's no need to get testy."

"What does Lindsay have to do with Angela?"

"There's been a deathbed confession in Regina from someone with insider knowledge, that Lindsay's death might not have been self-inflicted after all."

The glowing peach color of his skin drained, and he gripped the railing to steady his balance. "Wait. You're saying she *didn't* hang herself?"

"That's exactly what I'm saying," Pearson explained. "Now, I'm not trying to dredge up terrible memories, and I'm certainly not alleging anything."

Linus adjusted his position. "Okay."

"But rumor has it you and Lindsay called it quits about a month before her death. May I ask what happened?"

He hesitated to answer, and when Linus responded, it wasn't quite what Pearson expected. "People change. We changed."

"Care to elaborate?"

Just then, the screen door flung open again, and a petite, blonde-haired woman stepped onto the porch. "Babe, what's taking so—" She cut herself off at the sight of Pearson and Adam standing at the edge of the porch.

"This is Constable Pearson and . . ."

Adam cut him off. "I'm DS Prescott from the Regina Police Service."

"Nice to meet you both. Is there something we can help you with?"

Pearson explained the situation in full again.

"And may I ask who made this 'deathbed' confession?"

"Taylor Jackson. We're you acquainted with him?"

"I—yeah. We graduated together."

"And were you two friends?"

Angela shifted her eyes away and scanned the neighborhood. "Let's do this inside. I don't want any of our nosy neighbors to get the wrong idea."

"Sure," Pearson said.

Once inside, Angela led them towards the dining room situated between the living room and kitchen. "Make yourself comfortable."

Pearson and Adam each pulled out chairs across the table from the couple.

"You have a lovely house. How long have you lived here?" Adam asked.

"About seven years, right, honey?" Linus asked.

"Closer to eight, but who's counting."

"Well, you've done an amazing job. I'm not from here, but most of the houses in the area are drab, but yours, it's cheerful."

"Yeah, Angie must have color in her life. Isn't that right, honey?"

Her lip curled upward into a half-smile. "That's me, Little Miss Sunshine."

Adam carried on with his pleasantries, hoping he'd get them comfortable enough to hear some truths. "I can relate. I'm married to someone who's the same way."

For a moment, the tension whittled away, and after a friendly laugh, Pearson started in again with the serious questions. "Mr. Roussin, I realize I could ask anyone who graduated in 2009 this, but I want to hear it from you. Why did you and Lindsay end your relationship?"

Angela began to answer, but Linus reached for her hand and stroked her flawless skin. "Babe, you don't have to speak for me. Look, constable, Lindsay was a disturbed girl. She was always poking around in places she didn't need to. And, I'd had enough of the lies and games."

"Can you elaborate? What sort of stuff did she stick her nose into?"

"For starters, she stalked people. Badgered people with that damn video camera and recorder. She always said she wanted to weed out the bad in Cedar Lake, biggest crock of shit she ever said."

"Why do you say that?" Pearson asked.

"She was a hypocrite. Every other edition of that damn school newspaper was nothing but her lies in print. You have no idea how many lives she ruined. And when she came for the cheerleading squad, that was the last straw. I ended it the same day."

Adam smiled. "You broke up over the cheerleading squad? What exactly did she have against them?"

Adam already knew the answer from reading the unpublished article on Lindsay's hard drive the night before. Still, he wanted to hear it from Linus.

"She asked me to meet her at the sawmill one day after school."

"Why?" Adam asked.

"Said she had evidence proving that every member of the squad was involved in a cheating scandal to get their provincial exams 'fixed'. She even had Principal Lowry roped into it too."

"You say she had proof. Did she ever show you any?" Adam asked.

He shook his head. "Nothing. She was grasping at straws."

"Okay. And when did you and Angela begin dating?"

"Angela and I dated before, in grade nine. But we broke up over the summer between years ten and eleven, and that's when I met Lindsay on a volunteer project."

"So you dated Lindsay from year eleven until a month before graduation?"

"Yes."

Pearson glanced at his watch. The interview was dragging on longer than he expected, so he butted in and turned his questions to Angela.

"Now, Miss Martin, were you and Lindsay friends?"

"At one time, we were best friends. But she transformed into this person I didn't even recognize anymore."

"How so?"

"Everything became a conspiracy theory with her. Her quest to uncover stories that didn't exist consumed her. She let cheerleading fall to the wayside, and by the middle of year ten, we exiled her from the squad."

"And being the caring best friend—I imagine you were—you must have tried to get to the bottom of things?" Pearson asked.

She nodded.

"And?" Adam asked.

"She refused to see me. Every time I rang the doorbell, either Chad or her parents shooed me away. I tried to confront her in the halls at school, but she avoided me."

Adam locked eyes with Linus. "And what a coincidence the two of you just start things back up a few weeks before her death."

"Are you implying something?"

"No. Only an observation," Adam said.

Linus shifted in his seat. "I don't like where this is going. Are you considering us suspects?"

"Why would you ask that?"

"It seems like you're suggesting we did something to her."

"Not our intention. We came to figure out what was going on in Lindsay's life around the time she died. Nothing more."

"Yeah, well, your partner here believes we've done something wrong."

"How could I not? I mean, especially after what you did two years ago to DS Anderson at McGinty's."

"What in the hell are you talking about?"

"You're saying you didn't drug his drink and unleash your goons on him. If you'd do it to a constable, how can I be sure you didn't do the same to Lindsay? Hmm?"

"You're crazy, man."

"Perhaps you didn't want her to expose the cheating scandal because then you and your friends would be in serious trouble? You lured her out to the saw-mill, drugged her, and strung her body up in the rafters?"

Linus slammed his hands against the table, stood, and towered over the two constables across from him. "This conversation is over. I want you out of our house now!"

Blindsided by Adam's overflowing hostility, Pearson struggled to defuse the tension. "Mr. Roussin. Adam. Can we please calm down?"

Angela's lower lip quivered. "No, Linus is right. Neither of you is here to learn about our relationship with Lindsay. You don't want to hear the truth. You've both already made up your minds before you walked up the path. We're guilty until proved innocent; that's what this is."

"No, not even close," Pearson said.

"Well, I won't stand for this. Not in my home."

Pearson stuttered. "Ma'am, please, we're—"

She crossed her arms over her blue-checkered button-down shirt. "Am I un-der arrest? Is Linus under arrest?"

Pearson swallowed hard. "No."

"Then get the hell out of my house. Don't even think about coming back without a warrant," Angela said. She squeezed her eyes tight and pointed for the front door.

Pearson scooted the chair away from the reclaimed wood table and stood to his feet. Inside, the gruff man's irritation boiled. Yet, on the outside, he remained calm and collected.

"It's been my experience that innocent people don't say things like that, Miss Martin. We'll go, but don't leave town."

The chair flew out from under Angela, and she jumped to her feet. "Are you threatening me? You don't want any of this. One call to my dad and your ass will be lucky to get a job working mall security."

Angela Martin. The daughter of Ennis Martin, the mayor of Cedar Lake. She sure flaunted that surname for such a timid girl, accustomed to using it as a privilege when it mattered most.

"No threat. Just stating a fact, ma'am. Come on, Prescott, I think you've done enough damage for one day."

Pearson tapped him on the shoulder, but Adam stared deep into the beady eyes of the man who very nearly ruined his husband's career two years earlier.

The lead constable tapped again. "Prescott, let's go and leave these nice people to the rest of their day, eh?"

Adam exhaled loudly and spread his hands against the table and hoisted himself to his feet.

"Don't worry—this isn't over."

Adam stormed away without waiting for a reply with Pearson hot on his tail. Adam made it to the screen door, and with a violent thrust, it swung outward. He marched for the SUV parked along the curb.

Pearson turned back towards the house, and Angela and Linus hovered near the door. How had he allowed things to spiral out of control? As his head swiveled back forward, Adam was already in the vehicle, waiting for the ass-chewing he deserved.

And as Pearson closed the door of the SUV, he held nothing back. "Not sure how you guys do things in Regina, but you're on my turf now, and that's not how I run questioning."

Adam remained silent and let the man carry on with his rant.

"Also, I'm not sure what you thought you were going to—"

Adam turned and stared him straight in the eyes. "Accomplish?"

Pearson threw his head back, and it hit the headrest. "For Christ's sake, do you know who her father is?"

"Don't know; don't care. I did what I came to do, and I succeeded."

"And what's that?"

"Ruffle some feathers," he said. He turned his head towards the door just as

Linus wrapped his arm around a visibly shaken Angela. "And from the looks of it, I'd say mission accomplished."

SIXTEEN

BEING BACK HOME WITH GEMMA WAS like returning to a simpler time. Sure, Christian never had a clue what to expect when the two of them zig-zagged all over Cedar Lake, but they sure had fun. That's why what came out of her mouth after leaving the café should not have come as any surprise to Christian.

"We should pay that scumbag a visit," she said. There was a hint of wicked excitement in her voice.

"Which one?"

She cocked her head and gave that famous eye roll. "Don't play dumb."

Lee was the last person Christian wanted to encounter on this trip.

"But why?"

"Why not? After watching that video, it's clear he's hiding something."

"Yeah, but what?"

"That's what we need to figure out."

Christian gripped the steering wheel and let out a sigh. "Not sure this is our brightest decision."

Gemma mumbled under her breath as she glanced up from her phone. "Admit it; you're scared."

"The hell I am," was Christian's immediate reaction. Then he had time to think. "Well, a little."

"Finally. You admit it. You've encountered someone who puts the fear of God into you."

"Gemma, please. It's not like that."

"Then what is it?"

Christian pondered a few seconds. How would he answer her question? What was it about Lee White that made his anxiety flare? It didn't take him long to remember, and he blurted out, "For starters, the last time I questioned that man, he tried to have me killed."

"Killed? Babe, those guys just gave you a good ass-whooping. Trust me, if they wanted you dead, we sure as hell wouldn't be here having this conversation."

"And then there's what his son did to your sister. Got her hooked on drugs and ruined her life. And, well, we know what else happened because of Lee White and his family."

She crossed her arms over her chest. "Don't need the reminder."

"Sorry. My point is, do we really need to go poke the bear again? What added information do you think Lee White's going to offer on what happened to Lindsay?"

Gemma refused to entertain his constant questions and wasn't taking no for an answer. Her badgering continued. "Do it for me. Plea-a-a-a-se."

Christian gritted his teeth but did as he always did; he caved.

"If it'll get you to stop begging . . . fine. All I'm saying is this little excursion better yield something useful."

Gemma smirked. "Knowing him, I'm sure he has his dirty hands all up in this mess."

CHRISTIAN TRAVELED ALONG THE FAMILIAR COUNTRY road towards the White farm. While the weather may have improved from the frozen wasteland, he remembered from the last visit, the anticipation left a troubling twinge in the pit of his stomach.

The sedan rolled forward along the extended driveway. Christian stopped a few yards from the front porch, a popular perch where he first saw Lee White's face peering through the front door two years before. But this time, he was nowhere in sight.

Christian turned to Gemma, who unbuckled her belt and reached for the door handle.

"Hey! Not so fast. What's the plan?"

"That's the beauty of this. There is no plan. We ask him questions; gauge his responses. Not everything in life can be planned out."

As he watched her cross the front of the vehicle, Christian killed the engine and muttered under his breath, "Damnit, Gemma. How'd I let you talk me into this again?"

His sneakers hit the gravel, and he raced to catch up with the girl who was on some sort of suicide mission. "Wait up," he hollered.

It was too late; she was already on the porch banging at the door.

"Lee?" she yelled inside. "It's Gemma. You home?"

As Christian approached from behind, only a haunting silence remained.

Christian smirked and turned for the stairs. "Well, we tried."

She placed a hand on her hip and cocked her head. "He might be cooking up his special brew out in the barn."

"Yeah, you're on your own for that one."

"You're here in an 'unofficial' capacity. You have no jurisdiction, and now he knows who you are. So what's the problem?"

"The problem is, I don't want to be around any of that nasty shit he's brewing."

"Will you at least wait outside the door for me then?"

He nodded, and they headed off towards the massive barn on the east side of the property.

The entire way, his heart pounded in his ears. It was so like Gemma to live on the edge and jump head-first into situations like these. Perhaps that's what Christian loved about her. Was it her free spirit attitude? Or her ability to pull him away as he clung for dear life to rules and regulations?

He couldn't point to one particular trait. Still, somehow, one thing remained true—her ability to make him a happier person and an even better investigator.

Gemma tugged the heavy barn door and slid it aside.

"You got a flashlight?" she asked.

"Here," he tossed his iPhone, and she fumbled to catch it. "Use this."

She clicked on the bright LED light and laughed. "Phew, that was close."

"Just be careful in there. And holler if you are in trouble."

"Yes, Dad."

She disappeared into the barn, and Christian stood guard outside. The last thing he needed was trouble sneaking up on them. And it didn't take very long before the disruption he expected reared its ugly head.

A scream sent Christian into protective mode, and he rushed inside. A few feet from the entrance, he found Gemma, terrified, and standing over something on the floor.

"Gemma. You okay?"

Without saying a word, Gemma stepped aside and shone the light downward. He took a few steps closer, and lying on the ground was the lifeless body of Lee White. He rotated around with the flashlight to find a large pool of blood surrounding the body. This had been a brutal, unsuspecting attack.

Without hesitation, Christian rushed to her side, and he pulled her tight. "Is he dead?"

SEVENTEEN

CHRISTIAN YANKED HER CLOSE TO HIM and the scene brought back memories of the day they found Lindsay Ross in the sawmill. After all, she was the only reason he returned to Cedar Lake.

With a shakiness in his voice, he whispered. "Is he breathing?"

"I . . . I don't know."

"Well, you're the nurse-in-training; check his pulse."

Christian released his grip on her, and she crouched to the ground. Her hand shook as she reached out for his wrist but just before she made contact, the man's eyes flashed open, and he grabbed her by the forearm.

In a labored breath, he whispered, "Don't let me . . . die."

"Hey, hey. Relax. It's Gemma."

"Gemma?"

"Who did this to you?"

He closed his eyes and his grip on her relaxed.

These were the moments Christian excelled at. Chaos. Death. Composure during a crisis.

"Stay here. I have a first aid kit in the trunk."

"And do what?"

"Jesus, Gemma, I don't know. 911 would be a good start."

Gemma glanced down at her archenemy on the floor, bleeding out, and she retreated. Was this her subconscious way of getting her revenge on the man who turned Cassidy into a child prostitute and drug addict? Regardless, Christian couldn't stand by and allow another tragedy to play out before his eyes—even if the man was a piece of trash.

He reached down and grabbed the phone from her hand. He dialed and ran for his car with no hesitation in his actions while waiting for an operator.

Halfway to the car, a feminine voice pierced through the speaker. "911, please state your emergency."

"Yes, I've found a gunshot victim at the White farm off the 905."

"Okay, sir. Is the victim conscious?"

The sprint to the car taught him one thing: he was out of shape. He caught his breath and responded with one word. "No."

"Does he have a pulse?"

"No idea. I made a run for the first aid kit in the car."

The questions carried on, back and forth, and Christian grew tired of it. Desperation seeped out. "Please, send help."

"Ambulance and police are on their way, sir. Are you trained in CPR?"

"I'm a detective sergeant; I better be."

"Okay, sir, perfect. Help is on the way. Do you want to stay on the line until the ambulance arrives?"

"I think I can take it from here."

Without waiting, Christian hung up and dialed Adam. Two rings and his husky voice answered.

"Hey. You miss me already?"

"We got a situation here."

"Whoa. Slow down. Are you in danger?"

Christian exhaled sharply. "No, we're safe, but Lee White, well, he's been attacked."

"What? Where?"

"At the farm."

"Shit. Is he dead?"

Christian crouched at Lee's side and grabbed for his wrist. "He's alive. Pulse is weak, and there's a lot of blood. Whatever you're doing—stop—and get here as fast as you can."

"Yeah, of course, we're on the way. And Christian?"

"Yeah?"

"The suspect or suspects might still be on the scene, so be careful."

***

CHRISTIAN CUT THROUGH THE MAN'S UNDERSHIRT and exposed the gaping hole in his abdomen.

Ugh, that's bad.

He tore open a thick gauze pad and pressed it against the wound with his bare hands. Right away, the bandage had soaked through, and with his free hand, he reached for a fresh dressing.

The barn was sweltering. Christian hadn't noticed until a single bead of sweat rolled off his head, splashing against his hand. He wiped his forehead against his tee and scanned the room for Gemma. His eyes focused near the door, and there she stood, trembling like a terrified child.

As the blood seeped through the dressing, he hollered across the barn. "Gemma! A little help here."

The trembling continued, but she inched closer. As she reached the body, she kneeled on the ground and stared straight into Christian's eyes. "What can I do?"

"For starters, you can open this damn packaging." He tossed it across the body.

Christian expected a long, drawn-out slew of weak excuses from his best friend. Instead, he watched as she tore the paper wrapper with her teeth and fumbled to remove the gauze. His lecture would have to wait until another time.

She reached out her hand, and Christian tossed the saturated dressing aside and applied the fresh one to the wound. Unexpectedly, her hand brushed his aside, and he jerked.

"What are you doing?" he asked.

"You need a break. Please, Christian. Let me help."

The first thing on his mind was sabotage, and he kept his hand over the gauze. "Gemma—listen, you don't have to do this if you don't want to. This is the last guy you'd want to give a second chance to."

She shook her head. "It's not that. I took an oath to set aside my bias and never do harm. Besides, I'd rather see him locked away for life than die. Death is the simple way out, and I want him to suffer."

Christian retracted his hands, shocked at how she stepped up to the plate. Just then, a barrage of sirens wailed in the distance.

Finally.

Moments later, four uniformed people rushed the scene: two constables followed by two medics from the Cedar Lake detachment. Christian stood aside. Nothing made him happier than letting the professionals take over.

Gemma ran into his arms. Her blood-stained hands wrapped around his neck, soiling his army-green shirt. Blood dripped from his fingertips onto the dusty ground, but at that moment, only her safety mattered.

She buried her face into his chest and said, "I'm sorry, Christian. I don't know what came over me."

He continued to console her, and they both allowed the chaos surrounding them to fade away. Then a tap against Christian's shoulder broke his concentration. He lifted his head, and standing next to him were Adam and Pearson.

"Jesus, Christian. Tell me you didn't shoot the man," Adam said.

Christian shook his head and pulled Gemma tighter.

"What the hell happened?" Pearson asked.

"We dropped in to ask Lee a few questions about the video," Christian began.

Gemma finished his sentence. "And we stumbled onto this."

Constable Miller hollered Pearson's name, and he and Adam stepped away, leaving them to get their emotions in check.

"Okay, Gemma, we need to pull ourselves together. Remember why we're back here. It wasn't for Lee White, and I'm sure as hell not going to stand here and mourn this man. We're here to figure out what happened to Lindsay, right?"

Gemma raised her head and dabbed her tears with the sleeve of her shirt. "You're right. Why am I wasting any tears on some irrelevant asshole?"

Christian shrugged. "I don't think it's irrelevant. I think your tears are your pent up anger spilling out."

"You always cheer a girl up."

"I better. I've had years of practice. So, now that I've boosted your spirits, and this is an active crime scene—"

A grin stretched across her face.

"It's like you're reading my mind. What d'you say we uncover what Lee White's been hiding all these years."

They ventured deeper into the dark shadows of the barn. And unlike the last time, there was no one to stop them. Christian held his phone in front of him, scanning the ground, and a folded piece of paper caught his attention.

He bent down for a closer look.

The page was non-descript, just something out of a notebook. But the more Christian mulled over it, his curiosity about how it got there grew. Lee White wasn't the type of guy who ever wrote anything down. So, where did it come from?

"Gemma, can you grab me a pair of gloves from the kit?"

She raced towards the red box and dug around for the gloves. With them in hand, she ran back.

"What is it?"

"Could be a clue."

"Jesus, are you Nancy Drew?"

He laughed at her. "Only a bit more handsome."

He picked the evidence from the ground and slowly unfolded it, section by section. As he opened the sheet fully, the message was just another confirmation to Christian that Lindsay's death was no suicide.

Christian's color drained from his face, and he wobbled. Gemma reached out and caught him. "Whoa. What does it say?"

He lowered the paper to his side, turned his head, and with his mouth agape, he hesitated.

"What?"

He lifted the paper and read it aloud. "Keep your mouth shut, or you'll end up like the nosy journalist girl. Consider this your final warning."

As the seriousness of the situation sank in, Christian caught Pearson and Adam as they made a beeline in their direction.

"Gemma?"

"Yeah?"

"You know what this means, don't you?"

"Yeah—watch our backs."

EIGHTEEN

CONSTABLE PEARSON PACED THE WAITING ROOM floor of Cedar Lake Memorial Hospital—a place he'd grown tired of loitering in.

As the paramedics shuttled Lee White down the emergency room corridor, Pearson jogged alongside the gurney. The scraggly man barely clung to life, and the doctors and nurses rushed him into surgery the moment he arrived.

That was two hours ago. And with no word yet from the scene, Pearson grabbed his phone and dialed.

"Hey. You guys find anything yet?"

On the other end was his dutiful protégé, Constable Miller. "Not much. A few shoe impressions, a lot of blood, but no shell casings."

He sighed. "There have to be casings."

Miller interrupted. "Well, I did some research and discovered that in these types of attacks, a lot of times, the killer will take the casings. Your best bet will be the slug they dig out of Mr. White."

Pearson hated it when the younger constable relied more on scientific facts and theories he learned in school over his preferred hands-on approach. But this time, instead of making a fuss, he let it slide. Was having Christian working around him again leaving a lasting impression?

"Hey, Miller," he said. "You're doing a great job."

Miller stumbled over his words but eked out a simple 'thank you' in return.

Pearson lowered the phone from his ear and raised his head. Marching down the corridor was the same nurse from hours earlier. In her hand, she gripped a plastic cup. The double doors swung outward, and he stopped pacing.

"Constable Pearson, I assume?" she asked.

He glanced into her eyes and nodded. Those mysterious eyes left him speechless. It wasn't every day in Cedar Lake he met someone as alluring as her.

He snapped out of his daze and caught the tail end of the sentence.

". . . Doc said you need this." She extended the plastic cup out, and he took it from her palm.

"Yup, exactly what I need."

She walked towards the doors, but Pearson's booming voice stopped her. "How's old man White doing?"

"Serious, but stable. Mr. White's fortunate the bullet missed all the major organs."

"Yeah, that's damn lucky. He out of surgery yet?"

"He's in recovery, but the anesthesia hasn't worn off, I'm afraid."

"Shame. I got some questions for him that can't wait."

She leaned in closer. "If you hang tight, I'll grab you when he wakes up. But you'll have to be quick and tell no one I let you in."

She pulled away, and the two shared a smile. "Yeah, not a problem. I'll just wait right here."

She turned and sashayed back to the double door. She threw her head over her shoulder and gave Pearson one last smile before she disappeared.

He muttered under his breath. "Damn."

But the piercing ring from his cell phone interrupted his fantasy, and he glanced at the screen. *Christian Anderson.*

"Hey, buddy. You guys get showered?"

"The outsides are clean, but Gemma . . . Well, she's not holding up too well."

"What d'you mean?"

"She's packing her bag to head back to Regina. Tonight."

"I don't reckon she should be alone tonight. What can I do to help?"

"Can you stop by and talk to her?"

He hesitated. If he left the hospital, he risked not having the chance to grill Lee White. But if he stayed, and Gemma left, he'd lose someone familiar with the list of suspects.

"Can you put her on the phone?" Pearson asked.

"Uh, yeah. Hold on."

Pearson pushed himself off the wall and paced the floor again. He'd never admit it, but there was something in her sassy voice and carefree attitude that kept him fascinated by Gemma. He didn't want her to leave.

After listening to her say no several times, eventually, that voice resonated through his ear.

"You won't change my mind, Pearson."

"Not even gonna try. But answer this—why leave?"

"Because."

"You can't use that tired excuse as the go-to answer for everything. Come on, Gemma, level with me."

The line went still, and eventually, every repressed emotion rushed from her mouth. "Every damn time something awful happens, I'm at the center. I refuse to let every disaster in Cedar Lake derail my plans for the future."

"And I'm telling you they don't have to. But we need you. I need you to stay here and stay strong. Do you think you can do that . . . for me?"

"I . . . What's in it for me to stay and help? More death? More buried secrets coming to the surface?"

"I can't promise you that; I mean Christian's here, so chances are there'll be more death. And I can't promise we won't dredge up more ugly secrets the deeper we go either. But this time is different."

"Yeah, how?"

He needed to play into her ego. "This time, you're not only helping me. You're helping Cedar Lake rid itself of the trash which has consumed this community for far too long. You, Gemma."

"I don't know."

"Think about it: you say awful things happen around here. What if we got rid of the awful people causing them?"

"Isn't forgetting this place ever existed easier?"

"Ask Christian how that worked for him. Listen, we could bring Cedar Lake back to its former glory, and I'd have you to thank for that."

"So poetic, Pearson."

He scoffed. "Now, you can leave and get back to the life you've built elsewhere. Or you can wait one more day and help us. Don't answer me now but think about it before you make a hasty decision."

"I'll think about it. No promises, though, okay?"

He chuckled under his breath. "I'd expect nothing less."

Christian returned to the phone. "Well, hopefully, that worked. But I need to get a few things at the grocery for this dinner with my dad's girlfriend this evening. Hey, if you have an hour to pull yourself away, drop in."

"Thanks, but I think it's better if you spend some quality time with your father and take a break from sleuthing. Just for tonight, though."

"Well, the offer stands. I guess we'll pick things back up in the morning."

Pearson turned his head. The nurse from earlier caught his eye as she walked down the distant corridor. "Gotcha. Hey, I got to go. Have fun tonight."

He ended the call and walked across the marble floor towards the double doors. They opened, and without a word, she gripped his arm and indiscreetly ushered him down the hall.

The third door on the left remained ajar, and she pointed. "Five minutes, constable. And remember, this never happened."

"What never happened?"

NINETEEN

THE DOORBELL RANG AT SEVEN SHARP. Christian and Adam put the finishing touches on the table while Gemma and Matthias wrapped up the food prep.

The bell rang once more, and Christian stepped towards the edge of the dining room. Without warning, Matthias breezed past, with a little spring in his step. A sight Christian was unaccustomed to seeing. *He's really in love . . . isn't he?*

The low rumbles of cheerful voices in the adjoining room signaled Christian needed to put aside his childish behavior and play nice . . . for now.

I should give her a chance.

Christian made one final adjustment to the plate at the head of the table and wiped his hands against his indigo-washed jeans. His father's gruff voice seeped through the walls, and Christian peeked his head out just as his father planted a kiss on Joanna's cheek.

He withdrew, painted a forced smile on his face, and raced to be next to Adam. "They're coming. Look like a nice guy."

Adam turned and scoffed. "I am the nice one. Remember?"

Christian reached over for Adam's hand, and he interlocked his fingers with his husbands'. Not only was it a sweet gesture, but it sent a clear signal to the newcomers of who he was, and he wasn't afraid of any judgment.

With a grin stretched across his face, Matthias rounded the corner first, then Joanna and at last, her daughter, Anwaatin.

"Joanna, this is my son, Christian."

She extended her hand. "Yes, we've met. But thanks for the proper introduction this time."

Their hands locked, and he smiled at her.

"Ah, and I don't believe you met my son-in-law, Adam, the other day, did you?"

She wagged her index finger towards Adam. "Yes, he was standing outside the car. Sorry, I didn't stop to say hello; I was running a bit late."

As the small talk continued, Gemma appeared at the head of the table with a large pot in front of her.

"I hope everyone brought their—" She glanced at the visitors' faces, placed the food in the center of the table, and dashed back for the kitchen without finishing her sentence.

Christian sensed something in the way she eyed Joanna and her daughter and rose from his chair. "Gemma's done so much already; I can't expect her to do everything."

"That's my son for ya—always saving the day."

Christian disappeared behind the wall as the lighthearted laughter continued in the adjoining room. As he entered the kitchen, Gemma stood at the kitchen sink. Both hands gripped the countertop, and her head was down.

What is wrong with her?

Christian drummed his fingers against the wooden trim of the doorway, and she spun around, clutching her chest. She whispered, "Jesus, you scared the shit out of me."

"Sorry. Everything okay? You sure raced out of that room faster than I've ever seen you move before."

She fiddled with her shirt collar and diverted her stare. Christian approached slowly and, in a reassuring voice, pestered further. "What? What is it?"

The two stood on opposite ends of the butcher block island. "I know her."

"Who?"

"Anwaatin, or as she prefers, Ani."

"Okay? And that's a bad thing?"

"For me, yeah."

He scrunched his eyebrows and tilted his head. "How come?"

She leaned her body weight onto the top of the wooden table and hung her head. "I may have threatened to kill her."

His jaw dropped, and he jerked away. "May have? Are you fucking serious?"

"I had a good reason. At the time. She—"

He blinked, never taking his eyes off her. She nibbled at the tips of her manicured hands and exhaled.

"She dealt drugs to Cassidy, and I caught her."

His voice raised from a whisper. "You're telling me that this girl, the daughter of my dad's girlfriend, is a drug dealer?"

"Not sure about now, but fourteen years ago, yeah, she was."

He pressed his hand to his face and swirled around in a circle. After a few seconds, Christian stopped. "You think she'll remember who you are after all this time?"

She swallowed hard. And then again. All the dead air in the room irked Christian. From the other room, his father's joyful voice cut through the silence. "Christian? Gemma? What's the hold-up? You guys need a hand?"

He leaned across the butcher block and locked eyes with her. "Look, we go back in there and test the waters. It's been over a decade; she probably forgot all about it by now."

"But—"

He cut her off and shouted from the kitchen before she could resist. "Pop, we just had a minor mishap. It'll be another minute."

He walked around, picked up a plate full of dinner rolls, and handed them over to Gemma. "Go, I don't want to give them a poor impression."

Gemma sighed and grabbed another bowl from the countertop, mumbled under her breath, but still advanced for the door. Christian followed, and they reemerged in the dining room to a room full of blank faces.

Awkward situations were Christian's specialty, and he brushed it off with a chuckle. "Sorry, I kind of, sort of, made a mess and didn't want to leave it."

He always had this knack to spoon-feed a line of bullshit, and everyone around him somehow believed the words that crossed his lips. But that's a skill you perfect when your father is the town drunk, and you're the only gay person around.

Matthias stood and wrapped his arms around his son in a show of appreciation. "Can you believe this kid? Doesn't even live here, yet still treats this place like it's home."

The grandiose gesture scored Christian a few more points. Soon, everyone had moved on to new conversation topics instead of wondering what was happening in the kitchen.

***

DINNER WENT OFF WITHOUT A HITCH. If Ani recognized Gemma from years before, she hid the fact well. As Christian and Adam collected the plates and silverware, Matthias and Joanna retreated to the living room, leaving Gemma and Ani alone in the dining room.

Christian fiddled with his collar while an oblivious Adam slid the dirty plates onto the countertop. Perhaps he shouldn't have left them alone? Christian needed to do something to quell the unease in his stomach, so he snuck up behind Adam, who stood at the sink, as a bright flash illuminated the sky. An earth-shaking thunderclap followed, and Christian wrapped his arms around Adam and squeezed.

"Thanks."

"For?"

"I don't know. For being you. For helping me get through this 'family' dinner without too many hiccups."

"Yeah, well, that's what I'm here for. And while we're on the topic of hiccups, you care to share what took you and Gemma so long out here?"

The color drained from Christian's face. "Always the conspiracy theorist. But it's like I said, I made a mess, and Gemma helped me clean it up. Nothing more to the story."

An eyebrow raised, and Adam dunked another plate under the scalding water. "Uh-huh. Then why'd that golden-brown skin of yours turn pale white? Come on, babe, you're only digging yourself a deeper hole."

Years ago, Christian admitted that marrying Adam was like marrying a smarter, more observant version of himself. But why did he need to challenge him every time he tried to sidestep uncomfortable topics?

Pinching his lips together, Christian spilled the secret. "Fine. There is something. It's about Joanna's daughter."

"Ani? You know her?"

He shook his head. "Not me."

Adam set the dish in the sink, and his eyes widened. "No. Not Gemma."

"Yup. I told you, she knows everyone around here."

"How, though?"

"Where else . . . school and through Cassidy."

"She didn't? Ani couldn't?" he struggled to convey a lucid thought. "She's a druggie too?"

"I don't think she uses drugs, but according to Gemma, she used to sell them."

Adam handed the dripping plate to Christian to dry. "How can a sweet, innocent woman, who I spent the evening sitting across from, be involved in that world?"

"Gemma has done many questionable things in our long friendship, but one thing she's never done is lie to me. And before you connect the dots, there's more."

Adam turned and pressed his back against the edge of the countertop.

"Gemma threatened to kill Ani last year of school."

Adam ran his shaky hand through his hair, and chatter filled the hallway. As he turned, Gemma and Ani were carrying the rest of the dirty dishes. They froze and stared the two down.

"Oh my God, what?" Gemma asked.

Christian let out a scoff. "Nothing."

Ani set the dishes on the butcher block and smiled. "I already know what you guys were talking about, and it's okay."

"What's okay?"

"I'll be the first to admit Gemma and I have a somewhat sordid history together. We've both said things in the past, which today make my skin crawl. But you can relax—we won't kill each other."

Christian gasped, and his eyes turned on Gemma. "She recognized me the moment I walked into the dining room. I suppose my dad was right all along."

"About?"

"I leave a lasting impression."

Christian muttered under his breath, "That you do." He returned to drying the dish in his hand.

"I told Ani why we're back, and she might have some insider information you'll find useful to your 'unofficial' investigation."

The circular motion stopped, and Christian placed the plate on the counter. "Oh?"

The room went quiet, and all eyes homed in on Ani, who stood tall and proud. "So blunt. I love it. So, around the time your girl, Lindsay, took her life—"

Christian interjected. "Allegedly."

"Right. She was working on a big story. I know because when I was working for Lee, she came around the farm. Lee asked me to step out, but being the snoop I am, I stayed behind and hid in the corner."

"So, you eavesdropped?"

She nodded as the sky lit up, and the earth shook again.

"Lindsay had damning proof Lee threatened Principal Lowry. Before I go on, do any of you know who his niece is?"

Everyone traded glances before they all shook their heads.

"Do you remember Heather Hale?"

The name resonated with Christian and his eyes widened. "Head cheerleader, the most popular girl in my grade. To sum it up, a real pain in the ass."

"Ah, so you *do* remember her."

He raised his shoulders. "Vaguely."

"Christian, stop. You know her very well. Isn't she the one who started that rumor about you and—" Gemma said before Christian cut her off.

"Yes, I know her. I was just being dramatic."

Ani smiled and continued. "Well, she married a guy named Peter Grant and ditched the Hale surname twelve years ago."

Adam cocked his head and struggled to keep up with the story.

"Heather was hell-bent on getting into the University of British Columbia. But as the three of us know, school was not about to impede her busy social life."

Adam smirked. "I remember a few people like that back in Quebec."

"Did your classmates ever devise a plan to cheat on the provincial exams?"

Adam cocked his head. "Nah. They flunked out. Not the type of people I surround myself with. But anyway, back to Heather. From what you're saying, she phoned in a favor from her criminal uncle, and voila, she's an incoming undergrad at UBC."

"Bingo. I'm not here to interfere in your investigation too much, and I'm no expert. Still, I recommend you visit Heather. It could shed some light on Lindsay's final weeks."

"Thanks for the tip. One last thing," Adam said. "You have any idea where we'd find her?"

"The place she's always at; Grant's Pharmacy over on First Avenue. Can't miss it."

"You're telling me that not only is her uncle the town drug dealer, but she works in the pharmacy. Great combo."

Ani grinned. "Oh, honey, she not only works there . . . her and Peter own it."

Christian caught Ani twist her wrist and glance down at her watch.

"Guys, it's been great catching up, but I need to get going. Tomorrow's an early day and with this damn storm, driving around these parts in the dark is miserable."

Christian walked her to the door, and as she ran through the downpour to her car, Christian couldn't help but wonder why she would so freely offer such information.

Does she know more than she's letting on?

He closed the door, twisted the deadbolt, and with that burning question lingering in his mind, he crept back to the kitchen. His mind needed a little more time to process the additional information.

PART 4

MONDAY
CEDAR LAKE, SK

"Evil enters like a needle and spreads like an oak tree."
—Ethiopian Proverb

TWENTY

THE STORMS RAGED MOST OF THE evening, leaving Christian exhausted from a restless night of tossing and turning. He sat up and sighed. *Can't stay in bed all day.*

He slid on his jeans crumpled on the floor, snatched his shirt, and crept for the door. With a glance over his shoulder, he smiled as Adam snoozed without a care in the world.

Too cute.

The early hours, before any rational person stirred, were Christian's time to mull over the decisions he'd made the day before. After the attack outside McGinty's Pub and surviving, Christian's therapist recommended meditation, and so far, it did its job. It might have reduced his anxiety but did nothing to fix his smart-ass attitude.

He lingered for ten minutes beside the coffeemaker. The machine had to be older than he was, and it was just another thing he added to his mental shopping list of things his pop needed while he was back in town.

With a fresh coffee in hand, he pulled open the door leading to the backyard and staggered onto the deck. The humid air slapped his face, and it woke him faster than the caffeine ever could. The sun crested in the horizon, giving off a medley of magnificent burnt oranges and reds across the clear sky. It was a sight he rarely paid attention to in Regina. Still, for some reason, the sunrise always took his breath away when he was back in Cedar Lake.

He leaned against the wall, bent his knees, and slid down until his ass planted against the damp wood. He closed his eyes and allowed his mind to wander back to those precious last weeks of high school.

Should he have noticed something was off with Lindsay? Was there something he could have done to prevent the tragedy? He rushed to quiet the questions and focused on his breathing instead. There was always time to think about this later, but right now, he needed to find his inner peace.

But through his hums, the creaking of the door dashed his hope. With one eye, he gazed around, and lingering in the doorway was Matthias.

"Boy, what are you doing out here so damn early?"

"Meditating."

"Med-a-what?"

"I'm clearing my mind, Pop."

"That's a relief. All you ever do is think. I'm sorry about taking off like I did last night."

"Why are you sorry?"

The man lowered himself onto the bench at the table, drooped his head, and scanned the wooden deck. "Take a break for a minute and have a chat with your old man."

Christian sighed. He unfolded his legs, opened his eyes fully, and gave his undivided attention to his father. "Pop, I know what you're going to say."

He flailed his hands. "No. I don't think you have any idea. I learned something last night that you should be aware of."

"What's that, Pop?"

"After you kids went to sleep, Joanna confessed who she *used* to be, and I need your advice on how to move forward."

His father's hands shook the entire time he spoke. Christian sensed the distress and sat next to him, resting his hand on the older man's shoulder. "Sure, Pop. Whatever you need."

Tears swelled in his eyes, and he broke down. "She was a whore. The woman I love sold her body to men for a few measly dollars."

Christian's jaw dropped, and he struggled to offer his grief-stricken father words of consolation. All he could think about was Cassidy. She was involved in the same business, and look what happened to her in the end—a strung-out junkie who died because she couldn't live with what her father did to his mother.

Christian stroked his hand against his back while Matthias kept his face buried in his hands. He couldn't tell just by looking at him which emotions churned in his father's head. All Christian wanted at the moment was to be there for his father.

Their exchange lasted only a few moments, but now it was clear to Christian he had to question Joanna about her past life. A secret he didn't need to bring up in a moment like this with his father.

Matthias wiped the sleeve of his pajama top against his reddened face and turned to his son. "What should I do?"

"Pop, every single one of us has a past. Some of our pasts are innocent, others, well . . . a bit more complicated. If you love her, you'll accept her for who she is now. Not the woman she once was. How would you react if she said the same about you?"

"What d'you mean?"

"She could easily say, 'look at this guy who was once a hopeless alcoholic and gave up on life.' Pop, give yourself a break. You're not *that* guy anymore, and chances are you don't want anyone to judge you by your past failures."

Matthias leaned back against the table. "I never thought of it that way."

"You and I both know, given our family circumstances, that you did the best you could. So you lost your way, big deal. It happens to every one of us at some point in our lives. You asked for my advice, and so here goes—stay."

Matthias grinned and reached out and pulled his son close to him. "Thank you. Thank you for never giving up on me. I know how hard it was for you to come back to the place *and* the father you walked away from so long ago."

"Since we're being honest, I didn't want to ever come back here. But you know how convincing Gemma is, and you and me, we never settled our past. I'm not going to lie, the last time I was home, when I walked in and saw how you were living, I wanted to walk right back out that door and forget I ever saw you."

"Why didn't you?"

"Because. Because you're my father, and I couldn't let you drink yourself to death. To die all alone is a depressing picture, not just for your life, but for any life."

"Well, I'm glad you gave me another chance to prove I'm not that guy anymore."

Christian squeezed the old man's hand. "No, you're not. Now, if this lady is the reason for your renewed outlook on life, then I wish you nothing but the best."

Their open discussion continued for ten minutes more, until a groggy Adam appeared in the doorway with a mug of coffee in his hand.

"Morning," he said. Their heads turned, and Christian smiled. "I'm not interrupting your father-son bonding time, am I?"

Matthias hoisted himself to his feet and walked towards the door. "Nope. Just catching up. You look tired, boy."

"Well, he's no picnic to share a bed with. If he's not ripping away the covers, he's kicking and talking in his sleep."

Christian grinned, and Matthias turned and glanced at him. "It's just a phase. Trust me, he'll grow out of it."

Adam plodded along the deck and sat down next to his husband. "You had one hell of a nightmare last night."

"They're all a haze these days, but sorry I kept you up."

"It's not that. I'm worried about you. Ever since that guy Taylor showed up in Regina, you've been on edge."

Christian scrunched his face. "It's your imagination working overtime."

"You're not eating right; you're short with everyone. Hell, even your night-mares are back with a vengeance. Tell me again how this hasn't changed you?"

Christian had no rebuttal to the evidence Adam presented. He had to own up to reality. "She deserves the truth to come out."

"Who? Lindsay?"

Christian leaned inward. "What have we learned in two days?"

"Lindsay was good at keeping her life private, and her family is homophobic to the extreme," Adam said.

"Not to mention that incident with Principal Lowry."

"Back up. What incident? You never told me about an incident."

Christian pulled away. How could he have forgotten to mention that? "Shit. Slipped my mind. After we found Lee, priorities changed."

"Yeah, a gunshot victim is way more urgent than an idle threat. But listen, shit like that happens. There's a lot of moving parts to this. Too many people with motives. So focus, and tell me what happened?"

Christian replayed the encounter moment by moment, not omitting even the slightest detail.

"And now you think after what Ani said last night that we should look more at Heather and Lowry?" Adam asked.

"I'm saying the reunion was weird. His phone kept ringing, and he wouldn't even look at it. But when he grabbed my arm and threatened me, that was all the confirmation I needed: he's hiding something. I mean, why tell me to stay away from the Ross family? Are they involved in their own daughter's death?"

"I mean, after what happened with Gemma's dad, I rule nothing out around these parts."

"Smart man."

Adam's cell phone rang, and he glanced at the screen. *Luke Pearson.*

"It's your friend," Adam said, shaking the phone in his hand.

Christian smiled as Adam raised it to his ear. Christian could only hear the one-sided conversation, but then Adam raised his voice, more than likely to stop the man from rambling.

"Hey, stop talking for a minute. Got a tip for you."

There was a moment of silence, and Adam continued.

"Yeah, Heather Grant. Maybe you and Christian could pay her a visit when the pharmacy opens?"

Christian watched Adam's head bob up and down. Why was his own husband volunteering him up to visit the one girl who made his life a living hell all through high school?

Adam resumed. "Perfect. See you in about two hours then."

He hung up and set the phone back on the table. Christian stared him down as their eyes met.

"Why would you offer me up like that? Didn't you hear me say how much I despised her last night?"

"Babe, you're not in high school anymore. These people hold no power over you. And you said you wanted to find out what happened to Lindsay. You. And to find that out, *you* have to do things that make you uncomfortable."

Christian clenched his jaw as the birds in the trees sang a beautiful melody. How could he stay mad when Adam was right? "Sometimes, I don't know about you."

"You love me, and you know it."

"Yeah, yeah. Next time, check first before sending me into these awkward situations."

***

THE DOORBELL RANG, AND CHRISTIAN TOOK his time walking across the foyer. The last thing he wanted to do was question Heather, but there was no way around it.

He tugged open the door, and Pearson stood in full uniform, not in casual street clothes like every other time he showed up.

"Ah, going official for this one, eh?"

Christian stepped aside, and Pearson stepped inside. "There's more beneath the surface than Lindsay Ross."

"I'll bite. What's going on at the town pharmacy?"

"We received intel a few weeks back that Lee White is using the pharmacy as a source for his meth-making empire."

"Well, let me put on my shocked face for you."

"The warrant was sitting on my desk this morning, giving me full access to their records. After Adam said you guys received more intel, I figured we could kill two birds with one stone. My guys and I can carry out the search while you pry all you want about Lindsay."

"Her and I, we have history."

Pearson rubbed the back of his neck and smiled. "Don't most people? If you could distract her, you'd be doing me a huge favor."

Christian's stomach muscles clenched, and not even the breathing exercises he'd grown so accustomed to doing helped. Why couldn't he send Adam? He and Pearson had a better working relationship anyhow.

But then it came to him. This was the moment he'd waited for since his menial existence in high school—the chance to get one over on the girl who tormented him.

His eyes sprung open. "You know what. Yeah. I *can* do this."

Pearson dangled his keys. "Then what are we waiting for? Let's go take out some Cedar Lake trash."

TWENTY-ONE

THE RIDE TO THE PHARMACY WAS quick. Ten minutes to any place in town. The SUV came to a stop outside the plain building that blended in with every other rundown building on the block. If it weren't for the two flashing neon signs in the window, one could easily overlook the place.

Christian unbuckled his belt and reached for the handle. Without warning, Pearson clutched his arm. "Hey, before we go, give me the Cliffs Notes version of your history with Heather Grant."

"Well, believe it or not, we were once friends, but that was eons ago."

"When did your friendship fizzle out?"

"In between grades seven and eight. Man, I'll never forget that summer."

Pearson leaned in; all his attention focused on Christian.

"There was this boy. Nathan. Well, long story short, Nathan and I both were in limbo about our sexuality, so one night during a sleepover, things got a little, err, physical between us."

"Oh, boy."

"Now I know you're thinking, Heather must have caught you two. But she didn't. Instead, she made up this rumor and spread it all over school that we were gay. All because we spent almost every waking minute together."

Christian noted the blank stare in Pearson's eyes. After ample time to process the information, Pearson leaned over the center console. "How can it be a rumor if it happened?"

"You're missing the point. She didn't know *it* happened; she just wanted to make trouble. Well, Nathan's parents got wind, and we were forbidden from seeing each other ever again."

"What happened to him?"

"He dropped out and got as far away from here as he could. It's sad, but the stigma of being labeled queer had consequences, and the fallout was too much for him."

"So you're holding onto a grudge because you wonder what might have been?"

Christian folded his hands in his lap. "Not quite. I'm holding a grudge because she's no better than Lindsay was. Except for one minor detail: Lindsay exposed the truth to make Cedar Lake better. Heather, on the other hand, made shit up on the fly just to win points to make herself look superior."

"I'm not taking sides, and don't get mad when I say this. But didn't Heather expose your truth also? Didn't she improve your life? I mean, look at you. You're successful. You have everything you've ever wanted."

Christian stumbled over his words, trying his damndest to respond with something creative.

Did he have Heather to thank for catapulting him from of the closest? Was she the reason he ended up where he is today?

He shuddered at the thought. "You're making sense, but I'm still holding the grudge."

"It's a free country. You can do whatever you want, buddy," he said. He checked the time on his watch and sighed. "Where the hell is Miller?"

"He'll be here."

And after a few more minutes of his patience waning, Miller pulled just ahead of the SUV. As the junior constable exited the vehicle, Pearson muttered under his breath. "About time."

He flung open the door, and the three men loitered outside the pharmacy. Miller handed another paper to Pearson, who read through it with record speed. "Looks in order. You guys ready?"

Christian and Miller exchanged a quick glance and nodded.

Pearson led the pack inside the desolate store, and from an office behind the counter, a tall, heavier-set blonde wearing a white lab coat appeared.

Her brows furrowed when she realized they weren't there for the daily Lee White special.

"Heather Grant?" Pearson asked.

"Yeah?"

"I'm Constable Pearson with the RCMP. I'm here to serve a search warrant for your receipts, bill of ladings, copies of original prescriptions, and all other paper and digital customer data."

Her lips quivered, and her face reddened. "On who's authority?"

Pearson handed over the document for her to review. "It's all in the warrant. Now, I assume a savvy businesswoman like you keeps all that stuff locked up in your office, eh?"

Sweat beaded along her hairline, and her head bobbed as she read carefully through the two-page document.

"I want my lawyer here," she proclaimed.

"That's your right, Mrs. Grant. But you can't stop the wheels of justice from turning. Now, if you'll show me where you keep the documents, this will go much faster."

Pearson and Miller followed her into the office, but Christian hung back. He paced the aisles of the tiny store and stared at the floor.

Just keep a level-head, Christian. Don't lose your temper.

A commotion at the counter caught his attention, and when he glanced up, there she stood with the warrant and cordless phone in hand. She turned her back and spoke in a hushed voice. Yet, Christian never took his eyes off her. He moved from one aisle to the next, doing his best to keep a low profile. Her voice grew louder and sterner, and as she slammed the document on the counter, she ended the call. With a shaky hand, she ran her fingers through her hair and swung around.

She still hadn't noticed him, which gave him plenty of time to study his enemy. The years since high school hadn't treated her well, and inside he celebrated. Karma caught up with the popular, bitchy girl for a change.

He lifted a vitamin bottle from the shelf, which fell from his hand and crashed against the floor.

"Shit." His attempt to keep a low profile backfired, and soon her shrill voice called out.

"You with them?"

"Kind of."

The blank expression soon changed to wide-eyed. "Wait a second. You look familiar. Where do I recognize you from?"

He swallowed hard. Her wheels spun, and it was only a matter of time before his identity was out. He saved her the hassle. "We graduated together."

The clanking of metal drawers slamming closed only a few feet away echoed, and her jaw fell open. "Christian. Christian Anderson."

"Yup. How've you been, Heather?"

Her eyes scanned him up and down, and she motioned with a head nod towards the back office. "Been better. What are you even doing here? Didn't you solve that Cassidy girl's murder and go back to Regina?"

"Yeah, that's over. I'm just in town to spend a little quality time with my dad, but Pearson asked me to join him as a precaution." He scanned the store and smiled. "Wow, I can't believe—I mean, look at you. You and Peter bought the old drug store, and you're still looking as good as the day we graduated."

Her fake smile faded, and she bowed her head. "What do you want?"

"What makes you think I want anything?"

"I'm not an idiot. You hate me, and I hate you, so let's stop acting all cutesy. Okay?"

And like that, he set his acting skills aside, and out came the realness. "Fine with me. Now that you mention it, I do need something."

Her eyes lit up. Even twelve years since high school, she never shook her superiority complex. "I knew it."

"You remember Lindsay Ross?"

Her fingers drummed against the counter. "Nosy bitch. What about her?"

"So you do?"

She bent her fingers and glanced at her nails. "Get to the point, Christian."

He pulled out his badge from his pocket and set it on the counter. "Well, I lied when I said I was here to visit my dad. I'm here to find out what happened to Lindsay in 2009."

"You're wasting your time. The way I remember it, that nutcase hanged herself. End of story."

He scooped up his badge and slid it into his pocket. "Yes, that's what we all believed. But none of us were even close. Lindsay had a little help getting into that noose."

"I always knew you had a few screws loose, but this one takes the cake."

He snubbed her botched attempt to rattle him and carried on. "How was your time in British Columbia? I bet being accepted to one of the most distinguished universities in all of Canada was a highlight of your oh-so-perfect life."

She smirked. "Best six years of my life."

"Funny thing is I don't remember you doing so well in science back in high school. How d'you manage to ace your provincial exams?"

"Unlike you, a washed-up copper, I studied hard and earned all the success I made for myself."

Christian clenched his fists. "Funny you say that since I have evidence that suggests otherwise."

Her stare was like a million razor blades slicing through his soul. She shifted her weight to one side and rested her hand on her hip.

"No wonder you and Lindsay Ross were friends: you're both insane."

Christian leaned on the counter and slammed both hands down hard. "Is that why you killed her? Because she was about to expose your phony life? Or was it the way she eyed Peter in the hallways? Maybe you killed her because her and Peter had a secret affair going on?"

Her eyes shifted. The beads of sweat dripped down her scrunched forehead. But she didn't say a word.

"It's fine, Heather. You don't have to admit what you did. But I know from experience you can only hide a secret for so long before it has an odd way of rising to the surface. Especially when this washed-up copper knows where to look."

She stopped fidgeting and clenched her jaw. "Get out. Get the fuck out of my store before I—"

"Before what? You call the police? News flash, sweetie: I am the police. Those two guys back there, the ones rummaging through your files, yeah, they're on my side."

"You can't prove anything. I got into UBC on merit alone."

Christian muttered. "Doubtful. But hey, whatever helps you sleep at night."

Heather lunged forward just as Pearson poked his head out of the office door. "We're about done here, Mrs. Grant."

She turned her head over her shoulder. "You guys will be sorry you messed with me. I know powerful people. People who can make this all go away."

"Is that a threat?" Christian asked.

Pearson sighed. "Mrs. Grant, I'd think long and hard about the next words that come out of your mouth. I doubt spending the morning over at the station is how you want to spend your time."

She crossed her arms across her chest. "You wouldn't dare."

"Yeah, it's the last thing I *want*, but I'm a man of my word. Now, please, let us do our jobs, and we'll be out of here much quicker."

Without a word, she stomped as far away from the counter as she could. Pearson exchanged an awkward glance at Christian and mouthed, "What d'you do?"

With nothing more than a shoulder shrug, Pearson returned to the office to finish collecting the items he and Constable Miller came for.

Soon the two men exited with a dolly full of boxes, and Pearson clutched a silver laptop sealed in an evidence bag.

"Mrs. Grant?" he called out.

Heather appeared from around the corner with her reddened face and flaring nostrils. "Yeah?"

"I just need your signature on this inventory sheet, and we'll leave you in peace."

Her lower lip curled down. Her eyes shifted away. And on her strut to the counter, she reached over and snatched the pen from Pearson's fingers. She lifted the handwritten log close to her face. As she scanned the listings, Pearson rattled off what they took.

"We're seizing your laptop and five boxes of paperwork."

She slammed the paper onto the counter and scribbled next to the 'X.' As she tossed the pen aside, she turned to Pearson and scrunched up her face. "I want all of this back without a scratch . . . or else."

Pearson swept aside her ongoing threats. To him, Heather was nothing more than another privileged white girl who found herself backed into a corner when she realized she wasn't above the law. "I'll do my best, Mrs. Grant. I'll let you know if and when you can retrieve your items."

Pearson gathered the paperwork, motioned for Christian as he perused the store, and seconds later, the trio exited the pharmacy.

Christian and Pearson watched as Miller loaded up the police SUV, and the Mountie turned his head. "I'm not even going to ask what you did to send her on a downward spiral."

"Good because I wasn't going to share. I will say this, though: it's interesting how every time I dredge up Lindsay's name, people fly off the handle."

"Yeah, the same thing happened with Angela and Linus yesterday. Funny how a seventeen-year-old girl had more enemies than I did at her age."

"Ditto," Christian replied. "From only skimming the surface of her files, it doesn't take a genius to realize Lindsay had dirt on every crooked person in this town."

"And isn't it convenient how their scandals faded away with her untimely death? You think any of them shed a tear at her funeral?"

Christian shook his head. "I was there. They were all there. And there wasn't a dry eye in the church. Doesn't mean that one of them isn't capable of killing her and fooling a seasoned coroner into ruling her death a suicide."

The two exchanged glances as Miller slammed the hatch closed. "Ready to go, boss?"

Pearson gave him a thumbs-up. "Lead the way, Miller."

Just as Pearson cranked over the engine, his cell phone rang: *Unknown Caller.*

He reached out and answered on speakerphone. "Pearson."

The voice on the other end trembled. Again, Pearson spoke. "Who is this?"

The trembling continued, but the woman mustered up a few words. "You said I could call if—"

Instantly, he recognized the voice. "Angela? What's wrong? Are you in trouble?"

She didn't reply to his questions and instead posed her own. "Can you meet me at the sawmill?"

A warm tremor shot down Christian's spine, and his heart pumped hard.

"Sure. When?"

There was a hesitation on the other end, but she squeaked the one word out. "Now."

"Are you alone?"

"Yes."

"And you're not in danger, are you?" he asked.

The call ended, and the home screen reappeared. Christian twirled his finger in a circular motion above his head. With the lights and sirens blaring, Pearson jerked the car into drive and sped along Second Avenue towards the highway.

Although Angela Martin didn't flat-out acknowledge it, she didn't need to. Something was amiss at the sawmill. But what awaited them when they arrived was anybody's guess.

TWENTY-TWO

CHRISTIAN CLUNG TO THE OVERHEAD HANDLE as the SUV weaved around cars along Route Four. What took fifteen minutes during a casual drive, Pearson slashed to nine.

With each rut that the SUV whacked, Christian's body bounced and jerked. He closed his eyes tight, not daring to open them unless he wanted to see his breakfast for a second time that morning.

Loose pebbles ricocheted against the undercarriage like someone spraying the vehicle with a machine gun. And just when Christian reached his breaking point, the rattling stopped, and he opened one eyelid. He surveyed the overgrown surroundings; the most obvious thing out of place was the silver Subaru Outback parked near the door.

A few clicks later and the vehicle registration appeared on the screen.

Owner: Angela A. Martin.

"It's hers," Pearson said.

Christian flung open the door and hoisted himself up over the roofline for a better vantage point, hoping to catch a glimpse of the girl who desperately called them for help. But Angela was nowhere in sight. He slid back into the seat and turned to Pearson.

"Where is she?"

Dread set in, and a sour taste crept into the back of Christian's throat and lingered. Pearson flung open the door, stomped his foot against the rugged earth, and with one hand hovering over his holster, inched forward.

"Angela?" he called out.

Nothing. Only the screeches from the circling crows bounced off the rotted wooden building.

Christian stepped away from the SUV and called out. "Angela? Are you here?"

Pearson pointed at the abandoned car and motioned for Christian to cover him as he went in. He nodded and rushed behind. Without a weapon of his own, he was an easy target.

A few feet from the driver's side, Pearson pulled his hand away from the holster and crouched.

"What is it?" Christian yelled out.

Pearson held up a smashed iPhone and waved it around. "Looks like she left behind her cell phone."

"Shit. You don't think . . . Nah."

"Worse things have happened in Cedar Lake."

Pearson handed the phone to Christian and stepped closer to the vehicle. He touched the hood. "Still warm."

Christian clung to the tattered phone and stopped just shy of the driver's side door. He bent forward and peeked inside the window.

"Got a purse. Most people don't leave that behind. You think someone got to her?"

Pearson shrugged. "Too early to say. All of this could just be a ruse to throw us off track. You missed it, but your husband dug in his heels yesterday, and they were rattled when we left them."

"They aren't that smart, Pearson. No, we aren't having a repeat of the events that led up to Cassidy's death."

The mean-spirited comment threw Pearson off-guard and triggered a backlash of hostility. "Never throw that in my face again. I live with those choices every day. I'm just talking out loud, trying to understand what's happening."

Christian barked back. "Then stop acting like everyone is covering this up. You and I both know you rule out foul-play first, then work your way down the list."

Before giving Pearson a chance for a rebuttal, Christian stepped away. His world spun, and he pinched the bridge of his nose to stop the vertigo.

I didn't come back for more bloodshed. I came to confirm Taylor's statement.

His mind raced as he moved around. The more he allowed the thoughts to swirl, he always came back to the one question he couldn't shrug off: How could this innocent inquiry spiral so out of control? From the moment his feet touched the soil of Cedar Lake, things had gone awry. It all started with his visit to the Ross family. From then on, every person from his past was either confrontational or uncooperative. But none to the extreme of Lee White, who was lucky to be alive. And now, the one person he suspected of killing Lindsay was missing herself. It seemed too convenient. But he didn't want to pull a Pearson and assume the danger wasn't real.

Pearson stood from his crouched position, and Christian stopped. Pearson swung around and broke the uncomfortable silence. "Look, I'm sorry."

Christian scanned the ground. "Me too. I shouldn't have been so harsh. We're here to work together, not tear each other apart, arguing over the past."

"Right. So what d'you say we get to work. How long's it been since you processed a crime scene?"

"A few weeks. Why?"

"With Miller tied up with those files, I can't call him away."

"So what you're saying is this is on us?"

"For now, yeah. I can request some reinforcement from Saskatoon, but we know it takes a few hours."

"I remember all too well. But while we're at it, we should get some boots on the ground. Any chance you guys still have community volunteers who do search and rescue?" Christian asked.

Pearson nodded. "I'll get Miller to set that up. And while I'm doing that, you get Adam on the line. For this, we'll need all the help we can get."

"On it."

Christian walked away with his phone in hand. As he dialed, he endorsed the improved Pearson. The first to apologize and bring in reinforcements without much ado? Organizing the search party? This wasn't the same man he first met when Cassidy disappeared two years earlier.

The area was eerily quiet. Too quiet. From the time Angela called to the time they arrived left only a small window of time; ten minutes. How does one disappear from such a remote place in that amount of time without a car?

He pressed his phone to his ear, and Adam answered before the second ring. "That was quick. How'd things go at the pharmacy?"

He groaned. "Don't ask. But that's not why I'm calling. We got bigger problems now."

Adam sighed, and an image popped into Christian's head. He was undoubtedly pacing the floor and running his fingers through his hair. "This town never ceases to amaze me. Don't tell me. You and Heather got into a fight, and now she's pressing charges?"

"I have *some* self-control. No, it's worse. Much worse. Remember Angela Martin?"

He groaned. "Yeah, Grade A bitch."

"Well, that Grade A bitch is missing."

"Missing?"

"She called, scared, and asked us to come to the sawmill. Her car's here. We found her cell phone smashed on the ground, and her purse and keys are still in the car."

"Have either of you been inside?"

"Not yet." Christian's eyes shifted upward, and the bright sun blinded him. He turned away. "I could use your help here with this one."

Adam scoffed. "I bet you could. Give us twenty minutes, and whatever you do—Christian—do not go inside."

TWENTY-THREE

CHRISTIAN KEPT HIS PROMISE. Although it took every ounce of strength to heed his husband's advice, he didn't snoop around inside. He had more pressing things to tend to, and walking into an ambush wasn't one of them.

Emotions from earlier had subsided, but there was a hint of elevated tension lingering. Christian had a knack for tearing open old wounds, even internal ones. Clearly, Constable Pearson bottled those emotions up for a long time.

Pearson turned to Christian as they leaned against the hood of the SUV. "How long are you going to hold Cassidy's death over my head?" Pearson asked.

"What? Jesus, Luke, didn't we already apologize?"

"I need to know."

"You're talking nonsense. Why would I hold the death of my best friend's sister over your head?"

Pearson shrugged. "You tell me. Why would you?"

"I wouldn't. I've dealt with the guilt. Even Gemma has. But you . . . what is it about that case you can't let go of?"

Pearson drooped his shoulders and stared at his feet. Anytime he cried, he always deflected his face. "Because . . . because I failed to save a human life. I wrote her off as a washed-up, drug-addicted, diva who would do anything to grab even an ounce of attention."

The dejected tone in the gruff constable's voice was enough to tug at Christian's hardened soul. He stepped forward and rested his shaky hand against Pearson's shoulder.

"We *all* failed her."

Pearson raised his head and wiped away the wetness from his rosy cheeks. "What do you mean?"

"This entire ratchet town betrayed Cassidy, and it all started with what her father did to my mother," Christian swallowed his emotions and continued. "I had this partner seven years ago. An older guy who believed he was some sort of spiritualist. I remember one evening he said something that always stuck with me."

Pearson leaned forward and flung his hand about, eager to hear the rest of the story.

"Every decision we make is like an earthquake under the seabed."

"Okay, interesting metaphor."

"Sometimes the energy fizzles, and a major catastrophe never comes to fruition, just small ripples. But every now and then, the event is so colossal those small ripples grow bigger, more powerful, and those waves get bigger and bigger until they slam ashore."

Pearson glanced up. "And they destroy everything in their path."

"Exactly. Most people don't consider if their decisions are a small ripple or a tsunami when weighing the consequences. If we did, we'd all drive ourselves insane."

Pearson smiled. "I get what you're saying."

"Luke, the only thing we can do is collect the pieces of whatever remains from the destruction and move onto the next crisis."

Pearson relaxed his shoulder and stood up straight. "I hope Gemma will forgive me."

"Is that what this is about? Gemma?"

He nodded and grinned. "Maybe."

A nervous laugh escaped Christian's mouth. "You like her—don't you?"

"What? Come on, man. That's not what I meant."

"You sure? Because I think it's *exactly* what you meant."

Before Pearson could defend himself, the recognizable clatter of gravel pinging against metal echoed from afar. And soon, Christian's sedan came into view as it stopped thirty yards away.

Adam and Gemma exited the car and moved their way. Christian leaned in and whispered in Pearson's ear, "Your secret is safe with me. But, if you like her, tell her. Maybe she likes you too?"

***

AN HOUR HAD PASSED. The loosely strung yellow crime scene tape flapped in the light breeze, and the team of constables stood outside the door after conducting a thorough search of the inside of the derelict property.

There were no traces Angela had ever stepped foot inside.

From the opposite side of the tape, Gemma hollered. "People are on their way to help."

For the past hour, she had reached out to her extensive list of contacts begging volunteers to come out and search for Angela. When she ended the last call, she had convinced twenty people to come.

Pearson strode across the soft dirt and stopped a few feet from her. "What would you say if I made you the lead volunteer?"

"Me?"

A goofy smile graced his face. "Why not? You did all the hard work getting people out here. And more importantly, I trust you."

Gemma nibbled at her lower lip. "You do?"

"I do. I knew there was a reason you couldn't go rushing back to Regina so quick."

She cocked her hip to the side. "Is that so?"

He reached across the tape and grabbed her hand. "I needed you here for this."

Their eyes met, and her olive skin flushed. At that moment, time stood still, and Pearson leaned forward. He closed his eyes, but the revving motors of several cars racing down the lane interrupted their magical moment.

Pearson pulled back and loosened his grip on her hand. "Well, seems like your friends have arrived."

"When Ennis Martin's daughter goes missing, people get fired up."

"Shit. I forgot she was the mayor's daughter. I better get you up to speed on how to run a search party then."

TWENTY-FOUR

AS GEMMA GATHERED EVERYONE AROUND, A straggler scrambled from the convoy of vehicles parked along the lane. The man waved his hands, and Gemma stopped mid-sentence and waited for him to quiet down before resuming.

With a bullhorn in hand, she called out. "Come on up, sir. We're just about to get started."

From a distance, it was hard to make out any distinguishable features. As the man shoved people aside and worked his way to the front of the pack, her hands trembled. He wasn't a concerned citizen. It was much worse. It was the man who at one time she loved. The man who she hoped she'd never meet again in her lifetime.

A lump in her throat swelled, and she scanned the ground. Gemma waited patiently for the slow-motion train wreck to be over, and all she could do was mumble under her breath, "Bastard."

Linus Roussin stood before thirty townspeople and wasted no time hijacking the briefing. "How dare you show your face in this town? What have you done with Angela, you psycho bitch?"

Hushed whispers rushed through the anxious crowd, but Gemma refused to bow down to him. Those days of allowing any man to silence her ended the day she left Cedar Lake behind. She took two menacing steps forward, and his warm breath washed over her scrunched-up face.

"How dare *I* show up here? How dare you? The man who cheats on his wife like a cat in heat. This entire town knows you're nothing more than a man-whore whose primary goal is to keep up your phony appearances."

Linus gnashed his teeth. "Stop it or else—"

A wide smirk stretched across her face. "Or else what? You'll hit me like you do your wife? And how can we all be sure you didn't do something to your wife? Hmm? After all, isn't this what you wanted all along?"

"I should smack that smirk right off your face."

"You haven't changed a bit. Still can't face the truth."

His lips parted and trembled. Gemma's words cut deep, and she wasn't even close to reaching the climax.

"If you love Angela, as you claim you do, then you'd keep your dick in your pants where it belongs."

The back and forth worked the bystanders into a frenzy, with many jeering at the theatrics.

The uproar caught Christian and Pearson's attention, who had a map of the search area spread across the hood of a car nearby. Pearson worked his way through the densely packed group. As the last person stepped aside, Linus raised his hand in attack mode.

Without time to think, the constable dug his heels into the soft earth and raced to her rescue. Linus raised his hand, but Pearson snatched Linus's forearm before he could get any forward momentum and twisted it behind his back. "Not today, buddy."

Linus fought to free himself, but the more he fought, the harder Pearson twisted his arm. Gemma crossed her arms over her chest and stared at him with a glint in her eyes. "You picked the wrong one today, my friend."

With the distraction now diffused, Gemma worked to refocus the search party as Pearson slapped the cuffs on Linus and dragged him by the shirt to his SUV.

Christian stood at the back door and opened it. Nothing gave him more pleasure than seeing the man who orchestrated his assault two years ago in cuffs. As Pearson tossed the skinny hipster into the backseat, Christian leaned down.

"Hey, sunshine. Remember me? Bet you didn't think I'd survive that beating, huh?"

Linus scoffed. "Have we met before?"

"How's McGinty's doing these days? Still slipping Diazepam in people's drinks?"

Linus shifted around in the backseat, but not once did he react to Christian's accusation. Pearson crouched and yanked at the man's t-shirt, digging his nails into the fabric.

"What the hell were you thinking?"

His eyes darted upward, and his nostrils flared. "How dare you let a civilian run the search party for my wife. Why is she even involved?"

Pearson took a few deep breaths and returned his icy stare.

"You know what, don't answer that. My father-in-law will be here soon, and you'll have to explain to him why I'm in cuffs instead of out searching for his daughter."

Nothing infuriated Pearson more than a name-dropper. Besides, Pearson didn't work for the mayor. He worked for the federal government of Canada. And no one would stand in his way of getting to the truth.

"Mr. Roussin, that's why we're here—to find your wife. With that said, I won't tolerate disruptions, and I sure as hell won't have you out here threatening to assault those who have volunteered their time to help."

His jaw clenched, and he enunciated his words clearly. "I didn't assault nobody."

"Thank God. Because from my viewpoint, you were about two seconds away from having your ass hauled off to the detachment. What's your beef with Gemma, anyway? Weren't you two friends at one point?"

"It's complicated. Stuff you wouldn't understand."

"Try me? I'm a lot smarter than I look."

His eye muscle twitched, and he stumbled over his words. "We . . . Phew."

"Spit it out already, man," Adam said.

"Gemma and I had an affair for over a year."

Pearson cocked his head to one side. "When?"

He jingled the cuffs in his lap and bowed his head. "Four years ago."

"Did Angela find out?"

His lips turned downward. "She caught me with my pants down, literally, one night at McGinty's. Let's just say you wouldn't have wanted to be there."

"I imagine not. So why accuse her of having something to do with Angela's disappearance? Did she ever make threats?"

His head twisted side-to-side. "No."

"So, you tell me, who would want to hurt your wife?"

His shoulder raised and dropped twice. "I have no idea. We live a quiet life."

"You ever do any work for Lee White?"

His eyes darted everywhere except where they should be. He remained silent.

"Linus, I'm not here to bust you for anything. If you did work for him in the past, I need to know."

His chest puffed out, and he exhaled. "I dealt for him from the bar. But after what happened to Cassidy, I stopped."

"Out of the blue, just like that?"

"Yeah. Just like that."

"Why?"

"In all the time I dealt, I never saw the after-effects. But with Cassidy, she was different. She was always around, and for the first time, I saw how what I was doing destroyed her life. Those drugs sent her deeper into a paranoid state. Then she died, and I swore I'd never have another person's blood on my hands."

"And Lee? He was cool with your decision?"

"Now that you mention it, no. He said I'd be sorry. You don't think?"

"Think he's responsible?"

"Yeah."

"The perfect patsy, but impossible."

"I don't understand."

Christian squinted his eyes and pulled Pearson back. "Is he being serious?"

Pearson returned his attention to Linus. "You weren't aware someone shot him in his barn yesterday?"

"What? No. I had no idea. Is he alive?"

"Barely clinging to life over at the hospital."

The news changed the atmosphere, and Christian gripped the top of the car door. He leaned in closer and stared into Linus's eyes. "What about the Ross family?"

His pupils dilated. "What about them?"

"I dunno. How well do you know Chad Ross?"

"I'd consider him a friend. Not the best, but not the worst either. Why?"

"Think he could be involved in this? Maybe he had a thing for Angela? Maybe it's something more sinister?"

Linus shook his head vigorously. "No way. Chad isn't that kind of guy."

"You'd be surprised how well people can put on a show. You know, to your face, act one way, but behind your back, it's a whole different story."

The conversation went back and forth for another five minutes, supplying no useful answers. Pearson dug into his pants pocket and pulled out a set of keys.

He unlocked the cuffs with two twists and slipped them back into their holster on his utility belt.

"I tell you what. I was going to send you away, but we need all the help we can get."

Linus rubbed at his wrists. "Thanks."

"There's a catch, though."

He sighed. "Isn't there always with you guys?"

"You and I, we're going to be attached at the hip."

Linus bowed his head.

"Do we have a deal?"

"Is there another option?"

Christian banged his hand against the door, and his titanium ring clanged. "I don't think you're in a position to make requests."

Linus mulled over his choices and settled on the escort. By now, everyone had lined up, and Pearson kept Linus at his side. From a distance, Mayor Martin hollered over the murmur of voices.

"Linus, there you are. I was looking for you."

The two embraced, and the mayor slid his hand around Linus's back. As they moved away, Christian slammed the door shut and pulled Pearson aside.

"You and Adam don't let him out of your sight. That's the face of a man who knows more than he's telling."

"It seems to be a recurring theme these days. But yeah, Adam and I will keep tabs on him. As long as you promise to do the same with Gemma."

"Trust me . . . I won't let her out of my sight."

TWENTY-FIVE

THE SEARCH HAD BEEN UNDERWAY FOR well over three hours. Thirty-five people spread out in a line formation and had already covered a vast swath of land. Yet even with the extra support, the search offered no clues as to what happened to Angela.

The outburst from earlier had earned Linus a coveted spot between Pearson and Adam. From the empty stare, it was apparent to Pearson that Linus was pissed. They walked in silence, but Pearson needed answers.

Pearson turned to Linus. "You gonna tell us what you know?"

"Huh?"

"After your dramatic scene yesterday, it's obvious that one of you has information on what happened to Lindsay."

"We don't know anything."

"Sure, and people just go missing without a good reason. Save it; we've heard it all before. So, did someone get to Angela?"

"You two are insane."

"Really?" Pearson asked. "Then why did she call us to meet her out here?"

Adam found his chance and chimed in. "I can tell you why: she was about to spill everything. And someone was one step ahead of us and got to her before we did. Linus, look, if you have information, this is the time to speak up."

A muffled ringing came from inside Pearson's vest. He ripped back the Velcro and glanced down at the screen.

Constable Miller.

"Hold up, guys." He pressed the oversized handset to his ear and paced. "Tell me you're making progress with those records."

"I don't know if those are of any use anymore."

The cryptic declaration aroused Pearson's interest. He stopped and pulled the mouthpiece closer to his face. "In English, Miller."

"I'm outside Heather Grant's house . . ."

"What? Why?"

"She. She's—dead."

"Dead?" There was a brief pause. "Miller, I swear, I don't have time for games."

"Boss, I'm not. A 911 call about thirty minutes ago from 37 Second Street. With you out searching for Angela, they send me out to investigate."

"Why'd she call?"

"Came across as an attempted burglary in progress. When I arrived, I found the front door kicked in and, well . . ."

"What?"

"How soon can you pull yourself away?"

Pearson covered the microphone with his hand and talked in a hushed voice as he passed by Adam. "Can you keep him out of trouble until Saskatoon gets here?"

Adam nodded, and Pearson uncovered the mic. "Miller?"

"Yeah, boss."

"Give me a few to nail down our timeline, and I'll call you back."

"Copy that."

He hung up and darted through people until he found Christian and Gemma. He forced himself between them, and when Christian glanced up, he jumped.

"Jesus. Pearson. What are you doing sneaking up on people like that?"

"Sorry. We got another problem."

"Problems. This entire town is full of them."

The color drained from Pearson's face, and Christian stopped in his tracks. "Who's dead?"

"How?"

"You were never good at hiding anything. It's your face. Whenever someone dies, you get pale. So who is it? Lee White?"

His eyes blinked, but he remained silent.

"No, please tell me it isn't my dad." The silence continued. "For the love of God, man, say something."

His eyes drooped, and he took a calming breath. "No, not your dad. And not Lee, either. Heather."

"Grant?" he asked and received a simple nod from Pearson. "Damnit. How? How did this happen?"

Pearson's shoulders lifted upward, and he spread out his hands. "No clue. Miller responded to an attempted burglary call and found her dead. I trust you can wrap this up on your own, yeah?"

"No problem. Adam and I got this," Gemma said. "With her help, of course."

Pearson placed a torn piece of paper into Christian's hand. "You guys are the best. And if Saskatoon shows up, can you send them to this address?"

"Sure."

Pearson turned away, but Christian reached out and clutched his forearm. "Hey. I'll call you when we finish up. But if you need me, you know where to find me."

"That I do. And thanks to you both for your help. If things like this keep up, I'm demanding they provide me with another constable."

TWENTY-SIX

PEARSON MARCHED THROUGH THE FORLORN GRASSLAND. Angela Martin's disappearance took a backseat, and now, as he trampled the ankle-high blades of grass, there was only one person on his mind: Heather. Twenty minutes passed, and he caught sight of the crumbling mill. He spotted a white van and two black Impalas with their lights flashing as he tore along the gravel road.

Thank God.

Help had arrived.

The meadow had soaked up all the moisture from last night's rainstorm, leaving the ground sandy. With each stride, Pearson kicked up a cloud of dust behind him. He could make out the congregation of cars parked along the gravel lane; then, a recognizable silhouette came into view. His frame, the wire-rimmed glasses, and that robotic-like walk—all the indisputable traits of DS Clark. The same investigator who unearthed Christian's mother two years ago.

Pearson skidded to a stop. His black combat boots slipped across the dry soil, and the two men swapped a mutual smile before Pearson extended his hand.

"DS Clark. Man, it's been a long time. It's good to see you again."

"Likewise. I wish it was under different circumstances, though. How have you been, Luke?"

Pearson scoffed and turned his head upwards towards the heavens. "Eh, it's Cedar Lake. You know our motto, 'criminals outweigh the manpower.'"

"Damn shame what this town has become over the years. Heard not only do you have a missing woman, but now a dead one, too. That's a shitty afternoon, no matter where you are."

He bowed his head. "Shitty doesn't begin to cover it. I'm tapped out here, so you have no idea how grateful I am to have your help. Even if it is only for a limited time."

"There's no time frame. It all depends on what we find. When was the last time you took a day off?"

Pearson scratched his head and stuttered as he tried to stall. "I don't know."

"Well, we'll stay as long as you need us."

"I was just about to head to the crime scene. The search party is under control. I got two constables from Regina leading this."

The older man smiled. "That's Anderson and Prescott, yeah?"

"Boy, they don't skip a beat in Saskatoon, do they?"

"Nope. How's Christian? We haven't spoken much since his mother's . . ."

"Eh, he's doing as good as expected. Just between you and me, he hasn't come to terms one-hundred percent with what happened with his mother."

A murder of crows flew overhead, squawking as they zoomed by. "Takes time. Overall he's good, though, right?"

Pearson smiled and nodded. "Overall, yeah. He's still the same straight shooter we've grown to respect. Not to mention, he's been a tremendous asset trying to get these thugs wrangled in around here."

"Tall order. So, not to cut this reunion short, but we've got a crime scene that won't process itself."

And as a gust of wind blew across the prairie, the two men parted and drove back towards town.

***

THE SUN STRUGGLED TO PIERCE THROUGH the wall of thunderclouds growing taller on the western horizon. Pearson let his left arm hang outside the window and the steamy air passed over his skin. And for a moment, he forgot about the task ahead of him at the Grant residence. But as he crossed over Third Avenue, the sight of the yellow tape transported him back to reality.

After seven years in Cedar Lake, he'd seen his fair share of petty crimes, drug overdoses, and minor infractions. But ever since Cassidy's death two years ago, the town had undergone a dark transformation. One that Cedar Lake may never recover from.

The rims of the SUV scraped the curb, and Pearson tugged at the steering wheel.

Shit.

He killed the roaring engine and stepped onto the freshly paved, quaint street lined with oak trees. With the two-story yellow house towering over the others, Pearson stopped and eyed the immaculate structure.

Pearson scanned the neighboring homes, and his eyes wandered back to the two high-end SUVs parked in the driveway. The place screamed 'we have money,' but Pearson couldn't understand why they chose this street to settle on.

Miller stood at the door with a canister of fingerprint powder and brush. For as much grief Pearson gave the poor kid, he'd come a long way over the last two years.

Pearson took a step and hollered out. "How's it going in there?"

"You made it."

He raised the yellow tape and made his way to the front porch. "Any updates?"

"Coroner arrived ten minutes ago; he's inside waiting on your permission to cut her down."

"Cut her down?"

The young constable stepped aside and used Pearson's mantra against him. "You'll see."

Pearson stepped over the threshold, and it didn't take more than two steps before Miller's words made sense. His eyes rolled up, and there she hung, an orange extension cord wrapped around her neck, dangling not even six inches from the ground.

He bowed his head, and all he could do was shake it from side to side.

He scanned the small entryway. Underneath the body lay one black shoe turned on its side. And if it wasn't for the splintered glass scattered across the floor, it could have been a carbon copy of the crime scene photos from Lindsay's death.

She put up a fight.

He stepped closer and examined her face. It was purplish-blue, and her open eyes bulged out of her head. Those eyes had a sense of terror in them, but still it wasn't any different than the other twenty-five deaths he'd responded to the last two years.

Waiting in the corner, jotting down his observations, stood the coroner. The man had either not noticed Pearson or wanted to finish his notes before he acknowledged his presence. The older man scribbled hard against the paper and pushed his wire-framed glasses up the bridge of his nose.

"Damn shame, isn't it?"

"I'm sorry?"

"Another young life . . . gone."

Pearson shrugged. "To be honest, doc, it's becoming such a frequent occurrence around here I'm numb."

"You gotta do what helps you sleep at night."

"So, what are your observations? Suicide or worse?"

The older, gray-haired man shook his head. "I can't say for certain until I get her on the table. But preliminary observations lean more towards homicide."

Pearson turned and faced the man. "Go on."

He motioned for Pearson to follow up the stairs. Once at the top, they stood behind the body. With his pen, the coroner pointed. "First, there's this nasty gash."

Pearson leaned in closer and examined the bloody gash in the back of her skull. "Yup."

"Blunt force trauma. Never appears in a suicide by hanging. Then there are the defensive wounds on her hands."

He leaned over the railing and studied the abrasions. Several dark bruises had formed around her wrists, and he stepped back. "She struggled."

"Bingo."

"Any other observations you want to share?"

"I'll leave the rest up to you and your team. If it's all right with you, I'd like to cut her down now."

Pearson nodded. "Yeah. I've got a lot of work ahead of me tonight."

Pearson descended the stairs and stepped back across the threshold. As he stepped onto the wooden porch, Miller lifted another set of smudged prints from the front door.

"You talked with any of the neighbors?"

He attached the tape lift to a white index card and turned his head. "No answers."

"And her husband, Peter?"

Miller shrugged. "Haven't seen him, boss. Word is he moved out weeks ago."

"Where d'you hear that?"

"Around. Rumor has it they're in the middle of a vicious divorce."

"Uh-huh." He glanced again at the two vehicles in the driveway. "Whose cars are these?"

Miller slid the card into an evidence bag and sealed it. "One is registered to Peter; the other is hers. You don't think?"

"I don't know what to think."

Before he could continue, the Saskatoon team arrived on the scene with a presence.

"I brought you some help. I'm going to canvas the neighborhood again, see if anyone knows anything."

As he stepped off the last step, Miller spoke. "How was the search? You guys find any clues as to what happened to Angela?"

Pearson shook his head. "It's like she vanished into thin air. But you and I both know that's never the case."

They swapped grins, and Pearson rushed along the broken-up sidewalk along the otherwise-picturesque street. Someone had to have seen something. But then again, in Cedar Lake, ratting out your fellow man was what got you a one-way ticket to the morgue.

TWENTY-SEVEN

BACK AT THE SAWMILL, THE SEARCH party was wrapping up. After five hours, not a single shred of evidence turned up. It was as if the earth opened and swallowed Angela whole.

Christian and Adam watched as Gemma hugged a few volunteers from the car's hood. Lucky for Linus, he bolted the first chance he had. After the spectacle earlier, Christian hadn't expected him to linger.

Christian scanned the area for stragglers. With the coast clear, he leaned over and planted a peck on Adam's cheek.

"What was that for?"

"Just a token of appreciation for everything you do."

"I didn't do much."

"You kept an eye on Linus and prevented him from hurting Gemma. That alone earns you brownie points in my book."

Adam leaned closer and whispered. "There's something off about him. I haven't figured it out yet, but underneath that charming exterior, something is festering."

Christian's lips curled downward, and he wrung his hands together. Linus Roussin was the poster boy of evil. Although they were nothing more than acquaintances in high school, the stories about him continued bubbling to the surface years after. And after the incident two years ago at McGinty's, Christian would do whatever to avoid being alone in the same room with him.

"I should check on Pearson," Christian said. He hopped off the hood and stuck a perfect landing against the earth.

"I'm sure he's got everything under control."

He pressed the phone to his ear. "Still . . . what if he needs our help?"

"Not to come across callous, but he's a big boy. And besides, I'd think the forensics team from Saskatoon is here by now."

Christian stepped away. He didn't care if the nerds in their Tyvek suits were there. He returned to Cedar Lake with one mission: to find out what happened to Lindsay Ross. And if Angela, Linus, or even Heather were involved, he had to be there, scooping up every piece of evidence they left behind.

The ringing tones screeched in his ear, and after the fourth ring, Pearson answered. "You find her?"

"Nope. Nothing."

"One can hope, can't one?"

Christian smiled and allowed Pearson to continue. "Any issues after I left with you know who?"

"Mayor Martin seemed less than pleased as he escorted him away. How are things there? What the hell happened?"

Pearson scoffed. "Somebody did a piss-poor job of making her murder look like a suicide. Like we wouldn't notice the front door kicked in, or the broken picture frames everywhere."

"So it's true. She's dead?"

"Unfortunately. Found her hanging from an extension cord in the foyer."

"So her killer strung her up? Just like Lindsay."

"I know what you're thinking. The same person got to her just like they did with Lindsay, but I need more proof other than your intuition."

As much as he hated to admit it, Pearson was right. He had to find the missing pieces of the scattered puzzle and put them in the correct order if he wanted to link the current events with the past. "I know, you're right, but damn, digging through her files is a tall order."

"You've got Adam. He's a powerhouse with all that computer mumbo-jumbo."

Christian glanced over his shoulder and eyed his husband, who sat on the hood of the sedan, fumbling with his cell phone. "That he is. So, we're about to head out. Any chance you need any extra help?"

Pearson's low rumbling groan painted a picture for Christian of the constable leaning against a wall, his hand under his armpit, shaking his head. It didn't take but five seconds before the expected response passed across the constable's lips. "What I need is you to scour her files and find something to point us in the right direction. Besides, the coroner has already removed the body, and the Saskatoon Police are here doing their thing."

"Well, I suppose I better let you get to it. I've got an all-nighter of Computer Forensics 101 ahead of me."

"You're smarter than you give yourself credit for. Tell you what, I'll drop in and check on you guys before I head home."

"Perfect, then I'll see you when I see you."

Christian lowered the phone and moseyed on back to the car. By now, Gemma had joined Adam, and the sea of vehicles from earlier had disappeared.

"So?" Adam asked.

His hand shook, and his eyes darted away. "She's dead. They found her hanging from the banister."

Gemma gasped. "She killed herself?"

Christian kept his gaze on the ground. "Nah, a murder made to make us think suicide. Remind you of another case?"

Christian paced the floor while Gemma stood by and processed the information. "You need a minute?"

His mouth quivered, and his eyes widened. "For what? She was a wretched person."

"It doesn't matter if she was the one who killed Lindsay; no one deserves such a horrific death."

"Right."

"What can we do to help?" Gemma asked.

"There must be something in Lindsay's files to connect everything. I hope you're both ready for a long night of scouring."

Adam squirmed and slid off the shiny hood. Christian appreciated the front lines were never his husband's forte. Even so, he beamed in the comfort of knowing this guy would do anything in the world for him.

"We can reconvene tomorrow to continue the hunt, but those files won't search themselves."

And with those words, the three loaded into the sedan and headed back for town.

***

THEY SWEPT THROUGH THE DOOR LIKE straight-line winds blowing across the prairie. A quivering voice called out from the adjoining living room.

"Christian?"

He crept towards the opening and leaned against the wooden trim. "Hey, Pop." He glanced around the room, and sitting on the couch were Joanna and Ani. "Ladies."

He studied each of their stoic faces, and a cold tingle traveled along his spine.

"Why are you all staring at me like that?"

Matthias inched closer to his son. "Is it true?"

"Is what true?"

"Angela. Is she . . ."?

Christian swallowed hard. A light touch against his back and his head spun around. "Hey, we're going to get things set up in the dining room. Okay?" Adam asked.

Christian reached out his hand and lowered his head. How was he going to answer his father's question? And even as he hunted to concoct an answer, his father carried on with the questions in rapid succession.

"I know something's going on. I overheard a call go out for volunteers over the police scanner. Is she okay? Has someone done something to her?"

Christian clenched his fists to quell his trembling hands, but the pressure only made it worse. Just when things couldn't get any worse, Joanna spoke up. "Matthias, hon, sit down. We don't want Christian to be uncomfortable, do we?"

All eyes focused on Christian. He reached out his hand and planted it against the wall to balance himself. "Joanna, it's fine . . . I can't say anything about open cases until we have all the facts."

Matthias snapped, "Screw the facts. Is she missing or not? Not a hard question."

He bowed his head forward and shook it from side-to-side. "Pop, please."

"What else are you hiding? Ani said there was quite a police presence outside the Grant house when she drove over. Is Heather involved in this too?"

Christian rocked back and forth on his heels, and from across the room, he watched as Ani sat still. That was until she smashed her hands against the rough cushion and jumped to her feet.

"Geez, Matthias, you can't take a hint, can you? Christian has said what he can say."

"He's my son, and if I want answers, he'll—"

Christian glanced up and cut him off. "No, Pop, I won't. This is a serious situation, and talking about it could only hurt the investigation. I'm positive if you go online right now, you'll find answers for those burning questions."

Ani held her phone in her hand and stood. "Here. All you had to do was ask me. Instead, you wait until he returns and pounce on him like a cat in heat."

Joanna gasped. "Anwaatin!"

"What? Just look at him."

A hush fell over the tense room, and Ani continued coming to his defense.

"I'm sure he's been out in this heat all day, he's probably starving, and not to mention has a shit ton of work ahead of him. So, maybe we ought to let him get on with it, hm?"

Christian exhaled the breath he'd held in. For someone he only just met yesterday, the fact Ani was the one coming to his rescue left him speechless.

He grinned, and without stirring the pot anymore, he made his escape towards the dining room. He pulled out the chair and shook off the guilt. Not divulging information about open cases was routine to him. Still, after the promise he made to Matthias after they found his mother, he hated having to stay silent now.

Deceit and secrets were at the core of his life. And they generated so much anguish, which not everyone had healed from. And that alone tugged at Christian's heart.

I should tell him. But I don't want to jeopardize the case.

He brushed the back-and-forth in his mind aside and opened the laptop. A heaviness fell over him, and he peered up from the screen to find two sets of eyes watching his every movement.

"What?" he finally asked.

"Nothing. I gotta admit, you handled that better than I would have," Gemma said.

"My father?"

She nodded.

"The less he knows, the better. I've once again returned and ruffled some feathers. I don't want to drag my pop into this. I can't."

Christian bowed his head and freed a shaky breath. Adam rose from the chair and hovered over Christian, putting his hand on his shoulder. "We're not going to let anything happen to your dad. Okay?"

Christian reached over his shoulder and grabbed his hand. "How could we stop it? There's not enough personnel to go around."

Adam squeezed Christian's hand but couldn't dredge up any words to comfort him. Meanwhile, Gemma fidgeted with her phone, and it slipped from her hand and crashed against the table.

Their eyes gazed at her. It was silent for a few seconds, but then she spoke up. "I'll stay with him."

"No offense, Gemma, but what are you going to do if the killer shows up?" Christian asked.

"You forget just how tough I am. Trust me, whoever this creep is, he doesn't want any of this."

Before Christian could rebuff her outlandish bragging, Ani appeared in the archway.

"Am I interrupting something?" she asked.

"Nope. Not at all. What's up?"

Ani stuttered and focused her gaze on Christian. "I hoped we could talk for a few moments. Alone."

There was a hesitation on Christian's part, but soon he realized that maybe Ani was becoming a key ally, and it must have something to do with Lindsay.

He slid the legs of the chair away from the table and stood up. Adam refused to loosen his grip on his husband's hand, but Christian turned and ran the back of his soft hand against his scruffy face.

"It's okay. She's on our side here."

Adam leaned forward. His lips were less than an inch from his ear. "Christian. I know you think everyone is on our side, but that's not how life works."

Christian scrunched his face and his eyes. "But . . ."

"Listen to me. All I'm asking is you to consider the damage you could cause if you say too much. That's all."

Christian pulled away and confirmed with just the look in his eyes. The grip on his hand loosened, and he turned back to face Ani.

"Let's talk on the back deck, hm?"

TWENTY-EIGHT

Adam watched as the two disappeared behind the wall, and he returned to his seat next to Gemma.

"How does this girl have so much intel about what's going on?"

Gemma raised her shoulder but refrained from adding an opinion. She wanted no part in spurring his mind down a rabbit hole, one from which he may never resurface.

"Don't you have anything to add?" Adam asked.

"Not really."

"Why not?"

"Because I've known Christian a lot longer than you. He's not an idiot. If she's duping him to get information, he's smart enough to see through it. Geez, sometimes I think you don't give your husband enough credit."

"I give him plenty of credit!"

Her head swayed. "I love you to death, Adam. You and Christian have been amazing and done so much, I'll never be able to repay either of you. I just think you need to stop and listen to yourself before you critique others."

"What are you saying?"

She picked up her phone and twirled it between her fingers. "I'm saying give him some space to breathe. This entire case is taking a toll on him."

"Is it?"

She scoffed at his brazenness. "You really think he wants to be back here? To investigate the people he swore he'd never lay eyes on again?"

"I . . ." Adam began, but Gemma cut him off.

"Sure, he's happy he gets to reconnect with his Pop—but the rest of it—he could have lived a lifetime without the added drama."

"What should I do?"

"You should keep an eye on him, but for the love of God, ease up a little. Not only did he find who murdered my sister, but in the process, he uncovered the truth about what happened to his mother. He's smarter than you give him credit for."

"Yeah, and almost got killed."

"That's a choice he has to make. Not you."

"Gemma, hold up. You think Christian has the right to control whether he does something crazy enough to get himself killed? No, I won't sit by this time. I'll do everything in my power to never have to hold his hand while he lies in a hospital bed ever again."

"Then you're a fool who's going to push a good man away. At some point, you gotta let go and let him do this. Lindsay was important to him, why I don't know, but he deserves our support in finding the truth."

"Why? Why is she so damn important to him?"

"That's a story for him to tell. Not me."

***

CHRISTIAN LEANED AGAINST THE WOODEN RAILING outside on the back porch and folded his arms across his chest. His eyelids drooped as he mustered up the energy to flash her a smile.

"Sorry about that back there," she began.

"Why are you, sorry? You came to my rescue."

She smiled. "Someone has to around here. Can I ask you something personal?"

He nodded.

"You're not happy about my mother and your father dating—are you?"

"I . . ." he hesitated to confirm.

"It's okay. I wasn't too thrilled, either. I mean, not because I don't believe in love and all that shit."

"Was it the race thing?"

She nodded. "Let's be real, it's not every day a Cree woman and a white man kiss and hold hands in public in Cedar Lake. That's bound to get you a few stares from the racists around town."

"And did it?"

"At first, yeah."

"And now?"

"There's new gossip floating around."

"Like?"

"Well. You."

"Me? What about me? Is it because I came back looking into what happened to Lindsay?"

"That. And you brought along your husband. I think both topics have carried the same amount of weight."

"Screw these small-minded assholes. I'm happy, and I can't burden myself with people who care more about my personal life than fixing their own miserable ones."

Ani grinned. "That isn't the reason I wanted to talk to you, though."

"Okay. Something else on your mind?"

"There's something I didn't tell you last night," she began. "There's more to the prostitution ring than you know."

He perked up. Could this be something useful to steer him in the right direction? "I'm listening."

175

"I may have left out one minor detail about Lindsay."

Christian clamped his jaw tight and never broke his eye contact with her.

"Now you must remember, I worked for Lee White back then. And when he told you to do something, you did it if you didn't want trouble."

Christian held back his urge to make a snide comment, and let her continue, uninterrupted.

"I was told to take care of the problem by whatever means necessary. So, one night I followed her."

"Why?"

"Lee gave me orders. Clip her using my car, but don't kill her. Guess he assumed it would send a powerful message to back off."

"But you didn't follow through. Why?"

"It was well after midnight, and Lindsay crept along the dark streets of town. I tailed her everywhere she went, and where she ended up was at the elementary school playground. I parked close enough to keep her in my sights but far enough away not to tip her off. She had a video camera and was filming three guys on the swing set."

"Who were they?"

Her shoulders lurched upward. "No idea."

"If you saw their faces again, would you recognize them?"

"I don't know. It was dark, and I wasn't like right there, you know."

"Gotcha. So, Lee White wasn't one of the men?"

She shook her head. "Lee? No. Lee White never gets his own hands dirty. That's why he has amassed an army to do it for him."

No wonder we can't pin anything on him directly.

"What happened next?"

"She kept hidden for a while, but that camera never missed a minute. Maybe she has some footage hidden somewhere?"

Christian already had the hours of hidden video footage, so this came as no shock to him. Yet, she didn't need to know about that.

He shrugged. "The search came up empty. Perhaps someone found out about her secret recordings and destroyed them?"

He studied her face as he broke the news—nothing. No twitches. No spasms. Her eyes remained focused.

"But, if you think there's some evidence she hid, we'll keep digging around. I'm sure it's bound to turn up somewhere."

"I'm not in any trouble, am I? You know, for admitting I was going to harm her."

"Thinking about hurting someone isn't a crime. If it was, I'm sure everyone on this planet would be locked away."

The two shared a chuckle and returned inside. Christian stopped at the archway, and Ani took a few more steps towards the living room.

"And Ani?"

"Yeah?"

"To answer your question; my blood boiled when my dad kissed your mom on the steps. It pissed me off more than you'll ever know."

"Why?"

"He kept her a secret from me, and, well, it broke my heart."

Ani cocked her head to the side and stared blankly at him. "Why would something so innocent break your heart?"

"Because he broke the biggest promise we'd ever made."

"Which is?"

"Always tell the truth and stop keeping secrets from one another."

"Ah, yeah, I'm with you now. But after spending more time with them, what are your feelings now?"

Christian smiled. "Well, they're in love. And in the end, isn't that what we all want?"

Ani smiled. "Some of us, but not everyone."

"Fair enough. I can't tell you the last time I saw my dad glowing like this. Maybe when I was four? Your mother has been a godsend, you know, keeping him away from the booze and focusing his attention on more productive things. So, any woman who has that kind of effect on him is okay with me."

Ani walked back, grabbed Christian's hands, and squeezed. "Who knows. Maybe there will be wedding bells in their future?"

Christian chuckled under his breath. "Let's not get too far ahead of ourselves just yet."

She turned towards the living room, and the smile on her face faded the further away she got. Inside, there were so many things swirling around Christian's head. But the loudest one pierced through all the others.

She knows more than she's admitting. But, for now, I'll keep letting her believe I don't.

TWENTY-NINE

WITH DISTRACTIONS AT A MINIMUM, CHRISTIAN clicked away through the megabytes of videos, photos, and documents on the screen in front of him.

If nothing else, Lindsay logged something on the flash drives every day in the six months leading up to her death. The problem was pinpointing the exact moment things turned sour. Was it in late November when she first started following Lee White around town? Or was it that time in mid-January when she recorded her brother, Chad, meeting with Taylor Jackson behind the laundromat?

There were far too many hours of mundane surveillance, too many flowery words in her documentary-style daily findings. Christian's eyes burned, and his head ached. It had all tumbled down over him, and he ripped his headphones from his ears, and as they landed on the table, the crash echoed off the walls.

He slouched in the chair and ran his hands up and down his face. He closed his eyes for a second, and when he reopened them, Gemma and Adam had stopped clicking and trained their eyes on him.

"You all right?" Adam asked. There was a tinge of hesitation in his voice.

His head wobbled, and he slammed his hands against the table. "No. How are we ever going to figure out who's responsible when all she writes about is Lee White?"

"Clearly, it has something to do with him."

"You think? But he's not the killer. He's still in the ICU. Be pretty damn hard to kidnap Angela and murder Heather from an induced coma."

"Good point. I've seen Taylor a lot in these videos. Too bad he died before he could give me a hint on where we should be looking. I remember he said, 'stop *him*', so we're for sure looking for a man," Gemma said.

"So let's take a few minutes and brainstorm. What male suspects do we have remaining?"

"Chad Ross," Gemma said.

"Yeah. I got a creepy vibe from him the day we visited. And there was something he said that I can't shake."

Christian's eyes widened. "You didn't say anything to me. What was it?"

"He went out of his way to dredge up that fight between Angela and Lindsay in the parking lot. He even mentioned McGinty's and Linus. Maybe it was a subtle way of dropping a hint?"

Christian avoided getting too involved in his theory. "Valid point. I'll mark down Chad and Linus, but before we get into the nitty-gritty, let's finish compiling our list."

Christian and Adam let out a sigh simultaneously as Matthias paced in the hallway outside the dining room. Christian glanced up. "Pop?"

Matthias peeked his head in. "Hey. Not here to be nosy, but Joanna and I are heading out for a bite to eat. When was the last time you took a food break?"

Christian eyed the room, but no one jumped at the opportunity to have another night of take-out food.

"Always thinking about others, Pop, but we still have so much to cover. We'll make a dinner run a little later."

"You have to eat something. You're pale, and I can't remember the last time I saw you look so tired."

"I'm good, Pop. You two go, enjoy some private time together."

The old man smiled and tapped his hand against the trim. The front door creaked open, and within seconds it slammed closed. Christian tiptoed through the hallway, unsure if they had the place to themselves or if prying ears were lingering in the shadows.

"Ani?" he called out.

No reply. Only a calmness in the atmosphere.

He entered the room. "Where were we?"

"Chad and Linus. Who else?"

"Well, after my uncomfortable run-in with Lowry yesterday . . ."

Adam scoffed. "How could I forget. Move that joker's name to the top of the list. Him and Chad Ross." He shook his head and banged his hand against the table. "I knew there was something off with Chad."

"Guys. Focus," Christian said. "What about some unfamiliar people? Like Peter Grant, for example."

Gemma shrugged. "What about him?"

"Convenient he's nowhere to be found after his wife is murdered."

"How much do we know about this guy?"

Christian shrugged, and his lips curled down. "Just someone from school we used to know. He grew up in the trailer park outside town, kept to himself for the most part."

"Trailer park? How'd two people from such different social classes end up marrying?"

Gemma planted her hand on Adam's shoulder. "So many reasons. Let's just leave it at desperate people attract desperate people."

"*Quoi?*"

"Gemma. Let's not bore him to death with their sordid past, hm? Let's add him and move on."

She grimaced. "I heard Peter and Heather are going through a divorce. The guy's been living down at their cottage on Sunset Lake ever since."

"Who told you that?"

"Someone from the search party. But let's add him to the list anyway," Gemma said.

"Noted. Moving on. What about Mr. Ross?" Christian asked.

"What about him? You can't believe that a father would murder his own—" Adam cut himself off.

"Not only do I believe it, but I also lived it."

The color drained from his face. "I didn't mean to dredge that up, Gemma."

"You can't walk on eggshells around me for the rest of our lives. It happened, I've accepted it, and I've moved on. All I'm sayin' is we can't rule David Ross out as a suspect."

Adam rested his hand on her shoulder. "And I'm sure even if he didn't do it, being the wealthiest man in Cedar Lake made him a target. You and I both know that you don't get to the top without making a few shady deals along the way."

Adam had a point. How did David Ross go from being a nobody in the late 80s to suddenly bursting at the seams with money? Christian pulled the chair out and plopped down hard against the wooden seat. So focused on her investigative journalism being the cause, he disregarded the possibility that Lindsay's murder might not have been about her at all.

"What if her death was retaliation for something Mr. Ross did?"

Gemma and Adam exchanged concerned glances. "Nice theory. But what gives you that impression?"

Anxiety kicked in, and Christian was back on his feet. He paced, and his hands flailed about while he mumbled to himself. Then he stopped.

"Maybe he wasn't directly involved. What if he made a dirty deal, and she was collateral damage?"

"Christian . . ." Gemma began.

"No. Listen. Adam, dig up what you can on this prostitution ring I keep hearing so much about. Gemma, find anything you can on David Ross and his dealing around town. Surely it should all be public information."

"And what about you?" Adam asked.

He reached for the chair. "Me? I have a date with the rest of Lindsay's videos."

Gemma chuckled, and her hand slapped against the table. "Can't be too bad. I mean, how many videos can a seventeen-year-old girl make?"

He scoffed, flipped around the laptop, and pointed at the bottom of the file directory. "Ten hours' worth."

Her lighthearted approach disappeared as her jaw thrust forward. A noticeable gasp escaped. "Shit."

THIRTY

CHRISTIAN GAZED OUT THE WINDOW INTO the darkness which had fallen over Cedar Lake two hours earlier. Twenty videos down and only forty-five more to go.

He hovered the mouse over the next video, titled Pre-Prom. He scanned through the metadata.

> Created: May 7, 2009, 08:02:26 p.m.
> Modified: May 7, 2009, 10:04:55 p.m.
> Accessed: May 9, 2009, 07:55:33 a.m.

His eyes trained on the haunting date: the ninth of May. The day was forever etched in his mind. He adjusted his position, and the chair scratched against the wooden floor.

Worried he'd attracted attention, he scanned the room. To his shock, no one batted an eye.

With the clip queued up, he pressed play. In the last fifteen videos, each had a running theme: Blurry. Outdoors. Voyeuristic.

But not this one.

This one was clear, crisp, and recorded in a dimly lit room. And each of those other videos had a repeated pattern—documenting others' actions, but never herself. Until now.

Her fair-skinned face filled the computer screen, and Christian gasped as he stared into the eyes of a ghost from his past. Lindsay Ross had turned the lens on herself.

He paused the video, closing his eyes and drawing in a deep breath. Twelve years was a lifetime ago since he experienced that goofy grin of hers. That smile flooded his mind with beautiful memories, and for once, he allowed himself a few moments to reminisce.

Contrary to the rumors about him and Lindsay, not to mention what Christian told people, the truth was, they *were* close. Especially during Gemma's rebellious phase. However, once Gemma outgrew her feistiness, he and Lindsay spent less and less time together.

He assumed he understood her life. Empathized with her every secret. Yet, the more videos he scoured, he discovered he never understood her life at all.

His hand shook as he hovered over the pause button. Was he ready to hear what might be the last words she spoke before she died?

Just press on, Christian.

With one quick click, the video continued. He leaned in closer to the screen.

He analyzed her disheveled hair, the black, puffy circles below her reddened eyes, and her lower lip quivered as she struggled to speak. After a sigh, her grainy voice sliced through the headphones, and his eyes widened.

"Hey, guys—it's Lindsay. But of course, you knew that. So, there's no simple way to say this, so I'll just say it. If you've gotten your hands on this video, I'm about ninety-nine percent sure I'm dead."

Christian refocused his attention away from the background and back on her face. He muttered under his breath. "No shit."

"And only three people will ever find this video: my father, Chad or Christian Anderson. If this is my dad or Chad, this video is doomed. But if by some miracle this is Christian," her voice cracked. "I need your help."

He mumbled out loud, "With what?"

"I've done it this time. Dug a little too far and unearthed something I never should have known about. The evil that runs Cedar Lake. Drugs are rampant, and prostitutes fill the stools of McGinty's. I just want to expose this and get the hell out of here in one piece."

Oh, Lindsay.

"If I'm dead, these are the people you need to focus on . . ."

Christian paused the video and scanned the motionless room. Gemma and Adam remained focused on their assigned tasks, oblivious to their surroundings. He slipped the headphones away from his ears and drummed his fingers across the table.

The vibration snapped Gemma from her zone. She glanced up. "Time for a break?"

"No, no, I'm fine. I did find something you two might find interesting."

"I'm glad someone has," she said. "David Ross either has nothing to hide, or he's damn good at covering his tracks."

Adam dropped his headphones onto the table. "You should know, Gemma, people involved in human trafficking and prostitution aren't the type of people who leave a trail. I sure hope you've uncovered something useful, Christian."

"Trust me. I did. It's Lindsay."

"Wait. She made a video of herself?"

Christian nodded, and without a word, they raced from across the room and clustered behind. There was Lindsay, frozen, mid-sentence on the screen. Gemma raised both hands and covered her mouth to muffle her gasp.

"Let me back it up."

For the next few minutes, their eyes remained glued to the screen. Then he reached the part—the part where she unveiled the names of those involved.

". . . I've been following Lee White, Taylor Jackson, Principal Lowry. And worst of all, I've been following my brother, Chad Allen Ross. How he got sucked into the seedy underworld of Cedar Lake baffles me."

Adam reached for his phone on the table. "I'll call Pearson." He peeled himself away from the emotionally draining video and stepped into the hallway. Christian and Gemma remained glued to the screen.

"I'm ashamed to call myself a Ross. Our family name is tarnished forever if this ever gets out." Lindsay gasped for air and made one last point.

"I'm not an evil person. But this town is. The people of this town are. I just . . ."

She choked back tears but persevered. "Never did I believe when I began exposing this, that one day it'd lead back to my own flesh-and-blood. But here we are. I'm sitting here making a secret video to rat out my brother. I can't tell you how deep this goes, but if I'm dead, then you know what you have to do."

Lindsay reached out her hand, and the screen went blank. Christian fell back against the chair as Adam wrapped up his phone call.

"Little Miss 'no one can intimidate me' met her match. I'd never seen her so rattled. Ever," Gemma commented.

"Same. Whoever these people are, they had her spooked near the end."

She crouched. Their eyes level. "But who killed her? We can cut Lee and Taylor from the list. One's dead, and the other is practically dying."

"So that leaves us with Chad Ross and Principal Lowry," Christian said. Just then, Adam returned to the room.

"You're in luck. Pearson is right down the street."

Christian briefly acknowledged him and returned to his conversation with Gemma.

"You heard her. Even she didn't know how deep this goes. And after twelve years, how many more people are involved in it?"

"I don't have an answer for you. I wish I did."

***

FIVE MINUTES LATER, A KNOCK AT the door interrupted Christian and

Gemma's heated exchange. After one too many times stepping in, Adam learned his lesson a long time ago and backed away. As he hovered outside the dining room, he mumbled. "Don't trouble yourselves. I'll get it."

He dashed away. Each heavy footstep pounded against the hardwood floor, echoing along the way.

"Who is it?" he asked.

"Pearson. Open up."

Adam flicked the deadbolt and tugged open the door. Pearson pushed his way inside; his breath was shallow and fast. His typically sun-kissed skin was whiter than an untouched snowfall, and the constable planted both hands against his knees and leaned forward.

Adam kept his eye on him as he struggled to collect himself. Seconds ticked by, and Adam rushed to Pearson's side.

"Everything all right, man?"

Those unforgettable blue eyes peered upward, and he managed a nod. "I'll be fine. We need to talk. All of us."

They loitered around the foyer, the voices from the dining room carried. The past few years, their opinionated behaviors had escalated, each of them believing they knew what was best.

"What's going on in there?" Pearson asked.

"Give 'em a minute. They're working something out."

They marched towards the dining room, and the commotion subsided as they grew closer.

"Is it safe?" Adam asked from afar.

"Don't be so dramatic," Christian replied.

Pearson rounded the corner first. Christian sat at one end of the table and Gemma at the other. With their backs turned away from each other, like two spoiled children who couldn't get along, Pearson inched into the room.

Gemma huffed and shoved her arms deeper into her armpits. "He's pissy because . . ."

"Because?"

"She's leaving. Tonight. We're on the verge of a breakthrough in the case, and she's going back to Regina."

Gemma twirled around and slammed her hand against the table. "I have a job, Christian. Or did you suddenly forget that? And who's idea was it for me to be more like you and get out of Cedar Lake? It sure as hell wasn't something I would have done on my own. But your damn begging drove me mad."

He slouched in the chair.

"But I did as you wanted, because why would my best friend steer me wrong? And for once, you were right. I made a life. The life I always dreamed of—"

He raised his finger, and she stopped mid-sentence. "And I'm ecstatic for you. All I'm asking is for you to stay around, just a few more days and help me out."

"Why? Why would I hang around this shithole town while you three snoop around trying to solve something from twelve years ago? Maybe Lindsay was lying? Hm? Maybe she did slip that noose around her neck and end it all."

He shook his head. "No. Impossible."

"What if we're wasting our time here hunting down a murderer when there isn't one to be found?"

Christian took a calming breath and rested his elbows on the table. "She didn't kill herself, Gemma. You watched the same video I did. That's a girl who was scared to the core, a girl who knew her fate. But go ahead, get back to your new, perfect life in Regina. Adam and I will manage just fine without you."

And with those hurtful words, Gemma slid the chair away from the table, blew past Pearson and Adam, and stormed off towards the kitchen.

Neither of the two men said a word. What could they say in a situation like this?

Pearson glanced towards the kitchen and back at Adam, who winked in a sign of approval. As Pearson lurched forward, his cell phone blared, and he stopped.

"What are you doing, man? Go after her," Adam said. He pressed his hands against his back.

"Hold up. It's Miller."

Adam sighed and backtracked to the dining room, where Christian sat alone at the table.

"You okay?" he asked.

Christian glanced up with a reddened face. His brows furrowed together as if the rage had not yet subsided. It was clear that everything wasn't okay. Yet, he had to ask anyway.

"I'm fine. She just knows the right buttons to push, you know."

Adam scoffed. "That's what best friends do. Tell me what's going on in that head of yours. And don't lie and say it's because she's going back to Regina."

His head lowered again. "Because she's not taking this seriously like I am. I lied earlier when I told you that Lindsay and I were mere acquaintances. We were more than that."

"More? God, please don't tell me you two were romantically involved or—"

His voice had calmed. "No. Nothing like that. I merely helped her dig up evidence for a few stories she sent to the newspaper anonymously."

"You what?"

"And some days, I can't help but wonder why she had to die and not me. It should have been me, Adam. Not her."

Adam wrapped his arm around Christian's neck and pulled his head onto his shoulder.

Secrets. They're a bitch. And the root of so much anguish for Christian. First, his mother's affair with Gemma's father, then his own pop lying to him about where his mother went. Lies always snowball out of control, and the only way to get beyond them was to admit everything. Cleanse his soul from everything he's kept a secret.

Before Christian could continue, the heavy pounding of Pearson's boots hitting the floor interrupted. The constable appeared at the archway, but his blank stare with white knuckles put Christian's soul-cleansing on hold.

"What is it?" Adam asked as he pulled away from Christian.

"There's a problem at the hospital. Someone attacked the coroner and snatched Heather's body from the morgue."

Christian snapped out of his self-pity and turned his head. "Come again?"

"I got to go, guys. I'm sorry. If the lights are on when I'm done, I'll pop back in. Otherwise, let's reconvene tomorrow morning at nine. Yeah?"

And without waiting for an answer, Pearson raced for the door. Before anyone could grasp the severity of the situation, he was gone.

"Shit," Christian mumbled.

"Don't worry about Pearson. He's got this under control. He might not get any sleep, but what's new?"

Christian pulled away.

"Where are you going?"

"To talk to Gemma. I can't let her leave in her state of mind."

Adam yanked Christian closer and wrapped his arms around his husband's waist. He leaned closer. The scruff of his unshaven face scratched against Christian's neck as he planted a kiss on his neck.

Time stopped, even if it was only a few seconds. They gazed into each other's eyes, and Christian smacked his lips. "I'll be back."

Adam nodded. "And I'll be here. And Christian?"

"Hm?"

"It'll all work out."

PART 5

TUESDAY
CEDAR LAKE, SK

"Tell the truth, or someone will tell it for you."
—Stephanie Klein

THIRTY-ONE

THE COUNTRY ROAD SAT DESERTED. The only source of light for kilometers shone down from the full moon hovering above. The green glow of digital numbers in the dashboard caught Pearson's attention: 4:45 a.m.

He drummed his fingertips across the worn leather steering wheel, but his eyes never wavered from the last house along the dirt road. The place was void of life except for the vehicle witnesses reported fleeing the hospital sat in the driveway. A black, late-model Chevy Tahoe. Saskatchewan plate BPN 009.

Pearson scratched his head. How was it possible this man, one idolized by so many as an upstanding citizen, was involved in the seedy underworld of Cedar Lake?

He waited on backup to serve Alan Lowry, the principal from Cedar Lake High School, with a search warrant and one for his arrest.

In the rearview mirror, the glow of two sets of headlights grew closer with each passing second. From the cupholder came a vibration, and Pearson glanced down.

Gemma Williams.

He wiped his hand across his sweaty face and hesitated. Reluctant, he reached down and pressed the green button.

"Shouldn't you be asleep?" he asked.

"I could say the same for you. Christian told me about what happened at the hospital. Is everything okay?"

He grunted. "Not really. The coroner is in a bad way, but he'll survive. Worse, they stole Heather's body along with any evidence on it. The only bright spot is we found a few witnesses."

"Thank God for that. Luke, you're a smart guy, and I know you'll find the person responsible."

"I think we already have."

"That's a relief. Listen, I wanted to make sure I apologized for not saying bye before I rolled out of town. It's just . . . Christian. He's . . ." Her voice quivered as if mentioning her best friend's name brought back a flood of grievances.

"You don't have to tell me. He can be a real pain in anyone's ass. That's part of his charm, I suppose. But don't forget, you guys are best friends and have been forever. Shit like this happens from time-to-time."

He glanced up again, and the high beams reflecting in the mirror blinded him. He squeezed his eyes closed and lifted his free arm to shield his face.

The glaring radiance eventually dissipated, and the only light remaining was the muted glow of the phone screen.

Gemma continued, not knowing Miller and DS Clark had just arrived on the scene. "I know. I know. He and I talked before I got on the road. He always does this. Presses my buttons until I explode, and then swoops in and tries to smooth things over after the fact."

"It's just who he is, Gemma. And it works for him. But then again, you do the same to him. It's a two-way street."

She huffed but never corrected his assessment.

"So, I assume since you're calling, you made it safely back to Regina?"

"About an hour ago. Listen, I know you're in the middle of something, and I don't want to keep you tied up. But I need a favor."

"Sure."

"Keep an eye on Christian for me."

The request was vague, and Pearson grew alarmed. "What for?"

"Nothing I can put my finger on. I just get this inkling he's scheming something. I just don't want things to end up like last time. You know, with him in the hospital."

"I won't let anything happen to him."

"You promise?"

Pearson paused. How could he guarantee something he had no control over? Yet, his crush triggered those two words she wanted to hear. "I promise."

The slamming of car doors rushed him to wrap up the call, and as the screen went dim, he tossed the phone back into the cupholder. He reached into the passenger seat for his Stetson hat.

Everything from that point was a blur, and before he realized it, the driver's door opened, and a blast of cool air brushed against his skin. He moved stealthily alongside the SUV, glancing into the eastern horizon as the rim of the sun crested the horizon. The eye-catching undertones of burnt orange and red left him in awe. But there wasn't time to take in Mother Nature's glory.

He leaned against the rear of the massive vehicle as Miller and Clark approached.

"Anything?" DS Clark asked.

"House has been quiet since I arrived at three."

"Well, we're ready when you are."

Pearson waved them on. DS Clark took the lead, and he and Miller flanked from behind as they move towards the one-story ranch. He kept his hand hovered over his nine-millimeter strapped to his side as Clark banged against the door.

"Alan Lowry, this is the police. We have a warrant for your arrest."

There was no reply. The area was quieter than the morning mass pews in Cedar Lake, and Pearson pulled his weapon from the holster.

DS Clark knocked again. The fifty-something officer, who usually spoke in a soft, meek voice, flipped the switch, and out came a booming growl. Pearson snapped to.

Damn.

"Alan Lowry. This is your last chance. If you do not reply, we will be forced to make entry."

A minute elapsed. With no hint that Lowry was eager to turn himself in, Pearson backed away as DS Clark and Miller positioned themselves near the door, clutching the battering ram.

They exchanged no words, and seconds later, the tip met the wooden door which stood no chance. The hinges ripped from the wooden frame as the hefty barrier crashed against the floor.

Clark and Miller rushed through the opening; their flashlights and guns were drawn. Pearson backed into the house, keeping his eyes trained on anyone creeping up on them while the other two cleared the scene.

DS Clark called out from deep inside the house. "Pearson, hurry."

Pearson zoomed through the unlit house with only his flashlight to guide the way towards Clark's booming voice. He got to the dining room and sidestepped a pool of blood, which trailed along a hallway towards the bedrooms. He slowed, doing everything possible to avoid contacting the drops. Nothing worse than a contaminated crime scene. As he reached the end of the hallway, standing outside the door were Miller and Clark.

"He's not?"

Their feet remained frozen in place, and neither of them confirmed anything.

"Is he dead?"

Miller raised his shaky hand and shined the light into the bedroom. Pearson took two steps inside and found Lowry slumped across the bed.

Two more steps.

He glanced at the man's face, which lay cocked to the side—closed eyes. Bruises and blood covered his face. And underneath him was a blood-soaked white duvet. Pearson rushed to the man's aid.

"Alan? Can you hear me?" Pearson called out.

The man didn't move.

Pearson moved closer, and as he hovered over the lifeless body, he reached out two fingers and pressed them against his neck. The stench of cheap booze wafted off the man's body.

There was a pulse. A weak one, but it was there.

"He's alive. Get an ambulance rolling."

Miller reached for his shoulder mic and slipped away while DS Clark moved closer to Pearson.

"What the hell happened here?" DS Clark asked.

"Retaliation?"

"Obviously. But for what?"

That was the million-dollar question. If Lowry attacked the coroner and snatched Heather's body, how did he end up clinging to life himself?

This goes way deeper.

Miller appeared in the door, struggling to catch his breath.

"Ambulance is en route."

And for the next fifteen minutes, Pearson stood guard over Lowry's body while the others searched the house for any evidence.

Pearson paced the floor. He crouched next to the body and reached out his fingers again to check for a pulse.

As he touched the man's wrist, he jerked awake.

"What the hell?" Lowry blurted out. "Where am I?"

Pearson reached out and gripped the man with both hands. "Alan, calm down. It's Constable Pearson."

For a moment, Lowry stopped struggling and locked eyes with the constable.

"You're home and safe."

"They're going to kill me," Lowry said.

"Who's going to kill you?"

Lowry hesitated, and his eyes darted around the room. Yet he evaded Pearson's question like a pro.

With a gentle touch, Pearson shook him. He was so close to getting a name.

All Lowry had to do was spill those two words, and everything could come to an end. Yet, it grew clearer after two minutes; that name was never going to cross his lips.

Pearson bowed his head and exhaled. "You're making a huge mistake by protecting whoever this animal is. I can't help you if you don't help yourself."

Pearson kept quiet as Lowry gazed at the broken picture frames scattered across the floor. "Even if I tell you who did this, it still won't stop it from happening again. I'd rather be locked away for the rest of my life than be a snitch."

"Suit yourself. But we'll figure everything out. We're not as stupid as you believe we are."

Lowry reached out and grabbed Pearson's forearm. "Christian."

Pearson worked to free himself, but it was no use. "What about him?"

"He needs to stop meddling, or he's going to end up just like Lindsay did."

The constable pried away Lowry's hand and gazed down on the broken man writhing before him.

What'd he say?

Pearson leaned in close enough for the liquor emanating from Lowry's breath to singe his nose hairs. "Excuse me?"

"That's what he told me to tell you. Tell Christian to back off unless he wants what's coming next."

"And what's that? Hm?"

Lowry wiped away a stream of blood dripping down his cheek. "You know exactly what I mean. These people . . . they're powerful. More powerful than you. Me. And even Christian. For everyone's sake, please, back off."

"Not a chance in hell."

Before Lowry could reply, two medics charged through the bedroom door and attended to their patient. Pearson backed away, giving them space to work.

"Don't say I didn't warn you," he said through the oxygen mask affixed to his face.

As the medics lifted his body onto the stretcher, Pearson reached behind his back and brandished a pair of handcuffs. With a smirk painted on his face, he attached the first cuff to the metal guardrail of the gurney.

"Alan Lowry, I am arresting you for assault and improperly interfering with a human body. You have the right to retain and instruct counsel without delay. You also have the right to free and immediate legal advice. Do you understand?"

The beloved school principal nodded as Pearson cinched the other half of the handcuffs around his wrist.

"I must provide you the following warning: You need not say anything. You have nothing to gain from any promise or favor and nothing to fear from any threat, regardless if you say anything or not. Anything you do or say we may use as evidence. Do you understand?"

Lowry gazed back at Pearson with a vacancy in his dark eyes. Gone was the kind, jovial personality Pearson expected from the man, with a malevolence in its place.

"Screw you, pig. I want a lawyer."

Pearson scoffed and shooed towards the medics. "Get him out of here and make sure they do a drug test on him."

The confrontational man carried on spewing hostilities as they wheeled him down the hallway, and all Pearson could do was hang his head in awe. Beads of sweat fell from his forehead and splashed to the floor. He reached up to wipe them away.

What in the hell is going on in this town? Kidnapping, murder, stealing dead bodies, and threats to keep secrets. For what?

Before he could answer his internal question, DS Clark entered with Miller hot on his tail.

"She's not here. And there aren't any signs she ever was," Miller said.

"I didn't think she would be. Lowry said someone was going to kill him if he talked. Perhaps it's the same person who took her body before he even got it into the house."

DS Clark ripped off his latex gloves and rubbed his smooth chin. "Perhaps. But who? Who are we looking for?"

All Pearson delivered was a shrug and a furrowed brow. "I don't know. But mark my words, it'll come out soon enough. Just wait."

Clark reached out and patted Pearson on the shoulder. "Well, still a lot of ground to cover. I'll arrange to have his vehicle towed to the detachment garage. Maybe there's some evidence there?"

"Good. Miller?" he said.

"Yeah?"

"Shadow DS Clark."

"Sure. What about you?"

"Someone needs a wake-up call."

***

HIS KNUCKLES BEAT AGAINST THE DOOR of 815 Fourth Street West. The birds nested in the tree in the front yard whistled him a relaxing melody as he waited.

"Sorry, little guys, it's not you. It's me."

The door cracked enough for Pearson to catch a glimpse of a disheveled Christian, standing in nothing but a navy-blue t-shirt and black boxer briefs. Christian dug his fingers into the corners of his eyes and flicked away the crust.

"Yeah?"

"Christian, you look like death. You gonna let me in or not?"

His mouth opened wide and out escaped an extended yawn. He raised his hands to cover it, so as not to offend. "Yeah, sorry, Luke. I didn't get much sleep last night."

"That makes two of us."

Pearson twisted the handle and gently closed the door. "What time is it?"

"Seven."

Christian's eyes widened. "Seven? Why on God's green earth are you here so early?"

"First things first . . . where's the coffee?"

Christian grinned and motioned at him to follow. Once in the kitchen,

Christian turned and faced Pearson. "I take it this isn't a social call?"

As Christian reached for the tin of coffee, Pearson blurted out what he came to say. "You'd guess right. We got him in custody."

The tin of coffee slipped from Christian grasp and clanked against the kitchen counter. Without hesitation, he spun around. "You have *who* in custody?"

"Alan Lowry."

"Lowry. I knew it. After that encounter at the café, something told me he was involved in this mess somehow. How d'you find him?"

"A couple witnesses spotted his vehicle fleeing the scene."

"Uh-huh. Why are you here if he's in custody? Shouldn't you be questioning him?"

He sighed and lowered his head. "If I can be frank, I can't question him. Not yet, at least."

"Why the hell not?"

"He's in the hospital and requested a lawyer. You know the rules."

"Screw the rules."

"Nope, we aren't playing this game."

"So, you found Heather?"

"Negative. We went to arrest him but instead found him unconscious."

"Was he drunk?"

"He was, but then someone got to him afterward. Beat him bloody. It didn't take long, but he snapped out of whatever stupor he was in, and that's when it happened. Something I've never experienced in all my years of policing."

The water cascaded from the urn into the reservoir and Christian pressed start. "And that is?"

"Do you believe in dissociative identity disorder?"

"You're talking about multiple personalities? Sure. There's enough scientific evidence to suggest it's real. And as a man of science, I have no reason to question the experts. But what does that have to—"

The realization washed over Christian's face. "And you believe Lowry might suffer from it?"

Pearson shrugged his broad shoulders before reaching out for the cup of coffee. "I don't know what I believe anymore. One thing I can say with certainty is the entire atmosphere changed in an instant. He wasn't the same Lowry. He turned into a heartless maniac. Even called me a pig."

"Stress, maybe? I mean, if I attacked the coroner and fled with a corpse, I'd be stressed to the max."

"Didn't you say you had a run-in with him just the other day? How was he then?"

"At first, pleasant and interested in hearing all about how Gemma and I had been doing. But then—"

"Then?"

"Gemma walked away, leaving just us two at the table. And things got dark. He told me to stay away from David Ross and the entire family. And if I didn't, I'd regret it," he paused. "Shit. I'm in danger, aren't I?"

Heavy footsteps descended the stairs and distracted Pearson from answering the question put to him. All eyes in the room focused on the hallway. After a minute, Adam rounded the corner from the staircase.

"Pearson?" Adam asked.

"Morning, sunshine."

"Eh, what are you doing here? Is everything okay?"

Pearson glanced at Christian and back at Adam. "Yeah. I just needed some coffee."

"Uh-huh, and Tim Horton's was closed? Nah, something's going on, so spill it."

Pearson leaned against the countertop. "He always this cranky at seven in the morning?"

"Only when he hasn't had eight hours of sleep."

Christian dished out the mugs of coffee, and as Adam slid his fingers through the ceramic loop. Before he lifted it to his lips, he scrunched his face at Christian. "You're no delight yourself, Mr. Ray-of-Sunshine. Now, tell me what's going on. You need a favor, don't you?"

Pearson pressed the rim of the mug to his lips but didn't say a word.

"Luke, I'm about five seconds away from—"

Pearson choked on the liquid in his mouth and held out one hand in front of him. "Whoa, let's not get violent. We have enough of that going around. Look, I'm bringing David and Chad Ross in for questioning later."

"And this affects us how?" Christian asked.

"If you'd let me finish, you'd find out. I hoped you guys could observe my interrogations, and we could compare notes afterward."

Christian's shoulders raised, and he cocked his head. "Couldn't hurt."

"I'm down. I said it from day one; there's something off about that family."

Pearson clapped his hands together, and a genuine smile appeared on his face. "Perfect. Meet me at the detachment at ten. On the dot."

"We'll be there."

THIRTY-TWO

THE OBSERVATION ROOM WAS PRECISELY HOW Christian remembered it from two years ago. The lingering musty odor in the air, the accumulating dust stuck to the edges of the furniture. While the RCMP gentrified the common areas, they hadn't updated the electronic equipment.

"Pearson needs to hire a janitorial service or something," Christian said to break the tension.

"For Christ's sake, Christian, it's a police station. Not a resort. People aren't supposed to get comfortable here."

His lips curled downward, and he shot Adam a stare like no other he ever had. "Unfortunately, some of us have to."

"Cut the poor guy a little slack. Spending time with a Swiffer in his hand is not the best use of his time. Locking up the trash ruining your hometown; that's better. Besides, wasn't it you who told me your motto for this place?"

Christian grinned.

"Hmm, I think you said, and I quote, 'Cedar Lake—more trash, less class.'"

"Am I wrong?"

Adam flashed him a coy smile just as the door to interview room B opened. First in was David Ross, followed by Pearson, who, for some strange reason, appeared refreshed and down to business. Christian approached the one-way mirror, twisted the knob to the speaker, and pressed his hand against the cold glass.

"It's showtime," Adam said with a hint of sarcasm.

***

SOMETHING ABOUT THE WAY MR. ROSS carried himself unsettled Christian. Was it his slouch? Or the puffy, dark circles under his eyes? Maybe it was the man's untrimmed black beard. He couldn't pinpoint it, but one thing was evident: something about his appearance changed in the last few days and didn't align with that of a successful business executive.

With no time for mundane small talk, Pearson delved right into questioning. Christian watched Pearson slide a folder across the table and pulled out the chair.

"Thanks for coming in today, David."

"Sure. You were so vague on the phone it piqued my curiosity."

Pearson flipped open the file, pulled out a mugshot of Lee White, and tossed it across the table.

"Ever run into this guy?"

Mr. Ross retrieved his glasses from the pocket inside his sports jacket and lifted the photo. Christian paced, unable to suppress his anticipation. They were getting into the particulars now—which he hoped would reveal more information than they had, which at that moment was zilch.

Christian glanced over his shoulder and smiled at Adam. "He knows him. Everyone in town knows everyone. And when you're the town's biggest supplier of drugs and sex, well, I don't need to finish that sentence."

Mr. Ross studied the photo for a few seconds and slid it back across. "Never seen him."

Pearson smirked and flipped the photo upside down on the left side of the folder. He plucked the next mugshot: Taylor Jackson. "And how about this guy?"

Again, Mr. Ross slid his fingers under the photo and pulled it closer to his face. Christian studied the older man's face. A quivering lower lip, beads of sweat coated his hairline.

"He looks familiar."

"How so?"

"There was this punk kid that Chad hung out with during high school. But, God, that's fifteen years ago."

"Does the name Taylor ring any bells?" Pearson asked.

"Taylor. Taylor," he whispered under his breath. "Is his last name Jackson?"

The constable nodded. "You mentioned he and Chad were friends, yeah?"

Mr. Ross slid the photo back across to Pearson and folded his arms across his chest. His body slouched further back in the chair. "I mean, back then, sure. Don't all high school kids 'know' of each other. I wouldn't say they were best friends or anything. They ran in two totally different circles."

"Right. What you're saying is Chad was more of a cheerleader type, and Taylor, well, he was more interested in staying high."

Mr. Ross shrugged. "You know more than me. Why are you asking about this kid anyhow? Is he involved in what happened to Lindsay?"

"I'm asking because he's dead."

What happened wasn't like what the movies would have you believe. David Ross wasn't shocked. He didn't grasp at his chest. Instead, his jaw remained clenched. Not even a slight twitch or restlessness. Nothing. He either didn't give a rat's ass about another dead junkie, or Taylor's fate was sealed before he headed off for Regina.

After taking a second, Mr. Ross leaned forward and rested his elbows on the metal table. "Pity. Kids these days are a lost generation. Correct me if I'm wrong, but this town has gone to shit these last few years, hasn't it?"

Pearson kept things professional. He neither confirmed nor denied his comment. "Mr. Ross, I know talking about Lindsay may be hard, but I need to ask a few questions about the week leading up to your daughter's death."

"Sure."

"Was there anything out of the ordinary?"

"How so?"

"Was she more skittish? Did something happen at school to make everyone assume she committed suicide?"

He slammed his back against the chair and wiped the moisture from his forehead. "There were so many things out of the ordinary. I wouldn't even know where to begin. I've already told that guy, um, DS Anderson, everything we know."

"While helpful, Detective Sergeant Anderson is voluntarily assisting but doesn't have jurisdiction here. He's a concerned friend of your daughter's, who only wants to find out the truth."

"That's what we all want."

"Which is why I've officially reopened her case. So, I'll ask again. Is there any information you can provide to help us figure this out, once and for all?"

"There were a few major incidents. Someone got ahold of her journal and slipped photocopies into everyone's locker," he leaned forward in the chair. "Those were her private thoughts. Her notes on stories she was working on. It left her devastated. We all assumed that sent her over the edge."

"That was in the report. I'm more interested in personal vendettas she may have had with some locals. You know she did have a way of rubbing people the wrong way with her snooping for a story. Is it possible her *investigations* got her killed?"

His brows raised, and he appeared genuinely taken aback. But it was a response. Something Christian had patiently waited for.

"Investigations? What investigations? You make it seem like my daughter was working undercover for you."

"Come on, you must have known about the piece she was writing on the cheating scandal involving the, how should I put this, the more affluent students at Cedar Lake High."

He shrugged. "News to me. Any other shit you guys failed to mention twelve years ago?"

Pearson twirled a ballpoint pen between his fingers. It was clear to Christian that things could take a wrong turn by how David Ross stared the constable down. Yet, the twirling stopped, and Pearson rested his hand on the table. "We've only learned this in the last twenty-four hours. We're still uncovering a lot about Lindsay, but from the look on your face, so are you."

Mr. Ross flicked his wrist and glanced at his oversized watch. "While staring at pictures of nobodies is fascinating, and all, was there some particular reason you rushed me down here?"

"I thought you'd never ask. Yes, there is," he said, pulling another photo from the folder and laying it face-up on the table. "This man right here. You ever dealt with him before, you know, professionally?"

Christian repositioned himself, trying to get a better look. And the face in the photo was one he recognized all too well. It was Thomas Campbell. David Ross gave the picture a brief glance before he pushed it away. "Nope. Doesn't look like someone I do business with. Look, constable, unless this is going some—"

Pearson interrupted. "Somewhere? Trust me, it is. I'm trying to figure out who murdered your daughter and why. You may have missed the memo, but the world of forensics has advanced in the last decade."

"So, you must know something you're not telling me then?"

"Perhaps. But for now, I want to stay focused on these faces," Pearson spread the photos across the table. "Have you ever, recently or back then, seen any of these people snooping around?"

His nostrils flared, and he clenched his jaw tight. "I said no. And no matter how many times you show me, the answer is still no."

Pearson shuffled the photos into a pile and returned them, face down, inside the file. The room fell silent. Mr. Ross fidgeted in the chair, all while Pearson calculated his next move.

From the other side of the glass, Christian paced and nibbled at his fingernails. Adam glanced up from the laptop and sighed. "Babe, you're working your-self up, and for what?"

Christian glanced away from the action. "He's lying. This town is like those dotting the prairie. So small everyone knows everyone. Now, whether you social-ize together, that's a different story. But people know of people."

"Let's see where this takes us before we jump to conclusions."

He grinned. "Your calmness irritates me."

"You love it."

Pearson stretched out and raised his arms above his head. "Mr. Ross, what can you tell me about the sale of the sawmill you once owned?"

"What about it?"

"Seems odd your daughter is found dead in a building you once owned."

The man shrugged. "The sale was straightforward. It was time to diversify my ventures. Back when I bought the place in the 1980s, the place was my cash crop. Over time, people started caring about the planet or some cockamamie bullshit. Sales declined, and I got out before I got more in the red."

"Still, you can understand my concern."

He stopped fidgeting and leaned across the table. "Except . . . I can't. I sold the property in 2005, and you all found my daughter there four years later. I don't get how either is connected."

"I'm trying to figure that out too. Could it be an old grievance of some sort?"

Mr. Ross shook his head and slid the chair away from the table. It scratched against the linoleum floor as the man jumped to his feet. "Constable Pear-son, you're wasting my precious time. Either you tell me what you know, or I'm walking out of here."

Pearson flipped the file closed and gestured towards the chair. "That's not how we're doing things, Mr. Ross. For once, you're not calling the shots here. I am. Now, please, sit so we can figure this out together."

Reluctantly, the man returned to the chair and cleared his throat. "Fine. Can you at least tell me what evidence you have to warrant the reopening of my daughters' case?"

"I suppose you deserve to know what we know."

The man smoothed out his dress shirt and leaned forward.

"We've got several videos Lindsay recorded in the days leading up to her death."

For the first time during the entire interview, Mr. Ross trembled. "How. Where did you find them?"

"That's not what's important. What is, however, is she was scared. Well, petrified is a better word. Said if we found the tapes, she was probably already dead."

"How did this happen right under my nose?"

From the observation room, Christian didn't hold back his opinion. "Because you were an awful parent. So consumed with your own life."

"You're doing it again?"

Christian stood still. "What?"

"You're working yourself up. You swore to uphold the law and be unbiased. We don't have the entire story . . . yet. You know, for one of RPS's best, you get wound up a lot."

"Only when it involves people I know. That's why we're here 'unofficially.' This isn't my case; it's Pearson's. You and I are merely here to add insight and support."

"Still, Christian. I shudder to think what'll happen when he brings Chad Ross in next."

Christian scoffed and refocused on the ongoing interview.

"And so that's why I showed you the pictures. These are a few men we think might be involved in the piece she was working on for the school newspaper."

"Why in the hell would a bunch of high school students be interested in a cheating scandal? Or this prostitution ring you referred to? You sure you haven't mixed up your facts?" Mr. Ross asked.

"We're sure."

"Who is this 'we' you keep referring to? Is it that meddling kid, DS Anderson? Is he behind this investigation, and you're just his puppet doing all the hard work?"

"Funny you mention that. Did you know Christian when he was in high school?"

He nodded. "He was around all the time, for a while. Then he stopped visiting. Good kid back then. Smart. Going places, you know. But now . . . I probably shouldn't say this."

"Say what?"

"I think after what happened two years ago, maybe it messed him up. Learning his best friend's father murdered his own mother and his own daughter. Not sure how I'd react, but one has to admit it would mess you up."

His mother was a touchy subject, but David Ross bringing her up was all it took to send Christian bolting into the hallway and busting in on the interrogation.

Christian stood at the edge of the table. His finger wagged in the air, and his nostrils flared. And Pearson's attempts at controlling him failed. "Lousy son-of-a-bitch. How dare you say anything about my family when you couldn't even keep your own family under your control?"

The outburst rattled Mr. Ross, who pulled his body into a tight ball as he sat, speechless, in the chair.

"I asked to have this case re-investigated because I cared about her. She didn't have to die for exposing the truth about this God-forsaken town."

"Why is he here?" Mr. Ross peeked around Christian's body and stared at Pearson.

"Christian. Sit down."

"No. This is going to end right here."

Pearson's voice raised and deepened. "I said sit, Christian. Now."

Christian backed off and slammed his hand against the table. David Ross had struck a nerve. But, given as this wasn't his station house and he wasn't calling the shots, he obeyed orders and pulled out the chair next to Pearson.

No one in the room exchanged words, only reddened faces and tension so thick it sapped the air from the room. It carried on for another two minutes before Mr. Ross stood, snatched his sports jacket from the back of the chair, and moved for the door.

"We're not done," Pearson said.

"Am I under arrest?"

"Well, no. But—"

"Then, this interview is over. And a piece of advice, the next time you want to drag me, or anyone in my family, down here, I suggest you speak with my lawyer first." He pulled a white card from his wallet and tossed it onto the table in front of Pearson.

The metal latch clanked as the door closed. A shiver coursed through Christian's body, just like every time the metal jail doors closed at the station.

After the mental image dissipated, he opened his eyes and glanced in Pearson's direction. His face was red, damn near purple, and his pupils were swollen and homed in on him.

He's not happy.

And he wasn't. Pearson wasted no time reprimanding him. "Damnit, Anderson. I don't know which one of you is worse—Adam with his outburst with Linus or this. I'm warning you, Christian, this can't keep happening. Otherwise, you'll leave me no choice."

"I'm sorry. It's just . . . I can't believe he said all that."

"Listen to me," Pearson paused. "Hey, are you listening?"

He nodded.

"If we're going to continue working together to uncover the truth, this sort of shit can never happen again. You're going to jeopardize the case if you go off on every suspect because they said something bad about you."

"I know."

"I've written off your rogue stunts as part of trying to get shit done. But now, your actions are preventing me from bringing Chad in for questioning without a lawyer. What if he's our killer? I could have broken him into confessing."

Christian took a shallow breath and pressed his fingers into his temples. "There has to be something I can do to make this right?"

"Get back to watching those videos and find me something, any shred of evidence that I can use as leverage to get him in here for an interview."

"What exactly are you looking for?"

"Anything that proves Chad was involved."

He had that one video, the one of Chad, Taylor, and Lee White behind Mc-Ginty's. But that alone wasn't enough to bring him in for questioning in the death of his sister. And with Pearson still raging, Christian didn't dare mention it, not yet at least.

"I'll find something."

"You better. You owe me, big time, for your little stunt."

Christian nodded as the door swung open, and Adam appeared in the doorway.

"Luke, I'm so sorry about that. I should have stopped him."

"It's not your fault, Adam. While it shouldn't have happened, I anticipated it and should have done a better job of keeping him as far away from here as possible."

Christian stood to his feet. It took everything in his power to steady his walk and keep his head held high after the unwelcome critique.

"You ready?" he asked, turning his attention to his husband.

"Actually, leave him with me. We have a few people we haven't alienated that need to be questioned."

Christian hesitated. His eyes darted back and forth between the two, and he continued until Adam opened his mouth.

"Hey, it'll be fine. I'll only be a distraction if I'm there."

"But."

"Seriously, focus on the videos and find us what we need. If Lindsay is as meticulous as you've described her, she undoubtedly left you clues. You have everything you need; you just need to slow down and look for them."

As Christian reached the door, he turned one last time and studied their faces. Little did he know this uncomfortable moment might be the last time he'd ever see them again.

THIRTY-THREE

IT HAD BEEN THREE HOURS SINCE Christian sulkily entered through the front door of his childhood home. Still frustrated with allowing David Ross to provoke him, Christian had a colossal task ahead of him. Pearson needed something more concrete so they could get answers. And it was up to him to find that one piece of damning evidence.

After the eleventh video stopped, his eyes burned. He tossed the headphones onto the table and struggled to rub away the burning. It didn't work. Three lonely hours of Lindsay's silent movie-ish crap she was known for was taking a toll. Yet, for all his efforts, nowhere had he found a shred of evidence, no tangible proof, to give them cause to call Chad Ross in for questioning.

He glanced around the room. It was still. Eerie. Uncomfortable, even for Christian, who most times welcomed the peace and quiet. But now, left to only his own mind, the hairs on his arms stood on end.

He shook off the discomfort and stood. He needed some fresh air if he was going to survive another three hours of these amateur videos. Two steps towards the hallway, his cell phone rang.

He jerked and fell against the cream wallpapered wall. "Shit. I need to turn off the ringer."

He approached slowly; his head hovered over the illuminated display. Expecting it to be either Adam or Pearson, begging him to return, instead, the words on the screen were the last thing he expected.

Blocked Caller.

"What the hell?"

Under normal circumstances, he'd ignore it and carry on with his life. But times weren't usual, and without hesitating, he reached for the phone and pressed it to his ear. "Hello?"

"Hello, Christian," a distorted voice on the other end said.

"Who's this?"

"Not the right question. The right question is, are you ready to know what happened to Lindsay Ross?"

The word flew across his lips faster than a speeding cheetah. "Yes."

"Meet me at the sawmill. You have one hour. Do not tell your husband or that nosy constable."

"How do I know this is real?"

"You don't. Either you want to know the truth, or you don't."

Christian's hand trembled as he shook his head. "Nope, no deal until you tell me something that proves you know anything about this case."

"How's this for proof: I was there when they drugged her, slid the noose around her neck, and strung her up. But then again, you were there, too."

Christian's breath increased, but he suppressed the noise. He stuttered, trying to think of some way to deny he was the one who found her body and phoned in the anonymous call.

"Think long before you say anything else. I know you were there because my eyes don't lie. That knocked over chair underneath her body was smooth, huh? Sure did fool those stupid constables into believing her death was a suicide. That was until Taylor couldn't keep his damn mouth shut."

"Shit. Did you murder Taylor, too?"

"You have questions. And you'll get your answers. But not over the phone."

Christian's hands grew cold and sweaty. His next words caught in the back of his throat. "What . . . why now? After all these years, what do you want?"

"This isn't about me. This is about you. You want the truth, don't you?"

He breathed out a curt response. "Yes."

"One hour. And remember, come alone."

The line went dead, and Christian stood in the middle of the dining room. He glanced at the darkened screen of his iPhone, and only his shocked reflection greeted him.

"This is it. The break I've been searching for," he spoke aloud to himself. Something he had become quite good at lately. "But alone. At the sawmill. I hated that place even when I wasn't alone."

His first instinct was to call Adam, to at least tell someone where he was going. But he stopped mid-dial and set the phone on the table.

"No. They said to come alone. And if I tell Adam, he'll talk me out of going."

Twenty minutes passed, and he paced, weighing the pros and cons of moving forward. But then it was too late, there was no more time left.

He slid his phone and car keys into his pocket. He gave the room one last glance-over, and quickly jotted down a note and posted it on top of Adam's laptop.

> *I got a lead, a meeting at the one place I wouldn't visit alone, yet I am. Don't get too worried. I'll be back in a few hours.*
> *I love you.*
> *Christian*

And before the ink dried, he raced out the door, unsure what awaited him on the other side of town.

THE THICK STORM CLOUDS HUNG IN the sky as the potholes along the worn-out path consumed the tires of his sedan.

With each morbid flash of 'what-if' that crossed his mind, Christian's stomach tightened, and his breaths grew shallower. But here he was, on the verge of getting his answers, so there was no point in turning back now. And even if he wanted to, the killer already had his information and suspected it was only a matter of time before he unmasked them. Leaving now would only delay the inevitable face-to-face meeting. At least walking directly into the fire, Christian had a slim chance of finding a way out if things went sideways.

He crept the car as close as he could to the main door of the facility. With a shaky hand, he shifted the car into park and studied the facade of the building. A decade of extreme weather had taken its toll on the dry-rotted batten, leaving several long strips peeling away from the wooden structure. One long strip caught his attention as it slapped in the stiff gust that swept across the barren land.

He scanned the area. No car. No apparent signs of life anywhere for as far as he could see. For a split-second, he had doubts this was the right way to go about this.

"I should call Adam, and at least tell him where I am," he said to himself, but then the rogue side of himself reared its ugly head. "No. You're doing the right thing. You're getting justice for Lindsay. That's what you came here for, and by God, you're going to follow through."

He pressed the button, and the loud engine subsided, leaving nothing but the whistle of the wind and his overactive mind. Before he had the opportunity to back out of his commitment, he stood at the door and pulled it open. Armed only with a flashlight and his cell phone, he peeked his head inside.

The building moaned at his presence, but he pressed onward.

One step.

Two steps.

The wind slammed the door closed behind him, and he powered up the light before he moved any further inside.

"Creepy back then, creepier now."

The unmistakable aroma of sawdust from his visit two years ago had vanished. And in its place, a new, powerful earthy stench enveloped the building. A cough he had tried to hold back escaped.

He called out. "Hello? Is anyone here?"

But only a low hum of creaking wood echoed against the rafters above.

"Hello? Anybody there?"

Something metallic fell to the ground behind him, and Christian spun around faster than he had ever in his life. His heart pounded against his ribcage, and he could only manage steady, short breaths. Someone was there, but why were they hiding? Then a voice from behind called out.

"So, you *are* braver than I gave you credit for."

Christian flashed the light towards the voice, but the man was too far away for him to make out any distinguishable features.

"I'm here, just like you asked. The least you can do is reveal who you are."

"In time." The shadowy figure walked closer. "First, I have some rules."

"Seriously? Rules?"

"I will answer what I know. I will not speculate, implicate, or divulge information I do not possess first-hand."

"But you said you were there when they murdered her?"

"For all intents and purposes, I was. I was here, only a hundred feet behind you, but not as an active participant. More like security."

"So, you're not the killer?"

The man scoffed. "No."

"What's your name?"

The figure was halfway across the room, but a hood shielded his identity. "I won't answer that. You came because you had questions. And here you stand, asking questions that aren't really what you came here for. Think about what you're asking before you do."

Christian racked his brains, hunting for a new tactic. Then he had it.

"Was Lindsay murdered for what she knew about the prostitution ring?"

"Yes, and no. You of all people know that in these parts, some people don't welcome having their privacy invaded."

"What are you implying?"

"Lindsay was a damn good snoop. If she could have only waited just a few more weeks, she would have been long gone, far away from here. Out of the grasp of her killer."

"Was Lee White involved?"

"Yes."

A straightforward answer, for once.

"And Taylor Jackson?"

"He was. But he's why you're here, isn't it? Trying to clear his conscience by blabbing to Gemma. Yeah, well, look at what it got him. Stabbed to death in a piss-soaked alley in Regina."

"Taylor . . . did you kill him?"

"Wasn't me."

"Then, who?"

"Someone more powerful, whose only wish was for this tragedy to fade into the darkness like all the others. But some people just couldn't let the past alone."

"Who shot Lee White? Better yet, who attacked Lowry and left him for dead?"

"I'm the one who attacked Lowry. I received an anonymous text asking me to rough him up, you know, send a message to stop talking so much. But as far as Lee, I don't know who shot him. It wasn't me, nor the person who hired me."

"Who asked you to talk to me then? Let me take a guess, it was David Ross?"

"David Ross? Lindsay's father? You think he murdered his own kid? No, you're so far off track. David Ross is nothing like Liam Williams." The reference to Gemma's father shocked Christian.

"Then, who? For fuck's sake, stop wasting my time and give me something to work with here."

221

The man stepped into the beam of light and removed his hood.

Christian stepped backward. "Thomas?"

"Hello, Christian. So, we meet after all this time. You remember how your hunt for me ended last time, don't you?"

"Yeah, with a lot of bruises and you damn near ending my police career."

"Well, don't think I'll go any easier on you this time."

Before Christian could grasp what was happening, two bodies appeared from the shadows and secured his arms. Thomas walked closer with a white rag in his hand.

"Just as nosy as Lindsay was in her last days."

In one swift move, Thomas covered Christian's nose and mouth with a rag. The sickly-sweet odor came first, and then the haunting laugh jolted him back to the night of his beating outside McGinty's Pub.

Right before he lost consciousness, he managed to stutter out three words. "It was you."

THIRTY-FOUR

THE EVENING SNUCK UP ON ADAM and Pearson faster than they expected. But with three interviews down, all they craved was a quiet night in and hopefully a bombshell revelation from Christian.

Adam turned the doorknob. Instead of Christian greeting them at the door, excited to share any news, only an empty house welcomed them back. Adam called out.

"Christian? Matthias? Anybody home?"

Stillness.

"Maybe Matthias got a craving for A&W and took Christian along?"

Adam flaunted a half-smile. "Yeah. And I'd almost buy that, except Christian hates that place. Then again, after sulking all day, he might be seeking comfort in that artery-clogging crap."

"Hey, don't knock it. It's a delicious meal, cheap, and sometimes the only thing you can get late. I'm sure he won't mind if we see what he's been up to the last five hours."

As Adam rounded the corner, he noticed everything powered down. The files were stacked into neat piles. And Christian's headphones rested on top of the table next to his laptop.

"Strange."

"What is?"

"My husband is a good man, but someone who tidies up, he is not."

A bright, fluorescent pink Post-it affixed to the cover of Adam's laptop caught Pearson's attention.

"I think he left you a present," Pearson said as he pointed.

Adam walked over and peeled it away from the metallic cover. At first, he read the message silently to himself. And again. It didn't make sense.

"What's wrong?"

"He's . . ." Adam paused, trying to finish the sentence. "He's not out at dinner."

"Then, where the hell is he?"

Adam handed over the note. "Off chasing a lead. So typical of him to not give anyone else but himself consideration."

"Ouch. You two having trouble in paradise?"

Adam folded his arms across his chest. "Only when he pulls shit like this."

Pearson mulled over the jumble of words twice. "I don't understand what this means. The one place I'm afraid to go alone. Is that code for something?"

Adam shrugged. "Not his usual flair. What if—nah, never mind."

"No, that's not the deal. We agreed if something was bothering us, no matter how major, we'd say it."

"We did?" Adam asked as an eyebrow raised.

"Two years ago, while we waited for Saskatoon to show up at Liam Williams' place. Remember?"

Adam cocked his head to the side and tapped his index finger against his chin. "I vaguely remember that. But, if you say I said it, then I must have. Still, this note is pretty strange. What if he wrote it under duress? It's as if he couldn't flat out say where he was but left me a hint instead. He must have assumed I'd figure it out."

"Duress? You don't think they got to him? Do you?"

"Around here, anything's possible," Adam said.

"You know your husband better than me. Where is the one place he's afraid to go alone?"

Adam scoffed and flailed his hands. "Beats the hell out of me. I guess I don't know him as well as I should."

"Perhaps. It's still early on. Things like that take time to claw to the surface."

"I know who might know though . . ."

Pearson's eye lit up. "Gemma."

"You want to, or shall I?"

Without replying, Pearson had the phone out, his thick fingers tapped away at the screen. The constable's foot tapped in rapid succession against the hardwood until she answered. Adam assumed her voice startled him as he stuttered out a few words. "H-h, hi, Gemma?"

Her loud voice echoed across the room, and every word pierced through Adam's ears. "Luke! Tell me you got some sleep."

"Uh, no. Not yet," he paused. "But I will."

"You're gonna kill yourself working so hard. How's Christian? Better yet, making any progress on the case? Man, I wish I was there right now."

Pearson glanced at Adam, who spun his hand around, giving that all too familiar gesture he gave when he wanted things to move quicker. "Everything's good. But listen, I'd love to have one of our usual long chats, but we're sort of up to our necks in shit right now."

"Any breakthroughs?"

"That's why I called. I have a question for you."

"Fire away."

"Where's the one place in Cedar Lake where Christian is afraid to go alone?"

The line was silent for a moment, and her scratchy voice returned. "Wait. Why are you asking that? Has something happened to Christian?"

The pace in his voice grew faster. "We . . . well, no. Christian is fine. We're just playing a game. I call it, 'how well does your best friend know you?'"

"You're lying. Put Christian on the phone."

Adam shook his head, and Pearson gave him those sappy eyes. "Don't tell her," Adam whispered.

"Gemma, listen, Christian is out with his dad right now, and I just need the answer. It's some sort of riddle he left with us. Do you know where the place is or not?"

"Only an idiot wouldn't know the answer to that. He hates the sawmill. The place gives him the creeps; always has. Way back in high school when all the cool kids used to sneak out there and smoke up and get drunk, I practically had to threaten to spill all his secrets if he didn't come with me."

"Charming, Gemma. Well, you passed the test. I'm gonna go now, but we'll have Christian call you when he gets back."

Pearson hung up without waiting for a goodbye, switched the phone to silent, and tossed it onto the table. He ran his brawny hands across his scruffy face and grunted.

Adam stepped closer. "So, the sawmill."

"You know, if there's one thing I hate—more than psychos running the streets of Cedar Lake—it's lying to her."

"That's because you're in love."

Pearson parted his hands, and he peeked through the cracks. "What are you jabbering on about?"

"I said you're in love. The way you guys talk for hours. How she can't talk about anyone else other than you when we have her over for Sunday dinners."

His eyes lit up as they moved for the door. "Really?"

"I'm not a betting man, but I'd lay down a hundred that after nursing school, she'd move back here. That is if you asked her to."

"You're talking nonsense."

Adam opened the door. "Am I?"

"Yes. And besides, we need to focus on your missing husband. That's a bit more urgent than who I may or may not be in love with."

"Whatever you say. Luke and Gemma, sitting in a—"

"All right, that's about enough of that. Get in the car."

"That's wasn't even the best part."

"When we find Christian, you can sing until your throat closes up. Until then, we focus."

***

PEARSON'S SUV ROLLED UP OUTSIDE THE derelict building that not only annoyed him but weirdly captivated him. It was the one place that attracted chaos like a bee drawn to the sun.

The city council held a vote last summer on what to do with the eyesore. They had two choices: Leave it standing as a reminder to the citizens of everything they lost when it closed years ago. Or—the preferred alternative—tear it down and give the land back to the earth.

Too bad the seedy criminals running Cedar Lake had more power than he did. You know the type: the people you *think* you know but really lie in wait behind a phony smile—the ones who would murder their own mother for even an iota of control.

Those corrupt, power-hungry posers influenced some of the weaker council members. And while no one on the council would ever outright admit someone bought their vote, they made their final decision only two days later. The building would remain standing, at least for another year, while the town persuaded investors. That was the plan anyhow.

Pearson returned to the here and now. The council's promise meant nothing, except another memory added to his long list. That's because even after a year, the area sat deserted. No cars. No humans. Nothing except the waves of golden canola fields for klicks and the squawks from the crows circling overhead.

"I'm beginning to doubt how well Gemma knows her best friend," the constable said as he slammed the gearshift into park.

"This has to be right. You remember when we found Gemma here, he said, 'every tragic event in this forsaken town over the last ten years was tied to the sawmill.'"

"Vaguely. But he's not lying."

The two remained fixed to their seats. The very thought of going inside brought back memories from their last visit. Each of them had their own recollection of that February day, which affected them both differently.

Time was slipping away the longer they hesitated. But soon, Adam flung open the door, and his white tennis shoes kicked up a cloud of dust as they slammed against the dry earth.

"We aren't going to find him sitting here paralyzed by fear."

Pearson puffed out his chest. "I'm not afraid."

Adam rested one arm on top of the truck and leaned inside. "Yeah? Prove it."

Adam slammed the door closed. As he waited, he paced, trying to defy the negative voice in the back of his head. The voice that told him his instincts were off and that Christian was somewhere else, alive and well. But the thing about his inner voice: it was wrong. Every. Single. Time.

If this is where Gemma said he'd be, then he's here—car or no car. He ran the palms of his hands across his face. *Snap out of it, Adam, and find Christian.*

He glanced at the ground, and it didn't take long before he spotted the unique tire treads of his husband's sedan channeled into the dirt.

He crouched and leaned closer. In the distance, the door slammed closed, and the sound of Pearson's radio pierced through the wind blowing in his ear.

"He's been here," Adam said.

"I believe you. But where is he now?"

Adam stood and brushed the dust from his jeans. "You don't think they got to him . . . do you?"

"Around here, anything's possible."

THIRTY-FIVE

DRIP. DRIP. DRIP.

Christian's eyes flutter open. His vision was blurry, and his head pounded from the after-effects of whatever they drugged him with. He scanned the area. The windowless room was dim, and an overpowering moldy stench swirled in the air around him. To his left was an old wooden door. The paint on the walls had given up years ago and now the chips collected on the concrete floor in piles.

Except for the relentless drip of water slapping against the floor, the room was otherwise void of life. For a split-second, the tranquility put his mind at ease. That was until he tried to stand.

Christian thrust his body forward and wiggled his hands, but nothing budged. As he peered down, he discovered the culprit: every limb was zip-tied to the chair.

Where the hell am I?

He yelled out. "Let me out of here."

His voice echoed off the walls as he struggled with loosening himself. Then a faint feminine voice sliced through the air. "Christian, save your energy for the actual fight ahead."

Startled, his eyes opened wider. "Who's there?"

"Angela."

"Martin?" he asked.

"Yes."

"The entire town has been looking for you. What the hell happened? Better yet, where the hell are we?"

Before she even had the chance to respond, another weak voice pierced the tense air. "I can't believe my own boy got duped by them."

"Pop?"

Matthias released a long sigh. "Yes, Christian, it's me. They got to me too."

"Who are *they*?"

"I have no idea. Some guy called; his voice was disguised. He said to come to the sawmill so we could talk about Lindsay. Next thing I know, here I am."

"And where is here? What is this place?"

"You don't recognize it?" Angela asked.

"If I did, you think I'd ask?"

"Fair point. We're in the underground bunker of the sawmill. I'd been here a few times, but back when this place wasn't so, eh, gross."

"So wait, we're still on the grounds of the sawmill? You said you drove here. There wasn't a car out there when I got here."

"Yup, they didn't take you far. But I can understand how anyone not familiar with this place could overlook it; it's sort of tucked away. And as far as the car, yeah, I'm sure it's gone. Whoever these people are, they're good at making things disappear."

"So, I'm screwed."

"We're all screwed. These guys are pros."

"Not what I wanted to hear. Pop?"

"Yeah?"

"How'd they con you?"

"I wasn't. I was snatched."

"Snatched? You make it seem like a UFO swooped in and sucked you up into their craft."

"Why do you always have to be a smart ass, boy?"

"Part of my charm."

"Well, it's not cute," Matthias sighed. "It all started as Joanna and I finished our supper at the diner."

"The one you always go to. Off the highway?"

"I'm a creature of habit; what can I say. Anyways, so we get out to the car, and Joanna remembered she left her purse in the booth. I tried to be a gentleman about it and offered to get it for her, but she insisted she was fine."

"Let's get to the part where you were snatched."

"I'm getting there. Yeesh. As I was saying, I waited outside and paced outside the driver's side. Then someone grabbed me from behind. Before I could put up a fight, they covered my face with something."

"Chloroform."

"Chloro-what?"

"Chloroform. It's a—ugh—it's something that makes you pass out."

"Well, it did the job. I came to, Angela is crying, and I'm tied to a chair."

"This all happened last night?"

"Yeah. I'm shocked you didn't send Pearson out looking for me when I didn't come home last night."

"Why would I send Pearson to track you down? I knew you were with Joanna. And since we're all probably going to die, I might as well be honest."

Angela spoke up. "We're not going to die. We'll figure out a way to live."

"Look around. No one knows we're here except the psychos who put us here. Now, we'll figure something out, but can I at least get something off my chest with my father first?"

"Why not. Just how I expected to spend my last few hours on earth . . . listening to you and your dad bonding."

"Pop, I wasn't too keen on you and Joanna at first. But she makes you happy, and that's all that matters. I just assumed you two crashed at her place."

"Poor Jo. She must be in hysterics. How did she seem when she reported me missing?"

That question snapped him from his drug-induced haze. "Huh? She didn't, Pop."

"Wait? She hasn't been by the house or the detachment?"

"No-o-o. The last I saw Joanna was when you two left last evening," Christian paused as everything fell into place in his head. "You don't think they—nah—there's no way. It's impossible."

THIRTY-SIX

PEARSON PRESSED HIS TREMBLING HAND AGAINST the rickety door. It moaned as the wind violently slapped against the rotted wood. With Adam behind him, he pulled out his flashlight and shone it into the darkness.

"I'm getting bad vibes from this," Pearson said before his foot crossed the threshold.

A light from Adam's flashlight illuminated behind him. "We got this. Keep moving."

Pearson pressed forward. It wasn't as if he had any other choice. Christian was missing, and the sawmill was the only lead they had to work with.

Pearson stayed ahead of Adam, at least two paces. He relied on his partner to keep a lookout for any surprises from behind.

"Anything?" Adam called out.

"Just a bunch of nothing. You?"

"Same," he replied. He scanned the floor with the beam of light, checking for any disturbances. "Christian?"

Only the echo of his voice returned.

"God, what if they're holding him captive in the room Liam used?"

"Only one way to find out," Pearson said, picking up the pace. "God, I hate this place. I wish the damn town council had done the right thing."

"What d'you mean?"

They inched further into the belly of the rundown building. "They held a meeting last summer. The chief topic: this place."

"What about it?"

"A few people around town wanted it torn down, so, like any functioning democracy, they took a vote."

"Let me guess. The council voted to keep it up."

Pearson nodded his head. "Five of the six members voted to keep this place standing. Said it was a reminder to the townspeople to keep hope alive. That they needed to do better next time. Whatever the hell that means."

"Do better? How? It's as if they believe the people of this town caused all the work to dry up. And furthermore, how is keeping this decrepit building standing giving them hope?"

Pearson paused and turned his head. "It's not. It's only words. I'm sure it would cost the town too much money to just tear it down."

"You know, the more time I spend here, the more I get why drug and alcohol abuse run rampant."

"Usually what happens when people lose hope. And by keeping this building standing, the people aren't moving forward. They're stuck remembering the countless tragedies that occurred here."

"Let's keep looking," Adam said. Pearson moved deeper into the maze of collapsed timbers and outdated machinery. The hallway to the old offices was just ahead of him, but as Pearson kept walking, Adam froze in his tracks.

Pearson turned and backtracked through the maze of fallen timbers. He stood at Adam's side, but the distraught man only gazed at his feet. He began to speak, and what little optimism had crumbled. "What if . . . What if he's hurt? Or worse . . . dead?"

"Jesus. He's not dead. Okay?"

"I. I . . . " Adam paused. "It weighs on me, and I can't shake it."

Pearson planted his hand on Adam's shoulder. "We're going to find him. Alive. But listen to me, if Christian's hurt, we aren't helping him by standing around letting our emotions get the better of us."

Adam nodded.

"So, are we going to tear this place apart . . . or sulk in 'what-ifs'?"

Adam glanced up. The fire had returned to his wet eyes. "We're tearing this shithole apart."

"You're back. Thought I lost you there for a second."

They crept along steady, but cautious, towards the rear of the factory. As they neared the old loading dock, something on the ground caught Adam's eye.

"Wait up."

Pearson stopped and turned. "Whatcha got?"

"Over there," he said as he focused the spotlight onto a disturbance in the dirt. "A lot of foot traffic. And it looks fresh."

Pearson approached the area. Four clear shoe treads littered the ground. "Looks like chaos."

"And what's this parallel line running down the middle?"

"Curious, isn't it?"

They followed the trail all the way to the metal coiling door. Adam reached out and yanked down on the chain, which swayed in the calm air.

It didn't budge.

"What the—?"

Pearson shone his light towards the corner where the door met with the metal framing. "Save your energy. It's fused shut."

Adam rushed towards a side door, twisted the knob, and tossed his shoulder against the metal. It popped open.

He poked his head out, expecting to find Christian's car, but only overgrown foliage and an empty concrete slab awaited him. Pearson searched around for something to prop open the door and settled on a busted up concrete block.

He pressed against the door and dropped the chunk onto the metal staircase. "Anything?" he asked.

"Nothing. But someone's been here recently." Adam pointed at the two fresh tire treads burnt into the damaged concrete.

"Someone was definitely in a hurry."

Adam pulled out his cell phone and dialed Christian's number. The phone rang in his ear, but he pulled it away as the familiar ringtone Christian assigned to him blared from underneath an overgrown tangle of bushes.

He rushed down the rickety staircase and followed the ringing as it grew louder through the breezy, humid air. He dropped to the ground, and on hands and knees, Adam dug through the prickly bushes.

Seconds later, he pulled out his hand, and in it, he held Christian's iPhone. He yelled back to Pearson. "He was here."

"That's a start. But the next question is harder—where is he now?"

THIRTY-SEVEN

CHRISTIAN STRUGGLED FOR THE BETTER PART of an hour, doing anything to free himself from the constraints that burrowed into his wrist. It was a futile effort. He was like a seal clinging to rock as the sharks lurked in the murky darkness of the ocean, eager to pounce at the right moment.

The chatter between the trio of hostages subsided, and the silence gave Christian time to devise a strategy. Not only to save himself but also his father and one of the people who tormented him all through high school.

Yet, in those forty minutes, not a single brilliant idea materialized, and the optimism he latched onto of escaping dwindled with each passing minute. Then Angela's voice startled him.

"Christian?"

He sighed. "Yeah?"

"We're going to die. Aren't we?"

"We're not going to die. I'm thinking. Don't give up hope."

He often dished out advice like candy yet never followed any of it himself.

He carried on, rubbing the edge of the plastic tie against the wooden chair. *This always works in the movies.*

But his current predicament wasn't from an action movie, nor was it a terrifying nightmare he could shake himself from. This was reality. And the only thing the scrapping did was burrow the plastic deeper into his wrists' thin skin.

He scraped harder, ignoring the pain shooting up his forearm. This carried on a few minutes until the soft patter of footsteps outside the door stopped his efforts.

Angela whimpered in the distance. Based on her reaction, she'd already had a run-in or two with these people. The terror in her voice grew, and Christian reached his breaking point.

"Angela. Zip it. You're sobbing isn't helping."

"Why are you so mean? I was right about you all along. You're an asshole who hasn't changed since high school."

"I was never mean to you in school. Now, seriously, I'm trying to listen, and you're not helping. If we survive this, then we can rehash who was meaner in high school."

From outside the door, the soft murmurs carried through the poorly insulated room.

"Did you get rid of the car?" a female voice asked.

"It's at the bottom of Cedar Lake. I put Heather's body in the trunk to add some drama."

"Good. And his cell phone?"

"In the glove compartment of his car."

"Perfect. That should give us a few days to get this mess straightened out."

"And what about them?" the man asked.

"I can handle them. You just get things in motion. And get those two constables as far away from here as you can."

"How?"

"Use your brain, idiot. I don't pay you to ask questions; I pay you for results. Now grab your guys and send those two on a scavenger hunt. An anonymous tip to the police could set the wheels in motion."

"What about you?"

"Someone has to watch these three."

There was a brief silence, but then the woman spoke again. "You just make sure those coppers don't come back and let me and my guys handle things here. Okay?"

There wasn't a reply, only the stomping of two pairs of feet racing away from the door. Then the moment Christian had dreaded came. He was about to come face-to-face with the person, possibly persons, responsible for the mayhem.

The clanking of a metal key sliding into the lock sent a shiver down his spine. His heartbeat tapped his ribcage. He swallowed what little saliva lingered in his parched mouth, past the lump bulging in his airway. And then the door flung open, and a petite shadowy figure stood with a ring of keys at her side.

The woman stepped forward. The closer she got, the better her face came into view, and Christian let out an audible gasp.

"You."

"Hello, Christian," Joanna said. "I hope the accommodations are up to your lofty standards."

"How . . ." he stuttered. "How'd I miss this? How'd my father miss this?"

"You're not as smart as you've fooled everyone into believing. Are you?"

"Why are you doing this?"

Her laugh, devoid of soul, bounced off the damp walls. "You think I'd tell you? You're the spitting image of your nosy friend, Lindsay. Damn girl, always asked questions she had no business knowing the answers to."

"What d'you do to her?"

"Again, with the questions. I bet you were one of those children who asked 'why' all the time, weren't you?"

"If you're going kill us, the least you can do is tell me what I'm dying for."

The woman took another two steps closer but lingered in the shadows. "Eh, I suppose there's no harm in answering a few. I mean, you won't be my problem much longer, and you'll never have the chance to tell."

"You'll never get away with this, Joanna. Constable Pearson and my husband will figure this all out."

From behind, Angela launched into another whimpering spell.

"Doubtful. We've been operating under that inept constable's nose for the last seven years. No, he'll never put this together. And even if he does, you and your father will be long gone before that happens."

Christian winced at the tone of Angela's piercing sobs. He watched Joanna's annoyed face as she stood and took a few steps behind Christian.

"And you. You're a disgrace to everything I've spent years creating. Why would you want to destroy it?"

There was a tremble in Angela's voice. "I didn't. I swear. I only wanted to confront the person who was digging for information."

"Uh-huh. Right. You sure were quick to race out here. Alone. The rules were simple; those who blab end up on a slab. Or did you miss that memo after we stabbed Taylor to death in that revolting Regina alley?"

"But I'm not like Taylor. I didn't say anything. Ever. Not even when that Pearson guy showed up at the house. I kept my end of the bargain. I diverted the blame onto someone else."

Christian interrupted. "I suspected you knew more than you were telling, Angela. But never in a million years would I have tied you to Heather and Lowry."

Joanna returned and stood above Christian. "Maybe she was. Maybe she wasn't. Too bad Heather's not around to tell you herself. And chances are they've already locked Lowry up in the psych ward by now, too."

Christian wanted to jump from the seat and take Joanna down, but instead, he closed his eyes and inhaled sharply. His hands stopped shaking, and the lump in his throat loosened. "You agreed to answer my questions. And I have plenty of them."

Joanna walked across the room and snatched an empty chair propped against the wall. She dragged it across the damp, concrete floor, and as she hovered over him, she loosened her grip. All four legs slammed against the floor, and she sat only inches from Christian's face. "Well, someone never learned manners. Bad parenting skills, eh, Matthias?"

From across the room, Matthias's faint voice pierced through the thick air. "You're a vile piece of—"

"Now, now, Matthias. I'd watch what comes out of your mouth next."

"You used me."

She scoffed. "Well, of course, I did. I had to cover my ass in case your son ever got wind of what *really* happened to Lindsay. And, as usual, my instincts were spot-on."

Matthias wept in the distance while Joanna continued. "And your son is just as involved in this story as we all are."

"The hell are you talking about? I'm not involved with whatever this mess is."

"Not to the extent we are. But, still, you played a role, whether you'll ever admit it or not. So, sit back and pay attention to a tale of two teenagers sticking their noses in where it didn't belong."

THIRTY-EIGHT

THE RADIO ATTACHED TO PEARSON'S SHOULDER came to life, and the broken voice of Constable Miller carried over the airwaves. "Pearson, come in."

"Go ahead, Miller."

"Uh, we have a problem."

"What now?"

"I'm at the boat landing off Ninth Avenue East. And there's a dark-colored, four-door sedan floating in the lake. What's your twenty?"

"At the sawmill. We're en route."

"Copy."

Adam traded a glance with Pearson before they sprinted around the building and back to the SUV. "That sounds like Christian's car," Adam yelled, trying to keep up.

Pearson's head turned over his shoulder. "Less talking and more running."

They'd only spent a little under an hour at the sawmill. In that time, they explored the massive facility, room by room, however their efforts to find Christian turned up nothing. Sure, they had plenty of circumstantial evidence he had been there: the fresh shoe prints, the parallel lines gouged into the dust, skid marks, and finding his phone hidden in a bush. But none of those things suggested he ever stepped foot inside the building.

Now, with the request from Constable Miller for support, Adam couldn't shake the image of his husband, bound, gagged, and unconscious in the trunk of his own vehicle as it sank.

Pearson hopped into the driver's seat and threw the car into reverse, and the gravel sputtered out from underneath the rear tires. His cell phone in the cup holder illuminated, and he caught a glimpse of the screen.

17 Missed Calls

7 Voicemails

"Shit," he hollered as he tossed his cell phone into Adam's lap. "Can you see what the hell that's all about?"

"Huh?"

"The phone. Who are all the missed calls from?"

He stuttered. "Yeah, uh, of course."

Adam tapped against the screen, and the password screen appeared.

"Passcode? It's asking for your passcode."

"8-8-6-4-3-3."

The screen opened, and a big red dot displayed the number seventeen in the telephone icon's upper right-hand corner. Adam tapped again, and the same name highlighted in red came up.

Gemma Williams.

"She's been trying hard to get ahold of you."

"Who? Gemma?"

He nodded. "I'm gonna call her back."

"No. Wait."

"Why? The gig's up, Luke. The situation has shifted since we last spoke to her. It's been hours, and I bet she's been sitting by the phone, probably smoked through an entire pack of cigarettes, waiting for her best friend to call her back.

Guess what, he hasn't. And she's smart enough to figure out something's wrong."

Pearson banged his hand against the steering wheel. "Just—wait. We can't just call her up and be like, 'by the way, remember earlier when we told you Christian was out. Yeah, well, we lied.'"

"Fair point, but sooner or later, she's going to find out. And the longer you wait to tell the truth, the worse off it'll be."

"I . . . I just can't be the one to break the news. She'll never talk to me again."

Adam's jaw dropped, and a shit-eating grin graced his face. "You really are in love with her, aren't you?"

"No. We're just, er, friends."

"Yeah, okay. Keep telling yourself that, buddy. Look, I'll call her and break the news. I'll take the blame. At least it'll score you bonus points."

"You'd do that? For me?"

"You got a better idea?"

Pearson tilted his head.

"Then it's settled. Besides, once we bring him back unharmed, Gemma will forget this entire thing even happened."

Inside, Adam's rosy outlook shifted after the words crossed his lips. Christian wasn't bleeding in a snow pile alongside the street. No, this time was different. What if his car was sinking? He turned his head and gazed outside the window. "What happens if we don't—?"

"Don't even go there," Pearson said.

"—bring him home?"

Pearson's head swayed from side-to-side. "Nope. I said we're not going there. We can't. He's safe."

Adam kept his gaze fixated on the fields as they zoomed past. He didn't want to go there, but he also needed to prepare himself for the worst-case scenario.

I need to take a page out of Christian's playbook: find the positive in everything and stop the negativity.

FIFTEEN MINUTES LATER, THE TIRES SCREECHED as the SUV came to an abrupt stop behind a dark, windowless van parked at the boat dock on the edge of the town limits.

Their doors opened and closed in sync, and they approached the banks of the lake, the same one that gave the town its name ninety years ago. The constant battering of waves crashed against the shore, but the lake itself was empty.

A movement in the distance jerked Pearson's attention away from the water and onto the moving silhouette. It was Constable Miller, racing towards them with a pair of binoculars around his neck and a drenched, black police vest clutched away from his body. Out of breath by the time he reached the duo, he rested his hands against his knees and bent forward.

"Boss. It's . . ." he managed which gasping for air. "I didn't get the plate number before it went under."

"How long ago did it sink?"

"I . . ." he stuttered. "I'd guess no more than two minutes after I radioed you. It took longer than I expected."

"Any witnesses?"

Miller pointed towards an older man with a cell phone aimed towards the lake filming. "That guy. He told DS Clark he was sitting on his back deck enjoying a beer when an engine revved and the tires peeled out. He got up and walked to the edge of the deck just as the car went airborne and crash into the water."

"Doesn't sound like an accident to me," Pearson said.

The two local constables exchanged a few more words; however, Adam couldn't take his eyes off the vest in Miller's hand. His soft voice interrupted. "Where d'you get that?"

Their conversation stopped, and Miller raised the vest and turned it around. Adam studied the nuances. The word, 'police,' sewn into a strip of fabric, in all capital letters above the right pocket and situated just above the left pocket, was the all-too-recognizable shield issued to every constable of the Regina Police Service.

"The witness pulled it from the water. Said it washed up onto his property."

"That's . . ." Adam struggled to construct a sentence. "I recognize that vest. It's Christian's."

"How did it end up here?" Miller asked.

Adam wiped his hands across his face. "He always kept that damn thing in the trunk." Then the avalanche of emotions tumbled down. "Oh, God, Christian."

Miller reached over and caught Adam before his knees gave out, but they both ended up on the ground. "Adam, are you sure?"

Adam couldn't speak. All he could do was lay on the concrete and sob. Pearson crouched next to him and gave him a few minutes to compose himself. Then the locals began to congregate around the police tape. More focused on the detachment's public perception, Pearson dragged Adam out of their line of sight.

"Prescott. Snap out of it. Now, Miller asked a question. Are you sure this vest belongs to Christian?"

He uncovered his face, glanced once again at the vest, and sucked back his tears. "It's his. I'm positive."

"Shit. That means . . ."

"He's dead," Adam stood and walked away towards the shore. He shouted out to DS Clark. "How long before we can retrieve the car?"

"An hour. Maybe a little longer."

Pearson stood next to Adam. "Then, we'll wait. Prescott."

"How are you so sure?"

"He's more valuable to them alive than dead. No, there's a reason they lured us to this spot."

Adam jetted his left foot out and ran his fingers through his hair. "So, walk me through this. Why lure us here?"

"Because they needed us as far from the sawmill as possible. Why? I can't tell you."

"Man, we searched that place from top to bottom. There was no one there."

"Then we didn't look hard enough."

THIRTY-NINE

CHRISTIAN STARED JOANNA DOWN AS SHE shifted in the chair across from him. Her right leg swung over her left, and her arms folded tightly against her chest.

"Are you sure you want to know everything?" she asked.

"Yes."

"Once I tell you, I'll have to kill you."

His voice shook as he exhaled. "Yup. That's what happens most of the time in these situations."

Her voice shifted from polite to patronizing. "I just want to make sure you're aware of what you're getting yourself into."

He gnawed his teeth. "Cut this 'you care about me' crap. You played me showing up so well. Acting like you didn't know he had a son. You knew the entire time."

"Yup. Guilty. All part of the plan."

"What plan is so important it cost so many people their lives?"

"To know why we have to go back to 2006. You were just starting grade nine if I'm not mistaken."

He nodded.

"Lee White approached me with a proposition. One I could have walked away from, but then it hit me: why would I?"

A scoff escaped his mouth. "Of course, Lee White is involved in this story."

"Truth is, the town of Cedar Lake wasn't always here. The land you stand on, or used to, once belonged to my ancestors, generations ago."

"Right. Tell me something I didn't learn in my Canadian Studies class."

"My scheme was simple—reclaim the land stolen from our people by whatever means necessary."

"What does that have to do with prostitution?"

"Psh, that? You're still stuck on that. Nah, this goes deeper. Those girls were just the beginning."

"Of?"

"Reclaiming our land. Are you paying attention? Tell you what, you let me do the talking, and if you listen close enough, that lightbulb in your head may just flicker."

He rested his back against the chair and kept quiet.

"Where was I? Right. Lee's been cooking meth since 2004, and a lot of the young women around town couldn't afford to get their fix. So we concocted a way for us to make money, but it also worked out for them because they got free drugs out of the deal."

"Shady."

"When you're a junkie, you'll do anything to stop the pain."

"Right. Doesn't make it any better, Joanna."

"Look, I had an overall goal, but the prostitution ring was just the tip of what else I had up my sleeve."

"And I'm sure we're getting there, huh?"

"Your father was right. Patience is not your strong suit. The money flowed in, hand over fist, and then I had another idea. We began videotaping the encounters, you know, as leverage."

"Leverage for what?"

"You don't honestly think only low-life Cedar Lake trash were using our services, do you?" She laughed but cut it short. "No. We had city council members, constables, hell, even the previous mayor, were caught with their pants around their ankles at the Ridgeway Inn."

The lightbulb finally glowed in his mind. "Blackmail and extortion."

"Hey, a gal's got to make money somehow."

"You're sick. You know that?"

Joanna nodded her head. "An occupational hazard in my line of work."

"What about Cassidy Williams? Was she one of his *girls*?" he asked.

"One of? Cassidy was our prime girl. And this is how your involvement began."

"Stop saying that. You make it out like I aided and abetted. I didn't. I would have never helped with something like that."

"Always the upstanding citizen, isn't that right, Matthias?"

A drawn-out groan from the corner of the room was all the older man could muster.

"But you slipped along the way."

"How?"

Joanna stood from the creaky chair, walked around the back, and with both hands gripping it, she leaned in. "Let's take a trip down memory lane, back to the night you and your precious Gemma went to prom. You remember that night, don't you?"

He nodded and sighed. "All too well. Wait . . ." a fuzzy memory worked its way to the surface. "We spent the after-party at the Ridgeway Inn. There was a . . ."

"A brawl?"

A drop of water fell from the ceiling and splashed against Christian's nose. He shook it off. "Yeah, but how'd . . .?"

"How'd I know?" she released her grip on the chair. "Because I was there. Who do you think set the fight in motion?"

"Still doesn't explain how I'm involved."

"What did Gemma tell you to get you there?"

"She said Cassidy had booze and was having a party. That she had invited us to come have some fun."

"No, I think she told you more. Think harder."

Being in no position to argue, Christian closed his eyes. His shoulder muscles relaxed, and he allowed his scattered mind to remember that night. After a few seconds, images fired off in rapid succession like a movie of that evening playing on a big screen.

Gemma's big smile. The music. Walking down the middle of First Street West, passing a half-drank bottle of Jim Beam back and forth. The warm air brushing against his skin. Everything about that night was perfect. Until it wasn't.

The happiness soon faded as he replayed the moment those three men spilled out of Cassidy's motel room into the parking lot.

Punches. Empty threats. Blood spewing. All this chaos came to an end the moment Cassidy inserted herself between the three fuming men.

Then, through the whispers swirling around his head, Gemma's words cut through the chatter. *Chad doesn't own her like he wishes he did. I really hope she hadn't chosen this life.*

But those weren't the only words he remembered from that night. Cassidy had a few of her own also. *I'm old enough to make my own decisions now, and I don't want to do this anymore.*

His eyes sprang open.

"Ah, you remembered something."

His head rocked back and forth. "I was drunk out of my mind, that much I remember. But I assume you know, so let's cut the crap."

"Gemma told you she wished Cassidy hadn't chosen the life she did. Isn't that so?"

"You have no idea what she said. You're grasping at straws to implicate me in your sick game. That's all."

"No, Anderson, you had your hunches all along something was going on, yet you turned a blind eye."

"Hardly."

"My dear boy, yes, you did. I saw your face light up a minute ago. That undeniable expression everyone recognizes."

"What?"

"When your lip quivers and your eyes focus on everything else except the person in front of you. The classic indicator that you remembered something. It's what I call an 'ah-ha' moment."

He closed his eyes again and drown out her voice. He allowed his mind to go deeper. *Think, Christian, did you say something back?*

Then those haunting words came to him. *Who are all these guys, Gem? Wait, don't tell me your sister is working as a hooker now?*

One word crossed his lips. "Shit."

Joanna scooted the chair closer. "Ah, so you *do* remember what you said."

"Maybe. But neither of us proved if it was true or not."

"Doesn't matter. Your ignorance is what led to what happened next."

"I assume by next you mean what happened to Lindsay."

"Not her. She came into the picture later that year. I'm talking about how things after that night expanded and more people became involved."

"Look, I didn't come back to Cedar Lake to hear a play-by-play of your criminal enterprise."

"You're right. Because after what happened in 2009, you never had any interest in coming back here. Did you?"

He shook his head.

"Exactly. Let's look at the life of Christian Anderson. First, you find your friend hanging from the rafters, flee, leaving her to hang there. Next, you graduate and abandon your best friend. And worst of all, you left your father to rot in the bottle of whatever cheap liquor he could get his hands on. And why? Because you couldn't face the truth. When life gets too complicated, you do what you know best: you run away."

"Why I left doesn't concern you."

"It sure does. Because that day you ran to Regina searching for a new life, you left a void in this town. A void that gave me free rein to expand my blackmail scheme further. I hadn't expected it to work out so well, but that guy who was running the detachment was an idiot who drowned his sorrows with the bottle, just like your pops."

He ignored her flagrant attempt to ruffle his feathers and redirected back to the blackmail. "How many people are we talking?"

"Fifty or so. And that was in the first month alone. It got so detailed I had to enlist the help of more people just to keep up with all the dirt these poor souls were feeding me."

Christian's eye glanced away from her intense glare. "So you were operating like the Stasi?"

"A Nazi reference . . . can't say I expected that. But sure, I had people spying on everyone, digging up dirt."

"But why?"

"How do you take over a town, Christian? Hm? You turn everyone against each other until the point where they trust no one—except you. To you, you're the savior. The one who'll fix everything."

"Did it work?"

"Angela?"

The dehydrated girl cleared her throat. "Yeah?"

"Christian wants to know if it worked."

"I didn't talk when your snoopy husband and that lazy constable came around. Linus didn't either. Hell, even Heather kept her mouth shut up until her last breath."

"See. I have a way with people."

"But to take over an entire town? That takes a lot of infiltration. First, you'd have to get your people elected to the city council, the mayor's office. You'd also need to infiltrate the detachment. Yeah, we got two out of three covered. Pearson was supposed to be history by now, but that's another story."

"No, not so fast. You said I would get the whole truth."

"Fine. He's been harder to crack. He's too, how shall I put it, strait-laced."

Christian nodded.

"The plan was to dig up enough dirt on him to get him fired, or at least reassigned to another detachment. But he's a tough one. We've hacked his computer. All he does is play video games. No porn. No dating sites. Zilch. All that man does is patrol the streets looking for the next perp to snatch up."

"He's got what we call integrity. Someone you wouldn't know anything about."

"Oh, I know all about it. I just choose to live a different way."

"Well, I hate to break it to you, but the Saskatoon Police Service is onto your plans. Their lead DC informed Pearson this morning they were closing in on something."

She snorted. "News to me. I have people planted everywhere. In places you'd never expect. Anything that's about to go down, I know about before anyone else."

"And Ani?"

"What about her?"

"Is she involved?"

"She did a few things for me, but the overall picture I've left her out of."

"I know you sent her to murder Lindsay."

"You don't know anything."

"I know all about the attempt to run Lindsay off the road. Ani told me."

"Did she now? Well, that had nothing to do with me. That was all, Lee. He wanted her gone. But let's just say Lindsay wasn't who you think she was. I needed her alive."

"I don't get it."

"Of course you don't, you naïve fool. Lindsay worked for me. Until she decided to go rogue and threatened to turn over all the evidence to the police. I couldn't let that happen, now could I?"

"So you killed her?"

Joanna shook her head and raised her hands in front of her body. "It wasn't by these hands."

"Then, whose?"

"Hard to say. I have so many people working for me, any one of them could have had her whacked."

"Christ. How many people have you drawn into your deceptive web?" Christian asked.

She took a moment. She touched the tips of her fingers over and over. Then she stopped. "At this point, who knows anymore, maybe sixty, seventy."

The octave in his voice increased two-times. "Sixty? Seventy people? That includes people like Lowry, Lee White, and Taylor Jackson?"

"Especially Taylor. He was a good little soldier, until . . ."

"Until what?"

"All those years of drug-induced paranoia seeped into his brain. And, well, you already know what happened next."

"That's why he came looking for Gemma."

"He actually came looking for you. It should have never gotten that far. I told that idiot to just run him off the road but being stabbed near your station makes for a much better story."

"Wait. Hold up. Gemma was a fluke?"

"Coincidence is more like it. It's a shame about Taylor. The one thing I hate more than nosy constables . . . a traitor. Isn't that right, Matthias?"

Matthias had been waiting for his chance to speak, and he didn't hold anything back. "Hateful bitch. You made me believe you loved me; you sucked me into your sick little trap. Why? Why would you do this?"

"It was simple. Lost souls really are the easiest to convert. You just buried your wife after so many years, wondering what happened. Thanks to Christian, you gave up the booze—but you still needed something to replace that lost friend. You saw what we had as love, but I saw it as an opportunity. Let's chalk that up to a failure to communicate."

Matthias didn't have a snappy comeback for her; instead, he wept like a child.

"You are nothing but pure evil," Christian said.

"Guilty. Besides, dating your father allowed me to keep tabs on you. I need-ed to know if you were coming for a visit, you know, give my goons a heads-up to keep their eyes on you."

"But then I threw you a curveball. That entire scene on the steps was nothing but a fraud?"

"Sort of. It wasn't hard to pretend to be surprised. I hadn't received any intel you were planning a trip up."

"Worked out well for me, though. Got a chance to catch a few people off-guard, like the Rosses."

"Yeah, I hadn't anticipated they'd be your first stop. But Angela, Heather, and Linus knew you were around."

"Hm, a lot of good it did them, huh? But I gotta say, what Taylor did was heroic. He managed to do something worthwhile with his last few breaths."

Her face scrunched. "I didn't ask. A damn shame Taylor didn't take his last breath right there in that alley. Now, it just means I have another loose end to clean up."

Christian lunged forward in the chair. "You leave Gemma out of this."

She threw her head back and laughed. "Or what? You'll hurt me? Besides, it's too late. The plans are already in motion. Now, where were we? Oh, right. You came racing back because of Taylor Jackson."

"I did. When he told Gemma that Lindsay didn't commit suicide, I had to be sure. So let's skip forward to May 2009."

"What for? We have plenty of time to talk about Lindsay."

Christian lowered his head. "No."

"No? You'll ruin the entire story if you skip ahead."

"I don't want the entire story. I want the truth about Lindsay. That's all."

"You cared about her. Didn't you?"

A lone tear rolled along his cheek. "Yes. All right. Is that what everyone wants to hear? I cared about Lindsay more than I let anyone believe."

She shrugged. "How touching. However, if I knew death was knocking, I'd be more interested in getting the complete story. It's quite captivating. But, hey, it's your funeral. So, 2009. May. That was a tough year for you, huh?"

Christian raised his head. "You tell me. Seems like you already know the answer to your own questions."

"I liked Lindsay. She was a smart girl. Very dedicated. She should have just listened to her brother when he told her to back off."

That comment, and remembering what Cassidy said the night of the brawl, confirmed what he already suspected. Lindsay's brother, Chad, was involved in this somehow.

"So, you're saying her own brother murdered her?"

"Are you even listening, Christian? I said Chad warned her. Not once did I say he killed her. You're so damned impatient."

In the distance, the stomping of feet against the concrete floor rushed outside the door. After a quick rap, Joanna stood and whispered in Christian's ear. "Don't go anywhere."

The outline of her short body approached the door, but she vanished onto the other side before Christian could object. He focused his attention on the whispers permeating through the crumbling walls.

"And?" she asked.

"There's a problem."

"I don't pay you to bring me problems. I pay you to take care of them."

"There's been a change in plans. Those coppers already found the car."

"How? You guaranteed it bought us a day, two max."

"I hadn't factored in eyewitnesses, not to mention his police vest floated ashore."

"Never trust a man to do what only a woman can."

"Look, I'm sorry," the man began. "They'll figure out soon enough he isn't in the car and be right back here again searching. This time, they might bring reinforcements."

A loud thud against the door startled him, and her voice grew angrier. "Yeah,

I'm sorry too. I'm sorry I trusted you to run this operation smoothly. Your services are no longer needed."

It wasn't but a second later, and two ear-piercing bangs ripped through the air. Then a thud. Christian's breath increased, and he scraped the plastic harder against the splintered wood. He had to free his hands.

Matthias called out. "Were those gunshots?"

Christian didn't have time to respond before the door swung open, and Joanna reappeared in the door frame.

Joanna composed herself, running both hands along the front of her blood-soaked shirt. "Now, if you'll excuse me, I have a few loose ends to tie up."

"Why d'you shoot him?" Christian asked.

"He's not your concern. He's just a failure, like so many others I've entrusted with their tasks. Now, as much as I'd love to continue this, these tasks won't take care of themselves. So, hang tight, and when I return, I'll give you the authentic story about who your friend, Lindsay, really was. She was no saint."

"But . . ." he tried to interject.

She pulled out the gun and twirled it in her hand. "No, no. I have things to get done. This is an added measure, so you don't try to escape."

She clutched the muzzle of the gun tightly and tapped the butt of the pistol against her free hand. She stepped closer, and, with one hard whack, Christian slumped over in the chair as a stream of blood trickled down the side of his face.

FORTY

NINETY MINUTES HAD PASSED SINCE THE first call went out about the sinking vehicle at the lake. The underwater rescue team arrived moments after Pearson and Adam, and soon the town's only wrecker appeared. The daunting task of pulling the sunken sedan back to dry land had begun.

"I believe you," Adam said.

"That this is just a well-orchestrated diversion?"

"Yeah, but I need to make sure."

Pearson planted his hand on Adam's shoulder, and they gazed across the lake. "And we will. Should be any minute."

Without warning, the car rose to the surface aided by four lifting balloons, two attached to the front and two at the back. Adam stepped closer to the shoreline.

The anticipation sent Adam's heart racing at a dizzying speed, and a steady flow of moisture saturated his hands.

The tow driver lowered the tow hook into the water, and a diver grabbed hold and swam towards the vehicle. Adam clasped both hands together as if he were about to pray and held them close to his mouth. "Please don't be in there. Please don't be in there," he repeated.

No more than five minutes later, the wench motor quieted, and the water-logged vehicle sat a mere five feet away. Adam dug deep inside for the strength to not run up and tear the car apart, searching for his husband.

Somehow, he managed to fight the urge and waited as DS Clark investigated the wreckage.

Inside, the vehicle was empty. Adam poked his head inside the rolled-down driver's side window and noticed a wooden block wedged between the gas pedal and the driver's seat's metal casing.

DS Clark leaned in the passenger side and commented. "Oldest trick in the book."

"So, Christian wasn't behind the wheel when it drove into the water?"

"No. But someone went out of their way to make it appear so."

"And the trunk?" Adam asked.

"Was the next item on the list. You sure you're ready for this?"

Adam locked eyes with DS Clark and took a deep, shaky breath. "Do I have a choice?"

***

PEARSON PRESSED THE PEDAL TO THE floor and sped away from the lake and back across town.

"I knew he wasn't in there," Adam said. The hope had returned to his voice.

Pearson hung a sharp right onto Central Avenue and, with sirens wailing, sped through the one stoplight in town. Two more blocks flew by, and he skidded into an open parking spot in front of the town municipal building.

He pushed the lever into park and unbuckled his seatbelt. The door flung open, and before Adam could get out his words, Pearson leaned inside the window.

"We've wasted, what, two hours on a wild goose chase somebody designed to distract us."

"Yeah, two hours we won't get back. But I still don't get how that leads us here," Adam replied.

"Think hard, my friend. If you had just kidnapped someone and the cops were closing in, what would you do to throw them off your trail?"

"Create confusion. Get them as far away as you possibly could. Anything, just don't get caught."

"Bingo. We missed something at the sawmill. A trap door. A secret passage. Something. And there's only one way to get a better idea of what we're working with inside that place."

Adam's eyes widened. "The blueprints."

Pearson slammed his hand against the top of the SUV. "And your head is back in the game."

Adam planted his feet against the sidewalk. "We'll cover more ground if we both pitch in."

Pearson nodded, and the two raced up the marble stairs. Pearson reached out his hand and tugged at the glass door.

It didn't budge.

"You got another plan?" Adam asked.

Pearson sighed and tore the Velcro back from his breast pocket. His hand trembled as he slid out his cell phone and tapped against the screen a few times.

"Mayor Martin, Constable Pearson here," he began and paused. "Yes, sir, I realize the hour, but this is an emergency. Can you meet me at the municipal building with the keys?"

With the phone to his ear, Pearson turned away and paced up and down the stairs. Adam imagined the call would be quick. He didn't know Mayor Martin, other than by name and for the fact, his daughter was missing.

Then the begging stopped, and Pearson unleashed his infamous temper. "With all due respect, sir, I'm trying to find your fucking daughter. Now, you can try to block my every move, or you can get your ass down here and help me out."

FORTY-ONE

THE ROOM SPUN AS CHRISTIAN FOUGHT to focus his eyes. He let out a loud groan as he vigorously shook his head. The faint glow from the wavering rays of sunshine from before disappeared, much like his hope of Pearson or Adam rescuing him from this hellhole he found himself in.

He called out into the static void. "Hello? Pop? Angela? Anybody?"

Anticipating a reply, his heart dropped when only the echo of his voice returned.

"Are you guys there? Hello?"

Again, no answer.

He couldn't place whether the loss of blood or the adrenaline pumping through his veins was getting the better of him. Whatever it was, the atmosphere was heavy. It was like the world came to a standstill, leaving him the lone man to take everything into his hands. And now, abandoned in the dark, with only his own fears racing through his overactive mind, did it hit him.

"How could I let this happen?" he asked himself aloud. "You know how, Christian. When are you ever going to learn that you can't do these things alone?"

Indeed, he had built his entire career on taking chances and running with leads no matter how minuscule they appeared. If there was one thing he learned from Lindsay, it was to never squander a moment to uncover the truth.

He exhaled a long-held breath and focused on those happier memories that he shared with her. Immediately, a vivid autumn day near the start of grade twelve flooded his brain. He stopped squirming and allowed himself to enjoy the trip down memory lane.

"Hey, Anderson, wait up," her voice traveled down the crowded science corridor of Cedar Lake High. "Any plans this weekend?"

He paused and turned, giving her time to catch up before moving on to their Creative Writing 20 class. "Eh, nothing concrete. You?"

"Same. I was hoping you might want to—"

He cut her off. "Catch a flick? Sure, count me in, but only if it's gory. I can't get enough."

Lindsay chuckled. "Well, sure, maybe we can do that too. But I had something more school-related in mind."

"Oh, yeah, of course. Whatcha need my help with?"

"I've been working on this piece the past two weeks, and I really could use a fresh set of eyes to read it over."

"Yeah, absolutely. What is this, like, some story for the school paper?"

She grinned and bobbed her head up and down. Then as quick as it came, the memory faded, and Christian opened his eyes.

"Damnit! I'm such an idiot. She was working on that story and wanted to show me. I blew her off to focus on getting my shit together to flee this God-awful place."

PART 6

WEDNESDAY
CEDAR LAKE, SK

"Nothing is easier than to denounce the evildoer; nothing is more difficult than to understand him."
—Fyodor Dostoevsky

FORTY-TWO

ADAM PULLED HIS HEAD AWAY FROM the fist he'd rested it on for an hour. He watched his unofficial partner comb through the messy boxes scattered around the basement of the municipal building.

"Ah-ha," Pearson exclaimed.

"You got something?"

A thin layer of dust floated in the air after Pearson blew against the cylinder container. "I found 'em. The original plans for the sawmill."

"Thank God," Adam said, standing to his feet. "Let's get out of here. This place gives me the creeps."

"Eh, old places tend to give off those vibes, don't they?"

"That, and it doesn't help with Nosy Nancy outside waiting."

"The mayor? He's harmless."

"Nah. There's something weird about him. I don't like how he keeps peering through the glass."

Pearson slipped the documents from the cardboard cylinder and unrolled the bundle of papers across the table in the center of the room. "Prescott. Sit down."

"But we really should go."

"Go where?"

"Anywhere but here."

"Man, look. We need to figure out where they're hiding your husband in this place," Pearson jabbed his thick finger against the paper. "I'd think someone like you would have better self-control over blocking out their paranoia."

"You're right. You're right. It's just, eh, this town and the people in it make my skin crawl. It's like they watch your every move."

"Didn't used to be this way."

"Yeah, that's the same line Christian feeds me any time we bring up Cedar Lake. He'll say, 'before all the jobs dried up, things around here were semi-normal.'"

He glanced up, and Pearson stared him down.

"Sorry, I'm rambling on about nonsense, huh?"

"It's okay, man. I get what you're saying. It's sad how quickly this town went from Pleasantville to what it is now. Tell you what, let's focus on these plans and figure this out. The quicker we do, the quicker we can get the hell out of here and find Christian. Deal?"

For a second, Adam relaxed his shoulders and paid attention. "Deal. Let's do this."

Adam snubbed the badgering voice in the back of his head and concentrated on the set of complex blueprints laid out in front of him. "Do you understand this shit?"

"I'm no expert, but I did work a case ten years ago in Moose Jaw. A hostage situation," he pulled out a chair and sat. "These babies came in real handy when the time came to raid the place."

"Never had to do it . . . a raid that is."

Pearson glanced up and grinned. "Never? I'd expect things to be a bit rowdier in Regina."

"Sorry to disappoint, but most of my time has been spent in the virtual world. Christian, on the other hand, he's seen a lot more than me."

Adam's face scrunched up as if the dam holding back his emotions was about to burst through the brave persona he'd built up. Pearson reached out his hand and rested it on his shoulder.

"We're going to save him. All right?"

Adam scoffed. "We have to. I still have so many things to tell him."

The two men scoured through the plans for well over an hour. Pearson's watch chirped. 2 a.m.

"None of this makes any sense," Adam said.

Pearson flipped to the next page. And staring him in the eyes was the answer they'd hunted for all along. Typed in all caps at the top of the page. *Storage and Overflow.*

"Hey, did you ever come across any storage rooms?" Pearson asked.

Adam pulled his hands away from his face and cocked his head. "Offices, sure. Storage rooms. No."

"We overlooked something. Something crucial."

"What?" Adam asked and tugged the paper towards him. After a minute of browsing, he fell back in his chair. "I'll be damned. How'd we miss this?"

Pearson shrugged. "Weren't looking for it. I have a few people to wake."

Adam reached for his cell phone.

No bars meant no service.

Adam shook his phone. "I don't have a signal down here."

"Me neither. Hang tight. I'll be right back."

Pearson slipped through the door. Adam watched as he breezed past the mayor, and with the answers they needed, he rolled the papers up. Just as he was about to slip them back into the container, the door flung open.

"That was quick. Everything good?" he asked without looking up.

"You tell me. *Is* everything good?"

It was Mayor Martin, blocking the doorway.

"Sorry, I thought you were—"

"Pearson?"

"Yeah. We're almost done here; I'm just waiting on him to return."

"Well, I wouldn't stress about him right now. He's, shall we say, out of commission."

Something in the tone of his voice forced Adam to back away from the table. He clutched the cardboard cylinder. "What do you mean?"

"He won't be a problem much longer."

He eyeballed the man up and down, and it shot a prickling up Adam's legs. "What do you want?"

"What we all want. For all of this to go away. Quickly and quietly."

"I don't understand. Make all of what go away?"

"All the meddling. Lindsay should have stopped when we warned her. Christian, Pearson, you. All of you should have stopped while you were ahead."

"It's you. You're behind all of this?"

"I'll take partial credit. The real mastermind is much closer to home than you think."

Adam jerked to the side, but the older man kept up with his quick reflexes.

"There's nowhere to go, my dear boy," he pointed at the door behind him. "This is the only exit, and it'll be a snowy day in hell before I let you out of here alive."

The tingling shifted, and now a cold, clamminess washed across his entire body. His eyes darted from right to left, in search of anything he could use to fend off the menacing man who Pearson referred to mere hours before as harmless.

A few books, a chair, and the flimsy table were the only things within arm's reach. These weren't the makeshift weapons Adam had in mind to inflict severe damage and escape. Instead, he opted for his gift of stalling to buy himself a little more time.

"Why are you doing this?" he asked.

"It's complicated. You want the short version or the full version? We've got all night, which is more than I can say for your nosy husband."

"What have you done with him?"

"In a matter of minutes, it won't matter anymore what we did with him.

Now, you asked why we're doing this. Simple answer: we want our town back."

Adam retreated a few steps. "Back from who?"

"The outsiders. The ones who had no business here."

"I still don't get it."

The mayor stepped closer. "Your accent. You're not from around these parts, hmm?"

Adam ran his shaky hand through his hair as his back touched the wall. "No. Born and raised in Quebec." Adam's eyes darted around the room. "Does that matter?"

"It does. Let me give you a quick history lesson. Ninety years ago, the first Germans settled in the area. Bringing with them their own ways, which meant our ways were set on the back burner. They took our land and used us for everything they could."

"It's been my understanding from history they had treaties for these types of things. Wasn't there one of those?"

"A treaty? You can't be as naïve as you appear."

"Well, was there?"

"Sure. Still didn't mean they obeyed it. And what could our people do? Nothing. Our ancestors sat back and watched as the land they'd cherished for generations slowly eroded away from them."

Adam kept his eyes locked on the man, hoping if he showed even an ounce of remorse, maybe he'd let him go. *Say you're sorry. Even if you're not, just say it.*

He listened to the voice in his head. "I'm sorry to hear about your ancestors' troubles. Truly, I am. If there was something I could do, I'd do it. But that was so long ago, and there's no correlation between them and me."

The man bowed his head. "Yes, long ago, but still fresh in every one of our minds. I've told you too much already. I didn't want things to be this way, but you've left me no other choice."

Mayor Martin reached behind his back and pulled a revolver from his waistband. He inched closer to Adam, who trembled as he buried his head between the bookcase and the wall.

Through his heavy panting, the cocking of the gun only increased the sweat building on the palm of his hands. He squeezed his eyes harder, and for a moment, Christian's face appeared, and the deafening chatter in his head subsided. The only thing he could hear in that millisecond was Christian's voice. *Yank the bookcase. Do it . . . now.*

Without hesitation, Adam mustered up the last few ounces of energy he had in his reserves. He yanked the heavy bookcase away from the wall. His own grunting muffled the advancing footsteps, and seconds later, only a deafening crash of metal slamming against the linoleum floor filled the air.

His eyes shot open. The bookcase had crashed into the middle of the room, taking years of records with it. As he stepped around the heaping pile, the revolver once pointed at him rested atop a leather-bound ledger. And lying underneath the twisted metal was the body of Mayor Martin.

It wasn't how he pictured it. No gruesomeness. No blood splashed all over— just the lifeless body of a man who no longer posed a threat.

He stepped closer. With the tip of his shoe, he nudged at the man's leg.

Nothing. Not even a grunt.

He reached down and snatched the gun from the floor and backed away closer to the exit. Amongst the mess, he spotted the cardboard cylinder concealed beneath a pile of books. There was no time to waste. He reached down with his free hand, snatched the plans, and raced for the exit.

His speed only increased as he slammed against the door, sending it flying open. His head never turned back as he sprinted up the stairs, taking two steps with each stride.

The excitement of freedom didn't last long. As he neared the top of the stairs, he found Pearson slumped over.

"Shit."

He leaned down, shaking his arm. "Pearson, come on, man. You gotta wake up. He's going to kill us."

He remained unresponsive.

"Guess we're doing this the hard way."

272

Pearson easily weighed forty pounds more than Adam, but he refused to allow that tiny detail to hinder him. No matter what, never leave a fallen brother behind.

FORTY-THREE

IT TOOK LONGER THAN EXPECTED, BUT Adam persevered and dragged Pearson from the building, down the stairs, and hoisted him into the SUV. The door slammed closed, but that persistent sensation of someone watching over his shoulder still lingered. He turned back, only to find a deserted street.

He sprinted around the front of the oversized vehicle and slid into the driver's seat.

The keys. Where the hell are the keys?

He glanced into the passenger seat, and the voice in his head grew louder.
Check his pants pocket.

Minutes ticked by, and after some maneuvering, he had the keys in hand. The engine purred to life, and without looking, he pulled the gearshift into reverse.

The tires screeched as his foot slammed hard against the accelerator. His head turned towards an unconscious Pearson. "We're not dying tonight."

He sped along First Avenue, exceeding the posted speed limit by double digits. He had to get help. And then the illuminated green numbers of the police radio caught his eye.

"Come in," he said.

"Go ahead, Pearson."

"Eh, this is Prescott. Pearson is . . ." he struggled to find the right way to put it. "Pearson is injured. I need you to listen to me closely. There's a situation out at the sawmill. I need any available constables to meet me out there. Do you copy?"

"10-4. Sending all available units and medical to the sawmill."

"And someone please get DS Clark and his team out of bed. We'll need as much help as we can get."

Adam glanced up and tugged the steering wheel to the left to avoid hitting a car parked along the side of the road. The mic fell from his hand onto the floor. "Pearson? Man, come on, wake up. I really need you now."

Still nothing.

With each intersection he blew past, his heart thumped faster inside his chest, and his hands trembled as he struggled to keep his grip on the steering wheel.

"I'm coming, Christian. Just hang on."

From the passenger side, a soft moan broke Adam's concentration on the road. He glanced over just as Pearson pulled his head away from the window.

"Adam? What . . . Where are we? How'd we end up in the car?"

"You're safe. That's more important."

"What happened?"

"Yeah, your harmless mayor. He's not as innocent as you've been telling yourself."

"What are you talking about?"

"He attacked you. Left you on the stairs."

"Nah, that's impossible. He's like seventy years old."

"Oh, right. So why'd he come after me? Hm? Had a gun pointed at my chest, and he was about to shoot until—"

Adam paused. The fight or flight had worn off, and the magnitude of what happened in the records room sunk in.

"Until what?"

"I killed him. Oh, shit. I think I killed him."

Pearson's stupor wore off faster than a drunk sleeping it off in the holding cells. "You what?"

"It was self-defense. I swear."

"I believe you. I believe you. I'm just shocked. That's all."

"We've got bigger issues, though."

"All these different suspects are making my head spin."

"Heather, Lowry, the Rosses, they're all just puppets. There's someone else pulling all the strings."

"Who?"

"All he said was the person was closer to home than we think. Whatever the hell that means."

"You don't think—nah, that's impossible," Pearson said.

"Matthias? No way. Close, but not that close. Ani perhaps?"

Pearson cocked his head. "Christian did mention she'd been inserting herself in the investigation."

"I should have never left him alone with her."

"What else did the mayor say?"

"Uh, just shit about how the Germans stole their land, and they wanted it back. But he also said he was tired of all our meddling."

"Into Lindsay's *staged* suicide?"

Adam shrugged. "Things didn't get that far before he pulled the gun. But I can say with certainty Christian is alive. For how much longer, your guess is as good as mine."

Pearson leaned across the center console. "The sawmill. The blueprints. Shit."

Adam pointed at the package on the floorboard between Pearson's legs. "Got 'em. Hopefully, Miller and DS Clark will be there before we arrive."

"I'm not too confident about this," Pearson confessed.

"What choice do we have? Either we act, or Christian dies. And letting him die isn't an option."

***

THE AURA OF CITY LIGHTS GLOWED in the rearview mirror as Adam sped along the dark, bumpy road leading to the sawmill. As usual, the area was quiet, which only increased his heart rate.

"Shit. Shit. Shit," Adam blurted out.

Pearson gripped the bar above his head, holding on for dear life. "What?"

"They're not here."

"They'll be here. Now, don't go doing something stupid like bursting in there like the macho man you aren't."

Adam stuttered. "H-he could be dying."

"Yes, he could be. And if you go in without backup, you might be joining him on the other side."

Adam focused on the road and kept quiet.

"I refuse to let these criminals claim another victim. Christian needs you. I need you."

Adam swung his head and glanced into Pearson's eyes that emitted a genuine caring. Adam suppressed the imminent eruption of tears and got serious. "You're right. I can't do this alone."

The vehicle rolled to a stop just shy of the concrete slab where Adam found Christian's phone earlier. Adam killed the engine and headlights, and they waited under the shroud of darkness that engulfed the desolate land.

The only noise for kilometers was from the prairie wolves and owls singing their songs for only the other animals to hear. An icy shiver ran down Adam's back. The same kind he'd get when the weight of someone's eyes pierced through him. That was at least one thing he was never wrong about. He leaned across the center console and whispered, "We're not alone out here."

FORTY-FOUR

HOURS PASSED SINCE JOANNA VANISHED OUT the door. And those long, lonely hours gave Christian uninterrupted time to reevaluate the many choices he'd made over his lifetime.

He muttered a barrage of questions under his breath. "Was leaving this town the best decision? And if so, what is it about this dreadful place that keeps sucking me back in?"

He didn't answer the questions and instead rattled off a few more. "Was risking my life all for the sake of finding answers about Cassidy, Lindsay, even my mom, worth it? And then there's Pop. If I had stayed, would he not have fallen prey to Joanna?"

Every question he asked had an influence behind it, one that steered every decision he'd made over the last few days. Every rationalization led to two more questions. First, if he had stayed, would he have located his mother? And second, would his father have given up his vice? His constant guilt-based thought process kept him questioning one thing: "If I had made just one choice differently, would things have changed?"

He hung his head in shame. Still, the overall answer never wavered: he'd have left again and again no matter what tricks his mind wanted to play.

For the first time since they drugged and locked him away in the makeshift prison cell, Christian released his pent-up emotions. Tears rushed down his face like the turbulent rapids of the Churchill River.

The breakdown was long overdue. Two years passed since he buried his mother after all the years spent wondering where she went. After the funeral, he never shed a tear. Any time his mind wandered to her, he dove into his work instead of confronting reality.

The sobbing continued for ten minutes until the pressure in the room dropped. He opened his eyes and raised his head. The faint pattering of footsteps against the floor grew closer. Then the hushed voices pierced the walls. Then all the noise stopped, and his breaths grew deeper and louder with anticipation.

The door jerked, and the metal chains clanged together. A soft whimper escaped, and he squeezed his eyes closed as tight as he could, afraid of what lurked beyond.

This is it. This is how my life ends. I'm not ready. I still have so much left to do.

The door blasted inward, and Christian let out an ear-splitting scream. "No."

Exhausted, his voice trailed off, and he choked on the sawdust swirling in the air. He detected the heaviness of someone's gaze, and as he loosened his eye muscles, the brightness of lights aimed in his face blinded him.

"Just do it already," he called out.

The familiar sound of a radio snapped him to. They weren't there to kill him. They were there to rescue him.

"Hawkeye to Clark," an unfamiliar voice said.

"Go ahead."

"We got him."

"Copy. Retreat. Medics are standing by."

The array of headlamps illuminated the room, and a constable, dressed from head-to-toe in all black, kneeled before him. "DS Anderson?"

Christian sucked back his tears and nodded.

"I'm Constable Murray. We've been looking for you."

Christian struggled to get out his words. "Wh-where's Adam?" he asked.

"DS Prescott?"

"Yeah."

"He's waiting above ground with Constable Pearson. There was a slight incident before we arrived, but it's been neutralized."

"Neutralized?" Christian asked as the officer cut away the first plastic tie.

"Yeah, some guy decided tonight was the right one to ambush a few constables."

Christian's eyes widened. "Are they—"

"No, no. They're both fine. Can't say the same for that idiot. The guy was creeping up on the SUV when we arrived. One shot and he went down."

Christian hung his head and sighed. "Death. There's so much death in this place. I'm so sick of it all."

"Hey," Constable Murray raised his voice and snipped away the last plastic tie from Christian's leg. "You're safe now. And all that other noise is just that: noise. I'm telling you, today wasn't your day to die, brother. It just wasn't your day."

***

THREE CONSTABLES CARRIED CHRISTIAN FROM THE dingey room, along the corridor, and up the steep stairs. Surfacing from the underground bunker, the glow from the six floodlights erected blocked his view. As the warm, clean air hit his face, he shielded it and gasped.

"Fresh air."

Ready to get to work, two medics wheeled over a gurney. And as they laid him down, Christian gazed up at the star-lit sky. There was only one face he wanted to lay his eyes on, and after a few seconds, his wish came true.

"Adam," he whispered.

Adam grabbed his hand and walked along the side towards the awaiting ambulance.

"I'm sorry."

"For what? I'm the one who's sorry."

"I should have been there."

Christian smiled. "This was meant to happen. Did they find the others?"

"What others?"

"My pop and Angela. They were there with me, but then they weren't. Did they find them?"

"When?"

"I . . ." he stuttered, "I don't know. There was still light under the door."

"Jesus." Without another word, Adam released his grip and raced back towards the building. Christian could hear him hollering over and over. "Pearson? Pearson? Hey, we got a problem."

"Wait," Christian said. The gurney stopped, and Christian eavesdropped on their conversation.

"How's Christian?"

"Alive. But there's something even bigger."

The pause was more prolonged than Pearson expected. "Well, man, spit it out."

"Matthias and Angela were in there with him. Now they aren't."

"Shit."

"Yeah. I'm going to ride with him to the hospital and try to get some more details."

Christian turned his head towards the voices as Adam raced back to be at his side.

They slid Christian in first, and Adam hoisted himself into the back of the rig. It wasn't until the lights illuminated his face did the inflicted damage become clear.

Deep gashes in his wrists from the binds, the purplish hue under his left eye, and the knot on his temple were only the wounds visible. Adam shuddered at what lurked under Christian's tattered clothes.

The medic inserted an IV into Christian's arm as Adam scooted closer.

"Hey," Adam said, choking back his emotions.

"Hey. Are you crying?"

A chuckle mixed with a scoff came out. "No. Why would I do something like that?"

Christian reached out and squeezed Adam's hand. "Because you love me."

"A little."

The ambulance rocked, and Adam glanced at the rear doors. With one arm clinging to the handle, Pearson pulled himself inside.

"Scared the shit out of me," Adam said.

"Miller's got this under control," Pearson said as his eyes scanned Christian. "Christ, they messed you up good."

"Yeah, but it seems they did you too."

"You know I never bring comforting words with me. I hear your father and Angela Martin were down there with you. Right?"

Christian nodded. "Were. Did you find the dead guy?"

"Dead guy? Oh, you're talking about Charles White? Nah, they hauled him off a while ago."

"Not him. The other dead guy . . . down there," Christian said, pointing towards the building.

Adam and Pearson swapped puzzled glances. "No, we didn't find another body down there, did we, Adam?"

"Nope. Just you."

The beeps from the heart rate monitor increased, and Christian tried to sit up, but it was too much for his weak body, and he plopped against the gurney. "This guy, he was shot right outside the room I was in."

Adam held his hand against Christian's chest. "Hey, take it easy. Right now, you need to rest. Let us handle everything else. The mastermind is dead. Of course, this means finding your father and Angela will be harder."

Christian choked back his words as Pearson spoke over him. "Right. But we'll find them, and we can put yet another Cedar Lake nightmare behind us."

His heart rate continued to increase. "She's dead?"

Baffled, Pearson and Adam traded glances. Pearson spoke up after a few seconds of dead silence. "She? She who?"

"Joanna. You said the mastermind was dead."

"He is, but . . ." Pearson stretched out the word. "We're talking about Mayor Martin—"

"Why would you think Joanna—" Adam stopped before another word came out. "She's the one who held you captive down there?"

He made a circular motion around his face, and his sarcastic nature came out. "You think I did all this damage myself? But it wasn't just her. Thomas Campbell is the one who lured me out here in the first place, and he had help. Two other guys restrained me. They must all be working with her."

Pearson made his way towards the back doors of the rig. "Prescott, we got evidence to collect. They're getting sloppy."

Christian shook his head. "No. Stay."

Pearson returned to Christian's side. "Buddy, if Joanna is in on this, then we've been investigating this all wrong. Now, if you want us to find your father and Angela, we need to get down there and scour that room."

"Get to the hospital, and we'll come check on you later," Adam said.

Christian gripped Adam's hand. He never said a word, but he didn't have to. He had that look in his eye, one Adam had grown accustomed to over the years. Christian pulled Adam closer with what little energy remained. "Christian, please. I can't help you. You need a doctor to get you patched up."

That hidden fear of abandonment inched up, and like a water spigot, the tears flowed.

Adam didn't give in this time. "Do you want that joyous reunion with your father?"

Christian nodded, and the tears shut off.

"Then you gotta let us do our jobs and get down there and hunt for clues. I can't do any of that sitting in the back of an ambulance babysitting you."

Christian released his hold on Adam's hand, and without another word, reached over and ripped the IV from his arm. The attending medic raised his hands and backed away. A few dribbles of blood rolled down his arm, and Adam scrambled to get as far away as he could. "The hell, Christian?"

Pearson rushed in. "Stop being so damn stubborn. Do I need them to sedate you?"

He sat up. "No. What I *need* is to find my father and that bitch, Angela. You know she's in on everything too."

"I've lived with him long enough to know, arguing with him is pointless. In the end, Christian does whatever he wants," Adam said.

Pearson stepped forward and crouched at Christian's side. "Look, I'll make a compromise with you. You'll stay here, relax, and get some fluids. If he says you're good to go, and you're concussion-free, then we'll take you along."

"But?"

"But . . . if he says you're not fine, then you're going to the hospital to get better. Is that something we can agree on?"

A grin graced Christian's face, and he nodded. "Yeah. I like that plan."

FORTY-FIVE

ADAM JOINED PEARSON AND THE SASKATOON team while they huddled near the cellar door. For Adam, the decrepit space where Joanna beat and left his husband for dead was the last place he wanted to be.

But this wasn't the moment to allow his emotions to kick in. They had to find Matthias and Angela—even if she was complicit in the whole thing. And the only clues to their whereabouts rested solely on what evidence they found below the surface.

As they approached DS Clark shouted out, "How's DS Anderson?"

"He's alive but stubborn—nothing new," Adam said.

"Stubborn is how we get shit done. He'll pull through."

"So, what's the plan?" Pearson asked.

"The team just gave the green light. No suspects or hostages on site. Now comes the daunting task of collecting all the evidence."

"Need a hand?"

"I'll take all the hands I can get."

The six-member team from Saskatoon led the way while Pearson and Adam hung back. They stayed close, but soon they descended the stairs. His right foot reached the first step, and the nauseating stench of decay assailed his nostrils. He turned and let out a cough deep from the back of his throat. He paused, braced his hand against the wet wall.

"Breathe through your mouth," Pearson shouted back.

The coughing stopped, and soon, he found himself at the bottom of the stairs. Ahead of him was a long, narrow hallway lined with five doors.

He approached the first room. The door was busted in, and he peeked around the corner. Empty. He took a few more steps and found himself standing outside the second room. It was the room where Christian endured unrelenting torture at the hands of someone he should have trusted. Inside, nearest to the door was a single, wooden chair. Hesitant, he stepped inside and scanned the room with his flashlight. In the rear of the large room were three more chairs spread feet apart.

He returned the spotlight to the floor in front of him. In front of the chair laid four plastic ties, two of them covered in blood. His head dropped forward, and his mind wandered.

How'd Christian survive this? How'd I let this happen?

Before he could ask more unfathomable questions, a gentle touch of a hand against his shoulder saved him from himself. He turned his head over his shoulder and standing behind him was Pearson.

"You good?"

"You want the truth, or what I'm supposed to say?"

"I get it. This is hard. But unless we press on, we'll never find the clues we need to lead us in the right direction."

With a simple nod, Adam turned for the door and followed Pearson into the hallway. He stopped, and Pearson glanced back.

"Thank you. Thank you for refocusing my attention. I'm so focused on Christian I'm missing the bigger picture. And that is finding this bitch so we can end this."

"That's what I'm here for, man."

Two steps away from the room and a constable rushed from the fourth door down. The slender man stumbled down the hallway, with his hands covering his mouth. The retching echoed down the hall, and Adam clenched his jaw and closed his eyes. Even with his eyes obscured, it didn't prevent a cold tremor from crawling up Adam's spine as the vomit splashed against the floor. When the unpleasant noises ceased, he opened his eyes in time to find two fellow constables rushing to the man's aid.

"Shit. That's never a good sign," Adam whispered.

"Nope. Think you can you handle this?"

His shoulders arched upward. "No. But what other choice do I have?"

They raced for the door, and standing on the edge of the jamb, they found the culprit behind the sudden illness.

Three worn-out mattresses lined the outer wall, but the real culprit was inside the two white, five-gallon buckets situated in the center of the room. There was no need to get any closer, as the pungent odor revealed everything they needed to know about their contents. Adam stepped away as fast as he could and remained moving backward down the hallway. Soon, Pearson followed.

Far enough away, Adam stroked his nose and scrunched his face. "Damn. I never imagined anything more putrid than a decaying corpse. But human shit is ten times worse."

"Nah, this has nothing on decomp," Pearson said. "The stench of shit goes away in a few minutes, but decomp, that seeps into your pores and lingers for weeks."

Adam didn't reply and continued rubbing at his nose.

"I'm gonna dig around for clues. You'll be okay out here?"

Adam straightened out his back and fidgeted with the ring on his finger. "Yeah, I'll be fine. I'm glad one of us has the stomach for this."

After flashing a quick grin, Pearson raced back like a hero to the room. Adam leaned against the wall. His internal thoughts once again consumed him. However, this time his focus wasn't on finding Christian or blaming himself. He needed to nail down the precise moment everything about this investigation spiraled out of control.

Was it when he agreed to help? Or was it their presence at the Ross home that set everything into motion? Or could it have been finding Lee White dying on the hay-strewn floor of his barn?

Whatever the turning point, he never imagined returning to Cedar Lake would uncover another disturbing case which better suited a horror movie than real life.

I should have known better coming back here. Christian needs to let the past stay in the past.

The wait was agonizing, and soon he found himself standing outside the second room once again. Something about that room kept drawing him to it. And even though the voice in his head was always wrong, his gut was quite the opposite. His worthless flashlight was insufficient to comb the poorly lit room. He needed something more powerful if he was going to find anything. But where was he going to find an alternate light source?

He stuck his head into the hallway and hollered. "Pearson?"

"Yeah?" he shouted.

"You don't happen to have an ALS in your SUV, do you?"

There were a few seconds of silence. DS Clark poked his head out of the room a few doors down. "Got one in the back of the van. You never know when they'll come in handy."

Adam wasted no time scrambling up the stairs. He flung open the rear doors and sifted through the mounds of equipment. There it was, and he muttered under his breath, "Gotcha."

With the case in hand, he raced back into the bellies of the earth. He fired up the light and began his search in the corner of the room. Meticulously, he scanned the floor, praying something worthwhile could catch his eye. Yet, after twenty minutes, he'd searched the entire room, and the only thing that lit up was the bloody plastic ties.

No bodily fluids. Nothing to give him the faintest idea of where to head next.

He clicked off the light and hung his head.

Pearson's booming voice started him. "Anything?"

"Nothing. Damnit."

"Same here. They swabbed for DNA, but that'll be weeks before we get any results. I think our best bet is to get a warrant to search Joanna's house."

Then Adam remembered his distrust of Ani. He turned and faced Pearson. "Better yet, I think it's about time we drag Ani down to the detachment."

"Why her?"

"Who knows their own mother better than we do? Besides, she was a little too eager to pump Christian full of information before."

FORTY-SIX

CHRISTIAN WAITED WITH HIS EYES CLOSED in the rear of the ambulance. Unsure of how much time elapsed, his eyes sprang open as a familiar voice grew louder.

Adam's slid along the bench and reached out for Christian's hand. "Well, somebody got his color back."

Pearson hoisted himself inside just as Christian responded. "Still sore but getting better. Good enough to get out there and—"

Pearson raised his finger before turning to the medic. "No, no. The deal was *he* decides if you're good enough, not you."

All eyes focused on the medic, whose lips curled down. "I'm not a doctor."

"You're the closest thing we got. So, what's your opinion?" Pearson asked.

"Well, he doesn't have a concussion, and his blood pressure did stabilize. But—"

"I knew a but was coming."

"He's still dehydrated, bruised, and he needs rest at the hospital. Where a doctor can assess the situation better."

"So you believe he shouldn't return to the field?" Adam asked.

The medic shrugged. "Desk duty, sure. Chasing down suspects, no."

In a dismissive tone, Pearson said. "Well, there you have it."

But Christian was having none of the wimpy advice being dished out. "Take out the IV."

The medic remained stone-faced and didn't react.

"I said, take it out. Either you do it, or I will. And you know I keep my word."

Adam shook his head. "Just do it."

Hesitant, the medic reached over and stopped the flow of saline before removing the needle from Christian's arm. With a clipboard at the ready, he handed it over.

"Sign this."

"What?"

"It's a refusal form. Sign it."

Christian froze.

"You're not leaving the back of my rig until you do."

"I can't believe you're doing this," Pearson said.

"I'm aware of the risks. Let's say some crazed woman took your father captive, and you had no idea where he was, you'd do the same. Wouldn't you?"

Pearson hung his head in defeat. "Damn, you sure know how to lay on the guilt. But if we're taking responsibility for you, there are a few ground rules you will follow. If not, we'll drop your ass at the ER entrance."

"And they are?"

"You do what we say."

"That's it?"

"Not even close. If shit hits the fan, you will remain in the vehicle. I will not provide you a weapon, and your stubbornness ends right here."

Christian pondered the long list of demands, and he exhaled. "Anything else?"

"Excuse me? Christian, if you can't check yourself, tell me now. We can't afford to waste any more time looking after you when so many lives hang in the balance."

"Okay."

"Okay, you agree. Or okay, you don't?"

"You're right. I've been negligent. Just this once, I promise to control myself."

"Wise choice, my friend."

Those words dredged up a powerful memory, and Christian's eyes widened, and he whipped his head towards Adam, who sat at his side, holding his hand. "Wait. I remembered a few things she said."

His heart rate increased as every eye in the rig focused on him. "She was whispering outside the door and mentioned something about a forestry worksite. Could they have gone there?"

"Jesus. Do you know how many forestry sites there are within fifty klicks?"

"Too many."

Adam leaned in towards him. "What else do you remember?"

The beautiful face and smile of his best friend flashed before his eyes, and he could hear her voice in his head.

Don't forget me, Christian.

His body lurched forward. "Gemma. Where's Gemma?"

Pearson placed his hand on Christian's chest, and with a gentle push, Christian fell back against the stretcher. "Gemma's safely back in Regina. Why?"

"When was the last time you spoke to her?"

Pearson's once-calm demeanor shifted like the summer winds on the prairie. "Yesterday afternoon. Why are you so panicked about Gemma?"

Christian's eyes shifted around, and he lurched forward again. "Joanna. She—oh God, what have I done. What the hell have I done?"

Pearson yanked Christian by his tattered polo shirt, pulling him close to his face. "Christian. Listen to me. Are you listening?"

Christian flinched, and his eyes darted around.

"Should I be worried about Gemma? Is she in danger?"

Christian managed a quick head bob, but an already-strained Pearson gripped his shirt tighter. "Is Gemma safe?"

Christian stuttered through his words. "I . . . don't. I don't know. All right. I swear on my mother's grave."

Adam eased into the tense interaction. "What did you remember?"

"Joanna. She said she had one loose end to tie up."

"And by loose end, she meant Gemma?" Pearson asked.

"Yes. I pressed her to tell me what she had planned, but all that evil woman could say was, 'what's done is done.'"

Pearson yanked harder. "What is she going to do with Gemma?"

Christian froze. The hot air of Pearson's breath smacked against his exposed skin, and Adam interjected. "Pearson, man, back off. He's not the enemy. Joanna is."

Pearson didn't budge, and all it took was one glance into Christian's eyes for him to get the answer he needed. Gemma, the girl he'd allowed to penetrate his stony heart, was in danger.

The whites in Pearson's eyes disappeared, and he released his forceful grip on Christian. And without any warning, the constable smashed his hand against the rear door and jumped to the ground. The ambulance swayed back and forth, and Christian gasped and hung his head.

"He'll be fine. He's going to call, she'll answer, and he'll calm down. All Joanna wants is chaos."

Christian lifted his head and turned towards Adam. "You're cute and smart, just a few of the reasons I married you. But another thing you are—naïve."

Adam pulled back. "Excuse me?"

"You have no clue what these people are capable of."

"And you do?"

"They want to take over the town and will kill anyone who stands in their way. So, yeah, I think I understand what they're capable of."

"Well, Mayor Martin pulled a gun on me and gave me the rundown. So I've had first-hand experience of them."

Before Christian could apologize, a slew of swear words crept through the back door of the ambulance. Adam walked to the back door and peeked out. "I should check on him."

The moment he stood, Pearson appeared, looking genuinely distraught.

He mumbled under his breath. "She's gone. They got to her, and now she's gone."

His cell phone dropped from his hand and landed face-up on the gravel lane.

"What do you mean, 'she's gone'?" Adam asked. "Did she answer?"

Pearson pinched the bridge of his nose and shook his head. "She didn't, but someone else did."

FORTY-SEVEN

SANDWICHED BETWEEN PEARSON AND ADAM, CHRISTIAN hobbled away from the rig towards the SUV. Everything was a daze, but as he stared blankly into the eastern sky, the blends of pale blues and purples crested the horizon. This only heightened his appreciation for life and how precious it is.

He exhaled. He'd survived a long and lonely night, but his elation soon dwindled as he thought of the unknown whereabouts of his best friend and father.

For the second time in less than three years, Gemma found herself captured by another deranged lunatic from Cedar Lake. And no matter how much he wanted, he couldn't put a positive spin on his own rescue, not with too much at stake.

Unlike last time, when his impulsive mistakes cost him one night in the hospital, the outcome this time might not be as rosy.

To begin with, the circumstances now versus then weren't even on the same level. In fact, they were grimmer. This time there were more of *them*, each one blending in with the ordinary residents.

No, things were incomparable. The sacrifices were more sweeping. Gemma. His father. Lindsay. Each of them innocent victims in this dangerous game, who suffered due to the decisions he made without having the entire story.

I've got an impulse problem. Before I get anyone else killed, I must fix this shit.

Adam opened the rear passenger door of the SUV, and Christian slid into the cold backseat. The door slammed closed, and his eyes narrowed as he focused on his husband and Pearson traipsing across to rejoin the team from Saskatoon.

The meeting lasted only a few short minutes, and soon, everyone scattered with haste. Three piled into a black van, the other three into the white van, and their tires spewed pebbles across the landscape. Pearson spoke with Miller for a few seconds, and soon enough, the two raced back towards the SUV.

The doors flung open, and before Christian's head stopped spinning, the car tailed the vans along the dirt road.

"What's going on?" he asked. "Where are they going?"

Silence.

"Hey, has something happened?"

"Half of them are going to arrest Ani; the other half is going to the municipal building to check on Mayor Martin."

"And us?"

"We're going back to the detachment."

"Wait for what? Gemma. What about—"

Adam interrupted. "Christian. Chill. We have a plan. A plan that we need you for. So do us all a favor and relax for fifteen minutes."

"Relax?" his voice raised an octave. "Relax! How can I while my father is being held captive and my best friend is God only knows where?"

"Gemma's alive," Pearson said.

"How do you know? You said her kidnapper answered her phone."

"I heard her whimpering in the background. For how much longer she stays alive, I have no idea."

The haunting déjà vu moment sent a shiver up his arm and down Christian's back. "Then we should be out looking for her, not heading back to wait at the detachment."

"Look where? This Province is over six-hundred-thousand kilometers—squared—I wouldn't even know where to begin," Pearson said. "Besides, once we get Ani in and question her, she may shed some light on where to look. Hence why I need you to relax."

"But how?"

"Ani trusts you."

"She might be involved, though."

"She may not be. One thing is certain: who knows her mother better than she does?"

"Good point, but I don't know. There has to be something more we can do."

"I've already requested a warrant for Gemma's cell phone records. For right now, the only thing we can do is pray we get to her in time."

"Warrants take too long. There has to be another way."

Then he remembered. There was something at his disposal he'd never used, but now was a better time than any. "I know how we can find her," he shouted.

"How? Right now, you can barely form a coherent sentence," Pearson said.

"I have this app."

Adam turned his head and stared at Christian. "What app?"

"You know that thingy, the one where you can track your friends," he began. "And don't give me that look. I have no idea what it's called, but after what happened last time, we both agreed for our safety, we'd both have the ability to track each other."

"You're talking about *Find My Friends*?"

"If you say so," Christian patted against his body. "My phone. Where's my phone?"

Adam reached into his vest and dangled it in the air. "You mean this?"

"Where . . . why do you have it?"

"Your friend Joanna isn't as smart as she wants you to believe. Someone tossed it into a bush behind the sawmill. Power on and ringer on. Either they wanted us to find it, or they made a mistake."

"My money's on a mistake," Pearson said.

Adam tossed the busted-up phone into the backseat, and Christian barely caught it with his shaky hands. He tapped against the screen, but the screen remained black.

"Shit," he cried out.

"What?"

"It's not working. Is it—?"

"It's out of juice, Christian," Adam said as he tossed a white cord into the backseat. "Charge it up and try to get her location."

The last ten minutes of their return to the detachment was quiet. The phone remained in a dormant slumber, and Christian's jaw ached from clenching.

He ripped the charger from the cigarette lighter and followed them inside the building. Without greeting the constable behind the glass, he raced through the door and for the first available socket he could find. If Gemma had any chance of surviving, he needed to get into that app.

Christian glanced up from the phone as the two men walked past. Pearson meandered around his desk and flopped into his oversized chair. Meanwhile, his husband squirmed in the same uncomfortable chair he endured years ago.

When his eyes refocused on the phone, it happened. The picture of him and Adam appeared. Christian paused for a moment and stared at the photo. Amid all the chaos, whenever he wanted a reminder of happier times, he'd take a moment and stare at his cell phone screen. The background was the selfie he took when they reached Mount Rundle's peak in Banff National Park.

You survived that journey together. You're lucky because you get to spend more time with this handsome, good-hearted man.

Now wasn't the time to get sentimental, not with lives hanging in the balance. He swiped his pointer finger against the smashed screen and entered his six-digit passcode.

"Aha," he shouted.

"You're in?" Pearson asked from across the room.

"I'm in," he replied. "Now, where is this app?"

He swiped, and on the third page of his vast library of apps, the icon he'd been searching for stood out more than any other. He tapped once, and it opened. Six device names filled the screen, but it was the last device on the list he needed most. There was no denying it was hers, especially with the smart-ass name she'd given her phone—*ball breaker.*

Always the charmer, Gemma.

A wheel spun as it hunted for her. But it continued spinning, and sweat seeped from his pores. *Am I too late?*

It stopped, and a dot on the map pinpointed the estimated location.

"South of Saskatoon," he shouted as he stood to his feet.

"Is it moving or stationary?"

"I don't know. I don't think it's live."

Everyone huddled around and stared at the blue dot. One minute passed, then two. Finally, another update. "They're on the move."

Pearson wasted no time getting on the phone to the closest detachments and issuing a Province-wide APB. But it was vague; after all, the app could only say where she was, but not what type of vehicle she was in, who had her held captive, or where they were even heading.

Christian paced the floor for well over thirty minutes. Even through the pain, the circle-walking was the only thing that brought him comfort and calmed his nerves.

A commotion from the lobby area stopped him, and he backed away from the door. Soon, it busted inward, and two constables from the Saskatoon team struggled to keep Ani cooperative.

"You can't do this to me," she hollered. "I know my rights."

Pearson stepped between the hallway leading to the cells and the combative girl.

"Anwaatin Carmack, I am arresting you on suspicion of kidnapping. You have the right to retain and instruct counsel without delay. Do you understand?"

"Asshole," she barked.

"Do you want to call a lawyer, Ms. Carmack?"

"I haven't done anything wrong."

"I'll take that as a no. I must provide you with the following warning. You need not say anything. You have nothing to hope from any promises and nothing to fear from any threat whether you say anything. Anything you do or say may be used as evidence. Do you understand?"

She continued struggling to free herself from the grip of the two hefty constables. "Screw you."

Pearson pinched between his eyes and waved his hand. "Just put her in interview room A. First door on the right."

Kicking and screaming down the hall, the three stood watching them struggle to get her into the room. After a few minutes, the door slammed closed, and the two constables reappeared in the hallway. Even handcuffing her to the table didn't stop her outburst. The clanking of the cuffs against the metal table echoed down the hallway.

"She's a feisty one," one constable said.

"Your team find anything at her house?"

"Not yet. But they're still searching."

His head tilted towards the interview room. "We should get back, but good luck with her."

"Yeah, thanks. Just get out there and find us something."

***

CHRISTIAN STOOD ALONE; A THICK piece of glass separated him and Ani. Twenty minutes had passed since the Saskatoon team cuffed her right wrist to the table, and during that time, it was non-stop disorder. That was until whatever energy she had puttered out, and now an exhausted Ani buried her head between her crossed arms atop the table.

Finally, some peace and quiet.

The door opened, and for a split-second, Christian turned to find Adam moving in closer. He folded his arms across his puffed-out chest. He returned to studying the girl who tried so hard to insert herself into the investigation.

"Wore herself out, eh?"

"Yeah," Christian replied with a grin. "I'm just giving her a few more minutes, and then I'll try to get those fireworks going again."

"You think she'll talk?"

"She's facing a minimum of five years in jail. I'm sure I can keep taking on charges, and that'll only make her more willing."

"Doesn't always work, you know. Ani's loyalty to the cause could be so deep-seated nothing you say will make her talk."

"Perhaps. But I get a vibe from her. Like she isn't as devoted to her mother's plans; if she has a clue about them at all."

Pearson crossed his arms over his chest. "She does."

"She could have been steering us towards her mother, but the plans accelerated when we showed up?"

"Nonsense. Ani did what they trained her to do: steered you away from the real criminals to buy themselves more time."

Christian shrugged. "We can debate this all night long. It doesn't change the fact that two people I love very much are in danger. I'm going in."

"I'll be right here watching."

Christian marched into the hallway. There was only one thing on his mind: his father and Gemma. As he stood outside the door to interview room A, his hands trembled.

Am I ready for this?

The negative thoughts didn't fester too long as Pearson's booming voice echoed down the hall. Christian rolled his head to the left, but Pearson wasn't there.

He's on the phone.

He lingered a few moments and listened to the one-sided conversation.

"Have you spotted her yet?"

Then a pause.

"Okay, well, keep looking. Her last known location was about fifteen kilometers south of Yellowhead Highway interchange, but that was forty minutes ago. They could be heading towards Cedar Lake."

He watched Pearson sigh and squeeze the bridge of his nose. "Fine. I'll be waiting for an update."

The constable slammed the phone down, and then the banging continued as Christian reached for the door handle.

This is it. Make or break, Christian. Don't screw this up.

With one swift move, he turned the handle and pushed against the door. Ani didn't stir.

"Hello, Ani," he said.

She lifted her reddened face from her arms and stared him down.

"Hope they didn't rough you up too bad."

"What do you care? And why am I here?"

He pulled out the chair and clasped his hands together. "You know why you're here, so let's cut the crap. Where's your mother?"

Her eyes didn't waver. "How should I know?"

"Come on, you expect me to believe that? Your mother abducted my father, then me, and I've endured hours of torture at her hands. So while you think your innocent act is fooling me, it's not."

"No clue what you're talking about."

"She told me; you know. Told me all about how she tapped you to divert our attention, all to buy her more time. The gig's up, Ani. Now, what I want to know is where would she take my father?"

She grinned. "Hmm, I never took my mother as someone who leaked her ambitious plans so easily."

His shoulders lurched upwards. "Probably presumed she'd have time to finish me off. That was the plan, after all, wasn't it?"

"I have no idea what you're going on about, Christian."

"You know, her little puppy Charles. Everyone has a task, your mother's words, not mine. And I bet that was his one task: take me out, and my husband.

Hell, she probably put a hit on Constable Pearson too," he said. He stretched his arms and interlocked his fingers behind his head. "But the joke's on her."

Her eyes widened, and she leaned in closer. "What do you mean?"

"Charles White, yeah, he's dead."

That word—dead—stirred a reaction in her icy glare.

"Now, I don't give a rat's ass about Angela, or Thomas, or whoever else is working for her. I only care that my father walks away . . . alive. Or else—" he balled his fist together just as the door swung open and Pearson appeared in the doorway.

"Ah, thank God, the tantrum stopped," he rubbed his temples. "I got a migraine thanks to you."

Christian glanced over his shoulder, and nestled under Pearson's right arm was a stack of colorful folders. As they dropped against the table, a gust of air blew in Christian's direction. He scanned the folders. Each one had a name written in Sharpie: last name, then first name. And as Christian scanned through them, one thing was obvious: these were the files of everyone Pearson suspected of being involved.

He pulled on the chair, making sure the metal legs scratched against the linoleum floor. "Where d'you leave off?"

"I was telling Ani it's better she tells us where her mother is. The court is more lenient with suspects who help law enforcement."

"Ah, yeah, she's not going to fall for that old trick. She's too smart for that. In fact, we don't need her. We got enough in these files to make sure she goes away for a long, long time."

Her eyes never wandered from the folders. All she could do was sit, stare, and tremble. And deep down, Christian enjoyed every minute watching as her future slipped away.

"So, I guess we can go get something to eat. She won't mind if we leave her in here for a few hours. Right?" Christian asked.

"Man, I could sure go for a nice, juicy burger right about now."

They stood up in unison, and the constable stacked the folders into a tidy pile before shoving them back under his armpit. Two steps away from the door, Ani broke. "Wait. Maybe I can help after all."

"Well, look at that, someone's had a change of heart."

"I want immunity. I want protection, or I don't talk."

Pearson clicked his tongue and shook his head. "Yeah, that's not how it works in the real world."

"I won't say anything else until I get immunity."

"She can't be serious, can she?" Christian asked.

Pearson leaned against the table. "Well, then, you're in for a long wait in silence." He pointed at the simple clock hanging above the two-way mirror. "It's ten, and the only person who can give you immunity has a full docket today. So my advice; get comfortable."

Christian pulled the door closed behind as the two congregated outside the interview room. Before Christian could begin to ask questions about the folders, Pearson's cell phone rang.

"Hello," the constable said. "Uh-huh. No, no, fifteen minutes is perfect."

He ended the call and slid the thin phone back into the breast pocket of his vest.

"Okay, don't leave me hanging."

"That was the nurse I met at the hospital the other day. She says Lee White has woke from his coma and is asking to speak to me, again."

"Again?"

"He wasn't in the mood to chat two days ago. But now, he's asking for me. That means this can go two ways: either he breaks the case wide open, or he's just another stall tactic."

"I'm trying to be more optimistic in life."

"You? More optimistic?"

"That's what everyone says. But I've been spending a lot of time watching *Super Soul Sunday*. All that positive thinking is rubbing off on me."

"Sure, it is. I'm sure it is."

"Anyway, I think we're about to get the answers we need to not only find

Matthias, but Gemma too."

FORTY-EIGHT

PEARSON SPED THROUGH A STOP SIGN on the quiet residential street only blocks away from Cedar Lake Memorial. Time was precious, and nothing was going to stand between him and the information he desperately needed.

Adam interrupted the silence. With a crackle in his voice, he said, "I don't know. Entrusting Miller to watch over Christian and Ani . . . isn't there anyone else?"

"He's competent. I'm more worried about your impulsive husband than I am about Miller."

"Still, there had to be another way."

Pearson kept his eyes laser-focused on the road but shook his head. "Nope, sorry, pal. There's just not enough of us to go around. With half of DS Clark's team at Joanna and Ani's place searching for clues, and the other half dealing with the incident in the municipal building, we're spread pretty thin."

Still unaware, Adam asked the burning question on his tongue. "Did they find anything in the basement?"

"Say what you really mean, did they find *him* in the basement?"

Adam swallowed hard, anxious to learn the consequence of his desperate actions. "Did they?"

Pearson's poker-face did nothing to help put Adam's rattled nerves at ease. But soon, the constable smirked and rolled his head towards the passenger seat. "The mayor's alive . . . barely. You really did a number on him."

"Self-defense."

"I know, I know. You did what you had to do. And when this is all wrapped up and the oversight board reviews, they'll come to the same conclusion: you did what you had to do."

"Uh, remember, I'm here 'unofficially.'"

"Don't stress about shit until it's staring you right in the face, kid. You'll be fine."

Pearson's attempt at putting Adam at ease ended when he slammed the SUV into park underneath the hospital's covered entrance.

They breezed through the automatic doors, past the waiting room, and stood outside the locked double doors which lead back to the patient rooms. Security had tightened since Gemma's father almost snuffed out several lives two years earlier.

Pearson peeked through the narrow, rectangular glass. Right on schedule, the nurse from a few days earlier sashayed down the corridor.

"She's coming."

And as expected, the double door swung outward, and the petite nurse emerged from the sterile hallway.

"Ah, Luke. Thanks for getting here so quick," she said, as a smile graced her face.

"Yeah, no problem."

They exchanged smiles. It was clear to Adam there was a subtle attraction between the two, but they weren't here to find a suitable mate for the lonely constable. They were here to find out what information Lee White could add to the already head-spinning investigation.

Adam mumbled under his breath, loud enough for the coy smiles to disappear from both of their faces.

"Right, sorry, Adam. You said on the phone he was alert, but I gotta ask . . . is Mr. White on anything that may make his statements inadmissible?"

The nurse shook her head from side to side. "A light dose of morphine, nothing out of the ordinary for a gunshot victim."

This was uncharted territory for Pearson. Never had he visited a potential accomplice in the hospital to question them. He turned his eyes onto Adam, hoping for some guidance on how to continue.

"You ever have to question someone under the effects of morphine before?"

Adam nodded. "A few, yeah."

"And? Is it safe to go ahead?"

Adam released a low-spirited laugh under his breath. "Look, if the man says he understands his rights, then he understands. Just to be safe, I'll videotape everything. Better safe than sorry in case his lawyers try to claim forced confession."

Pearson grinned. "See, this is why I surround myself with people smarter than me."

They lingered outside Lee White's hospital room. What would he say? Was this the break they needed to fully understand not only what was occurring now, but what happened twelve years ago on that warm, spring evening?

Pearson rapped his knuckles twice against the door, and without waiting for a response, he lowered the door handle and pushed his way in.

Lee White, the tough man around town, the nightmare every person cowered away from, now laid there in the adjustable bed, powerless. With tubes, electrons, and an oxygen mask covering his mouth and nose, no longer was he a man in charge of anything. Adam let the door slip from his hand, and it softly closed.

Lee pulled the plastic mask away from his face. "Ah, so, you made it, huh?"

Pearson shielded his mouth and mumbled under his breath to Adam as he inched closer to the bed. "This better be one helluva story."

Lee let out a wet cough, the sort a pack-a-day smoker would have after years of abusing their lungs. "It will be."

"Why come clean now?"

"I knew my days were numbered—especially when our efforts to run you out of town failed. But the doc broke the news to me this morning: lung cancer—stage four. Regardless of what I say, I'll never live long enough to see the inside of a courtroom. And besides, kidnapping Gemma was never part of the plan. Even though she was a pain in my ass, I owe it to her to make sure she walks away from this alive."

Pearson wasn't one for heartbreaking endings, even if this man was scum in his eyes. To watch as another human suffered pulled at his heartstrings. And after spending months by his own mother's bedside as cancer snuffed out her life, he couldn't help but foresee a slow, agonizing death for Lee White.

Even so, Lee had put the residents of Cedar Lake through hell over the past three decades. Maybe this diagnosis was a blessing, not only for a troubled man but for the residents who could now resurface from the dark corners he'd backed them into.

Pearson managed a simple comeback. "Sorry to hear that."

Adam, on the other hand, wasn't as considerate. "Mr. White, I am Detective Sergeant Adam—"

Lee interrupted. "I know who you are. Detective Sergeant Prescott—you're Christian's husband. You rushed up here during Cassidy's murder investigation."

"I did. Do you object to me video recording this interview?"

"Nope, facts ain't going change regardless, so film away."

Adam lifted his cell phone and pressed the record button.

Pearson resumed. "I must provide the following warning: You are not obligated to say anything, but anything you do say may be given as evidence. Do you understand?"

"I do."

"I also must inform you that you have the right to obtain counsel, in private, without delay. You may contact a lawyer at any time. Do you understand?"

"Can't no damn lawyer do me any good now."

"At least you admit it."

"You're wasting time. Precious time. I could be dead while you stand here, stalling. You're here because you hope I can help you find Gemma . . . and Matthias."

Pearson squeezed his eyes. Lee was trying his damndest to infuriate him, but this wasn't the time to lose his cool. "How? How would you know Gemma is missing?"

"Just because Lowry tried to off me, you didn't think that meant she had lost faith in me, do you?"

"Lowry shot you?" Pearson asked.

"He was sent, but not by her."

"By her, you mean Joanna?"

"Who else? But you already know that. So, you came for a story. Which one do you want first? Matthias or Lindsay's?"

"First? How about who do you think put a hit on you? But listen, this is your time to talk."

His coughing fit continued as he struggled to catch his breath. "I'll start with Lindsay, her story's easy. That traitor, Taylor, he told you the truth. She didn't commit suicide, but man, we did the perfect coverup to fool all of you into thinking she did."

"I've seen the report. I don't need a play-by-play. I came for the why. Why you murdered her."

"Why do you think?"

Adam stepped forward. "She uncovered your plans. The prostitution ring, human trafficking, the drugs. She was about to expose it all, and your little clan couldn't let that happen, so you killed her to keep her silent."

"Kid, you're so far off, we're not even on the same planet anymore," he said, replacing the mask to suck in a few breaths of oxygen. "Let me guess, Christian made her seem like this gentle, harmless girl. Yeah?"

Adam nodded.

"And I bet Gemma painted her as quite the opposite. A monster, perhaps?"

"A dramatic word choice, but yeah, their opinions of her are different. So what?"

"So what, he says. Lindsay wasn't the girl Christian built her up to be. No, that little girl wasn't no saint. And neither is her brother, Chad."

Adam paused and remembered the weird interaction with Chad Ross on their first day in town. but he played it off and probed further. "How so?"

"They worked for us. My little brother–sister team who recruited for me."

"Recruited?" Pearson asked.

"You know, they went on the hunt for guys looking for a good time."

"I see."

"And I'm not talking about your average Joe from down the block, though. No. We needed men with power."

"Why?" Adam asked.

"How else do you convince someone to do what you say? You have to hold something over their head, something shameful that they'd never want to get out."

"So blackmail?"

"Straight-shooter, I like that. But, yeah, we recorded their 'sessions' with the girls and waited. When we needed a favor, one of us paid them a visit."

"How many guys are we talking?"

"In the beginning, a handful. But we hooked the biggest fish first."

"And none of these big fish ever fought you on it? Not one of them ever said 'I'm going to the cops'?"

His laugh turned into another coughing fit. "If you broke the law, and someone had hard proof, would you run to the police?"

"Point taken. So you used Lindsay and Chad as your helpers. Doesn't explain why you killed her and spared Chad."

He raised his hands inward and touched his chest. "Whoa, hold up now, I never said *I* killed Lindsay."

"If not you, then who?"

311

"We'll get to that . . . in time."

Adam bowed his head, and it shook from side to side. "Man, this guy's just wasting our time. All he's doing is buying Joanna more time."

"No offense, Pearson, but if these two fruitcakes are as good as rumor has it, then me taking up fifteen minutes of your time won't matter. Can I continue my story, hm?"

Adam's nostrils flared. Insults were nothing new in Adam's life. He could live with names like pig, oinker, or the ever-amusing Queen's cowboy, but when a suspect threw gay slurs his way, his blood boiled. He stood to his feet and kicked the chair away from the bed. "Screw you, man. I don't have time for this bullshit."

As Adam marched for the door, Pearson gripped his shoulder, and he stopped. "Hey, don't let this loser get to you. Okay? What if he's telling the truth, and he knows something? The least we should do is listen to what he has to say."

Adam walked to the chair and dragged it back next to the bed. "You're testing my patience. So what d'you say we get to the point, yeah?"

"Speedy version it is, then. We left Lindsay and Chad in the dark about the rest of the operation. All we asked them to do was convince people to come to the Ridgeway Inn. Nothing more, nothing less."

"So, what happened?" Pearson asked.

"Lindsay. Best damn snoop I've ever met. It didn't take long before she flung around the one dreaded word: why?"

"She wanted to know why she was doing what she was?"

"Yeah. Of course, we lied. Must not have convinced her, because she didn't give up and then it happened: she uncovered the goal."

Adam leaned in. "Which was?"

"Joanna wanted the town back. The town she and her followers claimed was stolen from them."

"And I take it those plans didn't sit well with her?"

"Something like that. Lindsay started following our guys around, videotaping them. She flew under the radar for a few months, but soon Chad grew suspicious and followed her."

"And that's when he turned her into Joanna?" Pearson asked.

Lee nodded. "Joanna was furious. 'Traitors will die,' that's what she told the crew. We all thought it was a scare tactic, but she kept true to her word. Six days later, Lindsay was dead. Everyone played their part, just like she instructed us."

"For example?"

"The diary leak, that was all Chad. The fight in the school parking lot a week before she died, that was Angela. Even Linus got in on the action."

"All that to throw the investigators off?"

He nodded. "They assumed the girl with a bright future ahead of her couldn't take the heat and did herself in."

"And David Ross?"

"What about him?"

"Was he in on this, too?"

"Man, you can't compare what happened between Liam and Cassidy to everything, you know. No, David Ross had no clue what was going on under his own roof."

"Was he on your blackmail list?"

Lee's eyes darted away.

Adam slammed down his hand, and his ring clanked against the railing. "Hey! I asked you a question. Was David Ross on your blackmail list? Yes or no." His frustration grew more visible with each syllable.

"Yes. Okay. We blackmailed him."

"Tell the truth, for once in your miserable life. Joanna didn't kill Lindsay; you did. The moment you found out she didn't want to play your little games anymore, isn't that right?"

"I'm telling you; it was all Joanna. We were just puppets following her orders."

Then something Gemma and Christian discussed a few nights earlier finally registered. *Stop him.* Those were Taylor Jackson's dying words.

Adam stared the frail man directly in the eyes. "You're lying." The accusatory remarks fell from Adam's mouth with ease. He could spot a liar, and nothing Lee White proclaimed was close enough to the truth for him.

Lee's eyes widened, and his face scrunched. "Excuse me?"

He turned to Pearson. "Did I stutter?"

"Nope."

"Mr. White, there's no way Joanna killed Lindsay."

"Everything was on her command."

"Sure, I'll admit, she probably did orchestrate the recent kidnappings, and I'll go as far as to say she murdered Heather. But I'll believe the words of a dying man over those of a proven liar such as yourself."

He stuttered. "Wh . . . what are you talking about?"

"'Stop him.' That's what Taylor said. He didn't say her. So let's try this again. Who murdered Lindsay?"

Lee White folded his arms across his chest and turned his stare outside the window. "I've said what I had to say. Believe me, don't believe me. At this point, I don't care. What's done is done."

Before either of them could grill him any further, a jingling emitted from inside Pearson's vest. Hesitant, he allowed it to ring a few times. But this only irked Lee White even more.

"Answer the damn phone."

"Pearson," he said.

On the other end was Constable Miller.

"I know you're busy, but there's been a development," the young constable said.

"Yeah?"

"Search and rescue helicopter spotted a burning vehicle out near Sunset Lake. I didn't want to interr—"

"We're on the way." Pearson ended the call and slid the phone back to its resting spot.

He locked eyes with Adam. "We gotta go."

Pearson approached the bed and pulled a pair of handcuffs from his belt. "Lee White, I am arresting you on suspicion of murder."

"Yeah, yeah, I know, I can call a lawyer. Like I told you, ain't no lawyer gonna help me now."

The cuffs clicked, and he double-checked to make sure they were secure. As they turned and moved towards the door, Lee expressed one final thought.

"They found the burning car, didn't they?"

Pearson stopped in his tracks, and his head spun around. "Yup. And let me guess; you knew this was going to happen."

He grinned and nodded. "She's following the plan to the letter. And fair warning, she doesn't plan to go down without a fight, so be ready."

Pearson walked back for the bed. As he hovered over Lee, Pearson placed his hand on the man's shoulder and leaned down. "I despise you. You've made my life a living hell these past seven years. But I wish you nothing but the best. Get better and take care of yourself."

And without much ado, Pearson patted the man on the back, rejoined Adam, and exited the room.

FORTY-NINE

WITH SIRENS BLARING, PEARSON PRESSED THE limit as the SUV zoomed along Route 54. Neither he nor Adam could predict what they'd stumble upon. With every available constable within a fifty-kilometer radius racing to the scene, all they could do was pray for a peaceful end to a tumultuous week.

Amongst all the chaos surrounding him, the last thing Adam needed was anything else on his plate. Then his phone rang. There was no need to check the caller ID, yet he did it anyway.

Christian Anderson.

"Someone can't live without me." A wide smile appeared on his face, and he tapped the screen before lifting it to his ear. Skipping the small talk, Adam dove right in on the one burning question. "Where are you?"

"In Miller's car."

"Why? Jesus, Christian. Didn't almost dying teach you anything?"

"It showed me I need to be there more for my family. For my friends. If Pops and Gemma are there, they'll want me there when you rescue them."

Adam glanced over at Pearson, who eavesdropped on their conversation. "Put him on speaker."

The quiet car soon filled with Christian's rambling voice. Pearson interrupted. "Christian, stop."

Christian's voice trembled before trailing off, leaving only an awkward silence.

"What have I been repeating since we saved you from that hellhole prison?"

There wasn't a response; instead, only Christian's shallow breathing confirmed he was still on the line.

Pearson banged his hands against the steering wheel, and Adam slid away. "I knew this was going to happen. I just knew it. I should have made them haul your stubborn ass off to the hospital. At least if you were there, I could focus more on the case and less on you."

Christian remained speechless. And before Pearson could inflict any more damage with his sharp tongue, Adam interjected. "Christian? You still with us?"

"Yeah." There was dejection behind that single word. Christian paused for a few seconds to steady his fluctuating voice. "Look, I know I shouldn't come . . . but my pops needs me. Gemma needs me. And even though neither of you will ever admit it, you guys need me."

The anguish in Christian's voice forced Pearson to reconsider his hostile attitude. Matthias and Gemma would indeed want to see his face when, and if, everything had a happy ending.

"You promise you'll stay in the car?" Pearson asked.

"I promise. And for the record, it's not that I don't want to get in there and kick some ass; it's that I'm in no shape whatsoever to do so."

"Wait, did Christian Anderson admit he can't do something? Did almost dying a second time break through that wall of invincibility?"

"Not cute," Christian said.

"Do you even know where you're heading?" Pearson asked.

"I have the coordinates Miller gave me. I'll see you there."

Fifteen kilometers down the two-lane, desolate highway linking Cedar Lake with the many lakes in the area, a tower of black smoke and helicopter hovered over the dense forest.

Adam rubbed his hands together. This had to be it—the end. There wasn't another option.

Pearson glanced over. "You all right over there? You're awful quiet."

"Just thinking."

"About?"

"Wishing this was all some demented nightmare, but I know it can't be."

"It'll be over soon."

"I hope so, at least for Matthias and Gemma's sakes."

He rubbed his hands harder. "There's something else on your mind."

"Christian."

"He'll be fine. They'll be fine. We're going to bring everyone out alive. You trust me, right?"

Adam rested his hands under his thighs. "Yeah. I mean, after everything we've been through, how could I not trust you with my life? But that's not what has me concerned."

"Then what?"

"What if we're walking into a trap? Or worse, what if we're too late?"

Pearson shook his head. "She has a plan, but we have one thing working in our favor: more bodies armed with weapons."

He hung a sharp right turn onto a gravel country road. With each pothole Pearson hit, the car shook. Adam reached up for the handle as the turbulence bounced him around like a rag doll.

Two minutes passed since the turn, and to their right, a rotted fence appeared along the roadside. The closer they got, a beat-up, wooden sign appeared.

Sunset Forestry Group.

Pearson braked hard and turned the wheel, barely missing the pull-off area. Thanks to the loose gravel beneath the tires, the car barely skidded to a stop. Pearson swerved to miss smashing into the back of the parked fire truck from a nearby village.

"Shit," Adam exclaimed.

Pearson ignored his wimpy outburst and stared straight ahead at the charred carcass of metal and rubber. "That'll get your adrenaline pumping."

Without cutting the engine, he flung open the door. Pearson gazed at three firefighters standing around bullshitting, two of them with cigarettes hanging from their lips. They must have somehow missed the ruckus since it wasn't until he slammed the door that their eyes shifted his direction. Their jovial mood ceased on the spot.

"Which of you are in charge?" Pearson asked, pointing his finger at each of them.

It didn't take long before a thirty-something man with soot covering his face to step forward. He removed his helmet and tucked it under his armpit. "That'd be me. Who's asking?"

Dressed the part of an RCMP constable, Pearson still pulled out his credentials and flashed them. "Constable Pearson from the Cedar Lake detachment. This is DS Prescott from the Regina Police Service. Can you tell me how long ago the fire started?"

"Thirty, er, forty minutes ago. Chopper called it in," he said. "Strange though, I didn't request police back-up."

"You didn't have to. Someone else did it for you. Have you seen the occupants in the area?"

The man glanced over his shoulder at his two colleagues and back at Pearson. "No, sir. Ain't seen anybody since we arrived. Why?"

"Any idea who the car belongs to?"

The man shrugged. "You sure are asking a lot of questions for a simple car fire."

"Did you run the plates?"

"No plates to run," he said, stepping aside.

Pearson approached the rear of the vehicle and scanned the bumper. *He's right. No plates.*

"You gonna tell me why you're here asking all these questions?"

319

Pearson tugged at his tight collar and barked back. "This car might belong to a person of interest in the murder of two people up in Cedar Lake. She's armed, dangerous, and is holding two hostages. Any other questions?"

With each step Pearson took closer, the firefighter backed up. He fell back in line with his colleagues and stuttered. "I . . . I had no idea. What can I do to help?"

"I need the VIN number. You *can* manage that much, can't you?"

Without haste, the man rushed towards the front of the vehicle and pulled out a pocket notebook and pen from his turnout gear. Engrossed in watching the man, Adam snuck up next to Pearson. "God, I hate small towns."

Pearson jerked. But before Pearson could catch his breath and defend the positive qualities of living in one, the shrill of sirens sidetracked his flow. It wasn't long before two more RCMP vehicles skidded in.

"At least this time we got back-up," Pearson managed to get out.

The fire guy arrived back and tore the paper from the metal coils. An annoyed Pearson snatched it from the man's hand. "Thanks. Prescott, keep an eye on them."

Pearson returned to the SUV and typed the seventeen alpha-numeric characters into the vehicle registration database. It didn't take but a few seconds for a hit to return.

What popped up on the screen came as no surprise. *Joanna Carmack.*

"Anything?" Adam asked.

Pearson stepped back and scanned the area. The two new constables waited near their vehicles. "It's her."

"She clearly wanted us to find her. Do you believe Lee?"

His head bobbed. "She's planning something. And now, more than ever, we have to stay vigilant to any traps she's set up along the way."

"That's why we have them," he said.

The pointing must have caught their attention, and the two officers approached the SUV. A younger, shorter constable asked, "Constable Pearson?"

"Yeah?"

"I'm Constable Greene, and this is Constable Sweeney. We're from The Battlefords detachment."

"The Battlefords? Damn, you guys got here quick."

"Open highway, blaring sirens; that helps. So, what do we know? Radio call said something about hostages."

Pearson nodded. "As far as we know, two hostages and one abductor. You know anything about this place?"

Constable Sweeney nodded and stepped out from behind Constable Greene. "Was owned by Russell Erickson."

"Was?" Adam asked.

"Guy did a nosedive from the Yellowhead Highway bridge. Splat. Took a few days, but a couple of hikers found his washed-up body about ten kilometers downstream from where he jumped."

"Damn. Why?"

"Why what?"

"Did he kill himself?"

"Time is running out, so I'll give you the short version. This place used to be the most profitable forestry operation in the area. Then the protests started, the money began to dry up, and we all know what happens when people get desperate for money."

"Usually involves shady dealings."

"Bingo. Mr. Erickson found himself wrapped up in a lot of illegal shit. Wire fraud, forgery, the list goes on."

"And these shady characters wouldn't happen to be from Cedar Lake, would they?"

"You know a guy, Lee White?"

Pearson and Adam nodded their heads.

"Yeah, he's been on our radar, along with two others, for a while now."

"I hate to ask, but their names don't happen to be Chad and David Ross, do they?"

"David Ross, sure, he's in on it. But the other guy is Peter Grant. He been on your radar?"

Then it hit Adam. Joanna didn't choose this place at random; she picked it because it was familiar, somewhere she could have an advantage over the RCMP.

Adam turned to Pearson and said, "We're screwed."

"Nah, you're in luck. I've spent a lot of time in these woods. Between the bunkers, abandoned living quarters, and dense forestry, the places to hide are endless."

"That's not what I mean, but don't let me stop your flow."

"If I were holding someone hostage, I'd hide them in one of the underground bunkers. They're concealed, easy to miss if you don't know where to look."

Pearson opened his mouth. But the words never had a chance to cross his lips. The pinging of gravel bouncing against metal and a revving engine filled the air. He turned his head as another vehicle slid in behind his SUV. It didn't take long to distinguish who was behind the wheel—Christian.

"Hang tight, guys. We have more back-up on the way."

Pearson strolled towards the back of the SUV and intercepted a panicky Christian as he raced towards him.

"Have you found them?" Christian asked, out of breath.

"Whoa. Whoa. What's the rush?"

Christian ran right into Pearson's arms, which extended beyond his broad chest. He stopped, bent forward, and rested his hands on his knees. "Where are they?"

Adam crouched next to his husband, and they locked eyes. "We haven't even started looking yet. But the burned-out car is Joanna's, so that's a starting point."

Christian kept to his word and didn't dare push the agreed-upon boundaries. Instead, he stretched his arms and dropped them to his side. "Okay."

Pearson loomed over his weakened friend and smiled. "You *are* keeping your word."

Christian gazed up. "I said I would. I'll wait here, but all I ask is you keep me updated on what's happening."

"I will. There are more constables on the way, but we're going to get moving if we have any chance of finding them before dark."

"I'll send them your direction."

As Pearson and Adam walked away, Christian hollered out. "Be careful."

Adam flashed the smile that melted Christian's heart years ago. And before he knew it, the four of them disappeared behind the wooden fence that surrounded the property.

FIFTY

THEY TRAIPSED ALONG THE RUGGED PATH, their awareness in overdrive. Constables Greene and Sweeney held a significant lead, in no part thanks to Adam checking over his shoulder every five seconds.

As he turned his head forward for the umpteenth time, his heart stuttered, and he froze as he watched as the darkness of the forest swallowed Greene and Sweeney.

He forced the hard lump in his throat down, but the adrenaline coursing through his veins had dried up every ounce of saliva remaining.

Adam stopped, bent forward, and rested his palms against his knees. He widened his nostrils and sucked in the fresh, moist air. His eyes darted upward as Pearson carried forward, somehow unaware he had stopped.

He glanced back down, shook his head, and took a couple deeper breaths. A voice interrupted his meditative state. "Are you coming?

Between gasps for air, he lifted one index finger and extended it upward. "Hold up."

Pearson folded his arms across his chest and his left foot tapped in rapid succession against the dirt. "Don't tell me . . . the spooky woods are a problem for you?"

Adam shook his head. "What? No. It's just . . . shouldn't we wait for more back-up?"

Pearson extended his arm and tapped at his watch. "Man, time's running out."

"I know. I know."

"We have two choices: we can turn back and wait for back-up, which could be hours, or we press on. Your choice."

Adam mulled over the cut-and-dry options. He closed his eyes, and a faded image of Christian sitting on the hood of the car appeared. His husband had already lived most of his life without a mother, and the last thing Adam wanted was for Christian to live out the rest of his life as an orphan. That was all the motivation he needed to gear himself up for the battle that lay ahead.

"Let's go."

They sprinted down the path, but with each stride, the items on Pearson's duty belt clanked against his body.

"Wait," Adam said.

"What now?"

Adam pointed at Pearson's waist. "Your belt."

"What about it?"

"You do know what incognito means, yeah?"

Pearson paused and cocked his head upward as if trying to search through his head for the right answer.

"It means to avoid being noticed in layperson's terms. Right now, with your noisy ass clanking along, you're anything but."

"So, what, we walk now?"

"Yeah. We'll catch up with those two at some point. But let's not alert the entire forest you're here."

"Gotcha."

They continued along the path. The air was still and motionless, and the temperature had dropped at least ten degrees the further they ventured in. Pearson broke his silence. "Let's use our time wisely."

"We could start by admitting we focused on the wrong suspects."

"Nah, they're all involved. Each one to a certain degree," Pearson replied. "But I would have never suspected Peter Grant, well, not until we found Heather hanging from the banister."

Adam nodded. "And we listened to rumors instead of hunting him down. Always suspect the husband, no matter what people try to convince you of."

"Rule number one: The husband's always the prime suspect—always."

Adam recalled what Sweeney said earlier. "That Erickson guy, you believe he's tied to Joanna?"

A shrug and grin graced Pearson's face. "He's tied to the others, so yeah, makes sense he's involved with her."

"And I never did get a straight answer from Lee about who the guy was who killed Lindsay Ross. Is it possible this Peter guy did it?"

"Anything's possible. But I don't even know if they knew each other back in those days. Peter graduated two years before Lindsay; he was older—"

Adam interrupted. "Yeah, but has he always lived in the area?"

"Call Christian, give him something to research while he waits."

Adam dug into his jeans pocket and pulled out his phone. "Siri, call Christian."

The phone rang twice, and Christian answered. "That was quick."

Adam stopped, completed a three-sixty turn while keeping a lookout for any movement between the trees. "Nothing yet. I do need a favor, though."

"Yeah, what's up?"

"How well do you remember a guy named Peter Grant from back in the day?"

"I knew of him, but we weren't friends if that's what you're asking."

"What kind of guy was he?"

"Quiet. Reserved. Smart. Why are you asking about Peter?"

"Was he living in Cedar Lake when Lindsay was murdered?"

There was a brief pause. "No. Peter was living in BC."

"Damn, there goes that theory."

"Wait, I wasn't finished. He didn't live here but was back the week before prom."

"Are you sure?"

"Sure, I'm sure. I remember seeing him wandering the halls one day waiting for Heather. He gave me a half-wave, smirked like the jackass he was, and breezed past Gemma and me."

"And he's still missing, right?"

"Yeah? What's going on?"

"It was something Constable Sweeney said."

"Spit it out, Adam."

"The owner of this property, before he killed himself, was mixed up with Lee, David Ross, and one Peter Grant."

"Huh? If that's the case, then . . ."

"Then we've been looking at all the wrong suspects this whole time. Stop him. Taylor wasn't referring to Lee, David, or Lowry. It's been Peter this entire time."

"But why? Why would he murder Lindsay?"

"You said Joanna told you she was running the show, yeah?"

"Right."

"Do you think she wouldn't say that to take the heat off Peter?"

"Well, sure, she could have said anything, and I'd have taken it at face value."

"They were never going to kill you. They kidnapped you to throw our trail away from Peter. Change of plans."

"Okay."

"Get back to Cedar Lake—"

Christian, as always, interrupted. "What? No. I'm staying—"

"You're doing it again, Christian. I need you to link up with Miller and DS Clark. I want everything you can dig up on Peter. Phone pings. Text messages. Phone calls. Bank transactions."

"That'll take too long."

"Come on, Christian, think about it."

"About what?"

Adam sighed. "Remember that little thing called the Missing Persons Act? I'll phone ahead and have Miller put together the application."

"Then why do they need me? I should wait here."

"No. I need you to make sure this happens. By now, Peter has a two-day lead on us. And as much as I respect Constable Miller, he'll never be as good as you are at making things happen."

That's all it typically took for Adam to get his way. Sprinkle a few well-placed compliments, and he had Christian ready to do whatever it took to get things done.

"Right. Yeah, I'm on my way back."

"Hey," Adam said.

"Yeah?"

"Are those firefighters still hanging around?"

There was a pause. "Um, yeah, yeah, they're lingering by the car."

"There's more backup on the way, so do me a favor, and tell them to stay put so they'll know where to go."

***

AFTER ENDING THE CALL, ADAM JOGGED ahead past Pearson. It wasn't long before he caught up with Constables Greene and Sweeney. Adam waved his hands, and they froze when they caught sight of him.

"What happened to you two?" Greene asked.

"Long story. Look, we've been going about this all wrong."

The two constables exchanged puzzled glances. "Come again?"

"Are there hostages here? Yes. Is the person holding them captive the mastermind behind everything? No."

Pearson strolled up, and Greene glanced in his direction. "What's he talking about?"

Puzzled himself, Pearson shrugged. "Not sure, but let him finish."

Adam carried on. "It didn't hit me until you said a name. A name none of us batted an eye at . . . until now."

"David Ross?"

"No, not Ross—Peter Grant."

"He's small time. David Ross is the one you want."

"From the moment I stepped foot in this town, I was adamant David Ross was behind his daughter's death. Shady business dealings, extravagant lifestyle, and he gave off an uncomfortable vibe. He fit the typical profile of either a drug dealer or a con man."

"That's great, but right now, our primary mission is to rescue the hostages. So, why are we even discussing this?"

"Because. This is all a distraction to buy the real mastermind more time."

"I don't know, Peter Grant doesn't fit the profile at all," Sweeney said.

"Forget all those years of training. The countless hours our superiors drilled into our heads that only people who display certain indicators are guilty."

Only three blank stares gazed back at Adam.

"Let me put this another way. If *you* were running an illegal criminal enterprise, would you put your mastermind out on display?"

"Can't really say," Greene replied. "A lot to consider."

"Not really. You always put your dodgy characters, the tough guys, the ones nobody messes with on display for cover."

"What you're saying is, they fooled us into believing Lee or David were running the whole thing."

"And we're back on the same page," Adam said. "Now, here's another wrench. Joanna inserts herself. She kidnapped Christian, fills his head full of lies, and for what? To make us believe she and Mayor Martin were calling the shots. The sad reality: they're both just pawns."

"Let's say your hunch is right, and Peter is on the run; what are *we* going to do about it?"

"Two steps ahead of you. Christian is on his way back to Cedar Lake, and I've got Miller working on getting a warrant for Peter's records."

"Excellent. Then I guess that means there's only one thing left for us to do here," Pearson said.

***

THE FOUR MEN TREKKED FURTHER INTO the woods than they expected. Twenty-five minutes had passed since Adam sent Christian back to Cedar Lake.

Hopefully, he's almost back.

A few hundred feet ahead of them, the path split. One veered to the right, the other to the left. The shafts of sunlight pierced through the thick canopy above. If Adam wasn't so focused on rescuing his husbands' father, he would have taken more time to appreciate the beauty. But there was no time. He had to keep focused on the mission.

Adam took a few steps forward. As he scanned the moist soil, he found the first signs of human activity since leaving the burned-out remnants of Joanna's vehicle. Footprints.

Adam yanked up a pant leg and got closer. His eyes shifted from one tread to the next. In all, he counted five distinct designs, all moving in a uniform pattern towards the right path—the same one which led to a clearing in the dense trees.

"We're getting closer," he said as he stood.

"Of course, they chose the furthest bunker."

"How far?" Pearson asked.

Sweeney pointed. "Four or five hundred feet that way."

"Lead the way," Pearson said.

The hike took only minutes, and soon they all stood around a rusted-out iron door in the middle of the forest. Adam stared at the wheel, questioning himself if there had been a mistake. He glanced at Constable Sweeney's face.

"You sure about this?"

"No. But you found the footprints, and this is the closest one."

"For Christ's sake, Adam, let's just get down there and check it out," Pearson said. He reached out and gripped the wheel. What Adam expected to take forever took mere minutes. Someone had used it recently.

The hatch opened, and a pungent blast of mildew slapped them in the face. Adam sucked in his breath and held it.

"Deserted for two years, you said, yeah?"

Sweeney nodded. "Yup."

Waving the stench away, Adam replied. "Smells longer."

Pearson retrieved his flashlight and aimed the beam into the hole in the ground. This wasn't like any bunker Adam had ever experienced before. Instead of the typical iron-wrought ladder, a set of stairs descended three meters and spit you into a long, dark corridor.

Adam stepped onto the first tread and turned back. "Well, this is it. You ready?"

"As I'll ever be."

And like that, unsure of what awaited them, Pearson and Adam vanished into the belly of the earth.

FIFTY-ONE

A FAINT LIGHT AT THE END of the corridor caught their attention, and they inched closer.

"This is the place," Adam said as he followed in Pearson's tracks.

"Yup."

A single gunshot pierced through the corridor, and both Adam and Pearson slammed their backs against the cinderblock wall.

"Shit," Adam shouted and slammed his back against the wall. "You hit?"

"I'm good. You?"

"Nah, I'm okay."

"Should have seen that coming," Pearson mumbled under his breath.

"What's our plan? Storm the place and pray for no bloodshed—"

Pearson raised his finger to his lips and crept closer to the corner. He moved like a puma hunting its prey, doing whatever it took to keep a safe distance between himself and the trigger-happy Joanna.

Adam hung back and kept his eyes on Pearson. Then Pearson took a play out of the SWAT handbook.

"I know you're in there, Joanna. It's over. Constables are swarming all around this place."

Joanna didn't reply, but her silence didn't stop Pearson from continuing his dramatic plea. "This will go a whole lot better if you release the hostages. We'll work this out."

But as another bullet ricocheted off the ground, and Pearson retreated, it was clear that if Joanna was going down, she was hell-bent on taking everyone else down with her.

Adam's heart slammed against his chest. The adrenaline kicked up a notch, and he leaned closer to Pearson.

"Now what?"

"She wants to play rough; I can play rougher."

This was the situation Adam hoped wouldn't happen. Bloodshed.

"So? Were you able to make out anything?"

Pearson nodded. "Four people. Matthias, Angela, Joanna, and—" his voice faded away.

"And?"

Pearson hesitated. "And . . . Chad Ross."

"Chad? Christ, this keeps getting better and better. And Gemma?"

Pearson shook his head.

"Shit. Do they even have her?"

Pearson downplayed the severity of the situation with a simple shrug. "I'm just as lost as you are, buddy."

Adam loathed the disturbing thoughts filling his head, yet they always did. Expect the worst, and hope for the best. This was the mantra embedded in his DNA. "All right, smart guy. What's the next move?"

Pearson pointed towards the stairs. "For starters, we need Greene and Sweeney down here."

"And then what?"

"Then . . . I'm going in."

Adam's eyes widened, and his jaw drooped. He swayed his head back and forth. "Hell no. Way too risky."

"I have a plan, trust me."

"Is it one that doesn't involve getting us killed?"

"I said, trust me. I'll go in, set my gun down on the ground. They're predictable. Chad will rush over, retrieve it, and frisk me."

"So weaponless, brilliant plan. Where do the three of us fit into this?"

"I'm getting there. While Chad's doing all that, the three of you burst in and focus on Joanna. She's in the right corner of the room."

"Luke, I—"

"How's your shot?"

"My shot?"

"How d'you do on your last qualifying at the range?"

"Uh, perfect score. Why?"

"You'll need it with her."

"Anything else?"

"Matthias and Angela are tied to two chairs, and Joanna is standing behind them. Aim up, not down."

The realization that he might need to shoot her sent a chill down Adam's spine. Not once since he joined the police force had he ever discharged his weapon. This wasn't how he pictured his first time being.

You can do this. Just breathe.

His internal pep talk ended abruptly.

Adam flinched as Pearson grabbed his arm and shook hard. "Prescott! Do you understand?"

"Yeah, aim up, not down. Got it."

Pearson released his grip and stepped back. "Good. Let's make it happen."

***

AS PLANNED, PEARSON INCHED TOWARDS THE dim room at the end of the passage. He glanced over his shoulder back at Adam. With a smirk painted across his face, Pearson extended his thumb and shouted around the corner. "I'm coming in. I'm unarmed, and I just want to talk."

There was no reply, but more importantly, no more bullets flew. Confident, Pearson faded into the darkness while Adam huddled with Greene and Sweeney.

"Remember, right corner of the room. Pearson can handle the male suspect; we need to keep an eye on the female."

"Got it."

"And guys, no shots unless necessary."

Like planned, Adam waited for a little over a minute before he advanced towards the ninety-degree bend. He kept his back pressed against the wall, and Greene and Sweeney were two steps behind. He extended his head to get a better overview of the room. It was just as Pearson explained. Joanna hovered over the two hostages, and Chad frisked Pearson in the middle of the room.

He retreated out of sight, took a deep breath, and extended his hand. He raised three fingers, and with each passing second, one finger dropped. Finally, at the end of the countdown, he shook his fist, and the three constables barreled into the room.

"Police. Keep your hands where we can see them."

Adam aimed his gun and swiveled it back and forth. Time slowed, like being stuck in a nightmare. The kind you can't shake yourself awake from. Except this was far from fantasy; this was real life.

From the corner of his eye, Adam spotted Joanna hovering over Matthias and Angela. Someone had roughed them up, but it was better than the alternative—however, the who and why weren't his primary concern at that moment. The barrel of the gun aimed at his chest took a much higher priority.

He shouted, "Drop the weapon."

His order went unheeded. He yelled out again, "I said, drop the weapon. No one has to die here today."

His hands shook, but somehow, he buried his nerves and kept his eyes trained on Joanna's hands. They were callused, and rings of blood lined her nail beds.

Anxiety's a bitch.

Joanna scrunched her eyes tighter, and her lips curled upward. She had those psychotic eyes, the ones you could study and know something evil was about to occur. It happened in a millisecond. Her finger twitched over the trigger. His eyes widened, and he didn't hesitate.

Pop. Pop.

Two rounds hit her square in the chest, and her body flew back. But her warpath was far from over. Before she collapsed to the floor, her finger pressed against the trigger. An unaimed projectile exploded from the end of the barrel. Adam followed the visible trajectory and watched as Pearson fell to the ground as he clutched his shoulder. He released a scream, unlike anything Adam had experienced before. Still, he couldn't let it distract him, not until he knew for sure Joanna posed no more danger.

He turned his head back towards her and took two steps forward. She had landed on her back with her head tilted to the side. He took two more steps. The dribble of blood seeping from the corner of her mouth and fixed eyes told him one thing: Joanna Carmack was dead.

Adam pushed out the breath he'd held in. The once delayed sense of time returned to normal before Adam's eyes. As he twisted his head towards the other side of the room, Constables Greene and Sweeney had Chad Ross tackled to the ground and were just slapping the cuffs on. The giant didn't squirm. In fact, he gave up easier than Adam expected.

"Where's the girl?" Adam overheard Sweeney ask.

"Who?"

"The girl from Regina. Where is she?"

"I don't know. I swear. She's isn't here."

Pearson moaned in agony, and Adam rushed to his side. "Let me see."

He pulled Pearson's hand away and stretched his sleeve to have a better look at the damage inflicted. "It's a through and through."

Pearson clenched his teeth and winced. "Doesn't make it any less painful."

"I'll get help." He reached into his pocket and slipped out his phone.

NO SERVICE.

"Shit." He paced and ran his fingers through his hair. "Can you walk?"

Pearson winced. "Do I have a choice?"

Adam crouched and gripped Pearson's face. "Can you walk? This isn't a game, Luke."

"Says the guy who believed he'd magically get cell phone service underground. Yeah, I can walk. Geez, not even a little sympathy."

Adam relaxed his shoulders and bent his neck. "Don't turn into Christian. Besides, I've seen worse."

With Chad Ross in custody, Sweeney and Greene led the way along the dark corridor. Once they reached the surface and out of the mildew-infested bunker, the sweet fragrance of pine infiltrated Adam's nostrils.

"All in a day's work," he said under his breath.

FIFTY-TWO

THIRTY MINUTES EARLIER, BACK IN CEDAR LAKE, Christian rested his head against Pearson's desk, as the room was abuzz concerning their prime suspect: Peter Grant. After enduring forty minutes on the phone with SaskTel, only the agonizing wait stood between putting an end to this nightmare.

"If you were wanted by the police, where would you retreat?" Miller asked.

"As far away as possible," said another constable.

"No, he's close," Miller said. "He grew up here. He's comfortable here."

"Yeah, but didn't he live in Vancouver for a few years?"

"Christian?" Miller asked.

Christian raised his head and turned. "Huh?"

"Do you think Peter is close or on the run?"

"He hasn't been seen in days. But something tells me he's close. I can't put my finger on it, but surely he'd have to be near to keeps tabs on everything."

"But?"

"But it's also possible he slipped away before we even considered him a suspect."

"What about his house?" Miller asked.

"It's a crime scene, so, doubtful."

"The pharmacy?" DS Clark asked.

"Too obvious."

"Yeah, right. But when was the last time anyone checked?"

The room fell silent, and Christian rested his head against his forearms as the chatter continued in the background. He needed something, anything that would lead them to Peter's whereabouts.

Then a chime blared from the speakers. Was this it? Was this something he needed? He glanced up at the one unread message in his inbox.

SaskTel.

He straightened his posture and double-clicked the message. His eyes scanned through the legal jargon, but the attachment was more important to him at that very moment. It was twenty-four hours' worth of cell phone pings for Peter's mobile phone.

Between 5 p.m. yesterday and noon today, Peter had pinged six times. Each ping used the cell tower located near the elementary school, but the company provided more. They also provided the coordinates of the phone's probable location.

Christian opened his browser, typed in the latitude and longitude, and waited for the map to sharpen. The red pin on the map left him with more questions than answers. *Is this another ruse, or could Peter be there?*

There was only one way for Christian to find out.

He jolted from the chair: "I'll be damned. He *is* at the pharmacy."

Everyone in the room eyeballed him, but no mouths moved.

"Did anyone hear me? Peter Grant is holed up at the pharmacy."

Constable Miller shifted in his seat and spoke. "Are you sure?"

"Cell phone data doesn't lie. I haven't been to the pharmacy in two days, have you?"

Miller glanced around the room. "No."

"So then why couldn't he be there? They've had us running in so many directions, it'd be the easiest and most familiar place for him to be. Now, unless anyone in this room has a better theory . . ."

Minutes ticked by, but Christian grew impatient at the room full of blank stares. "Tell you what. Just appease me, and let's check out the pharmacy. We got nothing to lose but plenty to gain."

Miller stood and turned to the team from Saskatoon. "I'm with Christian. Just because it's obvious doesn't make it wrong. Stranger things have happened."

"And if he's wrong?"

Christian despised people talking around him, so he interjected. "If *I'm* wrong, then it'll be a quick trip and one more place we can cross off the list."

***

THREE VEHICLES SWARMED THE NONDESCRIPT BUILDING at the corner of First Avenue and Second Street. Christian flung open his door, aimed his weapon towards the front doors with one hand, and dialed the pharmacy with the other. The phone rang and rang, but no one ever picked up.

Constable Miller pleaded over the loudspeaker, but again, the same: no response.

Christian shoved his cell back into his pants pocket and shouted to Miller. "I'm going in."

"But . . . you promised."

"I did, but between us, who has more experience? Me or you?"

Miller huffed. "You."

"You can blame everything on me later. Wouldn't be the first time I've taken the heat."

"You better believe—if shit hits the fan—this is all on you."

Christian nodded. "Ten minutes. If I'm not out by then—storm the place."

"Anderson, are you sure?"

"You got a better idea? It's now or never."

Miller peeled the Velcro strips from his Kevlar vest and slid his head through the opening. "I can't stop you, but I'll be damned if I'm letting you go in there unprotected."

He tossed the heavy body armor over the center console, and it crashed against the passenger seat. Christian slid his head through the vest, and as he fastened the last strap, Miller spoke. "And Anderson?"

"Yeah?"

"Ten minutes. That's it, or we're coming in. And my motto: Shoot first, ask questions later."

"Got it."

With stealth in his step, Christian advanced towards the front door. The storefront was dark and empty of customers. From the corner of his eye, Christian noticed a small crowd congregating. He shook his head and reached for the door handle.

The door gave with no resistance, and Christian's arm hairs stood on end. *He's here.*

He slid through the gap into the building. The soft melody of new-age music filled the store as if today were like any other. But nothing about this was normal.

"Peter?" His voice echoed off the walls. "It's Christian Anderson. I just want to talk."

He crept closer to the half-open door beside the pharmacy counter. The same one that Pearson and Miller used to access the backroom when they served the warrant.

He gripped his weapon and used the muzzle to open the door.

Clear.

He stepped into the small vestibule with two closed doors: one straight ahead and another to his right.

Which one?

His eyes darted between the doors, but he remembered Heather's position that morning. Her head never turned right.

Straight ahead.

He approached and twisted the door handle. It popped open with force, and Christian jumped back, expecting an ambush. But it wasn't.

He metered his breathing and mustered up one of his favorite words. "Shit."

He hesitated outside the door. The sweat from his palms loosened his grip on the gun, and one by one, he wiped them against the front of his jeans.

"Peter. I know you're here. Let's just make this easy for once, yeah?"

However, Christian received no reply. In fact, the building was void of any signs of life. And this sensation only added fuel to his already over-exaggerated nerves.

He inhaled and held the air deep in his lungs for a few seconds. When he exhaled, he grabbed the wooden edge of the door and yanked. Expecting a hail of bullets, he slammed his back against the door jamb, but to his amazement, zilch.

He moved forward into the chaotic room with a flashlight in one hand and the gun in the other. The light swept past the desk, and Christian found the back of the desk chair facing the door.

"Peter, if you're messing with me, it's not cool. Turn around so we can talk this out."

And it didn't take long before the chair spun, and a familiar face appeared. It was Peter. His right leg rested on top of his left, and his fingers formed a pyramid shape near his face. "Hello, Christian."

"Where's the weapon?"

"No weapon. I've just been patiently waiting for you to catch up. And here you are."

"Stand up and put your hands behind your head," Christian ordered.

But Peter remained seated. "Come on, Christian, you don't think I've been waiting here to give up that easily, do you?"

"You have about seven minutes before they storm the place."

"Then you better ask quick questions."

"Why'd you do all of this? You tossed your entire life in the toilet, and for what?"

"Opportunity."

"I don't understand."

"Sure, you don't; it's not like we were ever friends. But, like everybody in this town, I'm sure you know my story?"

Christian nodded. "You grew up in a broken home. It was just you and your dad; your mother split early. That's probably why your father spent most of his time chasing away his blues in the bottom of a bottle."

"Hmm, sounds familiar, doesn't it?" Peter asked.

Christian didn't confirm his observation. "I know your life changed when you started dating Heather. You went from a nobody to somebody overnight. You two moved to Vancouver, graduated, and came back to Cedar Lake to run the pharmacy. I still don't understand why you murdered Lindsay and Heather, though."

Peter leaned back in the chair. "You know, Christian, you and I are so much alike. Both from broken homes, both of us spending years living in the shadows."

"Yeah, with one glaring difference: I've never murdered anybody."

"Not yet, at least. I've done some digging on you. Decorated constable, one of the youngest promoted to detective sergeant, you even solved Cassidy's murder and found your mother."

"Yeah, so? Speaking of Cassidy, were you involved in the prostitution ring? The blackmailing?"

Christian watched as a grin stretch across his pale face. "All my idea."

"Funny, Joanna claimed credit for it."

Peter slammed his hand against the desk. "I recruited her, she recruited Lee, and he recruited the rest. But it was me who called the shots."

"Then why would Joanna claim she did it, because she wanted the land that was stolen from her family back?"

Peter released a soft chuckle under his breath. "She's not lying. She did, but that side gig came up much later."

"How'd a kid from the wrong side of the tracks devise such a scheme?"

"The truth; I hated my life. Living in the slums, watching my dad drink himself into a stupor every damn day. That's not a life. That's misery. And Lindsay and Chad, always flaunting their money all over town like it didn't matter. It does matter. It matters to people like my family."

"I get it. You wanted the lifestyle they had."

"Who doesn't? I wanted to be powerful, but to get there, I needed money. Lots and lots of it."

"But the way you went about it, it's just wrong. I wanted money too, but I chose to invest in hard work instead," Christian said.

"You don't think blackmailing all those people was hard work? I invested a lot of time, sweat, tears. But in the end, I got what I wanted."

"And now you'll get life."

"Doubtful. But you're not back in this shitty town because you want to know the ins-and-outs of running a criminal empire. You came back because of what that traitor Taylor confessed to Gemma."

He nodded. "Yeah, so let's talk about that."

"Sure, because once they arrest me, I'm done talking. So, take a seat."

He shook his head and kept his back close to the door. "No, thanks, I'm comfortable standing."

"Suit yourself. Well, ask away."

"Why d'you murder Lindsay? Did she threaten to unravel your plans?"

"Eh, something like that. I know you love fooling yourself into believing your precious Lindsay was some pinnacle of morality. Am I right?"

"She did what she did to get to the truth."

"Ah, and you really believe that?"

Christian nodded.

"Then you're even more gullible than I thought. Lindsay did all sorts of shit you had no clue about."

"Like?"

"Like, for starters, I bet she never told you that she and I were sleeping together before I met Heather."

Christian kept his composure. "Excuse me?"

"More than once, I should add. I tried to make Lindsay my first target, but she caught on too quick."

"And she threatened to go to the cops?"

"Nah, more like she wanted in on it. She needed money to get as far away from here as she could. Just like I wanted."

"I don't believe you. Lindsay wasn't about that life. Her life was about exposing the truth."

"Sure, but that was after we broke things off, and Heather entered the picture. But the thing about conspiracies: you're just as guilty as everyone else involved. If she went to the cops, she'd only implicate herself, and she'd kiss her future goodbye."

"But she made a choice to go rogue anyway?"

"Ungrateful tramp. Should have just kept her mouth shut, left for Regina, and she'd still be alive today. But, oh no, she couldn't keep her damn nose out of my business. Sneaking around town with that camcorder. Asking too many questions."

"How'd you find out?"

"My one faithful soldier: her brother. He worked for me too, but then again, you already knew that."

Christian glanced at his watch. Four minutes remained. "Yup. So you killed her to stop her from going to the police? That's it?"

"That's it. Not the grand finale you expected, huh?"

"Four minutes, Peter. Who helped with her murder? Chad? Lowry? Lee White?"

He shook his head and lifted one hand in the air. "I did it all on my own."

"Impossible. It'd take more than just you to stage a suicide."

"Why? Because you think I'm weak? I'm not. But your sweet Lindsay was. She believed every word I said and came running back into my arms with all her sentimental bullshit."

"And then what? You drugged her?"

"Later, yeah. We shared a bottle of wine, fed her every lame line to convince her I was serious about starting over."

Christian grimaced. "That's how you got the Diazepam into her system."

"Shit works wonders . . . in large enough doses. Anyway, wasn't long before she passed out. I kneeled next to her. That voice in my head kept telling me to think about my future. Don't let a snitch ruin everything in your life. That's when I wrapped my hands around her neck and slowly squeezed the life out of her."

"You're a psychopath. You know that?"

He lurched forward, and his beady eyes locked onto Christian's. "There's a little psychopath in all of us, you know."

"Let's assume for a second that I believe what you're saying. Why didn't she ever tell me about you guys back then? I mean, I spent almost every day with her in eleventh grade. I never saw you two talking in the halls. You never came over after school. So when would you have had the time?"

"We had plenty after hours."

"Peter, get real. Are you sure it wasn't the other way around? Hm? You were secretly in love with her, but she wasn't with you? And that night, you lured her to the sawmill and tried to make your move, but she rebuffed you?"

He slammed his hands against the desk. "She loved me. Me. And I had her wrapped around my finger until the point she decided to double-cross me."

"Sure, you have your story, but I'm sticking with my version. So before my colleagues burst in here, I have one more question."

Peter slouched in the chair. He didn't shake. His nostrils didn't flare. "Sure."

"Was it your idea or Joanna's to involve my dad in this?"

"Ah, you saved the best for last."

Christian folded his arms across his chest. "I'm not playing these games. Who picked my father and why?"

"That was also me. In fact, I've kept up with you all these years through social media, through the newspaper. You're a local hero. You save lives and have the life I only ever dreamed of. Then it dawned on me one morning; if this shit ever hits the fan, who better to battle than the local hero, Christian Anderson."

"You've . . . you've been stalking me?"

"Stalking is such a legal term. I prefer to say I've admired from afar. I suspected if what really happened to Lindsay ever got out, you'd come running back to Cedar Lake. Just like you did when Gemma's sister went missing. So, yeah, I asked Joanna to insert herself into your family."

"You're sick." The time on his watch beeped. "But you'll have all the time to get the help you need when they lock you away for life."

Peter stood from the chair, but before he could get the words out, the pressure in the room changed. "They're here."

Shouts from the sales floor diverted Christian's attention. He backed out of the room, leaving Peter with both of his hands on the desk. Then it happened. The ultimate act that Christian didn't expect.

Boom.

Christian ducked, and his head twisted back towards the desk. He watched as the gun fell from Peter's hand onto the floor. He rushed towards the desk, only to have two constables restrain him before he got a running start.

Christian watched as Miller stepped closer and shone his flashlight into Peter's face. It didn't take but a second to realize what had occurred. Suicide.

Christian followed the beam of light. Blood splattered against the photo frames and diplomas on the back wall. Christian collapsed, still in disbelief that Peter, the psycho from his past, chose the cowardly route out instead of being a real man and accepting the consequences of his actions.

A few minutes passed, and DS Clark managed to wrangle Christian onto the sales floor away from the scene. Christian struggled to collect himself, but that didn't stop Miller from dangling an evidence bag in front of him.

For Christian.

"He left you something," Miller said.

Christian stared at the innards of the bag. A jewel case containing a disc. "Where d'you find that?"

"Right on the desk. What the hell happened in there?"

"He confessed to everything. Then you guys burst in, and I turned away for only a second. He was right about his prediction."

"Which was?"

"He said 'doubtful' when I said he was going away for life."

Before Miller could continue, Christian's cell phone rang, and a familiar smile filled the screen.

He answered. "You're alive. Thank God."

"We've got 'em. We got 'em."

The tension in Christian's shoulders eased. "Thank God. How're Pop and Gemma?"

"He's dehydrated and weak, and Gemma, eh, I'll give you two guesses."

"Pissed and raging?"

"You two really are best friends."

Then came an uncomfortable pause. Christian didn't want to ask because asking made it appear as if he cared. Regardless of how it seemed, he needed the answer. "And Joanna?"

"Neutralized."

"She fought all the way 'til the end, huh?"

"Yup."

The chatter in the background seemed chaotic, almost as if Adam was hiding something.

"Is everything *really* okay there?"

Adam cleared his throat. "There is a slight issue. Now don't freak out."

"Telling me to not freak out is going to make me freak out. What is it?"

"Pearson had a mishap."

"He what?"

"I told you not to freak. He's awake and talking. The ambulance is here to get him to hospital."

"What? What happened?"

"I'll explain later."

"Joanna did something to him, didn't she?"

"Christian, do we have to do this now?"

"Yeah, we do. Tell me what's going on."

Adam paused. "As Joanna fell to the ground, her gun went off and—"

"She shot him?"

"Yeah. She shot him."

Christian kept silent.

"But she's dead and Chad Ross is in custody."

"Did you say Chad Ross?"

"He's been in on the whole thing from the start."

"Damnit, conned yet again."

"She fooled all of us. But Chad spilled his guts, confirming everything we already suspected. Joanna was never the mastermind. It was Peter, and only Peter, the entire time. Everyone else were pawns."

"Did Chad confess to who murdered his sister?"

"Not yet. But hey, don't stress, we'll get everything out of him. Once we find Peter, I'm sure we'll get to the bottom of this mess. Speaking of, did his records come in yet?"

Christian glanced over at his lifeless corpse. "You could say that."

"Okay? And? You sent Miller and the Saskatoon team out to find him, yeah?"

"Sort of. Look, he's been found, and that's what matters."

Christian's vague answer did nothing to calm Adam's nerves. Before he allowed his blood to boil over, he stopped and asked a straightforward question. "Where?"

"The pharmacy."

"Uh-huh. And you are?"

Christian paused. "At the pharmacy."

"So he's in custody?"

"Eh, sure, if you want to call it that."

"Christian, my nerves are already fraying, so answer the damn question."

Christian exhaled. "Fine. I found him."

"And he's in custody, right?"

"Well, we had a chat. But then we ran out of time."

Christian swallowed hard. The brief lull let Adam interrupt. "What are you saying? Christian. It's a simple yes or no. Is Peter Grant in custody or not?"

"Yeah. Did you ever watch westerns as a kid?"

"What . . . no. Why?"

"Well, they used to have those wanted posters. The headline was always, wanted dead or alive—"

"Oh, Jesus. He's dead—isn't he?"

"Yeah," Christian sighed. "Shot himself in the head."

"Damnit. So now we'll never know why he concocted this elaborate scheme in the first place."

Christian glanced at the evidence bag in his hand. "He confessed enough before he shot himself, but he also left behind a present for me."

"Oh?"

"It'll be the first thing you work on when you get back."

On Adam's end, the commotion continued. Except now, the voices grew more frantic. "I gotta go but don't leave the pharmacy. I'll be there as soon as I can."

"But my pop, Gemma. I need to—"

"You need to stay at the pharmacy where Miller can keep an eye on you. Trust me, your pop is fine. Gemma is fine. For once, can you make things easier on yourself?"

Christian grunted. "Yeah. I'll behave."

FIFTY-THREE

NINETY MINUTES PASSED, AND CHRISTIAN'S ANXIETY intensified, waiting for an update on Pearson. The coroner's assistant zipped up the body bag and wheeled Peter's body past him as he waited near the counter.

He bowed his head in respect, and the moment he raised his head, Adam appeared in the entrance.

"Christian?"

He glanced up and stared into his husband's eyes. His body froze, but he mumbled a 'thank God' under his breath. For the guy who was a champion at keeping his emotions in check, seeing Adam there forced him to toss all those stupid rules out the window. Christian couldn't get to him fast enough, and like seeing an old friend after many years, he spread his arms and crashed into Adam's chest.

"You had me so worried," Christian said, snuggling his face against the borrowed police vest Adam wore.

"It's all over."

"And my pop?"

"At hospital, getting checked out. Doc said he needed rest, so I left him in their capable hands."

"When can I see him?"

"Soon. But there's someone I need to show you first."

Christian pulled away. "What?"

"It's outside," he said.

"But the scene?"

"Miller," Adam shouted. "You good if I steal my husband for a few?"

Miller stepped out of the office with a smirk adorning his face. "Yup. He could use some fresh air."

Christian exchanged glances with Miller, who shrugged his shoulders. *What is so damn important?*

By the time Christian turned around, Adam was already outside waiting on the sidewalk.

"What's the hold-up?"

Christian stepped out into the daylight, and his first observation was how the crowd doubled in size. However, the team had pushed them back and cordoned off the block. As he followed, he scanned each face, but none stood out.

I've been gone from here for too long.

He shifted his gaze away from the looky-loos, and Adam waited just ahead near the corner. Christian walked towards the crime scene tape, raised it, and came towards Adam.

"You want to tell me where we're going?"

His head turned enough to expose only the left side of his face. "You'll see."

They rounded the corner at Second Street. He was initially unaware that his best friend was there, leaning against the bank's facade. But then she pushed her body off the wall. "Fancy meeting you here," Gemma said.

Christian froze, and his lips parted. He struggled to find words, but he didn't need to. She rushed forward and wrapped her arms around his neck.

"I never thought I'd be this happy to see you again," she confessed.

He tightened his hold on her. "Thank God they found you."

"I know. Otherwise, God only knows what could have happened."

"Where'd they find you?"

"About twenty klicks south of Sunset Lake. How'd they know where I was? And how did they know I was in trouble?"

Christian pulled away. "Remember that app? You know, the one that tracks where we are?"

Her eyes tilted upward. "Yeah. Wait. That's how you found me?"

"Yup. But at first, kidnapping was the furthest thing from my mind."

"Oh? Did you think I was driving all the way back up here to deliver an apology?"

Christian smirked. "Would have been nice, but no."

"Then how'd you figure it out I wasn't returning on my own free will?"

"Pearson. He mentioned you hadn't called him for hours. And it clicked: Gemma, not calling, something wasn't right."

"But it's over. David Ross is dead," she said.

"Mr. Ross? It was him?"

"The one and only. But he signed his death wish the moment he pulled that gun on those constables—bang, bang. Two shots and he fell to the ground. And you, I heard you had some confinement time too."

"Don't remind me. But it's over now. And there's only one thing left before I get some much-needed rest."

"What's that?" Gemma asked.

Before Christian could answer, Adam stepped between them. "I hate to break up the reunion, but there's someone else who is asking to see you."

"Pop?"

Adam grinned. "So, what, are you waiting for an invitation?"

PART 7

FOUR MONTHS LATER

CEDAR LAKE, SK

"Courage is the power to let go of the familiar."
—Raymond Lindquist

FIFTY-FOUR

THE EXTENDED WARM SUMMER EVENINGS WERE far behind them. And with each day that passed, the sun barely peeked through the cloudy skies. Even the green leaves had expressed their beautiful autumn foliage. Still, like clockwork, they too drifted away with the wind as winter ushered in on the prairie.

By some stroke of luck, Christian survived yet another tumultuous chapter in Cedar Lake. But this one, this was it. There would be no more trips to this decaying town. No more haunting memories filling his head. This place would now only be a place he once called home, but nothing more.

He stretched, gripped the nylon strap fastened to the U-Haul's roller door, and yanked it down. Without haste, he slid the metal hook into the groove and secured it with a padlock. He glanced down at his rust-stained hands and brushed the grime onto his jeans.

His husband remained inside, finishing up a few things, but daylight was fading fast. He released a pent-up sigh, but a sudden movement outside his childhood home caught his eye. It was his father, staring blankly at the facade of the building he had called home for more than thirty-five years. The place where he raised Christian and shaped him into the man he had become.

The decision for Matthias to abandon the only town he'd ever known wasn't easy. Although Christian wanted him closer, never once did he press his father to make a choice. How could a son tell his father to leave behind all the memories to start a new life in an unfamiliar place? This was his father's call and only his father's.

Christian remembered clear what his father said when he called. "You know, boy, a house doesn't make a home. I think it's time to start the next chapter of my life, and I can't do that without you, Adam, or Gemma."

Though the bond between Matthias and Cedar Lake was strong indeed, unlike most life decisions, this one was simple: too many years of heartbreak, violence, and loneliness took their toll on the older man. And for Matthias, he had to rid himself of the toxic bond that consumed most of his adult life.

Minutes ticked by, and the gray-bearded man hadn't budged. He stood in the same spot, looking at the same area for what seemed like an eternity. And even though the road trip ahead was a long one, Christian did the unthinkable: he smiled, folded his arms across his chest, and leaned against the dirty box truck. How can you rush someone when they're letting go of a lifetime of memories?

A few more minutes won't hurt.

As Christian watched his father, Adam appeared at the older man's side and wrapped his arm around his back. The whipping wind drowned out what they discussed, but just from watching the body language, it was clear whatever Adam said, it worked.

Matthias sauntered down the stairs, and when he reached the bottom, he turned just as Adam tugged the door closed and lock it. Adam wrapped his arm around Matthias, and the two strolled along the walkway towards the street.

Christian pushed himself away from the truck and walked towards them.

"You okay, Pop?" he asked.

Matthias nodded his head, but there was a look of grief washed over his face. "You know, we'll get through this. Together. Besides, who doesn't love a fresh start?"

Christian wasn't prepared for the answer he received. "How did I not see all this evil manifesting? These people," he paused. "No, these monsters forced me to do the one thing I never thought I'd have to."

It wasn't the fact he was uprooting his life that saddened Matthias the most. It was the circumstances that led up to it that dealt a blow to his soul. Christian reached out and pulled his father in close to him.

"Pop, nothing matters other than you're alive. You still have me, Adam, hell, even Gemma. I think that's more than you'll ever need," he whispered in his father's ear.

Matthias pulled away and exposed his tear-stained face. "Yup. I have more than most, and I'm so grateful."

The embrace lasted a few more seconds, and afterward, Christian walked with his father around to the passenger side of the U-Haul. As he opened the door and hoisted his father into the elevated cab, a familiar vehicle crossed over Fourth Avenue and slowed.

He closed the door and turned just as the driver rolled down the window.

"So, this is it, eh?" Pearson said.

"This is it."

"Can't say I'm not sorry he's leaving, but he'll have all the support he needs in Regina."

Christian smiled and nodded. "Any place is better than leaving him here. So how are you? It's been a while."

"Yeah, back on duty. You didn't think I'd let a gunshot keep me down, did you?" Pearson asked with a grin across his face.

"It'll take a lot more than that to get rid of you. I haven't seen much in the news these past few weeks. Any progress?"

"There's a lot to process. I'm going to be up to my neck in paperwork for months to come."

Pearson's words weren't an exaggeration. The investigation had far-reaching implications. After all, five criminals were dead, and indictments for forty-six others on charges ranging from aiding and abetting to first-degree murder were handed down. Even though the disc was addressed to Christian, not once did he ever view it. It went from Miller's hands to Pearson's.

"So that disc was a gold mine then, eh?" Christian asked.

"That's the understatement of the year. He handed us the entire case on a silver platter. Their plans, who did what and why, and even—"

There was a moment of hesitation. "Even, what?"

Pearson shied away. "Doesn't matter. What does is he's dead, and everyone involved is going away for a long time."

Christian knew Pearson was holding something back, but perhaps it was for his own good he never heard what almost dropped from Pearson's mouth. When Christian returned to Cedar Lake, his overall goal was to uncover what happened to Lindsay Ross that night in May of 2009. Not once did he ever believe his persistence would uncover the most massive scheme in Saskatchewan history to overthrow a governmental power. But once again, his refusal to stand down stopped Joanna's master plan and liberated the small town on the prairie.

"I know Lindsay is looking down on you right now and smiling," Pearson said.

Christian's eyes darted towards the sky. Just the image of her face brought a smile to his. "You know what . . . I guarantee she is."

Adam crossed in front of the SUV, waving at Pearson as he passed.

"Christian," he interrupted. "I know you guys could sit here and chat all night, but if you want to be back in Regina before ten, then we gotta hit the road."

Christian glanced at his watch. 2:57 p.m.

"Right. Be there in a few."

Adam nodded and walked away without speaking a word to Pearson. With Adam out of earshot, he leaned closer to Christian. "The guilt's still eating way at him, huh?"

"A little. He thinks because of what he did, you almost died."

"Psh. Shit happens; it wasn't his fault. Make sure he knows that."

"I will," Christian said as he tapped his hand against the rubber of the window. "Well, I got a long drive ahead of me. You take care of yourself, and if you ever find yourself down my way, you make sure you let me know."

Christian turned, and as he took his second step, Pearson's famous grin came out. "Er, about that."

Christian stopped and turned his head.

"With everything else going on, you might have missed the announcement."

"Announcement?"

Pearson reached into the passenger seat and folded a newspaper in half. Christian extended his hand and took it from him.

"Well, are you going to open it?" Pearson asked.

Christian unfolded the newspaper. It was a few weeks old, and his eyes scanned lower on the page until a picture of Pearson plastered on the front page stopped his skimming. The headline read, "Moose Jaw detachment receives new commander."

"This? You? You're moving to Moose Jaw?"

"What? No 'congratulations'? No 'outstanding job, Luke'?"

"I mean, yeah, I'm just. I wasn't expecting this. I thought you were content in Cedar Lake."

He chuckled. "Here? You're kidding me? I believe the word you're looking for is complacent. And I'll admit, I'm pushing forty. It's time to get back on the horse, you know, fall in love, buy a house, those sorts of things. I'll never find that in Cedar Lake. Not now, after everything that's happened."

"Good point. The dating pool around here is, well, you know."

"All too well."

"I'm happy you'll be closer, but are you sure going back to Moose Jaw is the answer to finding happiness? You've rid the town of evil. The people here need you. They deserve someone like you."

He shrugged. "I've spent the past twenty years focusing on the job. And in those years, I've realized one important thing: it's not always about the job. I need a companion. I need something that excites me to come home after a long, stressful day. Besides, it'll do me some good to get back to my roots and press the reset button on my life."

"Well, you'll always have my support whenever you need it. And, well, I know someone else who'll be even more ecstatic."

"Possibly."

"Does she know?"

He nodded. "We've discussed it."

"And?"

"And we're taking it one day at a time right now."

"I'm sure you are. Well, until we meet again, my friend, do me a favor."

"Sure."

"Keep away from psychos with guns and try to rest up. Detachment commander is even more stressful than this place ever was."

Pearson beamed. "Stop fussing. I'll be fine."

Somehow over two years, he and Christian had gone from foes to friends, each learning something from the other in that time. There was no telling what the next two years had in store, but each had become better people for having met each other.

Christian stopped and stared one last time at the place filled with a lifetime of memories, and as his eye wandered the landscape, he focused on the rectangular 'sold' sign that swayed in the wind. Christian couldn't hold back the single tear that rolled down his cheek.

This is it. So long, Cedar Lake. May you heal from your years of neglect and come back stronger than before.

He pulled himself into the U-Haul driver's seat, shot his father a smile, and followed Adam along the narrow street headed for the highway out of town.

ACKNOWLEDGEMENTS

I must thank a few people who supported me along the way. Without their input and responses to my questions (to make sure I got every detail right), this book would never have come to fruition.

First and foremost, I must give props to my husband, Jesse. You always give me the right amount of space to write my heart out and rescue me from myself when I need a break. You push me every day to be a better person and comfort me in those times I want to give up.

And no author would be complete without a crew of beta-readers. To Jenn, Heather, and Melissa, you three have no idea how much respect I have for your input. You devote hours out of your life every year to provide your critical feedback. Because of your input, I can better navigate my books in the right direc-tion for a better reading experience for all.

To my longtime Canadian friend, David Armstrong: thank you for taking time out of your busy life to answer a few questions I had about life in Canada. You're the best!

Finally, to my fans: Your kind words and dedication are the driving force behind these stories. A heartfelt 'Thank you' to each of you who takes time to read, leave a review, or personally reach out to discuss the books. I hope to continue bring-ing fresh stories as often as possible to you all!

ALSO BY C. L. BREES

THE DS ANDERSON SERIES
No Place is Safe

THE ALEX JONES SERIES
An Unsettled Past

Dark Ending

STANDALONE NOVELS
Among the Ashes